MAGGIE GASPED FOR BREATH, BREATHING IN OXYGEN IN GREAT GULPS OF RELIEF.

Somewhere in the distance she could hear Edward screaming her name, but she had no breath to call back to him. She wasn't even sure how she had managed to find herself above water until a deep voice spoke closer to her ear.

"Try to relax. Hang on to me." The words were spoken firmly but gently, and Maggie held tightly to the strong arm that supported her. She pressed her face tightly to his shoulder. "Kick your feet a little, and relax as much as possible," came the voice again.

Her head cleared more as she continued breathing deeply, and she realized that the man supporting her was Rafe Morrisey.

"I'll get you to shore," he told her reassuringly.

Maggie shivered. "Don't let go," she cried. "I can't swim!"

"I would never let go of you."

LOVE ME TOMORROW

Rosanne Bittner

Zebra Books
Kensington Publishing Corp.
http://www.zebrabooks.com

ZEBRA BOOKS are published by

Kensington Publishing Corp.
850 Third Avenue
New York, NY 10022

First Printing: January, 1998
10 9 8 7 6 5 4 3 2 1

Printed in the United States of America

I'll love you forever,
Though it brings me great sorrow,
For our love is forbidden,
And must wait for tomorrow.

Chapter One

''I'm thinking of leaving, Maggie.''

Maggie Dumont McCahan lay quietly staring into the darkness, too tired to get up and light a lamp so that she could look at her husband as they talked. She had not slept in the three hours she'd been lying there, and she knew Edward had also lain awake. Another heated argument with his father had left him agitated. More than once he had gone downstairs to sit in his study to think about yet another disagreement with his very wealthy, very controlling father. After thinking all night . . . after realizing she, too, was lying there awake . . . he needed to talk. He always needed to talk, always about the same thing, never about her. Always him . . . and his father. How could she not have realized before they married that it would be this way?

''What do you mean, Edward? Leave for where?''

Edward breathed out a long, deep sigh that told her whatever he'd decided was final. ''West . . . California.''

Maggie felt as though someone had cut into her heart with a knife, and her body suddenly tingled with a mixture of emotions. California! It was so far away! She felt terror at the thought of going into a wild, untamed land; resentment that her husband could make such a major decision without asking her opinion; agony at the thought of leaving her beloved mother, her sisters.

"I . . . can't believe you mean what you're saying, Edward. You are a man of means. Why would you want to go all the way across the country into an unsettled land, leave all our friends, our families—"

"Since Mother's death I've had no family," he interrupted. "I knew it would get worse after she died. So did you. She was the only buffer between me and my father. It's strange, isn't it, that he insisted I call him father, as though it were his seed that produced me? If he hadn't loved my mother so much, he would have given me away and been perfectly happy never to see me again."

"I don't believe that, Edward."

"I do. I've seen it in his eyes. His blood sons come first. My half brothers get all the easy jobs, the plush offices down at the factories, all the praise and recognition. Whenever anything goes wrong, it's my fault, and he never listens to my ideas."

Maggie choked back a need to scream. She had known Edward McCahan all her life. They had grown up friends, and in that relationship she had sympathized with the problems he'd had with his father. The fact that he had never felt loved by the man was the very reason her heart had gone out to him. When he had voiced his love for her, his desire to marry her, she had not said yes just because he came from a wealthy family, although her parents felt that was reason enough. She had agreed to marry him because part of her did love him dearly, and because she feared that if she rejected him it would only add to what he had already suffered feeling unloved.

Deep, deep inside her inner self she knew it was wrong to marry for that reason. But she knew him so well, knew he would be good to her. How terrible could it be to marry your best male friend? He was a decent looking man, with blond hair and mustache, eyes as blue as the sky. She had always enjoyed his company, and because they had grown close over the years, she had supposed she could "put up" with allowing his husbandly rights. After all, according to her mother, becoming intimate with a man was simply a necessity for having children. A woman was not expected to enjoy it, so desiring the man in that way was not a requirement for marriage. In fact, desiring a man sexually was practically a sin, even with one's own husband.

Still, she had come to feel somehow cheated of something she could not even name. Her good friend, Francine Megan, had recently married, and all she could talk about was how thrilling she found her sexual encounters with her new husband, how he ''melted her bones'' and made her feel ''on fire,'' and how they made love almost every night and every morning.

Edward had never made her feel that way, and his incessant complaining about and arguments with his father had become irritating to the point where Maggie wanted to just scream at him to please talk to someone else about it. When they were growing up and seeing each other only socially, it was easy to understand and sympathize and want to help. But now that they were husband and wife, she heard the same complaints all day long, all night long, and it seemed there were never any happy, carefree moments together.

Now this. California! ''Edward, I can't . . . I can't just leave my family. My friends. All I've ever known is Pittsburgh. We have a beautiful home, and your brothers love you and are good to you. It's only your father who gives you these problems. Some day he'll be gone, and your brothers will be in control.''

''I can't wait for some day. I was ten years old when my mother married John McCahan, and from that day on I was ordered to gear all my studies and thinking to one day being an officer in one of his businesses, expected to love the work, to be grateful that he called me son and later made me the Vice-President of the steel mill. I hate it there. It's a dungeon, even my office. I pretended that I enjoyed it only for Mother's sake, but I have always wanted to do something that was just mine. I want to build something on my own, Maggie. You know that. I've told you many times.''

Maggie rubbed her eyes. She did not like the direction this conversation was going. Wherever her husband went, she would have to go. Wasn't that what was expected of a wife? ''I thought that you would take the money inherited from your mother and start something right here in Pennsylvania. I wouldn't mind that at all, Edward. Between that and the generous monetary gift my parents gave us for our wedding, you could do any number of things, and we could still be close to friends and family. California . . . is so far away. We might never see family again."

"What difference does it make as long as we have each other?"

Your mother is dead, she wanted to shout at him. *Mine is still alive, and I want to be with her. I want to be near my sisters.* "Why California?"

He snickered as though amazed at the remark. "My God, Maggie, haven't you been reading the papers? Listening to all the talk? It's eighteen fifty, and even more people are headed west. Last year *thousands* went. There's *gold* out there! And lots of it! Can you imagine how satisfying it would be to go out there and strike gold and become a millionaire on my own? I've been talking to other businessmen, and they all agree that if a man wants the opportunity to build his own little empire, California is the place to do it. Maybe by now most of the gold has been discovered, but even if I don't find gold, I can make a fortune just selling supplies in the gold camps. We could go across by land, and I could have ships take tons of supplies around the Cape and on up, meet us there. Hell, I could end up being the richest mining supplier in California! And it would be all my own! I could be my own boss, run my own company. My stepfather would have nothing to do with it, and that would be the sweetest part. I'd be happier than I've ever been in my life."

And what about me? What about my happiness? Was it selfish to think that way? Why was the wife supposed to be the martyr in situations like this? "It frightens me, Edward."

He turned to his side and moved an arm around her, kissing her cheek. "It shouldn't. I'd be with you. I'd buy the best wagons, and you could take anything you wanted, china, furniture, all your clothes, anything. Other women have done it. Think how exciting it would be, the wonderful letters you could write home, the experiences we would have to tell our grandchildren about. Your family and friends here would envy you such an adventure. I'm told you can hire guides who take whole wagon trains out, so you would have plenty of company on the way, plenty of help. It isn't all that dangerous, and I would make sure we had plenty of supplies. We can even take our servants with us, so it won't be difficult for you. I've checked out everything, Maggie, and just the thought of it gets me so excited I can hardly stand it! I want to go, Maggie. I *need* to go. It's almost March, so the timing is perfect. I'm told the best thing to do is head for St. Louis. That's where you can hitch up with others, and at a place called Independence you can usually find a guide. It's best to leave in early spring in order to get there before the snows get too deep in the Rockies and the Sierras."

He turned on his back then, giving out another long sigh. "Oh, Maggie, we can do it. I know we can do it. You're my wife and my best friend, and I love you so. I'll make sure it isn't a hardship for you. I've been thinking about this for a long time, but I wanted to be sure. This last argument with my father clinched it for me. I have to get out of here, Maggie, away from John McCahan."

A silent tear trickled down the side of her face. "I haven't had time to think about it, Edward." She swallowed back a lump that rose in her throat and threatened to choke her. "You should have told me about these thoughts. I thought we told each other everything."

"We do. I'm sorry, but in this situation . . . I don't know. I wanted it to be completely my own decision, without needing anyone's okay, not even yours. I know that sounds selfish, but that's just the way it had to be this time."

He turned on his side again and kissed her cheek, running a hand over her breasts, feeling them through the thin flannel gown she wore.

"Come on, Maggie-girl. It will be exciting. Just you and me, headed for a new life in California! I promise I'll build you a home as fine as this one. You'll still have servants, plenty of food, all those things. You'll be part of those who go down in history as helping build America. You're beautiful, educated, refined. Out there you'd be a queen. And they say the weather is beautiful in California, none of the cold, damp, ugly weather we get here in Pennsylvania in winter. It's always warm and sunny." He ran his fingers through pieces of her thick, auburn hair. "Please, Maggie. I know it's right."

Maggie thought what an adjustment it had been leaving home to marry, even though home was only a few doors away. She had always had her mother, her three sisters, the security of family. "I suppose . . . it would be good for you," she said quietly, forcing herself to pretend agreement.

Why was she doing this? Why did the woman always have to do the husband's bidding? It didn't seem right, but that was life. She had made a contract with this man to love him to the end of her days, "for better or for worse." She simply had no idea the "worse" would come after only one year of marriage.

Edward was feeling exhilarated from finally making a decision on his own, from the excitement of a move west. He kissed her cheek several times over.

"Thank you, Maggie," he said between kisses. "It's going to be wonderful. You'll see."

Why? Why did his kisses frustrate and nearly anger her now? She had never dreamed it would be like this. Becoming his wife had changed their whole relationship, at least inside her own heart, but Edward needed her emotionally, and this was not the time to try to explain her own frustrations. Besides, she did love him. She just needed him in ways he did not seem to understand.

"Please stop, Edward," she said, pulling away from him. "I have too much to think about."

He frowned, moving away from her again. "What is it, Pet?"

What is it? Didn't he see what this meant to her? He'd had all the time in the world to think about it, plan it. But she'd had only minutes. "I . . . what if I got pregnant? I can't be out on that trail carrying a child. I don't want to have a baby in the middle of nowhere. If you're really determined to do this, then we had better begin abstaining until we reach California."

Edward lay there quietly a moment, then turned over, his

back to her. "I guess you're right, Pet. You do still love me, don't you?"

Maggie closed her eyes, suppressing an urge to scream. "Yes, love. I still love you. I love you today, and I will love you tomorrow." Her tears began creating a wet spot on her pillowcase.

Chapter Two

"Edward says it won't be all that dangerous, Mother. He is having special wagons built that will ensure as much comfort and convenience as possible."

Charlotte Dumont turned to look at the dancing flames in the marble fireplace of her sitting room. She could hardly bear to look at her daughter, after hearing the news. To look at her and think that these could be their last days together was almost unbearable. Maggie was her "baby," the last of four daughters. All had married well and lived in fine homes with wealthy husbands who were respected in the upper class community. She would have accepted nothing less for any of her girls. She blinked back tears at the thought that her youngest would be trading this wonderful life for a life of unknown dangers and questionable success in a land so far away they might never see each other again.

"You are twenty-two years old, Maggie," Charlotte Dumont told her daughter, "yet it seems only yesterday you were a baby in my arms. I was so happy you married Edward McCahan, because you were always such good friends in growing up. His mother was a wonderful woman from a good background, but the first man she chose to marry was not fit for such a fine lady. Edward's real father could never seem to settle into a career and be content to run his own father's businesses and live a normal family life. He gambled away his inheritance and drank too much, finally losing everything. His death was the best thing that could have happened to Florence, and it's a wonder there was still something left for her to put away for her son.''

Charlotte dabbed at tears, and Maggie thought how lovely her mother still was, her gray hair always perfectly coiffed, her posture straight and proud, a kind and attentive mother, but also a wealthy woman who expected only the best for her daughters.

''Now that Edward has decided to do this foolish, defiant thing,'' Charlotte continued, ''I have to wonder about him. Is he going to be like his father? He has never been happy working in John McCahan's industries, in spite of how wealthy they will make him some day.'' She sniffed, nervously fiddling with a lacy handkerchief as she talked. ''I know Edward loves you and that he means well, Maggie, but he doesn't have to go all the way to California to be free of his stepfather, if that is what he is trying to do.''

Maggie put her head against the back of the velvet chair in which she sat. She looked around the familiar room, remembering playing here when she was small while her mother embroidered or played the piano. ''He thinks he *does* need to do this, Mother. He's going there because he says he can become the biggest mining supplier in California—wants to get in while everything is still growing. Edward has been a friend all my life. He will always be good to me, and he is determined to make this work. You needn't worry about his character. Surely you know that.''

Charlotte shook her head, studying her daughter's beautiful face, her auburn hair piled in exquisite curls on top of her head, her shape slender and delicate, her fingers long and lovely, her face so pretty, with soft brown eyes and a perfect nose. ''They say it's mostly desert out there, Maggie. What will that do to your skin? Too much sunshine isn't good for the skin. And there are no conveniences. I've heard stories about the journey to California. How will you bathe? What if you need a doctor? What if you become with child along the way? Even if you don't, you will eventually have children, and I will never see them. And what if you are in childbirth and need a doctor? There surely are none out there so far from civilization. I can't believe Edward would take you to such a place, and so soon! You have only been married a year. This will go hard on your father, and your sisters. And how am I to explain to my society ladies? They will never understand this. And what in God's name does Edward know about handling wagons and such?''

''He'll hire drivers.'' Maggie could not help secretly agreeing with her mother that this was a foolish, dangerous trip, but Edward was her husband and she had to stand by him. ''Edward told me he would take as many wagons as necessary so we could bring along most of our furnishings, china and such, and we will bring our servants. If the ones we have don't want to go, we'll hire others. They can help me bathe, and we'll take plenty of food and wine. Edward has promised to build me a lovely home as soon as the supplies he is sending by ship arrive. He would never let anything happen to me, Mother, nor would he expect me to live below my means once we are there. He simply feels he must do this, and I don't have the heart to argue with him about it.'' How she hated the look of devastation on her mother's face. ''Father will know soon. Edward has gone to the office to talk to him about it.''

Charlotte put her head in her hands. ''I can't believe this is happening.''

Maggie wanted to repeat the words. She studied her mother's wrinkled hands, and she ached at the thought of leaving her. Charlotte Dumont was always proper and dignified, always concerned about the best for her girls. Yet her daughters all felt a need to watch over their mother, whose world of manners and propriety was so important to her that she was nearly oblivious to the world outside her home, her daughters, and her circle of wealthy lady friends.

Maggie glanced up at a painting of the four Dumont sisters that hung over the fireplace. She sat a little taller than the others, had always looked different from them, brown eyes instead of blue, auburn hair instead of blond. The other three looked like their mother. She looked more like her father.

It pained her to think of leaving her siblings. They had always been close, all three older sisters doting on her all her life. She supposed that now it was time to truly leave all that behind and be a grown woman in every respect. She was, after all, twenty-one years old, well-schooled, and now married. She had made that choice of her own accord.

"Please be strong for me, Mother. If it doesn't work out, we can always come back."

Charlotte shook her head, looking up at her with eyes that were red now from crying. "Edward would never come back if he failed. He could not bear to face his father, then. He will only come back if he succeeds, and perhaps not even then."

Maggie looked down at the tiny ruffles on her pink linen dress. "It will work out somehow, Mother. I have to believe that or go crazy. Maybe someday there will be a railroad west, so it will be easier to come home and visit, or for you to come out to us."

Charlotte rose and walked to a window, feeling older, a little more weary. "I'll be dead before a project like that can ever be completed, which I highly doubt will ever happen." The woman sighed, staring out at a brick street that was lined with elegant mansions. This was the only kind of life her daughter had ever known. What kind of life would she have in the desolate West, on the terrible journey it must be to get there? Her own grandparents had come here from France, and back then it was this part of the country that was barely settled. Her grandmother had been murdered by Indians, but her grandfather had stayed on and remarried, started a shoe repair business that had grown into a shoe factory, from which she had herself inherited a good deal of money. It was important to her that her daughters have lives of wealth and luxury.

"I'll never forgive him for doing this to you, Maggie."

Maggie rose and walked over to her mother, embracing her. "There is nothing to forgive, Mother. You told me once that a man does what he must do, and his wife simply puts up with it. Edward has had good training working for his father. He has plenty of money to make sure we have the best of everything on the trip and once we get there. He will be making arrangements today for supplies to be shipped, and he plans to settle with John and with his brothers, so there are no attachments left here.''

Charlotte hugged her tightly. ''What about your home, your beautiful home?''

''Edward is going to ask his father to buy it so he will have even more money to take along. John can just resell the house. We have been in it hardly more than a year, so I am not all that attached. Besides, it is much too big for just the two of us.'' Maggie kissed her mother's cheek. ''Mother, ever since Florence died, Edward has changed. It's just as he said. Florence was the buffer between him and John. She is the reason John adopted Edward and gave him his own last name. With her gone, it is just too much for Edward to try to handle John alone. You know how John McCahan is, bullheaded, always right, demanding, unforgiving, especially where Edward is concerned. He seems to always find fault with everything he does, and Edward just can't take it any more. I don't blame him. He is doing what he must do, and I have to support him. The hardest part will be leaving you and Sarah, Elizabeth, and Catherine.''

Charlotte nodded, touching her cheek, hardly able to see her daughter for the tears in her own eyes. ''I am proud of how strong you are being about this, child. Get yourself some good creams, plenty of medicines, especially for women's common problems. You'll need laudanum for pain, in case you should get hurt, and tea, take plenty of tea. Take your wedding dress. You should always keep it with you. And take your grandmother's trunk that she brought over here from France. I gave it to you years ago, an heirloom you must always treasure. It will be something of the Dumont family you can take west with you, something from France that traveled all the way across the ocean and then across America. It will—'' The woman pulled away, putting a hand to her heart. ''Oh, dear, when I think of all the things that could happen . . . the terrible desert weather, Indians, wild animals, and wild mining camps . . ." She shook her head. "I will pray for you, my darling daughter. And I will pray that if Edward realizes his dream, he will come back here to live. Perhaps on the way he will realize the mistake he has made and will come back, anyway. It is all I can hope for."

Maggie felt sick inside. If she told her mother how she really felt, how frightened she was, how she dreaded the danger and discomfort that surely lay ahead, how unhappy she was with Edward as a husband, it would only make her mother's agony that much greater. For her mother's sake, for Edward's sake, for *everyone's* sake, she had to pretend she did not mind the idea, pretend to be strong, pretend to be excited. It would be the only way her family could bear to watch her go, and the only way she could bear to leave them.

The questions were endless, and Maggie could see pity in the eyes of some of her own and her mother's friends who had come to the grand farewell party Charlotte was giving for her. Maggie knew that her mother was struggling to pretend happiness and excitement over her daughter's western "adventure." She called her a true pioneer, a brave, strong young woman who intended to bring civilization to California and the Spaniards there.

Maggie loved her mother dearly, but in moments like this she sometimes wondered how far the woman would go to save face, to be perfect in every way and to make her daughters the most wonderful creatures who were ever born. Reputation, admiration, respect, all meant everything to Charlotte Dumont, and to Maggie's father, Henry. He, too, was strutting around bragging up his daughter and son-in-law. Both her parents were making sure no one laughed at the idea. Henry Dumont could not bear to have someone think that he or any of his own would do something foolish, something to be scoffed at. He and Edward had argued over Edward's decision, but Edward was more determined than ever now, and so Henry knew there was no keeping his daughter in Pennsylvania. She was a married woman now, and that was that. He therefore had decided to make the best of it and make sure his daughter and son-in-law were sent away with good wishes from everyone, and with the idea that Edward had made a wonderfully intelligent and brave decision.

Maggie doubted that the decision was either of those things. Deep inside she felt it was totally foolish, and she did not doubt that some of those here tonight felt the same. She watched her husband move through the crowd of well-wishers, shaking hands, laughing, happy . . . so happy. Maggie could not feel any happiness, and she was beginning to feel terribly alone. She smiled for others, pretended joy and excitement, while down inside she wanted to scream and weep and beg Edward not to do this. She could not help realizing that everything she was looking at tonight, every person she greeted, she might never see again after a few more days.

Her farewell party was held in the ballroom of the home in which Maggie had grown up. This great stone mansion had been a warm, happy place in which to grow, in spite of its size and the presence of many servants and two nannies. It was home to Maggie, and leaving to marry had not been so bad, since she lived only a few doors away. But to leave it to travel 2,500 miles was something else.

She struggled against tears as she studied the Greek leafwork carved into the wood that bordered the tops of the walls in the ballroom. She used to sit and stare at those carvings when she was little, but sometimes she just ran through the room, purposely screaming to hear her echo. She finally found a chance to get away and be alone for a few minutes, and, slipping downstairs to the main floor, she walked through the billiards room, smelling the rich scent of tobacco, the smell of her father's pipe. From there she walked over velvety carpeting to her father's study, with its rich mahogany desk and leather chair, walls of books, tall windows. She walked through the sliding doors of the study out into the great room, studying the marble floor, the strategically placed Oriental carpets, Chinese vases, and fern plants.

She moved through the great room to her mother's sitting

room, her favorite room. She walked up to the marble fireplace and touched it, again studying the painting that hung above it.

"Maggie?"

Maggie turned to see her oldest sister, Sarah, standing in the doorway.

"You don't truly want to go, do you?"

Maggie looked away. "No," she answered quietly. "But Edward is so excited about it, and he's my husband. He has promised me all the comfort that is possible on such a journey, and a big new home when we arrive."

"Oh, Maggie, we'll miss you so! Our baby sister, going so far away! You shouldn't allow it, Maggie. Tell Edward the truth, that it's the last thing you want to do."

Maggie shook her head. "I can't. He needs to do this, Sarah. We've only been married a year. I can't destroy his one biggest dream, force him to stay here and continue letting his father abuse him emotionally the way he does." She faced Sarah. "When he told his father his plans, the man simply told him it was probably best. He *wants* Edward to leave. He agreed to pay him several thousand dollars if he relinquishes any further ties to the family and signs a paper that he will never come back asking for more."

Sarah's eyes widened in surprise. "How terrible! I never knew it was that bad."

Maggie studied the sister who looked most like their mother. Her hair was beginning to gray at the temples. Sarah was thirty-five and had four children, nieces and nephews Maggie knew she would never see grow up. More pain shot through her heart at the thought of it, and she told herself she must stop thinking these things. She took a deep breath to keep her composure.

"Edward's father is very controlling, Sarah. Edward says that out west a man can truly be free to do and say whatever he wants. I suppose he's right." She dabbed at a tear that slipped down her cheek. "I'll miss all of you so much, Sarah."

Sarah put out her arms and walked over to embrace her sister. "I just can't believe this is happening." She kissed her cheek. "You must write, Maggie, as often as possible. Keep a diary. Let us share the trip by reading about it. It would help so much. Through your letters we could all still be together, in a way. I've heard tales about mountain men and Indians. Make sure you get a good guide, Maggie. It's so important. My God, we don't want something happening like what we heard about the Donners. Remember? It was two or three years ago when the news came by a ship that had been to California. Half those people died of starvation in the mountains, and it was rumored they even ate tree bark and leather and . . . and even the flesh of their dead!"

"Don't!" Maggie covered her ears and turned away. "That was just because they started too late and got to the mountains at a dangerous time. And they took the wrong route, they say."

"Oh, Dear Maggie, I'm sorry. I'm just concerned. Surely you'll come back, won't you? Once Edward gets settled and has his business flourishing and can hire people to run it, you could come home and visit for a winter, perhaps."

Yes. Perhaps. That was how she must think of it, that she would definitely come back. After all, they had plenty of money and would have more in no time. They could do anything they wanted. "I'll try to come back." Maggie faced her sister again. "We must both keep diaries, so that I won't miss any exciting thing that happens here, and you can read about my journey."

Sarah nodded, and again the sisters embraced. Maggie's other sisters, Elizabeth and Catherine, found them then, and they carried on in much the same way Sarah had. After tears and hugging and chatting, they all insisted Maggie rejoin them in the ballroom, where all the children were. A photographer was there to take a last family portrait.

"I'll be along," Maggie answered. "I just want a couple more minutes alone here in Mother's sitting room."

"Oh, yes," Elizabeth told her. "We understand." Their smiles fading to sadness, the three of them left, and Maggie walked over to her mother's favorite rocker. She touched the arms, knelt down to study the unfinished embroidery that had been left in the chair.

"Oh, Mama," she whispered. "I'm so afraid." She folded her arms across the seat of the chair and put her head down, letting the tears come.

Chapter Three

For two weeks Maggie fretted over what to take and what to leave behind. How could she leave *anything* behind? Everything had some sort of sentimental value—dolls from her sisters, a quilt from her grandmother, jewelry boxes, music boxes, jeweled combs, jewelry that sported real diamonds and other precious gems. She had a closet full of gowns that had been styled and sewn just for her. What use would there be for such pretty clothes on the trail west? She should at least keep them for when she arrived in California. She would have need of them when she joined San Francisco's high society, if there were any such people there.

Edward had promised she could take any personals she wanted. She would take most of her clothes and perfumes, three of her dolls, her diamonds and pearls, two music boxes, and the quilt. Edward was having their most expensive, imported furniture sent by ship, and much of it had already been removed from the house, leaving the fifteen room home echoing with emptiness.

"Shall I pack your personals now, Maggie?"

Maggie turned at the voice of Gretta, her personal maid. "Yes. I want my wedding dress and my most treasured valuables put into my grandmother's trunk. I'll show you.'' She began giving Gretta orders about which items to take to the trunk, and she laid the quilt into the bottom of it. She touched the flowery-design lining of the trunk, thinking how ironic it was that it had once been in France. Now it would travel clear across America to California. She had already hidden a considerable sum of money under the lining, money her father had given her to use as she might need if something were to happen to Edward. He had promised to send several thousand more with the things Edward was having shipped, hidden in a secret compartment in one of their wardrobes. Maggie had sewn more money into her grandmother's quilt. Edward himself was taking several thousand dollars in gold coins, hiding them in special compartments being built into the wagons they would take.

She studied the worn leather exterior of the trunk, the pale yellow flowers that were painted on the crown of the lid. She could still remember her grandmother, even though she had been only twelve when the woman died. She had been quiet and stern, and when Grandmother spoke, everyone listened. She had never learned English very well, and at home she always spoke French. Maggie's own French had been refined by her father and by schooling. She wondered now what use there could be for it in California. She would have been better off to learn Spanish.

She continued directing Gretta, who seemed unusually flustered this evening. She gasped when she dropped a bottle of perfume, but it did not break, and she looked ready to cry when she picked it up.

''Gretta, what is it?'' Maggie asked.

''Oh, it is just za excitement of za trip.'' The young German woman fussed with finding just the right spot in the trunk for the perfume. ''Za girls at za convent are so happy zat I am going into the wild West. Zey haf told me to write zem und let zem know all about za trip.''

Maggie took the perfume from her. ''Are you sure you want to do this, Gretta?''

''Oh, yes,'' the woman answered. ''Zey say, you know, zat

out in dis California, zer are many single and lonely men, t'ousands of zem. Maybe I can find me a husband, no?''

Maggie smiled, thinking how that would be the last thing she wanted now, if she had a choice. ''So, you intend to go out there with me and then leave me?''

''Oh, no! He could go looking for his gold while I work for you, you see? I would not leave you unless I found you someone as good as me at cleaning a room and picking out cloze and fixing hair.''

''Yes, you are very good at what you do, Gretta. I appreciate that.''

Gretta grinned proudly, a gap showing between her two front teeth. Maggie thought how pretty she would be without that gap, but even so, she had a nice complexion, pretty blue eyes, and dark blond hair. She was a little plump, but Maggie suspected, from what she had heard, that there would be plenty of men lined up to court Gretta Wheeler, who at twenty-seven, had never been married. And after spending several years as a convent orphan, this trip must be the most exciting event in Gretta's life.

Maggie could take some contentment in knowing this trip was making at least a *couple* of people happy . . . Edward and Gretta. The housemaid and gardener had been let go, since neither wanted to venture on such a journey, and both had families. But their cook, Marie, had agreed to go along, for which Maggie was grateful, since she knew next to nothing about cooking. Marie had admittedly agreed she was going because she also had heard how available men were in California, and she planned to find one who owned a gold mine and be rich for once in her life. She was thirty-two and a widow with no children. The woman betrayed how much she enjoyed her profession by her huge size. She was not what one would call comely, but Maggie decided that if all a man cared about was eating well, he would do well by marrying Marie Schier.

The house servant who ran errands and served meals refused to go, and Edward had replaced her by trading her to one of his brothers for his servant, David Whittaker, an adventurous young man of only nineteen who had left an abusive home at an early age to make his own way. He was very good at his job, but he had always considered it a stepping-stone to something better, and he was willing to go to California because he intended to look for gold himself once he arrived. Edward had always admired the fine job David did at his brother's home, and Edward seemed to actually enjoy the young man's company, which would make the trip itself more enjoyable for him. Their butler would not be needed because there would be no home to manage for quite some time, and Maggie suspected they would also lose their cook, servant, and her own personal maid once they made their destination, all in one way or another to gold fever.

They would have to rehire all new people, which would not be easy, since most men would be off looking for gold, and they had received reports that there were few women around except for those who followed the gold camps to provide men with one of their basic necessities. Maggie shivered at the thought of doing such a horrible thing for a living. Sex was dreadful enough with her own husband. She could not imagine how a woman could do such an intimate, embarrassing, humiliating thing with perfect strangers, and she dreaded ever running into the company of such a woman.

"Be sure to wrap my porcelain dolls carefully before putting them into the trunk," she told Gretta.

She had suggested to Edward that she stay behind and come later, but he had insisted he needed her with him, not just because he couldn't bear to be without her, but because he wanted to build a home right away and would need her help in designing it just the way she wanted it. Besides that, someone had to manage what to do with their personal furnishings when they arrived by ship. He would be busy getting started on his supply business, and he simply could not manage everything on his own.

This will be a wonderful adventure and learning experience for both of us, he had told her with boyish excitement. *It will draw us even closer, Maggie. Oh, I'm so glad we're married. We were always meant to be together, you know.* He seemed to be completely oblivious to what this trip was doing to her.

She was beginning to feel as if her world had become unreal, as though this was all just a bad dream and it would end soon, but when she pricked her finger on a straight pin caught in the doily, she was reminded this was not a dream at all.

Tomorrow! Tomorrow she would board a riverboat for the weeks-long trip on the Ohio River to the Mississippi, to St. Louis, then along the Missouri to a place called Independence. Their wagons were already loaded onto the riverboat Edward had specially rented. Maggie had to admit that the unique features Edward had insisted be built into the wagons were quite accommodating. Wagonmakers were burgeoning with business now because of the gold rush, and it had not been easy to find a wagonmaker with the time to build such large wagons. Edward had paid the best man he could find close to twice the actual value of the wagons, bribing him to drop his other work so the wagons could be ready quickly. All three wagons were built extra wide, and one had two decks. It was filled with basic household goods, books, even oils and watercolors, in case Maggie wanted to paint along the way. Painting was her favorite hobby. Another wagon carried a cookstove with its chimney sticking out the top, all kinds of pots and pans, enough food for an army, gourmet wines included, a table that folded down, tablecloths and candelabras. Edward intended to have a table set up every evening so that they could eat as graciously as possible, rather than sit around a campfire with tin plates. He would not have his wife subjected to such living. Yet another wagon would be brought for Gretta and Marie, their personals, and even more supplies and belongings. David had agreed to "tent" it along the way. A fourth wagon, large and quite luxurious as wagons go, would serve as "home" for her and Edward until they reached California. It also had two decks, the upper one for sleeping, the lower one for dressing. Edward had even brought along a copper tub for bathing, and he intended to use the drivers he had hired for hauling wood and water when necessary.

There would be six drivers, so that no one man had to overwork himself, and they, too, were willing to go because it was a way to get to California and get paid on the way. Teams of fine, strong oxen had been purchased, as well as two teams of mules and all the gear necessary. Two wagons would be pulled by the mules, two by the oxen, and four extra oxen and six extra mules would be tied to the wagons, as replacements for any animals that might not make it.

Maggie moved to look out a window as Gretta continued packing. Once, when she had gone to the loading docks with Edward to watch the wagons being loaded onto the riverboat, a few men had laughed and scoffed at the idea of taking such huge, heavy contraptions across the country, telling Edward he would never make it over the mountains with them. Edward had insisted that he certainly could. He had good drivers and strong animals. "I have a feeling you don't know what you're in for," one man had commented.

Maggie could not forget the words. Was he right? What lay out there to greet them? How tall *were* those mountains? Could they really haul such large wagons and so much freight over them? Edward was so sure, and the man's remark had only made him more determined. There was no stopping him now.

She watched a fancy carriage go by, the horse's hooves clopping against the brick street. Across the way was another opulent mansion. Tonight they would go to the opera house and would dine at an elegant restaurant . . . all for the last time, for who could tell how long? This life of luxury was about to end, and the tightness in Maggie's stomach was beginning to grow more painful.

A crowd was gathered at the docks, and Edward was glowing in the attention. Newspaper reporters were there to write about the son of one of Pittsburgh's wealthiest venturing off into the Great American Desert to make an even bigger fortune in the supply business in California. Maybe he would even find gold. His "loyal and brave wife" would accompany him. The reporters frantically scribbled descriptions of the wagons, the supplies that would be taken. Flash pans exploded several times as pictures were taken.

Edward's brothers and their wives were there, but his father was not. How sad. Maggie's mother and sisters were there, their families, and her father, who said little. Henry Dumont was not at all happy with his son-in-law for taking his daughter into such desolation, but she belonged to Edward now, and this was her wifely duty. He seemed to understand that, and there was a flicker of pride in his eyes at all the attention she was getting. The rest of the crowd consisted of friendly well-wishers, most close associates, some perfect strangers. A few of Pittsburgh's lower class gawked from a distance.

Maggie struggled against the fear that she would break down in front of all these people and show them she was not brave at all. She wanted to cling to her mother and beg her to not let anyone take her away, but she presented a happy face, accepted handshakes and hugs. Then came the nieces and nephews, all with quick hugs, then Edward's brothers and their families, then her sisters. Oh, this was so hard. She embraced each one as all began to weep with the fear they would never touch again, never talk again. It took several minutes to let go of each one, and a steam whistle blew. The boat's captain was anxious to get underway. There was no more time to linger.

Maggie turned to her father, and he embraced her strongly. "Never stop being our Maggie," he told her. "Always be elegant and moral and proud and refined. Don't let that untamed land change you."

Maggie could not imagine why he thought that could happen. This was the only life she had ever known. She would never change. "I'll be all right, Father."

He kissed her tearstained cheek, and Maggie was touched by the tears in his own eyes. She realized in that moment that she really hardly knew her father. He'd been such a busy man all his life. Now she would never get the chance to be closer. Oh, what a sad day this was!

She turned to her mother. This was the hardest part of all. Edward was already telling her they must get aboard. A band began playing "For He's A Jolly Good Fellow," and Maggie clung to her mother, now weeping uncontrollably. How could she let go, when this might be the last time to be in her mother's arms? There was nothing to say but "I love you," and then Edward was pulling at her.

"I'm sorry, Maggie. We really must go."

Reluctantly Maggie let go, kissing her mother's cheek quickly, then throwing kisses to her father, her sisters, shouting, "I love you." In the next moment she was on the boat deck, and the boarding plank was removed. The band was still playing, the crowd was cheering and waving. Charlotte Dumont had turned to her husband and was weeping against his chest. Sarah, Elizabeth, and Catherine were all crying, their children jumping up and down with excitement at the sound of the riverboat's steam whistle.

The boat's huge paddle began churning, and they were underway. Maggie watched the crowd of people as they began to fade into the distance, keeping her eyes on her mother's pale green velvet cape until she could no longer see it. The riverboat moved faster, past city buildings, smoking factories, away . . . away . . . away.

Maggie turned her gaze to Edward, and she could barely see him for the tears in her swollen eyes, but she could tell he was smiling. How could he smile at a time like this? How could he not understand what this was doing to her? In that one quick moment part of her hated him, and she wondered how she would ever rid herself of the resentment that was growing in her soul.

Chapter Four

Maggie watched the landscape change from the hills of Pennsylvania to the endless flatlands of central Indiana and southern Illinois. Here and there she saw a farmhouse, but most of the area they traveled along the Ohio was still sparsely settled. It seemed so desolate compared to the city, and dread engulfed her in unexpected waves whenever she realized that where they were going there were virtually no settlements of any kind, not even a farmhouse. The only living beings in that wild land were Indians, and weren't all Indians thieves and murderers? Rapists? She told herself that if they hooked up with a big enough wagon train, which Edward had promised they would do, she need not fear the Indians. Even better assurance would be to find a guide who understood them and could converse with them.

So far things had been bearable, a rather luxurious trip due to Edward reserving a suite on the riverboat and fine rooms for Gretta and Maria and for all the drivers, none of whom had ever lived so well. Both Gretta and Maria reveled in being waited on, and they gorged themselves on extravagant meals of beefsteaks, puddings, pies, ham, sweet potatoes, fine wines, and such, taking advantage of a life of luxury for the short while it would last. Edward's party was so large that there was room for only a few other passengers. All the talk was of the west and gold, and how soon they would reach St. Louis. At one time Pittsburgh had been considered the "Gateway to the West." Now it was St. Louis.

So far they had lived nearly as comfortably as at home, but the tales Maggie was hearing about what it would be like once they headed out by wagon were making her dread what was coming even more than she already had. One gambler on the riverboat had been part way west and had turned back.

"No privacy," he'd lamented. "The women will have to hold up blankets for personal duties, since there are no trees for miles."

Maggie could not imagine a land without trees. The man had also warned, "You'll find mosquitoes big as bats, and they are relentless."

Edward had assured Maggie he was prepared for such problems. He had brought along mosquito netting. Maggie told herself that the gambler must have been exaggerating. She shook away the thought, reminding herself that at least Edward was happier than she had ever seen him, and at least he did not go on every night about another disagreement with his father. Her resentment of him had calmed as she actually enjoyed the luxury of the riverboat trip.

Besides, Edward liked to pretend he knew all about what he was doing. He was trying so hard to make this all look good to her that she did not have the heart to complain about anything. He displayed nothing but excitement and self-confidence, and she wondered if that was really how he felt on the inside. Maybe he was just as frightened as she was. Maybe he had just as many doubts and was simply too proud to admit it. Maybe he, too, wanted to turn back. But that would mean crawling, under John McCahan's command, and he could never go back to that.

And so they would press forward, ever closer to the point of no return. Her life of luxury and balls and theaters and jewels and attention was fast fading. In its place would be heat and bugs and mud, and in spite of servants and all the comfort one could muster under such circumstances she was still miserable with homesickness, and she ached to be in her own spacious home, sitting in front of a fireplace or lying in her soft, four-poster bed. At home she had had her own private boudoir and sitting room, both places where she could go to be alone and read. Now there was no place to be alone. She and Edward shared a room and soon would share the cramped quarters of a wagon. She did not like the thought of being thrown in with all sorts of strangers and being exposed to the constant smell of mules and oxen and their dung. She was surprised that the prospect of such inconveniences did not disturb Edward, the way he was raised; but then he was a man, and men did not seem much affected by such things. Anyone who could bear the constant smell of cigar smoke, she supposed, could bear just about anything.

There was, however, one inconvenience she would apparently not have to contend with, and that was because Edward left her alone in the night. He had agreed it was dangerous to risk a pregnancy, and so they abstained. Edward had declared that if she were to lose a child on this trip, he would never forgive himself . . . and Maggie in turn knew *she* could never forgive him. Besides that, it would surely be embarrassing and humiliating to try to make love in the cramped quarters of a wagon, where someone else would surely hear what was going on. Edward had a habit of grunting with every thrust, which upset Maggie even in private. It was as though making love was work for him, and sometimes she wondered if he enjoyed it any more than she did. Even though she considered his rather clumsy fumbling at her nightclothes and body irritating, a little part of her was hurt that he found it so easy to abstain. She could not, of course, mention such things in her journal, but she made daily entries, writing about the towns and scenery they had passed.

We came to the wide Mississippi River several days ago and soon should reach—There came a knock on the door to her suite.

''Maggie-girl, we're in sight of St. Louis!'' Edward shouted from outside. He had been outside all morning with David, giving him further instructions about what was expected of him in his new employment.

Maggie moved off the bed where she had been lounging and went to the door, looking out onto the three story high deck. She stepped outside to the railing, standing beside Edward to see a vast settlement ahead. It looked nowhere near as developed as cities in the East.

"Do you see the dome, Maggie? That's the courthouse. They say that's where we go to get more information about the journey west and perhaps find others with whom we can travel, maybe even find a guide."

The domed courthouse stood out amidst a mass of brick and wood structures not nearly as striking. Steamboats were moored all along the river's edge, and more were making their way up and down the river, steam whistles blaring, smokestacks spouting black puffs of smoke.

There were far more boats than Maggie could count, and as they came closer she could see many of them were unloading wagons and oxen. Bags and belongings and their owners lined the docks, as well as children and dogs, chickens and horses, carriages and sailors. The docks were a bustle of noise and movement.

"Soon we'll be on the Missouri River headed for Independence!" Edward told her, an arm around her waist.

Maggie's heart fell a little at the sight of St. Louis. To her it was the symbol of no return. Once they left this city, all that was Maggie Dumont McCahan and the life she had known would be gone.

Everything seemed to be happening too fast now. As Maggie waited for Edward to find the information he needed, she stared in awe at the inside of the courthouse, the magnificent paintings on the interior of the dome. Voices echoed against limestone and marble walls and floors, and people milled about everywhere, most of them obviously excited about their upcoming journeys into "true freedom," as she heard one person say. "Gold," was the most heard word, "land" the second. "Indians'' was another word that resounded throughout the structure, which Maggie had to admit was as magnificent as any building she had seen back East. At least some form of civilization had made it this far, but only because of the Mississippi, which afforded endless transportation from the Gulf of Mexico and New Orleans all the way up into the northern Minnesota Territory. That much she knew from reading what she could about the land into which they would travel.

As she strolled through the courthouse and studied one of its magnificent spiral staircases, she supposed that if they stayed and went no further she could possibly make a home here. At least there were a lot of people, and bearable civilization. It seemed perfectly feasible that Edward might want to stay, for nearly everyone headed west passed through here first. He could make a fortune selling supplies. She hated suggesting it to him, for he had been adamant that they must go all the way to California and concentrate on supplying the miners. There simply was no talking to him lately, and she knew he would never consider stoping here.

On a stairway landing, Maggie turned to look for Edward in the crowd. That was when she saw him—a man she supposed must be what was called a mountain man. She had never seen anyone quite like him. He was tall, and his back was to her, broad shoulders, slim hips, long hair. Long hair on a man! She thought only Indians wore their hair that way. Maybe he *was* an Indian! He wore fringed buckskins, and a wide leather belt around his hips held some kind of handgun and a sheath that sported the handle of a large hunting knife. Instead of shoes, he wore some kind of soft-looking things made of what looked like animal hide. She had read about Indian footwear, which were called moccasins. Was that what he wore? His garb fascinated her.

Did he visit and trade with wild Indians, as she'd read some such men did? Some even married Indian women! This one was visiting with a man and woman who were most likely travelers. Was he talking about guiding them? Maggie wondered if the man had ever lived life in a normal society. He obviously knew little about etiquette, as he wore a wide-brimmed, leather hat while standing inside. A man should remove his hat when he came into a building. He talked, nodded, pointed, looked at a map the couple showed him, shook his head.

He must know all about that wild land, Maggie thought. What kind of man made his living hunting and trapping in such places, guiding wagon trains clear across the Great American Desert and over mountains, and then came all the way back to do it again? What possessed a man to do something like that? What attracted him to such a terrible place, and once out there why didn't he stay and look for gold, as most men wanted to do? Why was he content to just constantly travel, to make the trip over and over again, to never settle?

As though he sensed her staring, he suddenly turned and met her gaze. Maggie was surprised by his face, strikingly handsome, his skin tanned dark, his eyes also dark, and wide-set, high cheekbones, a square jawline. She quickly turned away, embarrassed that he had caught her staring, more embarrassed at the odd flash of attraction she had experienced when his eyes met hers.

What in God's name was it she had felt? She hoped he understood she had been staring out of mere curiosity. Surely he wouldn't realize she had been momentarily attracted! How humiliating! She kept her back to him and continued looking for Edward, wishing he would show up and rescue her from her embarrassment. She began walking around, deliberately showing she was searching for someone, anything to keep from looking back at that heathen mountain man and giving him the wrong idea.

"Do you need some help?"

Maggie turned at the words, feeling a flush come to her cheeks to see the buckskin-clad heathen had been standing right behind her.

"I—yes. My husband. He's here somewhere, getting information about traveling to California."

The man nodded, finally removing the leather hat. His dark eyes moved over her as though he knew everything about her, and she backed away a little, noticing the front of his shirt was unlaced several inches, exposing a good deal of his chest and a necklace that looked like it was made of leather and beads.

"You're dressed like a lady who should stay in the city," he told her.

Well, at least he knew something about proper ladies. "Personally I would *prefer* to stay in the city. But my husband has a dream of starting a supply business in California, because of the gold rush."

The man slowly nodded. "Everybody in this courthouse has a dream. Most of them won't find it in California, but they don't want to hear that." He looked around. "My dream is to *never* settle, so I make my living guiding people west." His gaze moved back to meet her own. "Excuse me for intruding. I just thought you looked a little confused, and I wondered if I could help." He put his hat back on and nodded. "Good luck on your journey, Ma'am."

He turned and walked away, and Maggie thought about calling to him to stop. Perhaps he was just the kind of man Edward was looking for to guide them, but she didn't know his name, and she was not about to make a fool of herself by running up to him or calling out, "Hey, Mister!" She let him go, but she could not help watching him walk, watch the way the fringes of his buckskin clothing danced with his gait. What a strange type of man. She could not help being a little bit attracted, and she thought how interesting it would be to sit down and talk to him, ask him questions about the strange land into which they were journeying.

He stopped at the courthouse entrance, and turned, looking back at her. Again he had caught her staring at him! She quickly turned away, feeling like an idiot, and she hurried away to find Edward.

Rafe Morrisey made his way outside, where he took a thin cigar from a pocket inside his buckskin shirt. He walked over to where a group of travelers had built a small fire while camped in front of the courthouse, and he stooped down to light the cigar. He took a couple of puffs and looked back at the courthouse, the picture of the beautiful woman to whom he had just spoken remaining vivid in his mind. Why, he had no idea. She was just so pretty, and behind those soft brown eyes he had detected a good deal of fear and anxiety. And there was an air of refinement about her that told him she was a step above most of the women around here. What was a woman like that doing headed for California? Something about her rang of wealth and education, of someone who already had everything she could possibly need. It just didn't make sense, but then it was no business of his. He shrugged and walked off to retrieve his horse. He'd taken on another summer's job of guiding a wagon train to California. He had things to take care of.

Chapter Five

We are camped outside the town of Independence, Maggie wrote in her journal. *Some call this place the "jumping off" point, where travelers "jump off" the states and dive into the wild territories farther west.*

People had stared and pointed as the huge McCahan wagons had lumbered off the riverboat and were driven to this place where they were camped. Maggie was beginning to feel almost embarrassed at the grand style in which they traveled, since all others brought along only average size covered wagons, bedding, and clothing on the inside, most other things tied or nailed or hooked to the outside of the wagons. Women wore simple calico dresses and slat bonnets, and, according to Edward, most of these women and the children would have to walk nearly the whole journey, because it was necessary to keep their weight out of the wagons.

"We won't have to do that," he had explained reassuringly. "I made sure I had good, strong animals, and enough of them, to carry the load. I won't have you walking fifteen hundred miles, especially not in the summer heat to come."

Even now a few people laughed and pointed as they walked by, and at a time when she needed the friendship of other women most, Maggie did not feel any warmth and friendliness from those camped around them. She mentioned it to Edward as Marie cleaned up from supper, which had been served on a table spread with a linen cloth and decorated with a candelabra.

"They are just jealous, Dear," Edward had tried to soothe her. "You're beautiful, and it is obvious you are a woman of wealth. Most of the women here are not accustomed to being around someone like you. I don't doubt their husbands are going west to look for gold, perhaps for free land, searching for their own wealth."

It hurt to think these women were unfriendly out of jealousy. Did they think she looked down on them for their plainer dresses and common wagons? She had never given much thought to how more common people would feel about her, simply because she had never been around such people before. She could not think of one family friend or relative who was not considered at least moderately wealthy.

She decided she must make friends with some of these people. After all, they would all have only each other for months to come. They would depend on each other, both physically and emotionally. She was lonely enough as it was. She could not bear the thought of being given the cold shoulder on the long journey ahead and having no one but Edward and Gretta to talk to.

She noticed an older woman struggling with the yoke to which her oxen were hitched. She lifted it from one side, but could not quite raise it enough to remove it from both oxen. Maggie hurried over to lend her a hand. "Would you like some help, Ma'am?"

The woman looked her over with a frown. "You look a mite skinny and weak to me."

"Oh, I'm stronger than you know. Please let me help you."

The woman shrugged and lifted. Maggie lifted from the other side, embarrassed to tell the woman she was afraid of the big oxen, even though she knew they were supposed to be gentle creatures in spite of their size. She gasped and nearly dropped the yoke when the ox standing next to her turned and nudged her at the waist.

"Oh, my!" she muttered, clinging to the heavy yoke and helping the old woman set it aside.

"My husband has gone off with some of the other men to see about a guide," the woman said, walking back to unhitch straps and chains so that the lead oxen could be free to walk off and graze. "The dang fool left these poor beasts still yoked, after making them pull all day yesterday and then leaving them hitched while we came down river on the steamboat. I tell you, mention gold, and all men become idiots."

I can agree with that, Maggie thought.

"Help me unhitch the next team," the woman told her. "You've got your own fancy drivers to do yours."

Maggie rubbed her hands together. They were dirty from handling the yoke, and she realized they had never been that kind of dirty before. She hesitated at the two oxen left hitched. "I, uh, I am afraid I don't know much about hitching and unhitching teams, Ma'am. I just thought as long as the other yoke was loose, I would help you remove it."

The woman faced her, putting her hands on her hips. She was short, but stout and strong looking. "Honey, you'd better learn how to do things like this, and lots of other things. You might end up *having* to know them before this trip is over."

Maggie folded her arms and rubbed the backs of them against a slight chill in the air. "Oh, we have plenty of help—a cook, drivers, plenty of supplies."

"That's obvious. From what we're told, you can't depend on all those things being with you all the way through. The drivers might quit or die, same with your other fancy servants. The oxen and mules might die, which would mean you'd have to abandon all your belongings because there would be no way to pull them. All kinds of things can happen."

"Yes, well, I suppose." Maggie felt awkward and inadequate. "Perhaps you could teach me a few things. And I could have my cook teach me what to do, in case I should have to do it myself."

The woman shook her head. "You're a wonder. Do you have any idea what we're headed for?"

Maggie felt like crying. "I don't think I *want* to know. I never wanted to make this trip in the first place."

"Well, join the party. I'd bet you won't find more than one woman out of this whole bunch who came along because she *wanted* to. Our husbands make up their minds, and that's the end of it."

Maggie nodded. "Yes. My own husband, well, he had problems with his father. He wants to strike out on his own, build a supply business in California. What are *your* husband's plans?"

The woman grunted a short laugh. "Find gold. Get rich. What else?"

"I see. Well, I wish you luck." Maggie started to walk back to her own wagons, but the woman caught her arm.

"What's your name, child?"

"I'm Margaret McCahan, from Pennsylvania. Most call me Maggie. My husband is Edward McCahan."

"Mmmm-hmmm. You say that like I should know the name."

Maggie blushed. "Well, I guess if you were from Pennsylvania, especially the Pittsburgh area, you *would* know the name. I am accustomed to people recognizing it."

The woman rolled her eyes. "Sure. Well, we're from Michigan, and we are obviously not from your class. I think you will find that once we're on the trail we all become the same, with the same dangers and the same hard work, the same needs. It won't make much difference that you're a cut above the rest of us. Trips like this have a way of equalizing things."

"Oh, I don't think of us as above anyone, Ma'am. To be truthful, I came over here because I am longing to make some friends. I've been feeling very lonely since leaving my family behind."

The woman finally grinned. "And the Good Lord only knows what kind of home you left behind. Quite grand, I suspect."

Maggie smiled in return. "Most would think so. My husband has promised to build a home just as grand once we reach California." She looked at her hands. "Oh, my. My hands are quite dirty."

The woman chuckled. "Honey, get used to it. Maybe where

you come from people have a different way of getting respect, but among folks like us, it's dirty hands that will get you more respect than those fancy wagons and your servants and all."

"Really? My husband would have a fit if he knew I had just helped you unyoke your oxen. But I do thank you for your advice. You never told me your name."

The woman stepped closer and put out her hand. "Hazel Schultz."

Maggie shook her hand, taking great relief in having made a friend. "I'm glad to know you, Hazel."

The woman looked her over again. "Well, I guess I'm glad to know you. I thought maybe you'd be pretty stuck-up, what with servants and those fancy wagons and all. Some of the other women probably feel the same way. People have notions about other people, you know, without getting to know them first. I have to apologize for that."

"Well, thank you. I am far from stuck-up, I assure you. And I have never been away from my mother and sisters before, let alone for such an undertaking as this one, knowing I might never see them again. Most of the women here will hardly look at me, and it hurts."

The woman still had hold of her hand, and she squeezed it. "Sure it does. I'll pass the word. They'll all come around. For a journey like what we're about to take, us women have to stick together. Our men are so caught up in the gold rush that most of them don't know which end is up. They've got big dreams, and we're expected to come along and feed them and nurse them along the way. I swear, God should have made woman first so she could be head of the household and keep the men from doing stupid things."

Maggie agreed, with a wider grin. "Yes, that would have been better, wouldn't it? Thank you, Hazel, for befriending me. Perhaps you could teach me how to unhitch the rest of the oxen."

"Sure!" The woman led her to the other two oxen and showed her which chains and straps to loosen first before removing the next yoke. Before they finished, Maggie heard Edward shout her name. She jumped and turned to see him standing there watching her. Beside him stood a taller, broader man, dressed in buckskins. To her surprise she felt a sudden rush of pleasure combined with an embarrassment she could not understand. It was the same man she had seen in the courthouse!

"What the heck are you doing over there?" Edward demanded.

Maggie felt immediately defensive. "I am helping Mrs. Schultz unhitch her oxen," she answered firmly. "I need to learn how to do these things, Edward. It might be necessary—"

"It *won't* be necessary! We have enough help for such things. You could have asked one of our men to help the woman." He paused and nodded to Hazel. "No offense, Ma'am. Any time you need help, you just ask. I just don't want my wife doing these things. She isn't used to it, and she's—"

"Edward!" Maggie interrupted, her anger with him growing. "I don't need you babying me. I am perfectly capable of helping someone if they need it, and I am going to need some women friends on this trip. You tend to your needs, and I will tend to mine!" For some reason his chiding and pampering her in front of the buckskin-clad stranger deeply embarrassed her.

"Maggie, I am just concerned about your welfare. You aren't used to—"

"I *have* to get used to these things. What if something were to happen to you along the way, or to the drivers?"

"Well, I—I would never expect you to take over such menial chores!"

Maggie glanced at Hazel, seeing the affront in her eyes. She turned back to her husband. "I do not consider them menial. Back home they would be, but on this trip such chores are a necessity, and I am no less able and no more special than any of the other women here." Maggie felt an odd pride growing deep within her, and she was surprised at her own behavior. At home she never would have considered getting near a big ox and unhitching it, getting her hands filthy in the process; and never had she spoken up to Edward in their short married life.

"Well, Dear, if you think it is necessary. I don't happen to think it is, but if it makes you happy, you help the other women all you want." Now it was Edward who seemed embarrassed as he turned to the stranger. "My wife has a mind of her own, something I didn't even realize until this moment," he explained, casting Maggie a disparaging look. "Maggie, I want you to meet Rafe Morrisey. He will be guiding the wagon train we will join. We leave the day after tomorrow."

Maggie walked up to the man, putting out her hand. "How do you do, Mister Morrisey?"

He shook her hand firmly, giving no indication he had already met her. "Nice to meet you, Mrs. McCahan."

Maggie felt an odd tingle at his touch. "And you, Mr. Morrisey." She quickly removed her hand. "Are we to assume from your dress that you are experienced at this?"

"Believe me, Maggie, I have already asked all the right questions," Edward told her. "You don't need to ask more."

Maggie could see her husband was clearly irritated with her. She was not behaving at all like the Maggie he knew, and maybe she wasn't. She had not felt like herself since leaving Pennsylvania. "You can't blame a woman for being concerned, Edward. This will not be an easy trip for any of us." She looked up at Rafe Morrisey. "Will it, Mr. Morrisey?"

"No, Ma'am." His voice was deep, with a sure tone. "And I *am* experienced. I've traveled the West since well before gold was discovered in California. I've trapped, hunted, even lived with the Shoshoni Indians one winter after being attacked by a bear. I wasn't in much shape to take care of myself."

"Oh! How awful! Will we be in danger from bears?"

Rafe grinned with a note of sarcasm. "Let's hope bears are the only trouble we encounter. You never know, Ma'am. Every trip is different." He turned to look over their wagons, and Hazel Schultz watched, wanting to chuckle at the sight of the McCahan wagons. Poor Maggie McCahan. Her husband seemed truly concerned, but much too confident, and too sure he knew all there was to know. He was obviously a man who hated admitting being wrong about anything.

"You'll never make it with those wagons," Rafe said, turning to Edward. "They're too big and heavy."

"I have the best and strongest animals for pulling them, Mr. Morrisey, and plenty of them."

Rafe put his hands on his hips. "For one thing, I expect everyone to just call me Rafe. The term Mr. doesn't set right with me. My real name is Raphael, but I don't ever use that, either. At any rate, maybe you don't realize that from here on, for the next fifteen hundred miles, the trip is pretty much uphill all the way. By the time we reach the Rockies we will be a mile above sea level. There will be times when it looks like we are heading along flat land, but when you look behind you you will see we've been going uphill and hardly realizing it. But you can bet the animals *will* realize it. They won't last, Mr. McCahan, no matter how good they are. And when we reach the mountains, *if* you reach them with these things, you'll never make it over them. Not with this kind of burden."

"Well, I insist that we try," Edward returned. "These are all things my wife needs with her, and we must have the spare wagon for her personal servant and the cook. We of course must have the wagon that contains all our food and the cookstove, and—"

"Cookstove!" Rafe frowned. "One of those heavy iron things?"

"Yes. Oh, I didn't bring the best. It's only a Concord range. I'm having an Irving range and oven shipped—"

"Cookstoves weigh far too much to haul one up the mountains," Rafe interrupted.

"We've gotten this far with it."

"Sure, on a riverboat, and the short trip it took to get here. If you want any oxen or mules left by the time we reach the Rockies, Mr. McCahan, the stove has got to go. Use a campfire."

"But . . . our cook doesn't know how to cook that way!"

"Then let her learn from the other women. No cookstove, Mr. McCahan. I'm sorry, but you'll have to get rid of it. While you're in a town you can probably sell it to a supplier. I'd hate to just dump it out there on the prairie somewhere, but that's what will happen if you don't get rid of it now." Rafe looked at Maggie. "And you, Ma'am. Do you have a lot of books along?"

"No. Only a few, I assure you. We are having most of them shipped by ocean."

"Good. How about furniture? Big heavy tables? Dressers?"

"A four-poster bed," Maggie answered. "It's taken apart and stored in the spare supply wagon. Also a table. We use it at mealtime. And I have a large trunk that holds my personals. And we have a copper bathing tub with us."

Rafe sighed. "Those things will also have to go. Far too much weight. You look well off enough to order things like that once you get there. Do they have sentimental value?"

"Look, Mr. Morrisey—I mean Rafe—we can't ask my wife—"

"Do they have sentimental value?" Rafe repeated, still looking at Maggie. She thought about the bed. It had belonged to her own parents and was hand-crafted by a local furniture maker who had done a remarkably beautiful job. "Just the bed. It once belonged to my parents. And the trunk was my grandmother's."

"Well, I'm afraid the bed will have to go, as will the table and the copper tub. You folks will have to learn to eat off the back of a wagon or holding your plates in your laps like other people do. And you'll bathe in the river like everyone else. The trunk isn't quite such a problem, at least not yet. We can decide on that later."

"I will not sell the trunk or leave it along the trail, even if I have to carry it on my back!" Maggie told him flatly. "It was my grandmother's, and it was brought here all the way from France. It is something I have always loved. My most treasured possessions are inside it!"

Rafe saw the determination in her eyes, as well as a look of desperation. This beautiful, sophisticated woman did not belong here. She belonged in a castle, wearing jewels . . . sleeping in that four-poster bed. Why did it disturb him to picture her lying in that bed, wearing a silk nightgown . . . "The trunk can stay. If there is a problem later, we'll figure something out."

"Rafe—"

"No arguments!" The words were directed at Edward then,

who was the one who had spoken up. Rafe had no doubt he was going to object to getting rid of the bed and table. "Anyone who goes with me as a guide has to do what I tell them. Believe me, Mr. McCahan, if you don't do what I say you risk killing your animals, maybe even yourself or your wife, because of the hardships you will encounter. These big wagons are just going to make matters worse, but if you unload some of your heavier items right now, it might help." He glanced at Maggie once more. "Sorry, Ma'am. I don't mean to sound harsh. I just know what will and won't work." He tipped his hat, then nodded to Hazel and to Edward. "I'll see all of you at the meeting we've planned for tomorrow morning. Everyone has one day to get things ready the way I instruct them." He turned and left.

"I'm sorry, Maggie," Edward apologized. "I didn't know he'd be so abrupt."

Maggie watched Rafe walk away, again fascinated by the way the fringes of his buckskins swayed with his gait. "He is just doing his job. We have to do what he says, Edward. He knows what lies ahead. We don't."

Edward scowled. "Just stay near our wagons, will you? I don't need you going around helping others and risking getting hurt."

She faced him squarely. "I need to help out or go crazy, Edward. And I need the company of the other women. Please just tend to getting us there safely and let me do what I must do."

Edward sighed, touching her face. "I love you, Maggie. I need you. I just don't want anything to happen to you. You aren't used to this life."

"And neither are you. We will learn together. We might as well gradually get ourselves acclimated to this new life. We have no choice. These aren't the bricked streets of Pittsburgh, you know."

Edward was surprised at her sudden spunk. "Just be careful, Maggie."

"I will. And send one of our drivers to help Hazel finish unhitching her oxen." Maggie walked to her own wagon, stopping to watch Rafe Morrisey talking to another couple. Why did his presence bring out in her a desire to appear strong and sure? Why did she hate looking weak and pampered in front of him? She supposed it was partly because men like Rafe Morrisey had no respect for weak women, but why did she care?

Chapter Six

Rafe Morrisey re-introduced himself to the emigrants he would take across the country to California.

"For those of you who don't already know it, I have made this trip several times already. I've trapped beaver, hunted bear and buffalo, lived with Indians, and in general I know the West about as well as anyone can know it."

He began pacing, reminding Maggie of a restless animal. Again today he wore buckskins, the gun and knife strapped to his waist. He looked as though he had bathed and shaved, his face clean and smooth . . . and uncomfortably handsome. He wore no hat, and his hair was slicked back into a tail, tied at the base of his neck and wrapped with some kind of furry animal skin.

Standing to the side were two men Rafe had already told them would accompany the wagon train as scouts. One was older, a very rugged-looking character with a gray beard and worn buckskins. Rafe had introduced him as Jack Latham, "a man who knows the mountains better than the eagles." Latham looked like someone who had never spent a night under a roof in his entire life, and although he did not appear terribly dirty he was certainly far from tidy. He, too, sported a knife and a handgun at his waist, and he leaned on a long musket. His hair, too, was long, and it hung in tangled, graying disarray beneath a floppy leather hat.

The other man was an Indian, "the only specie that knows the West better than Jack and the animals." The remark had brought a few nervous laughs, and it was obvious some of the people were a little upset that an Indian would be along. Maggie did not mind, deciding that if Rafe Morrisey thought he was trustworthy then he probably was. Her confidence increased when he explained that Wolf Hunter, as he was called, had saved his life once in a bear attack. She supposed it was the one that had caused Rafe to spend a winter with the Shoshoni. Wolf Hunter looked very clean, and he wore buckskins that had a lovely beaded design on the front of the shirt. His long, black hair was worn tied at the side of his neck with a beaded hair ornament. He, too, wore a knife at his waist, as well as a small hatchet, but no handgun, although he held a musket in one hand. Maggie thought he would be rather good-looking, for an Indian, if not for a long scar on one cheek, and pockmarks on his face, probably caused by measles or smallpox.

"Before we get started, I want to know right now if there are any women in this group who are carrying," Rafe announced.

Several women blushed, and some bowed their heads in embarrassment.

"Apparently not," Rafe continued after a moment. "Don't lie about it. If any woman is carrying, wait until next year. There are no doctors in this group, and I suppose there are a few women who could help with a birth, but this is a tough trip, and too often women lose their babies and sometimes their own lives in the process. I would rather start out with no such risks. If it happens along the way, I can't do much about that."

More women blushed, including Maggie. Some of the men chuckled.

"All I can say to you men is if you love your wives and want to arrive in California with the mother of your children still alive and healthy, then you had better think about abstaining along the way. Besides, I think most of you will be too damn tired to think about things like that once you get to lie down."

More men laughed, and several women gasped at the embarrassing words. Maggie felt strangely drawn by them, to think that a man could be so straightforward about such a thing and talk about carrying as though it were no more embarrassing than cooking a meal. He was matter-of-fact, and he was apparently a man who did not dance around words.

"Always wear shoes, and in high grass keep children inside the wagons." he said, as he proceeded with what he had said would be the "Rules of the road." "Snakes hide in the grass. No use of firearms without my permission. More people are hurt or killed from careless use of firearms than any other reason. Only experienced men will be allowed to hunt. I'll know when it's necessary and the best areas to hunt. No buffalo hunting. If you don't have experience hunting buffalo, you can get yourself killed real easy. Buffalo hunting is my responsibility, and Jack's and Wolf Hunter's. They will do most all of the hunting, whether it's buffalo or deer or bear. You men have the job of taking care of livestock, wagon maintenance, guarding your horses, watching out for your women and children, and in general obeying the rules and keeping yourselves alive and healthy until we reach California. I don't intend to get there with a bunch of widows."

There came a little more nervous laughter, as already a few people were beginning to wonder if they really wanted to do this.

"Once in Indian country, volunteers will be needed for night watch to guard the livestock," Rafe continued. "Horse stealing is the biggest problem with Indians." He turned to Wolf Hunter. "Isn't that so, my friend?"

Wolf Hunter grinned slyly. "It is so."

This time the laughter was easier, but a few studied Wolf Hunter with obvious doubt and distrust in their eyes.

"No firing at Indians. No insulting Indians. No attempting to converse with Indians," Rafe continued. "All contact with Indians will be handled by myself, Jack, and Wolf Hunter. Indians are easily insulted. Most of those we run into will merely want to trade with us. One wrong move and you could turn a friendly bunch of Indians into a war party, and believe me, folks, you don't want that. There are no better, more determined fighters out there than the people who know that land best and who think they own it. Always remember that in their minds we are intruding into their hunting grounds, and that is a big issue with them. So leave the Indian dealings to me. You mind your own business and stay close to your wagons whenever they are around."

He walked over to a campfire and pulled a small stick from it, using the burning end to light a thin cigar before continuing.

"Supplies," he went on. "Make sure you have plenty." He glanced at Edward. "And those who have more than enough may have to share before the end of our journey. I'll have no arguing about it." He walked in a circle, addressing everyone then. "You will need at least eighty pounds of flour for each adult, a good twenty pounds of corn meal, and plenty of ham and bacon, one hundred pounds, packed in lard to keep it fresh. Dried beef, twenty or thirty pounds, fifty pounds of coffee, maybe forty pounds of brown sugar. If you like tea, bring plenty of that, twelve to fifteen pounds of beans and rice. And bring dried fruit. I'm told fruit helps keep teeth from rotting and is good for the bones. So is cheese. Bring plenty of salt, at least ten pounds. When you get out on that prairie in hundred-degree heat and no shade, you'll sweat plenty and you'll need to replenish the salt you lose. Soap is your choice. Everybody has their ideas on the importance of bathing." He turned to Jack. "Jack here doesn't believe in it."

Everyone laughed then, including Jack.

"Scrubbing his face and hands once in a while is about as far as he goes, and I have no concern over how often any of you washes. Just don't expect to sit in a luxurious tub whenever you want. Most of the time there just won't be time for things like that, and at times not enough water to even consider it, but as long as we're near a river, which we will be through most of the plains, you can use river water. The quickest way to wash is right in the river. Bring eight or nine bars of soap. If you run out, sand and sage do just as well. Sand scrubs off the dirt, and the sage makes you smell good."

Was that how Rafe Morrisey washed? Maggie wondered

how he smelled. He looked perfectly clean and—*Stop it!* she chided herself inwardly. *What is wrong with you? You are a married woman, and not only that, Rafe Morrisey is not the kind of man any decent woman has fond thoughts about!* What disturbed her most was that she had never had for Edward these strange curiosities and whispers of desire that she felt tiny nudges of over Rafe Morrisey.

"You need soda, cream of tartar, so the women tell me, lard, crackers, water barrels. Out on the prairie there are no trees, except along the river. When we get to places farther west where there just plain are no trees at all, there will be no wood for cooking. Carry as much as you can when we leave places where there are trees, but my advice is not to use it unless totally necessary. There are certain places where it will be more important, and in between you can use buffalo chips for your fires."

"What are buffalo chips?" one woman asked with a frown.

Rafe looked at Wolf Hunter and grinned, then turned back to the woman. "Ma'am, buffalo chips are dried buffalo dung."

The woman drew in her breath and put a hand to her chest. "Oh, my! We have to pick them up?"

Rafe nodded. "Yes, Ma'am. Out west you learn to make do with what you have. Indians have used buffalo chips for generations, for fires. They pound them into a powder and put them in the bottom of cradleboards before putting the babies in. The powdered chips soak up the urine and they don't irritate the babies at all."

Another woman put a hand to her mouth in astonishment.

"How crude!" another commented.

"It isn't crude at all," Rafe told her. "The Indians have a use for every last piece of a buffalo—bones, blood, bladder, intestines, horns, hair, skin, hooves, teeth, everything, including their droppings. Without the buffalo I don't doubt some Indian tribes would literally die out. Don't judge them just because they do things a little differently from you."

Maggie thought Rafe seemed well spoken for a man who surely had had no education. There were so many things she wanted to ask him, like where he was from, how he had ended up in this wild land befriending Indians.

"We'll follow the Platte River most of the way through Nebraska Territory," he continued. "If we're lucky, we'll make fifteen to twenty miles a day, but rivers, mud, and accidents will often slow us down. In ten days to two weeks we should make Elm Creek, in another two weeks Ash Hollow, and on to Fort Kearny. If things go right, we'll make Fort Laramie in four to six weeks, by the end of June. After that we'll be in the Rockies. We'll head to the South Pass and follow the Sweetwater and the Green Rivers on to Fort Hall. That's where anyone going on to Oregon splits off and heads north. Some going to California prefer to take the Great Salt Desert rather than going up to Fort Hall. It's a shortcut, but not worth the time saved. The cost in animal and human life is too high because of heat and the lack of fresh water, so don't ask me to go that route. I won't do it. When we come to the forts, you can rest, mend whatever needs mending, stock up on a few more supplies."

Maggie shivered at the thought of being on the trail so long, through mountains and prairie heat.

"Between the Rockies and the Sierras is a lot of desert," Rafe warned. "No one takes a drink or waters their stock without letting me check the water first. There is a lot of salt water out there, and alkaline, water that can poison your stock. Once we get into the Sierras it will be cooler and we'll have trees again. But we will also have some tough mountains to scale, and in some places it will be very important to be as quiet as possible so you don't startle the teams. There are roads in the Rockies and the Sierras that will make you dizzy because of their height, and at places they are dangerously narrow."

Rafe puffed on his cigar a moment, glancing at Maggie again. What was it about her that made him want to stare at her? She was beautiful, that was sure, and she looked so out of place here. He supposed that was it. He felt sorry for her. She just plain didn't belong here, and he was sure her bravery and determination were only pretended. This was her husband's dream, not hers. But then, he supposed it was that way for most of the women along.

"Many of you have wives and children along, so I want the single men to be tolerant of some of the problems that will pose. And no matter what the argument, I tolerate no fighting. Disputes will be brought to me, and I will decide how they should be handled. What I say goes, or you will be left behind. Once we make it over the Sierras, we're home free. From there on you will be in beautiful, sunny, warm California."

Cheers went up, and men threw hats into the air. Maggie felt only a sick feeling in the pit of her stomach.

"Tomorrow we'll be on our way, Maggie!" Edward grabbed her then and whirled her around, kissing her. "Are you excited?"

She smiled for him. "Of course I am," she lied.

"Thank you, Maggie, for doing this. It will be worth it. I promise you. And I'll take good care of you the whole way."

She blinked back tears. "I know you will, Edward."

Chapter Seven

Much to Edward's chagrin, Maggie walked, simply because the other women were walking. She decided that if she was going to make friends with them she had better join them in their misery, and misery it was the first several days. Most of the other women appeared to be hardworking farm wives, yet even they complained of pained muscles and aching feet at first, as they trained their bodies to get used to walking from eight to fifteen miles a day, sometimes twenty. It was even worse for Maggie, who was not accustomed to anywhere near the hard work the other women had known.

By the fifth day her calf, thigh, and groin muscles brought sheer misery. Her feet were blistered, her calf muscles were cramping, and it became so hot she wanted to rip off her clothes and walk naked. During the day there was an endless variety of bugs that liked to sting and bite, and the nights were worse, mosquitoes bombarding them like vultures after blood. The mosquito netting helped, but still, many of the pesky bugs got through.

''Do you ride?''

Maggie turned to see Rafe Morrisey riding behind her to her left. ''Where I come from, Mr. Morrisey, women ride in buggies or coaches.'' She forged ahead, pretending to be just fine. For some reason she hated the thought of Rafe Morrisey thinking her too delicate for something like this.

''I'm surprised your husband didn't think to bring horses for riding.''

''He intended that I ride in the wagon at all times, and he wanted to walk with the drivers and learn how to handle the oxen, just in case. He was afraid bringing horses would make it too tempting for him not to learn this the right way, and Lord knows we already have enough animals to look out for.''

Maggie and a few other women had fallen behind a little, and Rafe had come to make sure everything was all right. He hated to see the women walking, knew that until they got used to this daily struggle they would go through many days of terrible aches and pains. For some reason, the thought of Maggie McCahan's misery bothered him the most. ''I don't think your husband planned things too well, but then I guess that's none of my business.''

''No, it isn't, Mr. Morrisey.'' She hated to realize he was right, and she didn't want to insult Edward by agreeing. ''This trip is very important to Edward, for more reasons than you know. He's doing his best.''

''I'm sure he is. I've noticed some of the women do ride once in a while, even each other's horses. I know for the most part the horses that are along have to be saved for times when they'll be needed for something more important, but the weight of a woman isn't going to tire them much, at least not most of these women. There are a couple along who probably weigh more than their husbands, but they'll walk the weight off soon enough.''

Maggie scowled. ''Are you trying to tell me to ride one of their horses, Mr. Morrisey?''

Before she realized what he was doing, Rafe had dismounted and was walking beside her.

''Yes. And please call me Rafe. You need to quit torturing yourself trying to prove to the other women that you can handle this just as well as they can. Or maybe you just don't want them to think that *you* think you're above them.''

"I *don't* think that I am above them."

"I know you don't. But they think you do. Most of them seem to be warming up to you. I just don't want you to kill yourself trying to make that happen."

"I am just fine."

"No, you aren't. I want you to ride my horse for a while."

"That isn't necessary."

He grabbed her arm and stopped her. "Yes, it is. I'm *ordering* you to ride."

Why did his touch send shivers through her? That angered her. "You can't order me to do anything."

"Yes, I can. How badly blistered are your feet, Mrs. McCahan? How bad do your legs and hips ache?"

"I am just fine." Maggie gasped when Rafe suddenly grasped her around the waist and lifted her as though she weighed nothing. He plopped her sideways on his horse. He took hold of the reins then and kept walking.

"Stay there for a while."

She looked over at some of the other women, most of whom were smiling. "You'd better do as he says," Hazel called out.

Maggie felt both embarrassed and stunned . . . stunned at the odd thrill she had felt when Rafe Morrisey's strong hands had grasped her about the waist. She had to secretly admit that it felt wonderful to be off her feet, and she decided she might as well take advantage of the situation. She crooked one leg around his saddle horn to brace herself better, then grasped the back edge of the saddle to hang on.

"Tonight you will soak your feet in warm soda water," Rafe told her, "and tomorrow, whether you like it or not, you *will* ride in your wagon. We're on pretty flat land right now, and it's surprisingly solid for spring. I'm sure we'll run into some fearsome mud soon, but as long as the burden isn't too terrible yet on the oxen, go ahead and ride. God knows the McCahan wagons are already carrying more than they should. And in case you think I am singling you out, I'm not. I intend to order a few more women to ride tomorrow. Then those who don't can ride the next day. We'll be coming soon enough to country where weight will mean everything."

Maggie sighed with resignation. ''Whatever you say.'' She rode on in silence for several minutes, watching Rafe Morrisey's shoulders, his almost graceful stride, thinking how his long, dark hair looked clean and shiny. ''Why do you do this, Mr.—I mean, Rafe?''

''Do what?''

''You know. Lead wagon trains. Make this trip over and over? Why do you keep risking the danger of it, the discomforts?''

He walked another minute or so before answering. ''Mostly just something to do. And there is a beauty and a peace out here that can't be matched anyplace else. It's easy to see why the Indians love it and want to keep it for themselves. You'll see. The farther west we go, the more beauty you will see, and the more attached you will become.''

''Don't you want to settle and live in a normal home? Don't you want to be in a city with bustling sidewalks, theaters, restaurants, doctors and hospitals, brick streets? Don't you want a wife? Children?''

''I've had all those things.''

Maggie was surprised by the answer. She wanted to ask how, when, why, who? Where were his wife and children now? But there was something about the tone of his voice that told her he wouldn't want to talk about it right now. ''I'm sorry if I have brought up something I shouldn't have. I've told you certain things are none of your business, and I've asked things that are none of mine.''

''It's all right.''

Some of the other women began gathering spring wildflowers and sticking them in their hair and making bouquets. It became a game with them, to see who could gather the most, and the air became filled with laughter and screams as some tried to race to certain flowers before others could get there. Maggie looked around, studying a sea of wildflowers for nearly as far as she could see. ''It *is* pretty, I guess, if you like the country.''

''It's pretty whether you like country living or not. I guess if you've never known anything like it, it's a little hard to understand why someone would like the openness. I guess for a man it's just a great feeling of independence. Is that why your husband came out here?''

''Yes. He doesn't really need to go looking for gold or to start a new business. He already has all the money he needs. But he has a very controlling father, stepfather I should say, who makes life miserable for him. He felt a need to go out and do something on his own, without John McCahan hovering over him.''

Rafe continued leading his horse, his back to her. ''Well, we all have our reasons for doing what we do.''

Maggie took a handkerchief from the waist of her dress and used it to wipe at perspiration at her neck and forehead. Her dress was unbuttoned from the neck part way down her chest, and she was certain she looked a mess, her hair, which had been curled into a neat bun this morning, beginning to fall out in wet strings about her face. She wanted dearly to take off the cotton bonnet she wore, which had a broad, slat brim, but she could not bear the thought of what the prairie sun would do to her skin. She had borrowed the bonnet from Hazel, since she didn't have such common bonnets to wear. Because she had expected to ride in the wagon most of the way, she had not thought much about sun protection. How foolish of her. She felt foolish about a lot of things, most of all for even allowing Edward to do this. They could simply have moved to another city, anything but this hideous trip.

Still, Rafe might be right about the beauty of this land. So far she could not appreciate anything good about it. One young woman who Maggie recognized as the oldest daughter of Mildred and Graydon Howell, who had five other children, ran over and handed her a fist full of daisies and an assortment of other wildflowers. ''Here, Mrs. McCahan!''

''Why, thank you! What is your name again?''

''Katie. I'm fifteen. What is it like to be rich, Mrs. McCahan? It must be wonderful!''

Maggie was at a loss for words. She had known no other kind of life. With nothing to compare it to, how could she describe what it was like to be wealthy? She had never been *without* money. "I . . . I'm not sure what to say, Katie. All I can tell you is that it doesn't feel much different to have or not have money, as far as I know. Certainly not when we are out here on a wagon train in the middle of nowhere."

"Oh, but I want to hear more about what life is like where you came from. How old are you? You don't look much older than me."

"Well! Thank you! I am twenty-two, Katie. I went to a special girls' finishing school before I married, and I traveled to Europe."

"Europe! You must tell me more! Will you walk with me tomorrow? My mother would also like to get to know you better. She talked to Hazel Schultz about you, and Mrs. Schultz says you're very nice. She says you want to learn to cook and to sew. I can teach you. You're welcome to walk with us and come and eat with us any time."

"Thank you, Katie. I will do that. And you must spend an evening with us and taste Maria's cooking. She is very good."

Katie laughed. "I can't imagine having someone do all my cooking for me. Don't you *ever* cook?"

Maggie glanced at Rafe, whose back was still to her, but she sensed he was smiling. She felt suddenly embarrassed and inadequate. "No, but, I do embroider." She noticed Rafe shaking his head.

"Mr. Morrisey, my mother said to tell you you are to eat with us tonight. You will come, won't you? Ours is the wagon with the flag on one end."

"I know which one it is. I'll be there. Thank your mother for the invite."

"Yes, Sir, I will."

Maggie did not miss the longing way in which Katie had looked at Rafe. Why did that stir an odd jealousy in her soul?

"One of our lead mules is my special pet," Katie told Rafe. "I raised her from a baby. Her name is Beaner. I'll show her to you."

"I'd like that," Rafe told her.

"We'll see you this evening, then. I bake good biscuits. I'll make some for you!'' Katie ran off then, turning and waving to Maggie.

''I've noticed you seem to eat with someone different every night,'' Maggie told him. ''Is that a custom, that the travelers feed their guide?''

''Most of the time, if there are women along.''

''Well, then, you must eat with us, also. How about tomorrow night?''

''That's fine with me.''

''Pork roast? Marie makes a fine roast. She told me she can cook a small one in about an hour in the Dutch Oven if she has a hot enough fire.''

''Whatever suits your fancy. It's always appreciated.''

Maggie looked ahead, into a horizon that seemed endless. ''What is that dark line out there, Rafe?''

''I've been watching it. It's a storm coming this way.''

''Do you think it's a bad one?''

''That's my guess. Spring on the plains and prairies is always a time for some pretty wild storms. I've seen streams turn into torrents in minutes. I've seen hail as big as those round pincushions I've seen ladies use. And I've been through more than one tornado.''

''Tornado! I've heard of them, but I have never seen one. Are they as terrible as I've heard?''

''Probably worse. I'm afraid you'd better get down. I've got to ride ahead and see if I can find a ravine or something we can settle in until the storm blows over.''

He reached up and grasped her about the waist again, lifting her down. Maggie could not help noticing the hard muscle of his arms as she grasped them for support. There was something enticingly masculine about him that she had never felt around Edward, and it made her feel guilty. ''Thank you for the break from walking,'' she told him.

''I have extra horses along. I would get one for you, but there's no time right now. I've got to find Wolf Hunter. I suspect he's already been looking for a place to lay low. The riverbank might be best, if there's nothing else.''

Rafe eased up onto his horse in one swift motion, not even

using the stirrup. He rode off, looking as though he and the horse were a part of each other. Maggie watched in fascination, realizing only then that the last few minutes were the first time she had not thought about her aching feet, or about missing home.

Chapter Eight

The calm morning soon turned into a mad scramble to find shelter. Animals were whipped into moving a little faster in order to get as many wagons as possible into a slight, rolling dip in the earth. "Probably won't help much," Rafe had shouted, "but anything low is better than the complete open!"

Maggie didn't know what to think. She had heard stories about tornadoes, and Rafe had only stopped them here as a precaution. There might be no tornado at all, but it was a sure thing that a mighty storm was coming. She huddled with Gretta and Maria, while Edward helped the drivers keep the animals calm. One other family's team had already bolted, running off with their wagon and probably all the possessions they had left in the world. Rafe had ridden after it, and neither had returned.

"What will we do if Mr. Morrisey doesn't come back?" Maria asked. All three women lay in the lowest portion of the ditch, covered with a quilt.

"We still have Jack and Wolf Hunter," Maggie assured them, although she, too, worried what they would do without Rafe. She already felt an odd closeness to him she could not explain, and she realized she would feel very sad if something happened to him, and disappointed that she had never gotten to know more about him.

The wind picked up to a furious howl, and the temperature seemed to drop several degrees in seconds. Maggie and the other two women ducked their heads under the quilt, but then Maggie felt something hitting her back. She raised her head to see small balls of hail hitting the ground as if in a fierce snowstorm, quickly piling into layers, bouncing madly and filling the air with the clacking sound of balls hitting each other.

"What is it!" Maria asked, as the weight of the balls of ice began to literally pile on top of them. She kept her head under the quilt and refused to look out.

"It's hail!" Maggie answered her. She ducked her own head back under, and she could hear women screaming and children crying up and down the ditch-like area where they all hovered together. Oxen bellowed, mules brayed, horses whinnied, and men were shouting curses at the animals to hold them still, as well as shouting orders to each other. Their voices were gradually lost against the raging wind and pummeling hail, which became very noisy as it fell in torrents.

The roar of the wind turned into a sound Maggie had never heard before, a thunderous rumble that seemed like the wrath of God Himself, come to destroy the world. She heard a crashing sound, dared to peek out from under the quilt, which was now weighted down with hail that was beginning to melt against the warmth of their bodies. "Dear God!" she muttered. A wagon, which had apparently been torn away from its team, was whirling in the air several hundred yards ahead. It was the strangest sight she had ever witnessed, and she stared in fascination until the wagon finally landed on its side, most of its contents still whirling in a funnel-shaped, black cloud that suddenly pulled up, dropping everything it had held and disappearing into a dark cloud overhead.

Suddenly the wind was calmer, but rain began to fall in a torrent, the temperature warming again and the hail melting so that they all lay soaked under a soggy quilt, the water penetrating right through the last layer of underwear the women had on. The rain lasted several minutes before letting up into a light drizzle, enough so that people could begin crawling out from under whatever shelter they could find or make for themselves.

At first all was quiet, but then one young woman broke into frantic sobbing. "All our things! All our things!" she wailed. "It's all gone, Willard. All gone!"

"Barney! You all right?" she heard Hazel call to her husband.

Maggie was impressed by the woman's devotion to her aging husband, and the love she held for two sons who had already gone to California the year before. She had learned over campfire talks that Hazel and Barney were determined to go and find them, join their sons in California, because "the boys" were all that meant anything to them.

"Maggie! Maggie!" Edward was calling for her. Maggie turned to Maria and Gretta.

"Are you all right?"

"Just drenched!" Gretta answered. "We must get you into some dry cloze, Maggie."

"Just take care of yourselves." Maggie trudged toward her husband, walking in water that had grown to about a foot deep in the low area in which they had waited out the storm. Her dress felt as though it weighed fifty pounds, and strands of hair that had fallen from the bun at the nape of her neck were now pasted to her wet face. "Edward! Are you all right?"

Edward hurried up to her, splashing through water. He grasped her arms.

"Maggie!" He grabbed her close. "I was so afraid. What would I do without my Maggie? I'm so sorry, Darling. Are you all right?"

"I'm fine. You didn't answer me."

He pulled away. "I'm fine."

"Edward! Your forehead is bleeding!"

He wiped at the small cut. "It's nothing. Something hit me when things were flying in the air."

Just as quickly as the storm had hit it had left them, and now even the rain stopped. The sun peeked out, and the air felt heavy and muggy. Maggie had hoped the rain would bring a break in the heat, but the momentary cool air that had passed through was gone, replaced by air just as hot as that they had been experiencing, only now more humid. She did not doubt that would make the mosquitoes worse.

"What is the damage?" she asked, looking around at clothes, pots and pans, barrels, and other belongings strewn everywhere.

"Willard and Susan Haggarty's wagon was blown away. We'll have to go out and see what can be salvaged." He grasped her arms again. "I'm afraid the top half of our own wagon is also gone, bedding and all. The men and I will see if we can repair it enough so that we can put canvas over the top of what's left. We'll have to rearrange things in the lower half, since we'll have to sleep there from now on. But right now everything is wet. I hope Rafe will allow us a day or so to put things out to dry, or clothes and bedding will become mildewed."

Maggie looked around at an endless horizon on every side. "If Rafe Morrisey is even still alive. He never came back."

"Oh, a man like that has survival intincts most common folks don't have. I'm sure he's all right. Why don't you bring Marie and Gretta over to the wagon and try to find something still relatively dry that you can change into? I'll help the men get the team moving and get the wagons out of this ditch."

Edward left her, and Maggie thought about his remark about Rafe. Yes, he was a man who seemed as though he could survive just about anything. That was what fascinated her about him—so skilled, so brave, so daring, a man of adventure, a man who could probably handle himself in any situation. She wanted to know about his wife and children, what had happened. Why was he so well-spoken, as though educated, yet out here in an untamed land helping people make this deathly journey to an unknown fate? Were they all fools? Was whatever lay at the other end of this trail worth the trip?

There was no time to think about Rafe then; only time to help others. She and Maria and Gretta took turns holding up blankets so that each woman could change her clothes. A few other women were doing the same, and from reports they were getting, no one had been hurt. Still, not much was retrieved from the Haggarty's belongings. They were a young couple off to find gold and get rich, but now they had little in the way of belongings, certainly not enough to make it all the way to California, not even a wagon. Two of their oxen had been killed when the wagon was ripped away, but they had two left. They would have to purchase another wagon once they came across a fort or settlement along the way. Several women were already getting together whatever supplies they could possibly spare, including clothing and blankets and precious food, to donate to the young couple to help keep them going.

"Edward, they need a wagon," Maggie told her husband. "Please let them use Maria and Gretta's for sleeping. Maria and Gretta can sleep with me, and you can sleep outside with the men. I'm sorry, Edward, but we have so much, and they have so little, now. We are obligated to help them."

Edward frowned, watching Susan Haggarty weep against her husband's shoulder. "Maggie, if we do it for them, others will expect it. What if there are more disasters?"

"There *will* be more disasters. We will handle each one as it comes along. There might be a time when *we* need *them*, Edward. I've never seen so much caring and sharing as I have so far on this trip. I've never given much thought to the fact that some people can't afford all of their needs. But we can. It's our duty to help those who cannot. Isn't that what they preach about in church back home?"

She missed church, missed hearing the bells toll hymns softly on warm Sunday mornings, beckoning all to come. She and her family would dress in their finest, all going to church together in a large carriage, wearing gloves and carrying parasols. She never thought then that life would ever be any different for her. Now she wondered if she would ever hear church bells again. The only way to worship out here was to offer help to others and obey God's command to do so.

Edward sighed, looking down at her. "You are turning out to be a wonder, Maggie. I never thought you would adapt to all of this the way you have."

Maggie studied his blue eyes, remembering his hurts all the times he'd cried over feeling unloved when he was little.

"Edward, you have a dream, and I know you can't go back now and face your father with any pride. You have to finish what you've started, and you are my husband. If this is the way life must be for a while, then I will just have to put up with it. Just don't keep insisting that I ride in the wagon. I need these women, and I will never win their friendship if I am not walking right beside them. Somehow we will make it through this."

He kissed her cheek. "I love you, Maggie. If you want to give Marie and Gretta's wagon to the Haggartys, feel free to do so. It will help us . . . well, you know. We agreed to be careful."

Maggie kissed his lips lightly, a tiny part of her wishing he didn't find it so easy to abstain.

"It's Rafe! He's coming!" someone shouted.

The remark drew their attention from each other, and Edward and Maggie joined others in watching Rafe approach, leading a team of mules. Jack, who had ridden out to find him, rode beside him now.

Maggie breathed a silent sigh of relief. If Rafe Morrisey were killed, they would probably all have to turn back for Independence, and then they might have to wait another whole year to start again, for timing was everything, according to Rafe. They could not be late in getting to the mountains. Still, she realized it wasn't the disappointment of having to wait and start all over again that would bother her so much as the thought that they would have to do it with a new guide, that she would never see Rafe Morrisey again.

She turned away as others ran up to him to ask how he had survived. She could hear him explaining that he had found the runaway team, but that by then the wagon had careened sideways and fallen over, breaking the hitch. He had caught the team of mules, then found a cluster of rocks behind which he ducked for protection from the debris-filled wind. The team had gotten loose again, but he rode out and found them after the storm. The wagon had belonged to several men, mostly single ones, some married who had left their wives behind, who were all headed for the goldfields of California. It had carried mining supplies, and Rafe ordered everyone to make camp. They would stay here tomorrow and pick up as many of their belongings as possible. The miners had two other wagons and had been sleeping outside, so they could survive without the third wagon.

Maggie felt a heavy wave of guilt at how relieved she was that Rafe had returned, for she knew she was not concerned just because he was their guide. There was something more to it, something she had no business feeling. She wished she had not asked him to eat with them. She would rather not have to watch how he moved, look at his dark eyes. She would rather not have to shake his hand, or laugh with him.

Why did she feel this way? Had this sudden total change in her life made her lose her mind? She never dreamed she could live like this, put up with such discomforts, worry about people less fortunate than she. She had grown up being taught that the "rich" helped the "poor" because it was a rather fashionable thing to do, something to brag about at parties, where the poor were also complained about as beggars and lazy scavengers. These people were none of those things. They all had a dream, just like Edward, only it was much harder for them to realize their dreams, because dreams often took money, more than most of these people had.

None of these feelings were natural for her, and she was not quite sure how to deal with them. If she knew some of these other women better, she could talk to them, but even at that she did not dare mention the strange feelings she had for Rafe Morrisey. She assured herself she simply was not going to know her own mind until this trip was over and she was back to living the way she had been born to live, in a comfortable home, with new servants, able to bathe every day, wear her good clothes again, have tea parties, embroider, with time to read and relax. Perhaps she could get some clubs started, raise funds to build a church. Her mother had always been a good fundraiser. Yes, this odd feeling of being removed from her real self would pass. She and Edward would share a bed again, be husband and wife in the fullest sense, share—"

"Are you all right, Maggie?"

She closed her eyes. It was Rafe's deep voice. She turned to see he was still on his horse and had ridden up behind her, and it struck her that he seemed able to do so without making a sound. "I'm fine."

Because he'd been drenched, and the heat had returned, he had removed his shirt. Maggie had never seen a man with his shirt off. She and Edward always made love in a dark room under the blankets, and she had always kept her gown on, and he his nightshirt. They had never seen each other completely naked. Why did that thought come to her at this moment, when looking upon the splendid form of Rafe Morrisey, his broad shoulders, dark skin, muscled arms? His hair was still damp, his deerskin leggings also damp.

"Your husband has offered to help the Haggartys get another wagon when we reach Fort Kearny. I have a feeling that was your idea."

She looked away, hoping he had not read the look of curiosity and desire in her eyes at seeing him half naked. "I felt it was our obligation. We have plenty, and they have lost just about everything."

"We'll round up as much as we can for them. Thanks for offering to help. You'd better get out the mosquito netting. They will be thick tonight, I'm afraid."

"Yes. We'll be all right."

Rafe rode off to check on the others, and Maggie turned to watch. She had so many questions to ask, yet she had no idea why she cared.

Chapter Nine

A muggy heat followed the tornado, which made drying clothes and blankets take longer than normal. Personal belongings were spread over the tops of wagons, over wagon wheels, barrels, wagon gates and seats, anything over which something could be hung. Maggie could not help thinking how comical it all looked, and if not for the sadness of what had happened to the Haggartys and the miserable heat, it would be easy to joke about the sight—especially underwear that hung from hooks on the sides of wagons.

We all took a moment to stand together and pray, thanking God that no one was killed or badly injured, Maggie wrote. *Donated items for the Haggartys will be held by others until they find another wagon to use. We will donate two extra oxen to pull the new wagon. I am impressed by the willingness of everyone to immediately come to the rescue of those in need, and I am glad to be a part of it. For the first time I am beginning to understand the true meaning of "giving."*

The rest of the day was spent with continued clean-up, the men unhitching teams, some of them going out to bring in more scattered livestock. Maggie stood back and counted the wagons—seventeen, now that the Haggarty wagon was destroyed. Their own wagons accounted for four of them, and one to Hazel and Barney, another to a married couple, Wilena and Bill Marks, who had three children, Sam, eight, Billy, five, and Rose, two. Maggie thought how difficult this journey was with young children along who had to be watched constantly because of the numerous accidents that could happen. Another young couple with children were Terrence and Beverly Maddox, who had a six-year-old boy, Joey, a daughter, Minnie, who was five, and a three-year-old boy, Rob. They pulled two wagons.

Single men, and married ones going to California without their wives, accounted for two more wagons, now that they had lost a third to the tornado. Two more wagons belonged to Matthew and Lucille Krueger, who had brought their sixteen-year-old son, Billy, and a daughter, Wanda, who was ten. The Kruegers were good people to have along, as Matthew Krueger was a Methodist minister, determined to go to California and preach in the mining towns, which he had heard were awash in the sins of gambling and drinking. It felt good to have a man of the cloth along, and every morning he prayed with all of them. Many were sure it was Reverend Krueger's prayers that had saved them from loss of life during the tornado.

Also along was a widower, Jeremiah Smith, who appeared to be in his forties. Two grown sons accompanied him, Will and Ben, both in their twenties, all three going to California to look for gold. They pulled one wagon. Three more were pulled by the Howells, Mildred and Graydon, the parents of fifteen-year-old Katie and five more children. Nettie was thirteen, Larry twelve, Kenneth nine, Sharon six, and Tessa, four. Maggie had written all of their names in her journal, and each family seemed to appreciate her interest.

The last wagon belonged to a man called Buck James, who appeared to be in his thirties. He traveled with a woman who claimed to be his wife, but Maggie and some of the other women wondered if she really was. She was very young, and they didn't look like the common farmer and his wife, the common anything. Buck James wore ruffled shirts and slicked-back hair, and Jenny liked to wear color on her lips and cheeks, and dresses with necklines lower than the average ''proper'' woman would wear. Some were sure Buck James was a gambler, for when he waited in the evenings for Jenny to cook his supper he spent more time toying with a deck of cards than he did helping the other men with chores. Jenny kept to herself most of the time, and sometimes she would sit at their private campfire brushing her hair for a half hour or more, and singing softly to herself. She had refused to give Maggie any details about her age or where she had come from.

''She is one of zose dance hall girls, I'll bet,'' Gretta commented softly as she and Maggie and Maria lay trying to sleep that first night after the storm. The night was hardly any cooler than the day had been, which only made the mosquitoes worse, just as Rafe had said would happen. Somehow some always managed to get around the netting. The only way to avoid them was to sleep completely covered, even the head, but that, too, was miserable, because of the heat.

As promised, Maria and Gretta's wagon had been given to the Haggartys to use until they got their own wagon again. The close quarters of what was left of Maggie and Edward's wagon made it difficult, if not impossible, for Maggie, Gretta, and Maria to keep from disturbing each other, especially since Maria was twice as big as either Maggie or Gretta.

Maggie was not sure how long she had been trying to sleep when Gretta made the comment about Jenny James, if, indeed, she truly was Buck James's wife. She took the blanket off her head for fear of suffocation, and she immediately had to swat at a mosquito.

''I have never been so miserable in my life,'' she commented, aware the other two women were also awake.

''Nor I,'' Gretta answered, uncovering her own head as she spoke. ''I had better find me one damn handsome man when I make California, and he had better appreciate all I suffered to find him.''

They all lay there a moment, saying nothing. Finally Maggie broke out in laughter at Gretta's comment. The other two women also began laughing.

''I feel the same way,'' Maria added.

They laughed more, and Maggie felt like a young girl laughing with friends, rather than a married woman forced to sleep with her servants. It felt good to talk about something that made her laugh and momentarily forget the misery of this journey, and how much she missed home and life the way it used to be. When she was a girl, her "overnights" were with sisters or with friends who knew the same life she did. It seemed strange to lie here with her cook and her personal maid, talking and laughing as though they were no different from she.

Maybe they aren't, she thought. After all, what was the true difference? Money? Education? What did that mean with regard to a person's value as a human being? One thing she was already beginning to see was that however this trip ended, or if she ended up back home, she could never look at people the same way again. Already she had learned so much about a life she had hardly known existed before starting this journey.

"You must be talking about Jenny," she said aloud then, referring to Gretta's original statement that had disturbed her effort to sleep.

"Well, zose dresses she wears, and za way she sings. You have to admit zose two are not your common pair. Buck James looks like a slick one to me, and he is pretty damn good at handling a deck of cards."

"Watch your language, Gretta," Maggie chided. "And we can't be judging people on this trip. We all need each other, no matter what any of these people's livelihood might be, or their personal lives."

"Well, now, that doesn't sound like Maggie Dumont McCahan talking, I'll say," Maria said. "Speaking of which, are you sure it is all right to sleep in the same wagon with you, Maggie? It just does not seem right. You should have a wagon to yourself."

"There is no wagon I can have to myself. The Haggartys need your wagon, and that is that. You have both been my friends for years."

Gretta's smile faded, and she suddenly felt like crying. "I never did know you considered me a friend, Ma'am. I am just your maid."

"Don't say *just.* It is simply an occupation, and a fine one. And of course I consider you a friend. Good heavens, Gretta, you've seen me naked! You've seen more than my own—"

Maggie caught herself. Should she be telling these women such intimacies? The other two began laughing again, and Maggie could not help joining them.

"Don't tell me Mr. McCahan hasn't seen you naked!" Gretta whispered.

Maggie laughed again, but deep inside she felt an odd sadness. "Let's just say he is very proper," she whispered in reply. "We are always covered, and I keep my gown on." Had she really said that? What on *earth* had made her share such a personal detail with her cook and her maid! This trip was indeed having a traumatic affect on her entire being. Her thinking seemed to be completely turned around, and she was doing and saying and thinking things she would never normally do or say . . . or think.

"When I find my handsome lover in California, I want to be *completely* naked when we make love, and I want him to be, too," Gretta told them with a deep sigh. "I want to feel his naked body against mine, feel him—"

"Ladies?" Someone gently tapped the wagon gate. Maggie recognized Rafe Morrisey's deep voice. She sat up. "What is it?"

"Just wondering if you're able to sleep. Most folks are having trouble with the mosquitoes. I have some bear grease here that you can smear on your faces."

"*Bear* grease!" Maggie wrinkled her nose. "What on earth is bear grease?

"The fat from bears. It smells pretty bad, but the mosquitoes hate it, which is the whole idea. The Indians use it all the time. When you live out here, you learn to adapt."

Maggie moved to the back of the wagon and opened the canvas flap, looking through the mosquito netting that had been draped over the entire wagon. "We'll be fine, Rafe. We are not so desperate that we have to smear our faces with smelly bear grease!"

"Just offering, Ma'am. I heard you laughing in there and figured you were having trouble sleeping."

Maggie could see his face in the moonlight, and in that half darkness he seemed even more handsome and mysterious than by day. "Oh, my! Are we keeping others awake?"

He grinned. "I don't think so. Most everyone is having the same problem."

"Are any of them using the bear grease?"

"A few."

"Well, no, thank you. If things get worse, we might have to resort to it."

"Suit yourself, but try to sleep. There will be a lot more work tomorrow, finishing the cleanup after the storm and getting things dried out. We leave bright and early the next day, whether things are dry or not. We can't afford to hold up for too long."

He started to turn away. "Rafe," Maggie called to him. He turned. "Don't forget you are eating with us tomorrow evening."

"Yes, Ma'am."

Rafe walked away, and Maggie returned to her bedding, lying back with a long sigh.

"You asked him to eat with us?" Maria asked her.

"Yes. Didn't I tell you? I want pork roast. Now that we're held up here, it's the perfect time to cook one slowly all day in your Dutch oven so that it is perfect and tender. You do make such a good roast, Maria. You should teach me to cook, in case I would need to know later on."

"Teach you to cook? I never dreamed you would ask such a thing, Maggie."

Maggie grinned. "I am doing and saying a lot of things I myself never dreamed before this trip," she answered. "At any rate, I want it to be a very good meal. Everyone else takes turns feeding Rafe Morrisey. I want ours to be the best."

"Why?" Gretta asked.

Maggie was glad for the darkness, for she could feel herself blushing. "I don't know. I guess because we're the only ones along who actually have their own cook. All the other poor women have to cook for whole families."

"Sounds to me like you are trying to impress Mr. Morrisey," Gretta teased. "I know I wish *I* could impress him! I have never seen a better specimen of manhood in all my days."

"Gretta!" Maggie chided.

"Well, it is true, is it not, Maria?"

"Oh, it's true, all right. What a face! And those broad shoulders and slim hips. And there is something about those buckskins he wears, the way the fringes dance when he walks. There is a sureness about him that makes a woman feel safe when she's around him."

"Safe from Indians, maybe," Gretta answered, "but are zay safe from Rafe Morrisey?"

Both women laughed.

"Hush, you two!" Maggie scolded in a whisper. "He could still be right outside!"

Gretta gasped. "Oh, my! What if he heard us earlier, talking about wanting to lie naked next to a naked man!"

They all laughed again.

"I'd *like* to lie naked next to that one," Maria said.

There came more laughter, but deep inside Maggie felt like crying, for she had had the same thoughts, wrong, sinful thoughts.

"You will let me sit nearby when he eats with you, won't you, Maggie?" Gretta asked. "I could watch zat man all day. I want to hear him talk. He is so mysterious. You must get him to tell you how he came to do what he does, where he is from and if he is married."

Maggie hated feeling the hint of jealousy she felt at the thought of Gretta catching Rafe's eye. It was ridiculous! Then again, perhaps she would encourage the attraction. That was the best way to make up for these feelings. "He was married once, and I think he had children."

"*Really?* How do you know?" Gretta asked.

"He told me, yesterday, when I was riding his horse. I can't remember how we got on the subject, but he said he'd had a wife once. He never told me what happened to her."

"Maybe she was Indian," Maria suggested.

"I don't know. I will try to get him to tell me."

"I saw him lift you up on that horse," Maria said then. "What was it like, having that man's strong hands around your waist and lifting you?"

"Maria! I am a married woman!"

"I could forget my husband with that one around," Maria answered.

They laughed again, but Maggie felt a painful guilt that made her stomach hurt. *So could I,* she thought.

Chapter Ten

For the first time in her life Maggie felt ridiculous being served by Maria and the new house servant they had brought with them, David. Because they'd had to leave their table behind, Maria had insisted on setting up something that at least resembled a table, which turned out to be two long planks from their supply wagon, set on top of water barrels. More barrels became chairs, and Maria had spread the "table" with a linen cloth and set a candelabra at the center.

Rafe had grinned skeptically when he walked to their campsite. He folded his arms and shook his head. "You folks are a bit too fancy for me," he'd said.

"We treat all our guests this way when we ask them to dine with us," Edward had told him, shaking his hand and welcoming him to their table. "At home it might be the president of a company or the governor of our state. Out here you are just as important."

His words had warmed Maggie's heart and made her feel less self-conscious. Edward gave him a "chair" at the head of the "table," and he had David pour Rafe some aged white wine, giving him some history about the wine, which had been shipped from France. After his first sip, it was obvious by the look on Rafe's face that he truly meant it when he said it was the finest wine he had ever tasted.

"The Spaniards in California make excellent wines," he told them. "The climate in most of California is excellent for grapes, and a lot of Spaniards have huge vineyards. Of course, the Americans took a lot of them over when we claimed California after the Mexican war, which didn't bode well with a lot of them. But many still own their own *rancheros,* as they call them. They aren't too happy about California becoming a state this year, but there are some things a person just can't control, and the expansion of the United States is one of them, I'm afraid."

"Afraid?" Edward took a sip of his wine, frowning. "You don't *want* the United States to grow?"

Maggie sat down across from Edward, so that they each sat on either side of Rafe. Young David and the men they had hired as drivers would eat on their own around the campfire, but Maggie had allowed Gretta to sit at the end of the table with them and their guest. Maggie took a sip of her own wine, still impressed with how well-spoken Rafe was, as well as apparently being knowledgeable about politics. He and Edward talked about the Mexican war and United States policies.

"Texas really should still belong to Mexico," Rafe commented. "They wouldn't sell it to us, so we just took it. But what the hell? History has a way of continually changing peoples' lives."

"You speak as though you fought in that war," Maggie put in.

Rafe took another drink of his wine, more of a gulp this time, as though suddenly upset. "I did," he answered.

"You were in za *war?*" The words came from Gretta, who immediately looked down after asking the question. "I am sorry. It is not my business to speak into your conversation, Mr. McCahan. I vas just . . . surprised. I could not help overhearing."

"It's all right, Gretta." Edward looked at Rafe and grinned wryly, leaning closer. "I think my wife's personal maid is quite taken with you," he said quietly.

"Edward!" Maggie scolded in a whisper. "You will embarrass the man! *And* Gretta!"

Rafe grinned. "She's a fine looking woman."

Gretta giggled and blushed.

"How did you end up in the Mexican war?" Maggie asked, anxious to change the subject.

Rafe sighed, hesitating a moment, as though not truly willing to talk about it. He took another drink of wine before answering. "I was living in Mexican Territory at the time. I raised horses and also was a gunsmith—sold guns, fixed guns, traded guns, you name it. I got along just fine with the Mexicans. In fact, I married a Mexican girl." He puffed quietly on the cigar a moment before finishing. "She was killed in the war."

Maggie glanced at Gretta, and if not for the sadness of the moment she would have smiled at the wide-eyed look on Gretta's face.

"You're a widower?" Edward lit his own cigar. "I'll be damned. I'm sorry about that, Rafe. How did it happen? If you got along so well with the Mexicans, you must have taken their side in the war."

"Actually I fought *against* them. Before I lost Nina, I wouldn't have cared either way. But it was Mexicans that killed her, just because she'd married an American and the child in her belly had American blood."

"She was *carrying?*" Edward asked.

Gretta gasped.

Rafe took several quiet seconds to answer. "It was a band of radicals, and I knew they didn't represent the whole Mexican government, but at the time I couldn't help joining the war against them. In spite of what happened, I still believe the Mexicans got the raw end of the deal. I still call some of them friend."

"I'm sorry for you," Maggie told him. "Losing a wife in such a tragic way must have been awful. And the war itself must have been a terrible experience, being full of revenge and sorrow."

Rafe set down his empty wine glass. "I shouldn't have talked about all that. You people are the first to get that out of me."

He met Maggie's eyes with a look that seemed to say he wanted to talk more, but Maria began serving then, and conversation turned to food. Edward bragged about Maria's cooking, and Maria urged Rafe to eat all he wanted. Rafe was soon complimenting Maria on the delicious pork roast, and Maria complained that she could not cook nearly as good a meal as she would if she were home and had fresh vegetables at hand, and if she had a proper wood stove for cooking the pork roast, proper serving facilities. She fretted over the plain white plates she used.

"Quit apologizing, Maria," Maggie told the woman. "This is wonderful, especially under the conditions in which you have had to cook it."

"I agree," Rafe added. "And the plates are fine. When you normally eat off battered tin plates, any kind of real plate is nice. Why don't you sit down and eat with us?"

"Oh, no!" Maria objected. "I never eat with the Mr. and Mrs."

"Well, then tonight will be a first for you," Rafe told her. "Makes me nervous being served while you wait for us to finish. I'm the guest, so you have to do what I say."

Maria put a hand to her chest. "Why, thank you, Mr. Morrisey."

Rafe looked at Maggie. "You don't mind, do you?"

"You said it yourself. You're the guest."

Maria brought more bowls of food to the table, then sat down with Gretta to eat, spending more time staring at Rafe than at her plate.

"You seem quite well spoken and enlightened for a man who has apparently spent a good many years out here away from the States," Maggie told Rafe as he finished his food. "Something tells me you have had some education." She glanced at Gretta and Maria, aware that both of them were dying to know something more about the man's background . . . just as she also wondered. "You must know we are all curious about someone like you. Where we come from, such men are mere—" She caught herself, glancing at Edward, not wanting to seem too interested. *Fantasies,* she was going to say. ''Fictitious characters who don't really exist,'' she finished. ''Back in Pennsylvania, the West itself seems fictitious, unreal. If it isn't being too nosey, I wish you would explain how you ended up out here, doing what you do, especially if you *are* educated.''

Rafe put down his fork and rubbed his stomach, commenting first about what a good meal Maria had cooked.

''I have a cake, too. Baked it in a separate Dutch oven, right over the fire. I never made a cake that way before, but I think it turned out just fine. You must have a piece. I made coffee to go with it.''

Rafe nodded. ''I think I will wait a few minutes, but I will have some.'' He looked at Gretta and grinned. Gretta giggled and looked away again.

''Gretta, please act your age,'' Maggie scolded, angry for reasons she had no business feeling. She looked back at Rafe. ''Do you mind answering my question?''

''Maggie, maybe the man doesn't want to talk about it,'' Edward suggested.

''I don't mind,'' Rafe told him. He picked up the cigar he'd been smoking before dinner. ''Mind if I light this up again?''

''I don't mind at all. I had it in mind to do the same.'' Edward turned to David. ''Get us something to light these with, David. I just used the last match I had on me the first time we lit these, and I don't feel like looking for more. They are probably all wet, anyway.''

''Yes, Sir.'' David rose from the campfire, returning with a burning stick as Rafe spoke. ''I am part Comanche,'' he said. He expected the gasps he heard from both Maria and Gretta.

''Comanche!'' Gretta repeated. *''Indian?''*

Rafe puffed on the cigar as David held the burning stick to it. Once it was going well he took it from his lips, and David helped Edward light his cigar. ''I never knew any *white* Comanche,'' Rafe answered Gretta.

''Oh, my!'' Gretta exclaimed, looking away again.

''I have to admit, you do look as though you have Indian blood,'' Edward spoke up, ''but I doubt any Comanche Indian speaks as well as you.''

Rafe shrugged. "Most don't even know any English. My mother was the product of a Comanche raid made on a Mexican village when Texas still belonged to Mexico. Her mother was Mexican, her father Comanche. Her father sold her to a wealthy white man from New Orleans for guns and tobacco."

"*Sold* her!" Maggie put a hand to her heart in horror, and Maria and Gretta listened in silent awe. "He sold his own daughter?"

"She wasn't a full-blood Comanche. If I tried to explain Indian thinking to you, it would take much too long, and you would probably never understand, anyway. Believe it or not, they are human, with human feelings just like anyone else. But they have a whole different way of looking at certain things." He puffed on the cigar again. "At any rate, she was only fourteen when he sold her, and my, uh, father, had no concern for age, if you get my understanding. I am the result of his . . . infatuation with her, you might say."

"Oh, dear!" Maggie looked away.

"Goodness!" Gretta said softly.

"Oh, the poor thing," Maria muttered. "Your father must have been a terrible man."

Rafe studied the cigar he held in his fingers. "My father was very wealthy," he answered, almost absently. "Women were almost a hobby for him. He had many, never married any of them."

Maggie felt heat rising to her cheeks. Rafe Morrisey was a bastard, and part Comanche and Mexican. Back home he would be considered hardly worthy of a hello. She glanced at Gretta, who had her hands to her cheeks, her mouth hanging open. When she finally found the courage to look back at Rafe, he was still staring at his cigar. "What happened to your mother, Rafe?" she asked. "And to you?"

He took a moment to answer. "Actually my father was very good to his women, took very good care of them, bought them the best of everything, raised the children he had by them like any father would. He had the means to do it. My mother had never known any life except with Comanche Indians, who were not kind to her, so she stayed with him. He saw that I was privately tutored. I was schooled until I was fourteen. That's when my father died, and because he had never married any of the women who lived with him, none of them could claim any of the estate. He had a brother who was also wealthy, and devious. He knew all the right people, and he ended up taking over my father's estate and kicking out all the women. None of them knew anything about having to support themselves, and because they had lived with my father, and most had Indian or Mexican or Oriental blood, other men would have nothing to do with them. My mother ended up prostituting herself to survive. She was murdered in an alley, and I was on my own."

"Holy Mary," Maria said softly.

"How terrible!" Gretta added.

"I'm very sorry for you, Rafe," Edward told him.

Maggie could not find her voice. Her heart went out to him. She could see the agony in his dark eyes.

"My mother didn't have many choices in her life, never had the chance to know anything but what my father taught her. She was a good woman, just uneducated and inexperienced. I *was* educated, enough to know there *were* choices in life. My first choice was to find the men who killed my mother and make them suffer and die, which is exactly what I did. I was big for my age, and I was determined. After I killed them I fled the States. I hooked up with old Jack, traveled the West, learned about Indians, tried to find my Comanche grandfather, but never did. Then I went to Mexico and found my mother's family, ended up staying there and marrying. Turns out that part of Mexico became United States territory. Then my wife was killed. That was six years ago. I ended up fighting in the Mexican war and then found Jack again and started helping him lead wagon trains."

He sighed deeply and straightened, glancing around at all of them. "So, here I am. By the way, this is a fine cigar, Mr. McCahan."

He pretended unconcern over what he had just told all of them, but Maggie suspected a hurt deep inside that would probably never go away. What a strange, unhappy, confused, unstable life he had led, compared to her perfect upbringing in a loving home with a real family and everything she could ever want.

''I'll take that cake now, Marie,'' he said then.

Maria jumped up, as though awakened from a dream. ''Oh! Yes, Sir!'' She hurried away to get the cake.

''I'm sorry for going on like I did,'' Rafe told Maggie and Edward. ''That isn't like me at all.''

''Well, we asked, and you told,'' Edward replied.

Rafe smiled rather sadly and nodded. He changed the subject to what lay on the trail ahead, and Maggie was sure he did so because it was too painful to dwell any longer on his past. He glanced at her occasionally as he spoke, and by the look in his eyes she guessed he was wondering what she thought of him now that she knew the whole truth about him. Why did he care? He ate his cake and drank his coffee, joking with Gretta a little, warning Edward about the dangers that lay ahead, including a dangerous river crossing.

''This time of year the rivers are swollen pretty good,'' he warned. ''Crossing them will be dangerous. It wouldn't hurt to try to shed even more weight,'' he told Edward.

''We'll make do somehow,'' Edward insisted.

''Just make sure the women go across separately. Jack, Wolf Hunter, and I will take some of them ourselves. If they're in a wagon and it gets away from you, they can get tangled inside and drown. We take all the women and children across first, then the wagons.''

Edward nodded. ''Whatever you say.''

Rafe finished his cake and coffee, then rose, picking up what was left of the fine cigar Edward had given him. ''That was quite a meal, Maria. I haven't had anything that good in a very long time. Mr. and Mrs. McCahan are lucky to have you for their cook.''

''Oh, thank you, Mr. Morrisey. We will have you again.''

''Yes, we will,'' Edward added, rising. He put out his hand again.''Thanks for the interesting story, Rafe. Helps us forget our own troubles. Heaven knows we all need any form of entertainment we can find, and listening to you is certainly that. Perhaps next time you can share some of your adventures with us, things that have happened to you on other wagon trains, that sort of thing.''

Rafe shook his hand. ''Oh, I don't think you want me to bore you with all of that.'' He nodded to the women and thanked them again, then walked off into the darkness.

''Lordy, Lordy,'' Maria muttered.

''Unusual man,'' Edward commented. He turned to Gretta. ''Help Maria clean up, Gretta.'' He walked closer to Maggie. ''You had better get some rest, dear. Lots of work tomorrow to get ready to leave out again.'' He turned away, and Maggie watched after Rafe. Unusual was only one way to describe him, that was sure.

Chapter Eleven

Maggie could not help wondering how lonely a man like Rafe Morrisey must be, but she almost wished he had not told them about his past, for now Gretta could not stop talking about him. She was completely infatuated, and Maria encouraged it, teasing her about finding "her man" before she even reached California. Their joking and fantasizing about the man every night irritated her, so much so that she had literally ordered them last night to stop talking and try to sleep.

"He is obviously not interested, Gretta, or he would be coming here to sit with us every night," she had barked. "The man seems far from wanting to settle, after losing his wife in such a terrible way. And how do you know he does not have that streak in him his father had? Perhaps he, too, would rather have many women than one."

"Well, he *did* marry once," Gretta had answered, sounding ready to cry.

Maggie felt awful now for having deliberately thrown Gretta from her height of daydreams, and the worst part was she had done it out of her own jealousy . . . a jealousy because Gretta was at least free to daydream, free to pursue and be pursued. She realized that courting was one of the more pleasant, exciting events in a young girl's life that she had never experienced. She had simply grown up with Edward, and seeing him socially had come naturally. She had always looked at it as attending social events with a friend, and when he asked her to marry him she had actually been surprised, never having realized he thought of her that way. He had been going through a bad time with his father again, and she had accepted out of pity. She realized that now, but now was too late.

"I am sorry I snapped at you last night, Gretta," she told her. They walked beside each other, headed for a river crossing.

"I do not mind, Ma'am. We haf become more like friends zan ever before because it cannot be helped on a trip like zis. And so I haf become careless and forget my place."

Maggie could feel the hurt. "We *are* friends, Gretta. You know that. It's just the heat and mosquitoes and the monotony of this trip that are making me irritable."

"Yes, Ma'am." They walked on in silence for a few minutes before Gretta spoke again. "Zat Katie Howell has also been making eyes at Rafe. And do you see how zat dance hall girl looks at him?"

"You don't know that she is a dance hall girl."

Just then they heard a woman's scream, followed by a gunshot. Wagons came to a halt, and moments later Rafe galloped past them to the last wagon.

"It is zat dance hall girl's wagon!" Gretta exclaimed.

"Maggie! Maggie! Are you all right?" Edward shouted the words as he hurried toward her.

"I'm fine, Edward. Something has happened at the last wagon."

Gretta was already running in that direction, and Edward joined Maggie in rushing down the line of wagons to see what had happened. Others were already gathered there, and a few women screamed at another gunshot. Maggie stopped and gasped when she saw Rafe pick up a large snake and toss it away from the gathering crowd.

"Someone's been bitten!" Edward exclaimed. He held Maggie's arm as they stepped closer to see Rafe bent over Jenny

James's left leg and cutting into it with his big hunting knife. Jenny lay screaming with pain.

"What are you doing to her!" Buck James demanded.

Rafe shoved his knife back into its sheath, his hand pressed tightly around the bleeding slits on Jenny's leg. "I'm trying to save this woman's life!" he answered, apparently angry that he was being questioned at such an untimely moment. He bent down and began sucking on the wound, then spitting out blood, an act he repeated several times while people stared.

"He's suckin' out the venom." The words came from Jack, who had ridden up behind the crowd. "You better make your wife quit thrashin' around, Mr. James, or she'll just make things worse. It's important to lay real still."

Buck James knelt down and pressed Jenny's arms against the grass, urging her to lie still.

"Make him stop! Make him stop!" she screamed. "Oh, God, I'm going to die, Buck!"

"No, you won't. We're going to California and get rich, remember?"

"I don't care any more! I'm going back . . . to Chicago." Her screaming began to fade. "You . . . aren't my husband. You can't . . . stop me."

Some of the women quietly gasped, and Gretta stepped closer to Maggie. "I *told* you so!" she whispered.

Buck James looked at the crowd with a scowl on his face. "She's delerious from the snakebite."

"I hope so," Reverend Krueger told him. "We cannot have our children exposed to an unmarried man and woman traveling together and sharing the same wagon."

"All that matters right now is that she doesn't die," Rafe told them. "Get me some whiskey, and something to wrap the wound with. We'll let her travel in her wagon." He looked at Buck James. "Prop up some pillows and blankets so we can lay her in there with her head elevated. If she gets through the next twenty-four hours, she'll probably be all right. We might have gotten it in time to get out most of the venom. The less that gets to her brain, the better."

Buck hurriedly climbed into his wagon and handed out some

whiskey and some cotton wrapping. Everyone had been ordered to have such things handy before leaving Independence. Rafe poured some whiskey on the wound, and Jenny moaned. She appeared to be slipping into unconsciousness. Rafe tipped the whiskey bottle to his mouth, swishing some into it and spitting it out, and Maggie could not help making a face at the thought of how awful the mixture of blood and snake venom must have tasted. Rafe took a swallow of whiskey then and handed the bottle back to Buck. He wrapped the wound and tied off the cotton cloth, then rose with Jenny in his arms. Maggie wondered how it must feel to be held in those arms, then turned away from the sight as Rafe helped get Jenny into her wagon.

Moments later Rafe was back on his horse, ordering everyone back to their places. "Get the wagons moving!" he shouted. "We have to cross the river later today before we make camp."

"Keep an eye open," Edward told Maggie. "I would want to die myself if something happened to you." He kissed her cheek and hurried away to help the drivers.

Rafe rode past then on a handsome black gelding, one of four horses he had brought on the journey. A second horse was used for carrying his gear, and the other two were spares, one a roan color, the other two gray and white spotted horses Maggie had learned were called Appaloosas. She had never seen an Appaloosa back east, and when she had commented about them once to old Jack he'd told her they were a favorite of the Plains Indians. Wolf Hunter rode an Appaloosa. All of Rafe's horses were geldings except one Appaloosa mare.

Why had she bothered to take note of such unimportant things as the kind of horses Rafe Morrisey rode?

"What a man," Gretta said with a sigh.

Maggie watched after Rafe a moment, shaking her head, needing to pretend she did not think the same way. "I will leave you to your daydreaming, Gretta. I am going to walk with Edward for a while." She hurried over to join her husband, deciding that from now on she must give no more thought to Rafe Morrisey. She was behaving like a foolish young girl, allowing the trauma of this journey to interfere with her common sense. She decided she was seeing Rafe in an unreal light, only because he was someone sure and skilled, and on whom they all depended to get them safely to California. She simply could not trust her own judgment when she was in this predicament where her life had been turned upside-down and she could not think straight.

Edward's remark that he didn't know what he would do without her had made her realize that all she felt for Rafe Morrisey was dependency. She needed and depended on him to keep her safe and to guide her well, just as everyone here needed him that way. That dependency had made her think she could actually love him. It was just the same as Edward depending on her. That dependency had made him think he loved her.

Yes, that was the answer. Once they were safely in California, these feelings would go away. The only trouble was, it felt good to think she might be able to lean on someone else, rather than someone else always leaning on her. Even Maria and Gretta leaned on her. In a sense her whole family had leaned on her as their precious, beautiful, special baby daughter and baby sister. Edward was the most dependent, constantly telling her he could never face life without her. She did not mind dependency in her mother and sisters, or her maid and cook. But she resented it in her husband. He should be the strong one, and he tried to be. But deep inside she knew he was not strong at all. She was his strength.

The river was dangerously swollen, and Rafe announced that if they did not cross now the trip could be delayed for days. The river would only get higher over the next couple of weeks. "In mid-summer the Platte gets down to practically nothing," he explained when he called them together before the crossing. "But snowmelt and spring rains can turn it into something mean. The current will be strong and swift. Right now it won't be any deeper than up to a man's neck, but it will be plenty strong and cold, and the animals won't be easy to manage. You men who are driving them will have to be firm, and you'll need your whips."

He walked in a circle as he spoke.

"The women and children will go across on horseback. Jack, Wolf Hunter, and I will take care of that. Then we herd across the spare cattle, mules, and horses, so those on the other side can watch them while we bring the wagons across, one at a time. Those of you with chickens in cages tied to the sides of your wagons should move the cages higher, up behind the seats at least. If you have sacks of seed along, place them as high in the wagons as you can. Same for flour, salt, sugar, any food items that would be ruined if they got wet."

"What about Jenny?" Buck asked. "She's too weak to help herself hang on to anyone going across."

"I'll set her in front of me and hold her myself. I'll get her over, don't worry." Rafe looked around at the others. "If we have problems because of weight, and I say something's got to go, then it's got to go. The river bottom is going to be muddy, an extra strain on the horses." He walked over and mounted his horse. "Get the women and kids lined up."

Jack and Wolf Hunter, who had both crossed over to check the current and depth, joined Rafe, both of them soaked from the crossing.

"It'll be up to our necks in places," Jack warned. "Nothin' we can do about it, but at least it's a hot day, so you'll all get cooled off right good."

There came a few nervous smiles and laughs, and Jack leaned down and lifted eight-year-old Sam Marks up to his horse in front of him. The boy wiggled up and down, laughing, feeling no fear. Wolf Hunter took up Billy Marks, and Rafe took two-year-old Rose.

"Oh, Dear God, get my baby across safely," Wilena Marks said, practically in tears. Rose began crying, frightened at sitting on a big horse with a dark stranger, and because of the anxious look on her mother's face.

"Don't worry, Ma'am." Rafe rode into the river after Jack and Wolf Hunter, and everyone watched anxiously while Sam laughed and screamed as the water rose around his neck. Five-year-old Billy sat in quiet terror, and Rose squealed the whole way. Wilena fell to her knees and thanked God when all three reached the other side.

There followed a procession that took all afternoon, while men worked at getting perishables to higher places. Rafe, Jack, and Wolf Hunter forged the river repeatedly, taking the three Maddox children, ten-year-old Wanda Krueger, and Jenny James, who was laid down to rest in the grass after the crossing. Then came the six Howell children, and it was obvious fifteen-year-old Katie was excited about being taken across by Rafe himself.

There was some laughter when Jack took Maria across, for, in spite of having lost some weight from walking, she was still hefty. She screamed in terror all the way across, exclaiming how she hated water and had never learned to swim. Wolf Hunter took Gretta, much to her disappointment, for she wanted Rafe to take her. When Rafe came back across from taking little Rob Maddox, he came for Maggie. "Let's go."

Had he chosen her deliberately? Oh, what a fool she was for thinking such a thing . . . for *wanting* to think such a thing. She obeyed his command, saying nothing as he took his left foot from the stirrup so she could put her own foot in and mount up behind him. This was no time to worry about straddling a horse with a dress on. It mattered little whether her legs showed, for once they were in the water nothing would matter but getting across.

"Hang on!" Rafe told her.

She moved her arms around his middle, having no choice but to hug him tightly as he rode into the river. She could not help thinking how solid he felt, and, in spite of her internal argument that she only had feelings for him because she depended on him, she could not help the sense of security she felt as she clung tightly while the water began to swirl up over her chest and shoulders and to her neck. She pressed her head against his back, squeezing her eyes shut. The horse seemed to stumble slightly, and Rafe kept talking to it in gentle commands.

"I'll have to change horses when I go back," he yelled to her. "This one is getting tired."

Now they seemed to be almost floating. "God help us," she whispered. The horse suddenly stumbled again and fell sideways, and Maggie screamed as she felt the current carrying her away.

Chapter Twelve

Maggie struggled against the cold current that quickly drew her under. Her dress weighed her down, and it quickly became tangled around her legs. She had never swum a stroke in her life, and she was sure this was how her short life would now end. She held her breath as long as possible, but panic made it difficult, and her lungs felt ready to burst. Her thoughts were of her mother and sisters when suddenly a strong arm came around her breasts and caught under her arms, pulling her to the surface.

She gasped for breath, breathing deeply in great gulps of relief. Somewhere in the distance she could hear Edward screaming her name, but she had no breath to call back to him. She wasn't even sure how she had managed to find herself above water until a deep voice spoke closer to her ear.

''Try to relax. Hang on to me.'' The words were spoken firmly but gently, and Maggie held tightly to the strong arm that supported her. She pressed her face tightly to his shoulder. ''Kick your feet a little, and relax as much as possible,'' came the voice again.

Her head cleared more as she continued breathing deeply, and she realized that the man supporting her was Rafe Morrisey.

"I'll get you to shore," he told her reassuringly.

Maggie shivered. "Don't let go," she cried. "I can't swim!"

"I would never let go of you."

Maggie could still hear Edward yelling her name, but his voice was growing fainter.

"Come on! Work with me, Maggie!" Rafe told her. "Hold on to my arm with your left hand and use your right arm to help swim. Come on! You can do it!"

Maggie turned slightly, grasping his right wrist tightly with her left hand.

"That's it! Swim, Maggie! Use your right arm!"

Instinct forced her to paddle and kick her feet.

"Grab that branch!" Rafe referred to a branch that had fallen from a cottonwood tree and lay partly in the water. Maggie grabbed the end of it, but that part was small and dead, and it quickly broke off. By then Rafe had grabbed a sturdier section. The current tried to drag Maggie away from him, and her hand slipped, but Rafe quickly grabbed hold of her wrist and held on tight as he dragged himself closer to the branch. He found his footing and pulled hard, dragging Maggie closer, until he could get his arm fully around her again. With his feet and his left hand he pulled and walked until he was out of the strongest current and Maggie was able to also find her footing. Together they struggled to shore, where both fell for a moment, breathing deeply.

They lay facing each other, and when their gazes met an unexpected jolt of something she could not even explain tore through Maggie, causing her to quickly sit up. What was it she had seen in his eyes just then? Only then did she remember the ring of devotion in his voice when he had hung on to her in the water. *I would never let go of you.*

Rafe turned onto his back, panting, and Maggie gratefully drank in her own gulps of air, pushing some of her wet hair behind her ears.

"I'm damn sorry," Rafe told her. "My God, you could have drowned. Are you all right?"

"Yes. Yes, I'm fine." Maggie looked down to see her dress was ripped at the waist. Her clothes were a soggy, muddy mess.

She looked across the river to see the rest of the party, and those who had already been transported across to the north side were several hundred yards away. The current had dragged her and Rafe a good quarter of a mile in the short time they had been in the water. "You have nothing to be sorry for," she told Rafe. "You saved my life. Thank you for being so quick to grab hold of me. I'm sorry I wasn't much help. I have never been swimming in my life. It just isn't something we ever did back home."

"Well, I've never lost a traveler out of something I felt was my fault, and I wasn't about to start with you," he answered.

"It wasn't your fault."

Rafe looked upriver himself to see his horse standing on the north side grazing calmly, as though nothing had happened. "I should have realized my black was getting too tired. I should have switched to the roan before bringing you over." Rafe rose and reached down to help her to her feet. He leaned over then and wrung out his wet hair. The rawhide tie that had held it had come loose and now was gone. He had worn cotton pants and shirt because they did not get quite as heavy when waterlogged as did his buckskins, and he had deliberately removed his boots earlier on this side of the river, before going over to get Maggie. He was glad he had taken them off. They would have inhibited his swimming as well, and could have cost Maggie her life. He watched her shaking and wringing water from her dress, and he thought how strange it was to realize he would have felt a sad emptiness if she had drowned. What annoyed him most was realizing the sadness would not be just from feeling responsible. He truly would have missed her presence. Why? He had never felt this strange attachment to one of those he guided on the trail west, certainly never for another man's wife. Maybe he would not have these feelings for her if it wasn't for what he knew about her husband. Did she have any idea what Edward really was?

"We'd better get back upriver. I'll get a ride back over with Jack or Wolf Hunter and get a fresh horse."

Maggie met his gaze. There it was again! That near worship in his eyes. Maybe she misread the look. Maybe it was just that he was so sorry for what had happened. "I'll never be able to thank you enough," she told him.

Rafe forced a smile, fighting the emotions this woman created in him. "Let's just say I've properly thanked you for a good meal."

Maggie smiled in return, and Rafe took her arm and walked with her. When they came closer to the others, Maggie could see Edward was nearly to shore. He had apparently asked one of the other two men to bring him over so he could see if his wife was all right.

"Maggie!" he called out before reaching shore.

Maggie waved at him, and Rafe let go of her arm. She looked up at him, thinking how safe and protected she had felt as she hung onto his strong arm in the water. "Thank you again, Rafe."

Rafe's gaze moved over her in a way that made her feel sensitive of the way her wet dress clung to her bosom and the torn waist exposed her slips.

"Just remember . . ." Rafe hesitated. What he'd seen, what he knew about Edward McCahan, was not his business. He was going to tell her to remember to come to him if she had any problems, but that sounded too personal. "Remember to relax in water, and use your arms and legs to stay afloat."

Rafe smiled softly and left her, and at the same time Edward reached her and grabbed her close. "Maggie, my Maggie! Tell me you're all right."

She kissed his cheek. "I am fine, Edward."

Edward clung to her almost like a child afraid he'd just lost his mother. "I'm so sorry, Darling. If I had lost you—" Edward pulled away. "I should never have brought you with me. It's just that I hate being apart from you. We haven't been apart since we were small." He put a hand to her face. "We'll get you into some dry clothes as soon as the wagons come across."

They walked arm-in-arm to where the others stood waiting, and Gretta and Marie ran over to Maggie and began fussing over her and pouring out questions. Maggie insisted they stop fussing and help others coming to shore, which was how they spent the rest of the afternoon. A few cattle, as well as two spare mules, two horses, and an ox were swept away, and some of the men who had made it across rode farther east to see if any of them had survived.

"What was it like, being rescued by Rafe Morrisey?" Gretta asked Maggie quietly. Both women and Maria sat in the grass trying to dry themselves off in the sun.

"Honestly, Gretta, what do you think? I didn't have time to care about who was rescuing me. All I could think about was trying to stay alive!"

"I wish it had been me."

"No, you don't! Don't talk so foolishly. I could just as easily have drowned!"

"Rafe Morrisey would never have let you drown."

"He isn't God, Gretta. He's just a man doing his job. I really do wish you would stop talking about him all the time. I especially resent your talking as though I am just another young woman looking for a man. I am *married,* and I don't care to be gossiping about the most eligible bachelor on this wagon train or sharing your daydreams about him. I have enjoyed being closer to you, and I don't mean to force my station over you, but I must order you to stop talking to me about Rafe Morrisey."

Gretta's eyebrows shot up in surprise, and she glanced at Maria, who shrugged. "Yes, Ma'am," Gretta told Maggie, wondering why lately she got angry every time she mentioned Rafe.

Now the three wagons brought by the prospective miners were led across the river, one by one, and keeping the teams under control was not easy. The wagons were heavy with mining equipment. Edward helped grab and lead the first team of mules to emerge, and once on shore the driver of that team jumped down from the wagon to help the other two come in. By now twelve wagons were across. All that was left were the four McCahan wagons and Buck James's wagon. Women were already dragging certain things out of their own wagons to air them out, mostly quilts and clothes.

"For heaven's sakes, if it isn't the rain it's the rivers," Lucille Krueger complained.

Maggie watched anxiously as the first McCahan wagon came across. She rose and left Gretta and Maria, and Hazel Schultz came to stand beside her.

"We're almost there," the older woman told Maggie, putting a hand to her waist. "Just a couple more wagons. You okay, Maggie?"

"Yes, I'm fine, thank you."

"You had a rough crossing. I was afraid for you, Honey. I'd have missed you dearly if something had happened to you."

"That's a nice thing to say, Hazel. I would miss you, too, if anything happened to you."

"Well, you're a nice young woman, in spite of being the richest little girl I've ever known." She gave her a squeeze. "But you aren't a snob like most."

Maggie realized it was Hazel's way of complimenting her, so she thanked her, putting an arm around her shoulders and thinking how amusing they must look, for she stood five-feet, six inches, and Hazel seemed barely five-feet tall. Both women watched as the first McCahan wagon, which carried a good deal of their personal belongings, made it to the north side. Gratefully, Edward helped lead the oxen farther off shore. Maggie was relieved. In that wagon was the precious trunk her grandmother had brought from France. It was strapped high on the inside on special shelves Edward had ordered built for stacking belongings, and she hoped it was high enough so that it had not gotten wet. So far she had been able to keep its precious contents dry.

By then the second wagon was on its way across, this one the wagon in which Maggie, Maria, and Gretta slept. Maggie winced at the thought that everything in the bed of the wagon, including all their bedding, would be soaked. It seemed to be stuck for a moment, but the drivers, who all worked together bringing each wagon across, managed to help goad the oxen into pulling harder, and finally the wagon arrived safely.

Nineteen-year-old David, who had turned out to be a very courteous, obedient house servant, helped bring across the third wagon, the heaviest supply wagon. Midway it faltered and began to tip. "Oh, no!" Maggie exclaimed, leaving Hazel's side to walk closer to shore.

The drivers worked frantically, two of them working with the oxen while the other four and David put their shoulders into the side of the wagon that was listing. Rafe charged into the river to try to help, but before he could reach the wagon it went over.

Edward waded into the water, and Maggie screamed at him not to go. "The current is too strong! There's nothing you can do, Edward!"

The rest of the women and those men who had already come across gathered on shore, several of the women exclaiming "Dear God" and saying quick prayers, while most of the men cussed.

"My supplies! I have to have my supplies!" Edward lamented.

"What about the men?" Maggie reminded him. "I don't see all of them."

The wagon began to break apart, and several barrels began floating downriver. The men who had been trying to support the wagon had been on the side facing upriver, which meant some of them could have been drawn underneath. Maggie's fears were verified when those left began shouting to each other.

"They're caught! They're caught!"

"Get them out before they drown!"

"The current's too strong!"

The base of the wagon remained mired where it had become stuck, and apparently more than one man was caught under it. Rafe, Jack, and Wolf Hunter all had ridden out to try to help, leaving their horses to swim ashore on their own. Rafe and one of the drivers dove under several times, as the other drivers worked with the oxen to get them moving and try to pull out what was left of the wagon. Because the top braces and everything that had been stored in the top half of the wagon had washed away, the wagon was lighter, and they finally managed to free it.

"Hold it! Hold it!" one of the men shouted. "Wait till they get Cal and David free!"

"David! Oh, no!" Maggie moaned. "He's so young, and was so eager and excited about this trip."

"Damn!" Edward exclaimed, looking ready to cry. "David! Dear David!" There were tears in his eyes, and Maggie could not help feeling sorry for him, as she always ended up doing. She moved an arm around him. "I'm sorry, Edward. I know how badly you need those supplies to get started in California, and how responsible you must feel for David."

Edward embraced her. "My God, Maggie, you almost drowned yourself. I almost lost my Maggie." He shivered in a sob. "I'm sorry, Maggie. It's just that this all means so much to me. And now it might have cost young David his life."

Maggie closed her eyes and clung to him as the men in the river kept shouting. Again she felt Edward was clinging to her, rather than she to him. She wondered how much longer she could continue being the strong one.

"He's dead!" someone shouted.

Maggie let go of Edward to see Rafe swim to shore, pulling a body with him. Others ran to help when he reached water's edge, while the other drivers brought in the remains of the wagon. One of them helped Jack bring another body to the shoreline, and everyone gathered around to see one of the drivers, who was called Lars, and young David, both lying lifeless on shore. Rafe and Jack both worked frantically over them, turning them facedown and pressing on their backs to force water out of their lungs, but to no avail.

"Forget it, Rafe," Jack told him. "They was under way too long."

Rafe tried a while longer, then stood up, panting, still dripping wet. Maggie was surprised to detect tears in his eyes. He turned away and picked up a rock, angrily tossing it into the water and walking away.

"He don't like losin' anybody on a train he leads," Jack explained to the others. "He considers it his responsibility. He thinks he shouldn't have brought you across, but you folks better believe he had no choice. That river is gonna' get deeper and wider, and we would have been held up a couple weeks or more if we didn't try to get across right away. A couple weeks late can mean disaster in the mountains, so don't none of you go blamin' him for what happened. It's all part of the risks you take tryin' to get yourselves to California.'' He ran a hand through his own wet hair. ''Right now you might as well start diggin' a couple of graves. We should bury these two yet tonight. Rafe is gonna' want to leave out first light.'' He turned to what was left of the drivers. ''Hate to say it, but we've got to go back across and get the last wagon plus Buck James's wagon.''

The other drivers looked down at Lars and David and shook their heads. ''Lars was a damn good man,'' one of them, called Marty, commented. He looked at Edward. ''Sorry, Mr. McCahan. We did everything we could.''

Edward wiped at silent tears. ''I know. I know.'' He knelt down and touched David's hair.

The rest of the men left, using borrowed horses to go back across the river to help bring in the last wagon. Once all the wagons were across, Rafe and Jack crossed once more to bring over horses that had been used for the crossings and had been left on the opposite shore.

It all happened so fast then. Graves were dug. Two men were buried, their personal papers and belongings saved to be shipped back home to their families, but as far as Edward and Maggie knew, David had no family. Reverend Krueger spoke over their graves as the sun settled into the western horizon, and Maggie noticed Rafe was not there. She looked around, finally spotting him. He was sitting alone upriver.

Chapter Thirteen

Yesterday we lost the young man, David Whittaker, whom we had hired as a servant and helpmate, Maggie wrote in her journal, glad to discover it had safely made the river crossing. *He drowned in an accident helping get one of our supply wagons across the river. Another one of our drivers, Lars Hansen, also drowned. There is really no time for mourning on this trip, as making every hour count is important. They were buried shortly after they drowned, and this morning we were again on our way.*

Maggie sat on a log while the others ate their supper. She was not hungry. Each day of the journey only made her more sure of how unhappy she was with Edward. It had been easier at home, for there she at least had her family. Now it was just the two of them, and she was beginning to feel as though she was simply accompanying a good friend.

It is almost impossible to describe the discomforts. Because another couple lost their wagon in the tornado, they have had to take the wagon meant for Maria and Gretta, who now sleep with me. Edward must sleep outside. The mosquitoes are outrageous, and I have so many bites I fear I will never look the same. Just yesterday morning a young woman was bitten by a rattlesnake. She survived, but only due to our captain, Rafe Morrisey, who cut the wound and sucked out the venom. The woman is quite feverish and somewhat delerious, but Mr. Morrisey tells us that since she survived a full twenty-four hours, she will live.

How can I describe Mr. Morrisey? I gave a physical description in an earlier writing, but I have come to know him as a very concerned man, who went off alone after the drownings because he felt responsible and was feeling very bad about it. He feels such accidents are his responsibility, but I personally witnessed him doing everything he could. In fact, when I myself slipped into the water upon riding across, Mr. Morrisey saved my life. Without his quick thinking and swimming skills I, too, would have drowned.

There is an interesting story to Mr. Morrisey's background, and when I have more time I will explain it. He is most unusual, wearing buckskins yet well educated; showing both patience and a temper, a man with Indian, Mexican, and white blood, and sometimes showing all three persuasions in dress and actions. I have seen him use his knife quickly and deftly, and he is equally skilled with rifle and handgun. We have seen him kill a fleeing rabbit with one shot, which I am told is very difficult to do with a handgun. He is a true mountain man, yet well-spoken and clean, and I must say, quite handsome.

Why had she written that? She started to cross out the last comment, then decided she was simply writing down facts about the man who was leading them west. There was nothing wrong with saying he was handsome.

She set the journal aside, thinking again about the way he had looked at her when first they landed on shore after her near drowning. What was it she had seen in his eyes? And the way he had spoken those words while rescuing her—"I would never let go of you, Maggie." There was something about the way he had said them. Was she simply wanting to hear such words from Edward, spoken in a supportive way, rather than because he was *afraid* to let go of her?

She could not forget how upset Rafe had been over David and Lars's deaths, and she was touched by his concern. Deep inside lay a man much more complicated and more capable of deep feelings than one would think of a wandering scout who called no place home. The one attempt he had made at settling had ended in disaster. Perhaps he had decided that he was not meant to ever be truly loved or to ever have a normal family. Tonight he was nowhere to be seen, although she had no doubt he was somewhere out there in the darkness watching out for them. She picked up her journal and finished her entry.

We lost a good deal of our supplies in the crossing accident, but some were rescued and there are still enough left to make a decent profit as soon as we arrive in California, as one of our guides named Jack told us the miners will pay outrageous prices for the smallest item, sometimes a whole dollar for a potato! The only trouble is, I worry what more will happen before we arrive. California is still so far away.

Edward came over to urge her to eat. ''Your body needs the nourishment for all the walking,'' he reminded her. ''Please eat, Maggie. The last thing you want is to get sick.''

Maggie had to agree. ''I'll try,'' she answered. ''I just feel so bad about poor, young David. He had such dreams. I feel as though he and Lars died for *our* dream.''

Edward sighed deeply. ''I can't talk about it, Maggie.'' He put his arms around her. ''I miss you, Maggie. It seems we never have time to be alone together and talk like we did back home, but I promise it will be that way again when we reach California.''

Maggie realized that would mean resuming their sex life, such as it was, and the horrible reality hit her that she had no desire for him sexually, and never really had. Perhaps once she had a child by him, her feelings would change.

Edward kissed her lightly. ''For now, I must be grateful for the difficulties of this journey, because it leaves me too tired to act on my desires for you.'' He laughed almost nervously and kissed her again. ''Maggie, Maggie. My wife, my good friend, so wise and accepting. Who would have thought my beautiful Maggie, with all her fine upbringing and comfortable life, would have adapted so well to the hardships of this journey? I will forever be grateful to you. Some day we *will* go home, and we will go in style and be able to tell our families about the millions we made in California.''

''Of course we will, Edward.''

Edward walked her back to their campsite, and someone else watched them from the darkness. ''Just how happy are you, Mrs. McCahan?'' Rafe muttered. This had never happened to him on any journey west. He had been around plenty of pretty young girls who were single, some of whom had even made it very clear they were interested in him, like the McCahan maid, Gretta Wheeler. But he had not been interested, and in his position, it was always wise to avoid involvement with any of the women.

But for some reason Maggie McCahan was different, and she wasn't even available. She was married to someone else, a man he knew did not deserve her. What a damned ridiculous situation he'd gotten himself into, allowing this attraction to her begin to get under his skin . . . and into his heart.

Maggie could tell she had lost weight, for her dresses did not fit as snugly as they once had. She was grateful that she at least seemed to be adjusting to her situation. Muscles no longer ached so badly at the end of the day, and the blisters on her feet had turned to callouses. She went through two pairs of shoes by the time they reached the higher plains of western Nebraska, and there had been several more river crossings . . . and more burials. Too many entries in her diary. . . .

Bill Marks drowned today, leaving a wife, Wilena, and three young children. Wilena is beside herself, having no purpose, now, for going on, yet unable to turn back. One of our drivers, Stuart Purdy, has been quite attentive to her, and Jack, who ate with us one evening, told us that often a woman widowed on her way west will marry a near stranger just so her children will be taken care of. Perhaps that is what will happen with Stuart and Wilena.

They had been held up for three days by a fever none could explain. Nearly everyone had suffered from it, including herself and Edward and Gretta. For some reason, Maria was spared, and she was able to help take care of the rest of them. Rafe said it probably had something to do with drinking the river water, perhaps just the constant exposure to the soaking waters when they crossed the river several times. Whatever it was, it had been miserable, and it had killed thirteen-year-old Nettie and nine-year-old Ken Howell.

More burials . . . the saddest kind . . . children. Mildred Howell had hardly spoken ever since, and her oldest daughter, Katie, had been forced to take over a mother's duties, doing most of the cooking and looking after her younger siblings, twelve-year-old Larry, six-year-old Sharon and four-year-old Tessa. Maggie greatly admired Katie for the adult way she had taken charge, and now the poor young girl was much too busy to find time to flirt with Rafe, as she had done so obviously on the first part of their journey. There would be little chance for trying to attract his eye, anyway, since Rafe had stayed much more to himself since that first river crossing. Maggie sometimes wondered if it had anything to do with the way he had looked at her that day after saving her, then decided that was a silly thought. Gretta was very disappointed that he kept to himself evenings and never again joined them for supper.

There were many more diary entries. Susan Haggarty fell and broke her arm. Her screams filled the open plains when Jack and Rafe set the bone, but she seemed to be doing all right now. Billy Krueger suffered a bee bite that made his hand and arm swell and turn purple, and the poor young man was miserable.

Then came the cholera. It hit hard, and slowed their progress. Somehow Maggie was spared, but Edward fell gravely ill, and Maggie nursed him faithfully, although inside she felt horror at both the strain of having to clean up after him, and the fear she would herself get the disease. Gretta was also somehow miraculously spared, but not Maria. Maria died.

Another sad diary entry. *We buried our faithful Maria today. After much suffering she died from what we are pretty sure is cholera. Many are still sick, including Edward, but he is improving.* Others did not improve. Jeremiah Smith died, leaving his two grown sons to go on without him. One of the group of single men heading to California to dig for gold also died. Three-year-old Rob Maddox died, and his mother had to be dragged from his grave in order to go on.

Nine dead, so far. *I shall miss my Maria forever,* Maggie wrote. A day did not go by that she did not shed more tears over her faithful cook's death. Now it was up to her and Gretta to do the cooking. Gretta had only a little experience, Maggie had none. Spirits brightened a little when her cooking mistakes brought friendly laughter from others. The women got together and began taking turns helping Maggie cook until she had learned enough to try it on her own, but she still made mistakes. The experience was frustrating, and yet in a way it was fun. It helped occupy her thoughts, and she began to feel proud of certain things she cooked, especially learning to bake bread in a Dutch oven. It was cause for more entries in her diary, more pleasant writing.

They passed Chimney Rock, an amazing sight about which Maggie also made an entry in her diary—*It truly looks just like a chimney. I have never seen such strange rock formations as out here, and we are beginning to enter the Nebraska Sand Hills. I thought they were mountains at first, but Jack tells us they are just "little hills" compared to the Rockies.*

Edward is well, thank God. Nursing him has been a nightmare, but it has made me a stronger wife and woman.

The wagons trudged on toward Fort Laramie, a constant, gradual climb that went slowly and wore out the animals. A mule and two oxen collapsed and died, and they were not yet to the mountains. One woman was forced to unload a china cabinet that had come from England with her parents. More of Edward's supplies had to be left behind. The Krueger family had to discard two church benches and a heavy oak podium the Reverend Krueger had planned to use in the church he would build.

Sad hearts were lightened when Rafe ordered the wagons to halt and told everyone to come to the ridge just ahead. He had something to show them, but warned that everyone should be quiet. Glad for the excitement and the break in monotony, everyone hurried up the hill, gasping at what they saw just over the rise.

Buffalo!

"There must be hundreds!" one woman said quietly.

"Thousands," Rafe corrected her.

It looked to Maggie as though they were so thick a man could almost walk across the next stretch of land on the backs of the buffalo. They were both beautiful and frightening, huge beasts, although a few little ones ran among them, kicking and playing, but staying close to their mothers.

"Can you and Jack get a couple for us?" Barney Schultz asked Rafe. "Looks like mighty good meat."

"I would, but someone else is after them, and I don't intend to cut in on their kill. It could make trouble for us. Look over to that ridge on your left, and stay low. They haven't seen us, and if we don't interrupt them, we'll be all right."

Everyone looked to where he pointed, spotting a group of Indians charging down a different bluff toward the buffalo.

"My God! Indians!" Edward exclaimed.

"They'll run them to the north, and the hunters on the ridge to your right will charge right into them for the kill."

It was only then that everyone realized there were even more Indians opposite those they had already seen.

"All we have to do is hope they don't herd them this way," Rafe told them. "I don't think they will, from what I can judge. That far hill ahead of us is even steeper than this one. They'll run them up that one to wear them out and slow them down. Makes the killing easier. Just lay low and watch, and you'll see a real buffalo hunt."

"What kind of Indians are they?" Matthew Krueger asked.

"Up in this area it is most likely Lakota. Whites call them Sioux. We leave them alone, they'll leave us alone. So far there hasn't been that much trouble, but things are going to get worse pretty quick, with so many going through their hunting grounds to get to California. That's why we don't dare try to down a couple of those buffalo for ourselves. To them it's stealing. This is their land, and that's their game. They couldn't survive without the buffalo. Nearly everything they eat, use, wear, fight with, whatever it is—it all comes from the buffalo.''

Everyone watched in fascination as the hunters closed in on the buffalo, killing several of them before the big, lumbering animals even knew what was happening. The herd finally began to run, and Rafe had been right. The Indians chased them up the hill ahead, downing several more with bow and arrow. Maggie thought it a beautiful sight, one she would never forget. These were the original people of the plains, and this was a moment about which she could tell her grandchildren. She could hardly wait to make tonight's entry in her journal. She could hear the yips and calls of the Indians, and she could not help thinking what a dreaded sound that would be if those warriors were after them rather than the buffalo.

''Are you sure they won't come after us?'' she asked.

Rafe lay watching, only a few feet away. ''I don't think so. A hunt is very serious business to the Indians. Once it's over, they'll go get their women, who are probably camped not far away, and the gutting and cleaning will begin. It's a lot of work that will keep them occupied for quite a number of days. The men will sit and enjoy their pipes and their full bellies from roasting some of the meat before the rest of it is smoked and dried. Some of it will be pounded into pemmican. That's a mixture of meat and berries and a few other ingredients, pounded together and dried. It makes a great staple for the men when going on the hunt or making war. Pemmican lasts weeks, even months.''

''When can we move on?'' Barney asked.

''Soon as they get over that rise. We'll swing around to the south and try to go around them. You'll have to watch for buffalo wallows. You can break a wagon wheel falling into one of those, and you might not get back out. When male buffalo fight, they leave big holes from their scuffling; and other wallows are formed just from the buffalo wiggling around on their backs to get a good scratch. Jack and I will make sure to guide you around them so we don't have any accidents. We'll make Fort Laramie within another week.''

They watched the buffalo charge up and over the hill, still

being chased, and behind them lay several carcasses, all killed with bow and arrow. Maggie thought it a splendid sight. She studied the far horizon, wondered when they would begin to see the Rockies. This was truly fascinating, dangerous, beautiful, big country, a place that could bring both great tragedy and great pleasure, a place of magnificent scenery, violent weather, yet day after day of sunshine. It struck her only then that she was learning to love it.

Chapter Fourteen

Wilena Marks has married Stuart Purdy, Maggie wrote in her journal. *The Reverend Krueger conducted the wedding ceremony here at Fort Laramie, and at last we have something to celebrate. Everyone has recovered from cholera and bee bites, and Susan Haggarty's broken arm is healing. There are traders and soldiers here, as well as a camp of Sioux Indians outside the fort. It is wonderful to be able to stop and relax a little, and get a few more supplies. The Haggartys were able to purchase another wagon, so at last Edward and I can be together again, but poor Gretta must sleep alone, now that Maria has left us.*

The Indians are interesting. They frighten me some, but Mr. Morrisey assures us they are quite harmless as long as we are near the fort. If we run into more after we leave, he says they usually only want to trade. Some of them are quite grand looking, with feathers and beads decorating their deerskin garments, but a few are not so clean, and they have apparently taken a liking to whiskey, which Mr. Morrisey says they call firewater. He has told us to be very careful around any Indian who has been drinking. We all have stayed to ourselves and left them alone, but it is interesting to watch Mr. Morrisey talk with them, using their own tongue as well as some sign language. Our captain is a man of many talents and many moods. So far he has done a good job in getting us this far, the deaths we have experienced attributable only to nature and our own carelessness and ignorance.

Maggie set aside her journal and pen to go and join others who had gathered today to present gifts to the newlyweds. The gifts consisted merely of useful articles donated by everyone that the new family Stuart Purdy had "inherited" could use once they settled, items no one could really afford to spare, but things that were given from the heart.

Maggie gave the newlyweds a set of crystal glasses from her trunk, which had been a wedding present to her and Edward. They were not something especially useful now, but she wanted to give something pretty, something Wilena could always treasure. Wilena nearly cried at the gift, declaring she had never owned something so beautiful or expensive, and that she would wrap them carefully and treasure them always. The poor woman was in almost constant tears from a mixture of still mourning her first husband and happiness at finding a good man to help her the rest of the way and to provide for her children.

Maggie could not help wondering what it must be like for a woman to marry someone she had known only two months, and only then by sight. She had not actually spoken with Stuart and gotten to know him on a more familiar level until Bill Marks died, which was a little less than one month ago. What must it be like with someone a woman had hardly known at all until just weeks ago? The thought brought Rafe Morrisey to mind, and she realized that wanting to be with a man did not have so much to do with knowing him a long time as with that strange, indescribable sexual attraction that made a woman feel things she felt for no other man. She had known Edward all her life, but she'd never had those feelings of true desire for him.

What a curious country this was, where strangers married, where people could watch Indians hunting buffalo, where men with exotic pasts risked their lives to lead determined but ignorant emigrants to a place they knew nothing about. The lure of gold could cause men to do incredible things, to risk their entire families for dreams that might never come true. She could only pray that after all they had been through, Edward's dream would be realized. He deserved that much, and she would help him all she could once they reached California. Maybe once they arrived, she would see him in a different light, away from the influence of his father. She did have to admire his tenacity on this journey, for he, too, was used to a much more comfortable way of life. Her heart had gone out to him during his sickness, and the whole ordeal had made her stronger.

Hazel had baked a cake for the party, and everyone gladly took a piece. She apologized that it was a little too flat and not as moist as it should be. "But out here, what can you expect?" she joked. "First thing I'm getting when we reach California is a real cookstove with a real oven."

Everyone joined in her laughter, and Maggie watched Wilena, seeing loneliness in her eyes, but she smiled when she looked at her new husband. She realized Wilena was a woman of true courage and strength. She had risked sacrificing her own happiness to make sure her children did not suffer hunger and danger. A woman with little children on the trail west needed a man's help, and that was that. Maggie hoped Stuart would be good to her. He seemed like a decent man who was truly happy to take a wife, and if it helped Wilena, then Maggie did not mind losing yet another driver.

They were down to four men and four wagons now, with no extras for taking turns and getting relief. David and Lars were dead, and Stuart had married. That left Marty, Ben, John and Bill . . . and Edward. Edward was learning and could do quite a decent job of driving the oxen, and because of that her own respect for him had grown, even though she still saw him more and more as only a friend.

She drew a deep breath, telling herself she must quit feeling sorry for herself. She should be happy to have made it this far, and she had seen and experienced wondrous things she would never forget. Women like herself would go down in history, wouldn't they? If she had to endure these things, then she would simply count herself lucky to have experienced something no other woman from the circle she had known back home would experience, and back home Edward would end up a hero.

"We have to get ready, Maggie!"

Gretta had interrupted her thoughts, coming to stand beside her while cake was handed out.

"Ready for what?"

"For za dance! Hazel told me zat among za traders and soldiers zere are enough men who know a few instruments to play some music, so we can dance and be happy for once. You shoot wear one of your prettier dresses, one of za special ones you have never taken out of your trunk. It has been a long time since you look pretty for Mr. McCahan. It would be goot for him to see his Missis looking beautiful again. I will fix your hair for you like we used to do back home. Und *I* will make *my*self as pretty as I can! Perhaps our Captain Morrisey will come! I want him to know I can look better zan what he has seen so far!"

A dance. What a pleasant thought. It *would* be nice to dress nice for once, fix her hair in something better than a plain bun. Maggie walked up to get her piece of cake, and she noticed Rafe Morrisey standing in the distance. *Would* he come to a dance? Did he even know *how* to dance?

Maggie chose a soft green day dress, not among the special dresses in her trunk. Those were *too* special for dragging their ruffled hems around in the dirt here at the fort, and none of the other women here would have anything fancy except, perhaps, Jenny, who was sure to wear something too low at the bosom. Her necklines were a source of constant remarks by the men, and gossip from the women.

Maggie's dress had a modest neckline, scooped only enough to show the soft, white skin of her neck and chest, but not enough to display any of her bosom. Her auburn hair was wound into a pile of waves pinned at the top of her head, and Gretta urged her to wear a pair of diamond drop earrings that were in the trunk. Edward gladly got it down for her, excited about showing off his beautiful, elegant wife. Edward wore clean cotton pants and a white shirt, but he, too, did not feel right wearing his best. Instead he wore a simple but well-cut cotton jacket that at home he might wear to the office.

It felt wonderful to taste a little bit of home by dressing for something special instead of wearing the plain calico and dark cotton dresses more suited for walking across the country. Maggie put on delicate white shoes that laced up to mid-calf. She helped Gretta fix her own lovely ash blond hair into a fancier do than was normal for a maid, and she let Gretta wear a pink cotton day dress that hung a little too long because Gretta was slightly shorter than she, but fit her nicely. Maggie's own dress was a little loose because of her losing weight, but she had no choice. She splashed on some lilac toilet water and let Gretta use some, and she hid her irritation at the way Gretta carried on about hoping to get a dance out of Rafe Morrisey.

Just at dusk the music began, and Gretta hurried off to try to attract the attention of Rafe, or perhaps one of the single prospectors or one of the drivers. At this point she really did not care which, although she still tended to moon over Rafe. Maggie took her husband's arm, and Edward kissed her cheek.

"You look wonderful, Maggie. When we get to California, you can take those fancy dresses out of your trunk and be a true woman of class and culture again. I promise you that."

"I know, Edward." Maggie walked with him to an area where a platform had been built by the soldiers for dancing, so that the women's dresses would not drag in the dirt. Men sat playing fiddles, guitars, drums, a flute, and a trumpet—an odd combination, but one that melded surprisingly well. Women exclaimed over how beautiful Maggie looked, and the men teased Edward about finally having his wife back. Maggie blushed at the hinting remarks, and Edward led her up to the platform to dance.

One thing Edward was, was a wonderful dancer, and they moved together to a waltz, enjoying night air that was cooler than normal, with just enough of a breeze so that the mosquitoes were not quite such a bother. There had been many moments when Maggie had considered using the smelly bear grease Rafe had once offered, but she never had. She had, however, taken his advice to stop using creams and perfumes that attracted the pests, and that did seem to help.

Tonight, however, she wanted to feel clean and lovely. She and Gretta had bathed in the river, and she wore her finest perfume. It felt wonderful to put cream and a little powder on her face, color on her lips, to wear the diamond earrings.

"I am so proud of you, Maggie, how you have come through this trip so far," Edward told her.

"It's called survival, Edward. We all do what we must for it. I will say one thing for this journey. It has helped me understand sides of me, and you, that I did not even know existed. Sometimes I don't even feel like myself any more, at least not like the Maggie who left Pennsylvania."

"It is the same for me, Maggie. There is a wonderful freedom out here, freedom from all the confines of the lives we once led, freedom from my father, freedom from having to do what is expected, rather than what is really in your heart to do."

Maggie frowned, catching something in the statement she could not quite name. "And what is really in your heart, Edward?"

He shrugged, whirling her around proudly. "You already know. To strike out on my own, build my own little empire, to find the real Edward McCahan." Did she know? What was that in her eyes? He loved her. He truly loved her, but now he knew for certain he dared not ever reveal the secret about himself. Maggie was the only one who might have understood. She was such a good friend. But now she was also his wife. To tell her now would break her heart. Because they had always been so close, he thought it would be easy to be the man he should be if he married her. But even his beautiful Maggie could not bring forth the true desire any man should have for such a woman. Oh, yes, he desired her as a friend and counselor, as the support he'd never found in anyone else. He treasured her for the kind and educated and eloquent woman she was, the perfect mate for a man of wealth. He greatly admired her strength and courage, her valiant effort to remain by his side through this awful journey. He'd thought that once they were on the trail west, and needed each other in ways they would never need each other at home, perhaps *then* he would find that part of himself that had been strangely missing all his life. But he had felt that kind of manliness only with young David, and David was dead. No one knew the real reason he had hired him, and probably no one ever would. He had not been able to mourn him in the way he truly needed to mourn him, for everyone would wonder.

"Edward, are those tears I see in your eyes? Whatever is wrong? You should be so happy tonight."

Edward took a deep breath. "Oh, I am, Maggie. I guess that's why I feel like crying. I am just so proud of you, and I worry so that something might happen to you before this trip is over. I could never forgive myself for that." *Or for marrying you under false pretense, for not being able to give you all that you truly deserve, to truly be a man for you in every way.*

The weariness from the journey, and having to give a wagon to the Haggartys, had combined to give him an excuse not to sleep with his wife. Now his only excuse could be the one they had always had, that she should not get pregnant before this trip was over. But he had to make her believe that was difficult for him. He could not give her any idea he did not desire her that way, and he could only hope that he could continue to dredge up enough of his manly needs to be able to make love to her once they settled in California.

"Nothing is going to happen, Edward. You must not think that way."

Edward smiled and turned her again and again, realizing how much the other men admired him for having such a beautiful, poised, sweet wife. Maggie in turn smiled, realizing her husband wanted to show her off. She would make this work. She had no other choice.

The dance ended, and as Edward led Maggie off the platform to join some of the others, Maggie looked past the crowd to see Rafe standing on the other side of a large, central campfire, watching her. He turned away.

Chapter Fifteen

The terrain has changed dramatically since leaving Fort Laramie. We have left the wide-open, treeless country and the sand hills of Nebraska Territory and have entered an even more beautiful area, hilly, rocky, with strange formations that make you wonder if perhaps God simply played with the rocks and threw them about, for there is no explanation for why some of them are where they are. And in the distance we can see the mountains. We are finally approaching them. The mosquitoes are not so bad here, and our captain promises it will be cooler when we reach the mountains.

Maggie leaned back, watching Edward sleep. He had hinted several times at making love, but had been agreeable when she insisted they wait until they reach California. She felt guilty for always denying the poor man, and yet a little part of her wondered why he did not insist. Sometimes she almost wished that he would, not because she desired him, but because it might *make* her desire him if he would be a little more aggressive and demanding, show some male instincts, tell her he could not go one more minute without being a part of her. Instead, he usually simply kissed her on the cheek and told her good night.

She set the journal aside, deciding she should be glad Edward had enough respect for her health to keep away from her. It was just that abstaining hardly seemed to phase him. Sometimes he seemed almost relieved that they had an excuse to refrain from lovemaking.

She pulled on a robe and climbed out of the wagon. Taking tissue paper with her, one of the luxuries she had brought from home, she searched through the darkness away from the light of a lingering campfire, looking for a place to urinate once more before going to sleep. Once her eyes adjusted to the dim light of a half-moon, she found a place behind a cluster of rocks. Looking around first, she then bent down to take care of things, shivering at the sound of wolves howling somewhere in the distance and, closer, the yipping of coyotes. She had learned to identify some night sounds and, knowing all the dangerous animals there were that prowled at night in these regions, the darkness made her nervous, but there were some duties that simply could not be avoided.

She rose to go back, stepping around the rocks.

"You should always let somebody know when you're going into the dark alone."

Maggie started at the voice. Her heart pounded painfully hard from surprise and fright, for she had already been nervous. She put a hand to her chest and took a deep breath when she realized it was Rafe.

"You scared me to death! My God, how long have you been there!" She could tell he was leaning against the rocks.

"Not long. From a distance I saw you come out here. I wasn't even sure it was you, Maggie. I just knew somebody had come out into the darkness. It's a dangerous thing to do. We're being stalked by Blackfoot Indians."

Maggie glanced around, then looked back at Rafe, although she could only see the outline of his big frame, not the details of his face, not those dark eyes. "Why didn't you tell us?"

"I didn't want to alarm folks. They might be harmless, just curious. Most likely all they want is to trade at some point. I don't think they'll try to make trouble."

Maggie shoved what was left of her paper into the pocket of her robe, then folded her arms across in front of her, shivering at the thought of possibly being watched right now by Indians. "How on earth did you see me from a distance on a night like this? There is hardly any moon. And how did you manage to get so close without me hearing you?"

He moved away from the rocks, closer to her. "I'm part Indian myself, remember? I'm used to keeping my eyes open at night, for one thing, and out here you *learn* to walk quiet. There aren't exactly a lot of places to hide yourself if you're stalking the enemy. That's what Indians are good at, and I guess I am, too."

Maggie was glad for the darkness, so that he could not see the blush in her face. "And just how long were you standing there while I was doing something personal?" She could feel his smile, but she could not see it.

"Don't worry. I was on this side of the rocks the whole time."

"Well, I certainly hope so!"

Both of them talked quietly, as most of the camp was asleep, except for two men assigned to watch the livestock.

"I wouldn't be surprised to wake up and find some of the horses and cattle missing," Rafe told her. "I just wanted to make sure there wasn't one of our *women* missing. Sometimes Indians steal women and hold them for ransome, trading them for tobacco and guns."

"That's . . . that's deplorable!"

"That's the Indian way. I have to say, though, you'd be worth a lot more than tobacco and a few guns."

Maggie could not stop a smile. Why didn't she go back to her wagon? Why did part of her want to stand out here and talk to Rafe Morrisey? They had hardly spoken since the river incident. It seemed as though he had been deliberately staying away, but she supposed it was because of his work. He had better things to do than socialize with the travelers.

"I guess I should thank you for that remark," she replied. "Is that a roundabout compliment?" She heard a soft chuckle, and she realized she had never heard Rafe Morrisey laugh before.

"I guess it is. Of course, we would be the only ones who

would know that. To the Indians you wouldn't be any more valuable than a horse."

Now it was Maggie who laughed. "Well, now, that is one way to shrink a swelled head, isn't it?"

He came even closer. "Everything is pretty much of equal value to the Indian," he answered, "except maybe sacred arrows and other fetishes."

Why did his closeness make her nervous? She turned away, walking over to lean against the rocks where he had stood. "Do *you* hold anything sacred, Rafe?"

He came to stand beside her, also leaning on the rocks. He lit a thin cigar before replying. "Not really, but then I wasn't brought up among the Indians. I've just learned a lot about them. I *do* believe that there are certain things that *should* be held sacred, and I understand how important that is to the Indians, how spiritual they are."

He drew on the cigar, and Maggie caught sight of his face for a moment in the glow of the red ashes. He seemed even more dark and mysterious and handsome at night. The quick thought came to her that Rafe Morrisey would not easily take no for an answer when he wanted his woman, and just as quickly she wondered why on earth she had entertained such a thought! She must get out of here and get back to the wagon. What would people think if they knew she was standing out here alone, in her nightgown, with Rafe? Before she could make an excuse to leave, he continued talking.

"There *are* some things I hold sacred," he said, "but not material things like the Indians."

"Oh? What do you mean, then?"

How tempting it was to tell her what he had seen on a near-dark night like this one . . . Edward McCahan and young David Whittaker. They never knew he was there. They were too lost in each other. How could he tell this beautiful, sophisticated, trusting woman something like that? What the hell kind of marriage could she possibly have with a man like Edward? How could he possibly fulfill her needs? Had she ever experienced the true pleasures of being with a man?

"Oh, I just mean things like marriage vows, promises, truth, a man's word, things like that. My father promised to always take care of me and my mother, but he didn't. When she died the way she did, in poverty, living like a prostitute to get money, I vowed then and there that I would always mean what I say and act on it.'' *I think I love you, Maggie McCahan. I mean that, and I sure as hell wish I could act on it.*

''Well, that is very noble, Rafe. I am surprised you shared such a thing with me. You certainly are a man of surprises.'' Again she could tell he was smiling.

''Sometimes I even surprise myself. I guess my life has been a journey of trying to figure out who I really am and where I belong, considering my background and mixed blood.''

''Well, I would say you are Rafe Morrisey, just a man like any other, and that you belong wherever you *choose* to belong.''

''I am a bastard, Mrs. McCahan.''

Maggie frowned, hating the ugly word. ''That is just a word, a description ignorant people give to children of unmarried parents, or unknown fathers. Why should the *child* be labeled, when it did nothing wrong? The child is innocent. How dare you think of yourself that way! You have been around, experienced a lot of things in a short period of years. You should know better than anyone that bastard is a useless, meaningless label used only by ignorant people.''

He chuckled softly again. ''The woman is also a preacher.''

Maggie grinned, leaning closer. ''I have never in my life thought of myself that way! I guess this journey and this drastic change in my manner of living has done something to me. I swear I am not myself at all.''

They both laughed, and not far away a coyote yipped, sounding much closer than normal. Maggie cringed and moved even closer, and before she realized what he was doing, Rafe's arms were around her.

''Just stand real still,'' he whispered, drawing her close. ''There's a coyote only a few feet away. He'll sniff around a little and leave.''

Maggie grabbed hold of his deerskin shirt with her fists and kept her head pressed against his chest, closing her eyes and waiting for sharp fangs to bury themselves in one of her legs. Rafe's arms came closer around her, holding her tightly.

"He's gone," Rafe finally whispered.

Maggie relaxed, but for some reason she did not want to let go of him. How wonderful it felt to have a man's arms around her in a comforting, protective embrace, rather than clinging to her like a child's. For the first time in years, probably since she fell once when she was young and her father held her to calm her, she experienced the pleasure of letting someone else be the strong one. It took her a moment to realize what she was doing—a married woman, standing out here in the dark with another man, clinging to him, his arms around her! She wasn't even wearing any undergarments or shoes, and her hair was undone!

"My goodness! I had better get back to my wagon," she exclaimed, starting to pull away. She looked up at him as she spoke, and suddenly his lips were covering hers in a sweet, delicious kiss, a kiss she did not want to leave, forbidden, yet so deep and satisfying. His arms tightened around her again, and wrong as she knew it was, she could not resist. It was as though he had some sort of power over her. She had never sensed this virility with Edward, this near demand that she allow the kiss, this sudden, fiery desire to know what it was like to be kissed this way.

She responded to his soft groan, the way he crushed her against himself, and as though she had no control over them she was moving her arms up around his neck, returning his kiss with wild abandon. He moved one of his hands down over her bottom, pressing his fingers into the cleft of her bottom and down farther, grasping her between the legs from behind. At the same time his tongue explored her mouth. Edward had never done such things. She didn't even know such things *were* done. She felt something hard as a rock pressing against her groin, and when she realized what it was, she wanted more. Dear God, she wanted more!

No! Not this way! This was wrong! Sinful! A woman was not supposed to have these kinds of desires. She turned her face away. "Let go! Let go!" she exclaimed in a frantic whisper.

He kept a tight hold on her. "It's all right, Maggie."

"No! It *isn't* all right. Oh, my God, what have I done!"

"Nothing! It's all right. Do you hear me?" He kept a firm hold on her. "I'm sorry. I'm damned sorry. Please believe me, I've never done anything like this. It's just . . . I care very much for you, Maggie McCahan. And you deserve a better man than the one you've got!"

"What?" She pushed at him. "How *dare* you talk about my Edward that way! And how dare you take privileges with a married woman! Oh, my God!"

He grasped her arms. "*Stop* it, Maggie!"

She broke into tears. "What must you think of me?"

"I think you're a beautiful but lonely woman who maybe didn't know what she was getting into when she got married. I think no less of you than I did ten minutes ago. In fact, I think *more* of you than I did ten minutes ago."

"Please let go of me!" Maggie jerked in a sob, mortified, ashamed. She covered her face. "My God, I've lost my mind! This trip has destroyed my common sense! I hate it! I hate everything about this land! And I hate you for what you just did, and myself for *letting* you!"

She started to run off, but Rafe grabbed her arm. "Don't go back in this condition. Edward will wonder." God, how he wanted to tell her the truth, but now would be an even worse time. Maybe she would think he was making it up, trying to turn her against her own husband. And she was already embarrassed and upset. How could he tell her such a thing now? He'd handled this all wrong. "I'm sorry, Maggie. Please forgive me. It's just that . . . I've admired your courage and your strength. I've seen you struggle to adapt, without complaint. You've got what it takes to live out here, Maggie, and you're a fine woman who deserves a man to match your strength."

She jerked her arm away. "There is no excuse for what either one of us just did! Mine is that I have just plain lost my mind out here! Yours is that you are just like your *father,* aren't you? I don't need the compliments, Rafe Morrisey! *Any* woman will do, won't she, single or *married!*"

She stormed away, and Rafe stood watching after her. Her words had cut deep. The last thing he ever wanted was to be compared to his womanizing father, who had had no true feelings of love for anyone in his life. Damn her! And damn himself for allowing his gut feelings and baser instincts to take control. Now he was in pain with the want of her.

The coyote snuck back, standing not far away and just staring. Rafe walked up and kicked at it. "Get the hell out of here!" he growled.

The coyote yipped and ran off.

Chapter Sixteen

There was only one way for Maggie to force herself not to care about Rafe, and that was to believe the last words she had spit at him. He was a womanizer. How did she know he had not tried the same thing with one or more of the other women? The man made these trips every year. He knew how hard and lonely it was for a woman, how most women on such journeys were probably fed up with their husbands for bringing them along and making them leave everything and everyone back home.

Yes, that was it. He was just like his father, and she had fallen for his words, his touch, his dark mystery, his damn good looks, his kiss, his exotic masculinity. Never had she felt like such a fool, nor been so ashamed. She could not bear to look at him for fear of what he must be thinking by now. He had declared what happened did not make him think less of her, but how could it not? Had he bragged to Jack and Wolf Hunter about it?

What a fool she was! How could she finish this trip with Rafe Morrisey around day in and day out, knowing what he must be thinking, knowing he must be laughing at her on the inside. She snuggled closer to Edward at night, trying to reassure him of her love. What if he found out? How could she have been so untrue as to kiss another man and let him . . . touch her? Edward would never do a thing like that to her. She had been the only woman in his life, and he considered her his best friend . . . but his best friend had betrayed him. She would never forgive herself.

She half expected Rafe to ride past them occasionally and give her a haughty look of victory, try to make her uncomfortable. But he didn't. In fact, he stayed away completely except for shouting an order once in a while as he rode past. None of the other women showed any signs that they felt any differently about him. Some often mentioned what a good job he was doing, and how respectful he was, how concerned about the well-being of everyone along, seeming almost apologetic whenever he had to order that yet another treasured item be left behind.

Gradually his words came back to her, making Maggie wonder if he truly did have feelings for her. *I care very much for you, Maggie McCahan . . . I think you're a beautiful but lonely woman who didn't know what she was getting into when she got married.* How would he know that? *I'm sorry, Maggie. Please forgive me . . .* He'd seemed so sincere. *You're a fine woman who deserves a man to match your strength.* What did he mean by that? Why was he trying to tell her Edward was not good enough for her? That was what angered her the most—that he would insult Edward. What did he know about their relationship?

She looked up now to see him riding hard toward her and the other women who were walking. "Get up closer to the wagons! Quick!" he told them. He rode off again, and Maggie felt frustrated that he had acted as though nothing had changed. On the one hand, she was relieved he was not paying any special attention to her or giving her looks to make her feel guilty. Yet a little part of her *wanted* him to acknowledge something *was* different . . . and part of her wanted to experience that kiss again. Much as she wanted to hate him, to put away all thoughts and memories of him, there he was every time she closed her eyes, pressing her close, tasting her mouth, touching her, waking something inside her, a place deeply buried, a place Edward had never stirred. As much as she hated what had happened, she had never felt so on fire and full of passion as she had in Rafe Morrisey's arms, and that was the hell of it.

"Hurry, Maggie!" Gretta shouted at her. "Mr. Morrisey said to get to the wagons!"

Maggie started running, and before she reached her own she saw the reason for halting the train. A group of painted warriors had lined up in front of them to stop the wagons. Rafe was talking with them now, shaking his head, using sign language in addition to speaking some of their own tongue. Jack was beside him, and Wolf Hunter stood at a little bit of a distance. Whatever tribe this was, perhaps it was one the Shoshone did not get along with. She raced to her wagon to join Gretta.

"What are they?" Gretta whispered.

"How should I know? Maybe they are Blackfoot."

"Blackfoot? I don't remember Mr. Morrisey mentioning that tribe. How would you know about them?"

Maggie looked away. *Because the other night, when I was with Rafe. . . .* "I remember Jack mentioning Blackfoot Indians sometimes come into this area," she lied. "I'm just guessing."

Rafe turned to the men, who had gathered nearby. "They need blankets for winter, and they want tobacco, whiskey, flour, and some meat."

"But we can't spare any of those things," Graydon Howell protested. "Tobacco and whiskey, maybe a little, but not blankets, and flour and sugar. We haven't even started into the mountains yet."

Rafe folded his arms and nodded to his right and toward the back of the wagon train. "We don't have a lot of room for argument," he answered. "Look around you, Mr. Howell. There are more of them than you realize."

Maggie looked in the direction of Howell and the others. "Dear God," she muttered. More Indians appeared on a ridge to the south, and more were riding up from the east. They were practically surrounded.

"These are Blackfoot Indians," Rafe explained. "And they

are not always terribly friendly. They are angry right now because a lot of their tribe lost their lives this past winter because of severe weather, and because of a wave of smallpox that swept through their village. They blame whites for that, and rightly so. I wouldn't argue the issue. I would get together as much of the items I mentioned as you can possibly spare and bring them out here.'' He glanced at the women, who stood farther back. ''You women can help by bringing some material, ribbons, anything like that, especially if they are brightly colored. Mirrors, jewelry, anything interesting that will greatly please their women, especially when they are things they didn't even ask for. They'll go away a lot friendlier.''

Everyone began climbing into wagons to see what they could retrieve, most grudgingly. Maggie grabbed a bright yellow dress from where some of her better clothes were packed in boxes, then took some ribbons from another box where she kept combs and hairpieces. ''Lord knows I don't need things like this out here,'' she muttered. She climbed back out of the wagon and nervously walked to where offered items were beginning to pile up. She held up the dress and ribbons to the man at the head of the Indians, with whom Rafe had spoken, and he smiled, apparently pleased with her ''offering.'' She felt as though she was presenting all her worldly possessions to a king, for he sat as proud as one, dressed in fancy beaded buckskins, feathers in his hair, his cheeks painted. Even his horse was painted. He looked fierce but was quite fine looking. Still, to be around him and so many like him was quite frightening, and she had to be grateful that Rafe knew how to deal with them.

''Aren't they even going to trade something back to us for all this stuff?'' Barney Schultz asked.

Rafe stood watching carefully. ''They are letting us go through their hunting grounds. They figure that's payment enough. You might call all this stuff our passage fee.''

''It's robbery,'' Terrence Maddox grumbled.

''They don't see it that way. Quit complaining and be glad you're alive.''

Just then a shot rang out, and Beverly Maddox screamed. Her husband cried out at the same time, and he crumpled to the ground, holding his foot. Frightened by the gunshot, others ran behind or dived under wagons, thinking the Indians were shooting at them, and Rafe went to Maddox to see what had happened. All of it happened in a matter of two or three seconds, and Maggie watched in horror. As Rafe hurried over to see what had happened, there came a quick whirring sound, and Rafe cried out when an arrow landed with a thud in the left side of his back.

"Oh, Dear God!" Maggie cried out.

More women screamed. Men scrambled to grab firearms. Rafe fell to his knees, grimacing with pain. The leader of the Indians whirled his horse, holding up a tomahawk. Jack waved his arms, trying to tell the Indian leader that what had just happened was some kind of accident. He shouted something to the Indian that apparently meant "Wait! Stop!" The Indian leader hesitated, but deep anger filled his eyes. He had apparently expected to be betrayed by these whites—probably had been in the past, Maggie did not doubt.

"It was an accident!" Beverly Maddox screamed, leaning over her husband, who was rolling on the ground holding his foot. "My husband had a gun just in case he might need it! It went off. He's shot himself in the foot!"

"Jesus God Almighty!" Jack swore. "He could have got us all killed! Rafe here had things set good! Now we *still* might all die! I don't know if I can convince the chief it was an accident or not. If he thinks your husband meant to shoot him, we're done for!"

Maggie feared for Rafe's life. He remained bent over. The ugly arrow had gone all the way through and was sticking out the front of his ribs. He grunted something in the Blackfoot tongue, holding out his arm as though to stave off further attack. The scowling Indian chief looked at all of them, then pointed to Terrence Maddox and said something.

Still on his knees, Rafe managed to straighten enough to look up at the man. "No," he said, shaking his head. He said something more in the Indian man's language. The chief spit something back at him, and Rafe, grasping at the arrow and the ugly wound in his side, managed to get to his feet. Blood poured from the wound and over his hand. "He wants . . . to punish Terrence . . . for trying to shoot him," he told them through gritted teeth.

"No!" Beverly screamed. "Can't he see he's *already* being punished? He's wounded! And he *didn't* try to shoot him! It was an accident!"

"Wait!" Maggie shouted, stepping closer, wondering if she, too, would feel an arrow slam into her. "Tell him to please wait, just a moment. I have something that will please him. I will give him a special gift if he will take the things we have already offered and leave."

She looked at Rafe, realizing when she saw him wounded that she was in love with Rafe Morrisey, for she could not bear to think of him dying. And she knew without asking that he had told no one about their encounter. She had always known. She had wanted to believe otherwise, that he was a worthless womanizer out to get what he could, but deep in her heart she knew better. "Try to explain," she told him. "It will take me a minute to get the special gift."

Their gazes held as Rafe stood there panting and bleeding. He nodded. 'I'll . . . try." He turned to the chief, while Maggie ran back to the wagon that held her grandmother's trunk. She ordered two of the drivers to climb inside and unstrap the trunk. Edward ran back to where she stood.

"Maggie, what are you doing?"

"Saving our lives . . . maybe. I don't know. It's all I can think of."

The men took down the trunk and brought it out. Maggie unstrapped and opened it.

"Maggie! Your most treasured items are in there!" Edward protested.

"What are *things* compared to our lives?" she replied. She rummaged through the trunk, taking out a pair of diamond drop earrings.

"Maggie!"

"It has to be something very unusual, and something Rafe can explain is very valuable to us. We have enough money to buy all the diamonds I could ever want, Edward, you know that.'' She lifted a few dresses, then took out the one she once thought was her most prized dress . . . her wedding gown.''

''Maggie! God in Heaven, not your wedding dress!''

''It's white, and satin. The lace and beading on it make it even more special. Their women will be thrilled to see and touch and cut up and share something like this.'' She looked at Edward. How could she explain the real reason she could no longer look at this dress? She had betrayed him, not just because of the kiss, but because of what else she had wanted from Rafe Morrisey in that moment, something Edward had never given her, and probably never would. ''Edward, this might save us. Remember it that way. Do you want to get to California and realize your dream? Or do you want to die a horrible death right here, along with your wife?''

He blinked back tears and turned away. ''Do what you must do.''

Maggie took the dress and earrings, boldly walking up to the Indian chief and handing the dress up to him. He frowned, fingering it, his frown slowly turning to a soft smile. He nodded. Maggie showed him the earrings then. She handed one to him, then put one to her ear, screwing the back of it so that it tightened and he could see how it was to be worn. His face brightened. Yes, this was quite a gift. His wives would like this! Maggie told Jack to explain to him how valuable diamonds were to whites. Jack proceeded to do so, and the chief nodded.

Maggie took off her earring and held it up to him, showing him how to screw and unscrew it. She jumped back in fright when he suddenly dismounted, leaving the wedding dress slung over his horse. He held up the earring, then pointed to his own ear, saying something to her.

''He wants you to put them on his ears,'' Jack told her.

Maggie could not imagine touching a real Indian. Would he grab her and make off with her? Would he kill her? He bent closer, and, shaking with nervousness, Maggie managed to screw one of the earrings onto his ear.

''Does he understand these are for women?'' she asked Jack.

''The men like jewelry, too,'' Jack answered. ''Makes no difference, long as you're pleasin' him.''

Maggie screwed on the other earring, and the Indian straightened, nodding and smiling. He said something to Jack, then mounted his horse, shouting some kind of order to some of the Indians behind him. They rode forward, gathering the items others had donated in blankets, then riding off with their makeshift sacks of goodies.

Their leader backed up his own horse, then turned and rode off, letting out a startling war whoop. The others who rode off with him let out their own war cries, and the air was filled with whooping and yipping, which gradually faded as they got farther away.

Everyone at the wagon train site waited, seemingly frozen in place, until they were sure the Indians had really gone. Then they breathed sighs of relief, some of the women breaking into tears from pent up terror.

"You might have saved all of us," Susan Haggarty told her.

"And your wedding dress!" Mrs. Krueger told her. "What a sacrifice!"

Maggie felt like a hypocrite. It was not so hard to give away something that was beginning to hold less and less meaning for her; but she did love Edward, and she would ever be true to him. She looked at Rafe, who stood nearby with his arm around Jack's shoulders. "Will he be all right?" she asked Jack.

"Don't know. I've got to try to yank out the arrow and pour some whiskey into the wound. Whiskey seems to help keep away infection. I don't know how, but it helps."

"You did . . . a smart thing," Rafe told her, his voice growing weak. "Thanks, Maggie."

There it was . . . the way he'd said it. He *had* been sincere when he'd kissed her. That made things even more complicated. "I just did the only thing I could think of. I hope you'll be all right, Rafe."

"We'll camp here the night," Jack shouted. "Somebody try to do somethin' about Terrence Maddox's foot. Douse it good with whiskey and wrap it tight. Make sure the bullet ain't in there. I've got to take care of Rafe!"

Everyone began moving at once, gathering the wagons in a

circle, unhitching teams, a couple of the men and Terrence's wife seeing what they could do about Terrence's wounded foot. Maggie hurried over to where Jack knelt beside Rafe, who lay on his right side. Jack braced a big rock under the part of the arrow sticking out of Rafe's back, then took a small hatchet from his gear and whacked off the back part of the arrow. Maggie winced when Rafe cried out at the little tug the chop created. Then he gritted his teeth and grunted when Jack yanked the arrow out from the front side of the wound, and his breathing came in pants, his face glistening with sweat.

"I'd like to help if I can," Maggie offered.

Jack looked up at her, surprised. "Sure, if you've got the stomach for it. We mainly got to get some whiskey into the wound and wrap it. You can help me with that. Then we have to hope it don't get infected. If it does, I'll have to burn it out. That ain't no fun, especially for the patient."

Maggie shivered. "We will have to pray that won't be necessary."

"Yeah, well, go get something to wrap the wound."

"Of course." Maggie looked down at Rafe. What was that in his eyes? Gratefulness? Love? What on earth had she gotten herself into? She turned away to go and get some wrappings.

Chapter Seventeen

Again Maggie noticed the scars. Jack had cut off Rafe's buckskin shirt, and doused his wound with whiskey. He managed to get Rafe to a sitting position, and Maggie helped wind cotton cloth tightly around his mid-section so that the wound would be wrapped. Rafe said nothing. He only breathed deeply, perspiration still showing on his face.

Maggie struggled against a desire to put her arms around him and hold him, the desire made even more tempting by having to reach around him to wrap the cloth. "What are all the other scars from?" she asked Jack, wanting to divert her thoughts.

"Well, the one on his left arm there is from an arrow durin' another Indian fight. The one up on his right shoulder is from a bullet wound in the Mexican war. There's one on his left thigh from a knife fight he had with an Apache Indian. The Indian lost. You ain't seen him in a fight, and you don't want to see it. Ole' Rafe can get mean and wild when it's necessary. He don't show it around decent folks like yourself."

"Don't make me out to be . . . even less civilized than they . . . already think I am," Rafe told him. Maggie tied the cloth, and he lay back down, wincing with pain.

"I don't think anything vital was hit, Rafe," Jack told him. "But you'd better take it real easy. Infection is the most dangerous thing we've gotta watch for."

"I'll be up and . . . leading this train by tomorrow morning," Rafe told him. "You tell them that. I don't want them . . . thinking they've lost me."

"Well, now, they've still got me. Ain't I good for somethin'?"

Rafe managed a weak smile. "I'm not sure."

Jack laughed and moved away from him to build up the fire nearby. Rafe looked at Maggie. "Why you?"

She dipped a rag in a bowl of water and wrang it out, using it to wipe the sweat from his face and cool him. "I don't know. Something happened when I saw that arrow hit you and thought for a second it might have killed you."

He closed his eyes. "I meant it . . . when I said I was sorry. But I'm only sorry . . . that I made you feel bad about yourself. I'm not sorry for the kiss . . . or for loving you."

Maggie sat back on her heels, flabbergasted he'd said he loved her.

"I just wanted you to know . . . so you wouldn't think . . . I'm like my father. I'm not. You have to believe that. I would . . . never use a woman like that. I saw too much of it . . . growing up."

Maggie moved her hand to take hold of his and looked around before squeezing his hand. "I believe you." She blinked back tears. "I don't understand how any of this happened, but it has to be ended, here and now. It can never go any further. Surely you understand that."

He studied her a moment. God, she was beautiful, even in a plain dress, sunburned, her hair pulled into a bun. He could not forget how she'd looked the night of the dance at Fort Laramie, and he knew without seeing that when she was truly done up in all her glamour, as the wealthy woman she was, she must be absolutely stunning . . . and deserving of a man far more sophisticated than he . . . and certainly a man who was *more* of a man than Edward McCahan. He longed to tell her the truth, but he could not bring himself to do that to her.

If she were to discover the truth, she had to do it on her own. She might never forgive him if it came from him, and if she in turn confronted Edward he might deny it, which would make her hate him even more for "lying."

"I understand," he answered. He winced as more pain shot through his middle. "Just don't be . . . going off alone at night. Then I . . . won't have to follow you and . . . get caught alone with you again."

Maggie smiled through tears. "I'll be more careful." She thought how pleasant it would be to sit and talk with him, share things with him. A man like Rafe understood another kind of world Edward knew nothing about, and he surely had a lot of stories to tell, about the Mexican war, about his other exploits. Just like Edward, he was a worldly man, but in a whole different way. And it would surely be a wonderfully satisfying pleasure to belong to a man like Rafe. A woman could lean on a man like that. With him she would feel totally protected, totally "owned." She wanted that feeling, to be with a man who knew how to take charge, who knew how to *be* a man for her, how to hold her, how to. . . .

She looked away. "I had better leave you now, or people will talk."

Rafe grinned. "We can't . . . have that."

Maggie started to rise.

"Wait." He caught her hand.

It felt so good to feel his big hand wrapped around her own. "What you did . . . giving Two Chins that dress and those earrings. You . . . might have saved all of us. It was very brave . . . and very generous. You're . . . one hell of a woman, Maggie McCahan."

She smiled softly. "I hardly knew what I was doing. I was just desperately trying to think of something—" She hesitated. "Two Chins?"

Rafe grinned more. "The Indians often give names like that . . . to their older leaders, who tend to sit around more . . . and grow fat. Sometimes they are called Big Bellies. This one's name was Two Chins . . . because of his double chin."

As she needed relief from all her pent up tension and her

agony over what had happened between her and Rafe, anything funny was enhanced for Maggie today. The name struck her as hilarious, and she covered her mouth in laughter. "Two Chins! What a great name!" She laughed more. "One thing you can say for Indians, they say it like it is!"

Rafe also began to laugh, but he grabbed his side and groaned with pain at the same time. "Didn't I . . . ever tell you how honest Indians are? It's a fact." He laughed more, along with her. "Oh, Jesus, please don't make me laugh," he finally told her. "Get the hell out of here."

Maggie cried as she laughed, needing so much to do both. She squeezed his hand, thinking what an exciting, fulfilling life it would be belonging to this man. "All right. I'm going." *I love you, Rafe Morrisey.* She could have said it so easily, and the temptation struck her hard, for she realized that was exactly what had been happening this whole trip. She had been slowly falling in love with him, a love that could never be truly fulfilled. "Please take care of yourself," she said, wiping at tears.

"What in the world is going on here?" The words were spoken by Edward, who had walked up behind Maggie. "I thought you were gravely wounded."

Maggie quickly rose, wiping at more tears. "Oh, Edward, we were just laughing over the name of that Indian chief. I don't know. I guess I am just so nervous and worn out that anything I find to laugh about is refreshing." She laughed again. "His name is Two Chins, because of his double chin. Can you imagine if all of us named ourselves after a physical attribute—or fault? Just think of the funny names some people could have. And just think of the arguments it would cause."

Edward grinned, then chuckled. "Well, that is pretty funny, isn't it?" He looked down at Rafe. "I'm glad my wife can make you laugh, considering what just happened to you. She's quite some woman, isn't she?"

More woman than a sonofabitch like you deserves, Edward McCahan, Rafe wanted to say. "That she is," he answered. "Your wife . . . did a very brave and generous thing . . . giving that dress to Two Chins. You should . . . be very proud of her."

"Oh, I am. Of course I would rather it hadn't been the

wedding dress, but then—'' He moved an arm around Maggie. ''She won't ever need another one. She'll have quite a story to tell our grandchildren about what happened to her wedding dress, won't she?''

Rafe closed his eyes. ''That she will.'' He wondered if there would ever really be any grandchildren. A man had to be a real man to his wife if he was going to plant his seed good and deep and expect it to grow. He would himself like nothing better than to plant his own seed deep inside Maggie McCahan.

''Well, I hope you recover quickly, Rafe, and with no problems. Too bad about Terrence Maddox.''

''How is he?''

''In a lot of pain. They got his boot off. The bullet went clean through and into the ground, and they figure it probably broke a couple of the small bones in his foot. He'll have to ride in their wagon for a few days. Maybe we can fashion some crutches for him, but it will be awfully hard for him to keep up that way. I offered one of my drivers to lead his oxen, which means I will have to drive one of my own teams myself, but I think I have learned the trick well enough by now to do it.''

''Good. That's good.'' Rafe figured he was the only who realized how proud someone like Edward would be to master such a ''manly'' job. It would make him look better in Maggie's eyes.

''Well, there is work to be done if we're going to set up camp here, Maggie,'' Edward told her. He looked down at Rafe. ''I'll talk to the other women and have them take turns helping you however you need it. I need our Gretta to help Maggie cook something for us, but I will be sure to send her over later. Gretta will be thrilled to help take care of you. I hope you know the woman has an eye for you, Rafe, and she's single and very pretty, a hardworking woman from good German stock.''

Rafe waved him off. ''I get this every trip . . . somebody trying to hitch me up with their daughter or . . . sister or somebody.''

''Well, do me a favor and give her a little attention of some sort. The woman talks about you constantly, so much so that my wife has had to tell her more than once to please change the subject."

Rafe met Maggie's eyes, understanding why such talk would upset her. "I'll see what I can do," he said.

"Well, just don't be marrying her and running off with her too soon. Maggie will need her the rest of this trip and for a few weeks after we arrive, until we can find someone suitable."

Rafe covered his eyes with his hand. "Don't worry. I'm not exactly biting at the bit to be a married man again."

Edward laughed and walked off with Maggie, apparently completely oblivious to any feelings between his wife and Rafe Morrisey.

Rafe closed his eyes, letting the warm sun penetrate his skin. "Damn you, Edward McCahan," he muttered. It would not be so hard to force himself to stop thinking about the man's wife if he was sure she was happy and fulfilled in her marriage, but he knew damn well she wasn't.

Before Chimney Rock the Platte River forked into north and south extensions, Maggie wrote. *Since then we have followed the North Platte through Fort Laramie. At roughly Independence Rock, the North Platte flowed off in yet another southerly direction, and we then followed the Sweetwater River. At Independence Rock we carved our names into the great, flat wall of rock, and I wonder if anyone else will ever see them and think about us and appreciate those who came first and paved the way for others.*

She wanted so much to write something about Rafe besides explaining how he had been wounded. She wanted to write about the kiss, how it felt, how *she* felt about Rafe Morrisey. But that would have to forever be her secret. She did explain about the wedding dress, but she could not write that she would not miss it. She had to say that it was a great sacrifice, but the real sacrifice would be staying with Edward and being a loyal wife. Thank God he was at least a kind and doting husband.

I am becoming quite adept at cooking over open fires, something I never thought I could do. We are now into the most beautiful country I have ever seen, surrounded by rocks and pine trees, forging through majestic mountains. It is a terribly dangerous area, and if not for Mr. Morrisey's and Jack Latham's skill in getting us through these mountains, we would surely all perish. The nights are very cold, but not freezing, thank God. So far, in spite of the tragedies we have suffered along the way, we are not terribly off schedule, and our captain tells us that we should not have to worry about a possible mountain snowstorm until we reach the Sierras. By then it will be September, and weather in the mountains will be very unpredictable. We know, of course, that the Sierras are where the Donners met their own disaster, but we are trusting our captain to get us through. Thank goodness, his arrow wound seems to be healing without infection. However, Mr. Maddox was not afforded the same luck. His foot became infected, and after many attempts to cure it, our captain and his assistant decided the foot had to be removed. May I never again be witness to such a horror, or hear such screams.

Maggie shivered at the memory. Beverly Maddox had been a sobbing wreck, and her husband was kept drunk for three days following the "surgery," which consisted of whacking off the foot at the ankle with an axe. It had to be done quickly, Jack said, and so it was. There was no sense prolonging the horror by sawing it off. Maddox still lay in his wagon in agony, and no one was sure the "operation" had helped; but all understood something had to be done, or death was definitely the only end.

In some areas the descent was so steep that we had to tie heavy logs to the backs of the wagons to help slow them, and we had to keep the reins pulled tight on the mules. For oxen, the men had to shout all sorts of orders to keep them from going too fast, and never was the air filled with so much sinful cursing! I hope the Lord was not listening, or all the men will burn in Hell for blasphemy, I am sure, even Edward, who is doing a surprisingly fine job of driving the oxen that pull the supply wagon. At times we had to unload great quantities of supplies and then lower them later by rope, so that the weight of the wagons would not push too hard on the teams, for then wagon and animals might all go tumbling. If you saw how steep some of these canyon walls are, you would surely faint dead away, as I have nearly done a number of times.

We are now headed through the South Pass, a high, flat area in the Rockies where we are experiencing a wonderful relief from steep climbs and descents. This area is normally called ''The Parting of The Ways,'' because it is here that those headed for Oregon veer north and on to Fort Hall. However, our entire party is headed for California, and I am glad, for we have become close to all of them and I would hate to have to say good-bye to anyone just yet. Soon we will veer south and stop at a place called Fort Bridger, then on through more mountains before reaching the desert, which I dread. We are told it is beastly hot, and there will be no shade and hardly any kind of life for several hundred miles. Most of the water is no good, for it is salt water. I am sure we will all be glad to reach the Sierras, no matter how dangerous they are. Heaven help us.

Maggie made no mention of the pain in her heart. Rafe kept his promise and paid her no more heed than anyone else, and she was sure that he was as glad as she was that the trip had caused everyone so much work and stress that there was no time left for relaxing and ''thinking.'' At night they were all so weary that sleep came easily . . . even for those whose hearts ached with a longing that could never be satisfied.

Chapter Eighteen

The wagon train rolled into Fort Bridger with fewer oxen and mules than when it left Fort Laramie. Several had died from pure exhaustion, and Maggie made another entry in her journal, expressing the concern that they were now all using mostly their spare animals. *And we have not even gone into the desert yet. If we are unable to replace some of the animals at Fort Bridger and we lose more in the desert, we will be forced to abandon some of the wagons. We are also getting low on supplies, no thanks to the Blackfoot Indians who took a good deal of them. We are worried we will reach the Sierras with a dangerously low supply of food.*

Maggie looked up from her writing at six men who were sitting around their own campfire drinking. They had ridden in just this morning, fresh furs and other animal skins on their pack horses. Maggie did not like the looks of them, or the fact that they were drinking. They were slovenly, obviously had not bathed or washed their hair or even their faces in weeks. One had walked past her earlier, and she could still smell his reeking body odor. They looked longer than necessary at every woman who walked by, old or young, and usually they said something to each other and laughed afterward. She had not looked at any of them long enough to distinguish one from another. In some respects they looked alike, with beards, long, tangled hair, soiled buckskins and big bellies, except for one who was tall and skinny.

Fort Bridger was nothing more than a collection of log and mud buildings, a supply post established by Jim Bridger, who Rafe had told them was one of the most experienced mountain men alive. The post consisted of a blacksmith barn and a supply post, with a few other small cabins where liquor, feed, and other such assortments were kept in supply for travelers.

Jim Bridger was not present, but those who stayed around and sold supplies and worked the blacksmith shop said another wagon train had just left two days earlier, some for California, others deciding to go to Oregon. ''You folks make about forty thousand passed through here so far this summer,'' the blacksmith had told them.

Maggie had written the figure in her journal, finding it astounding so many were willing to leave the comforts of home and family for the lure of gold. From the crowds back in Independence to the countless graves along the way and the piles of household goods left along the trail in order to lighten wagons, she knew many had gone before, and that there were surely many more behind them; but to realize there really were so many was still startling. ''Good business for wagonmakers and blacksmiths,'' the blacksmith had added.

It was refreshing to be able to sit in one place for two days, as all wagons were checked over and repairs made before heading into the desert. New shoes were put on horses, mules, and oxen, and loads were rearranged, supplies sorted and counted. Terrence Maddox was still laid up, but the pain in the stump of his leg was becoming more bearable, and it seemed to be healing without further infection.

Maggie watched Rafe walk up to the mountain men sitting and drinking nearby. They offered him some whiskey, but he refused. ''A little early in the day, isn't it?''

''Never too early for good whiskey,'' one of them replied. ''Ole' Jim keeps the best here. Hell, that's the main reason he's got to watch out for the Indians. They'd rather have this stuff than horses, and that's sayin' a lot!''

They all laughed, and Rafe grinned, walking around the circle of men. Maggie worried for his safety. Some of the women had complained that the men were saying embarrassing things and made them feel threatened. ''I save my drinking for when we reach California,'' Rafe told them.

''I bet you make up for it good, then!'' one of them said, taking another swallow during more laughter.

''Do you make up for lack of a woman in your bed, too?'' another one roared, ''or do you get a piece now and them from the poor, lonely ladies on this wagon train?''

Embarrassed, Maggie looked down, pretending to be writing in her journal.

''Well, it's like this,'' Rafe replied. ''The people on this wagon train are decent folks, and the women don't need to be hearing remarks like that. I only came by to to ask all of you to keep to yourselves and watch your language. There are young children along, and most of these folks can hear everything you're saying.''

''Hell, we ain't here to make trouble. Just celebrating a good hunt, that's all,'' one of them said. ''You've got no problem with us. Me, I got me a pretty little Indian gal waiting for me up in the Bitterroots. Soon as I sell my skins, I'm heading back up that way.''

''Rest of us are sellin' our skins here and goin' on to California,'' another said. ''Figure if we don't find gold, we'll have one hell of a good time in the minin' camps.'' They all laughed again. ''I hear tell there's plenty of whiskey and painted women in them camps! Things must get pretty wild, and we've all been holed up in the mountains quite a while. Figured it might be a nice change to go someplace where there's women and music and whiskey, dancin', singin', gamblin'—hell, I wouldn't be surprised of a lot of these folks was goin' there just for the fun.''

Rafe shook his head. ''They're brave, God-fearing people, most of them with families. I just came over here to make sure you all understood that. And like I said, watch how you talk. I'd appreciate it."

Maggie remembered what Jack had said about Rafe's temper, and intuition told her it was being tested right now.

"*I'd* appreciate you not comin' over here tryin' to tell us our business," one of the hunters replied.

"Leave it alone, Beaker. The man is just doin' his job," one of his cohorts said. "He's right. We'd best watch what we say."

"Why, hell, it's just the whiskey talkin'," another said, looking at Rafe. "You don't have to worry about us."

The one who had acted offended rose, standing as tall as Rafe, but even wider, a big, burly man who looked as though he could wrestle a bear. "You know, I don't believe you don't drink till you get to California. I just think that *you* think you're too *good* to be drinkin' with us."

Rafe stood his ground, facing the man squarely. "Where and when I drink is none of *your* business, Mister, but taking care of the people on this wagon train is more important to me right now than a swallow of whiskey. I only came over here to ask you to be careful how you talk and to leave the women alone. A couple of them have complained."

The hunter turned and spit tobacco juice onto a wildflower. "Well you can tell the stiff-corseted, tight-assed old hens along that we—"

The man was not able to finish his sentence. Rafe's foot came up into his groin in a swift kick that cut off his words. The big mountain man grabbed his crotch and sank to the ground, howling. Rafe turned to the rest of them. "Do the rest of you understand what I'm asking? I didn't come here to make trouble. I asked you kindly to watch what you say, and some of the women have complained that you stare at them and laugh at them. Keep to yourselves. Understood?"

They all looked at each other, and Maggie could tell they were considering challenging Rafe. After all, it would be five against one. They seemed to think the better of it, since Rafe faced them all squarely and gave the appearance of a man none of them wanted to mess with.

"Understood," one of them answered.

Rafe turned to walk toward Maggie, and that was when she saw the movement. One of the other five men rose, pulling a knife from its sheath on his wide, leather belt. "Rafe!" Maggie shouted, starting toward him.

Rafe whirled and ducked, and the knife flew past him and landed with a thud in Maggie's left shoulder. For one brief second it seemed that everything stood still, and Maggie did not even feel any pain at first. She simply looked down, wide-eyed, at the huge iron blade and the handle, which was wrapped with some kind of animal skin, taking a moment to realize it was sticking out of her own shoulder. She looked back at Rafe as she sank to her knees, and Rafe, fury in his eyes, headed toward the five men.

"Rafe! No," Maggie tried to protest, but too late, and her voice carried no strength. As Gretta and Edward rushed to her side, Rafe landed into the hunters. The one he had kicked was still bent over, groaning, but the others were ready for a fight. Edward tried to take Maggie to the wagon, but she clung to his shirt, telling him to wait, so stunned and in shock that she still did not feel the full force of the pain in her shoulder. "Rafe!" she muttered. "He'll be killed!"

Women hurried their children into wagons, not allowing them to watch the fight that ensued.

"Wait! Wait!" she told Edward and Gretta, as again they tried to help her. "You must help him!"

No one stepped in, none of the men willing to get involved in a fight with men experienced in such things, men, including Rafe, who were waving huge hunting knives and lunging at each other. Jack and Wolf Hunter were nowhere to be seen. Rafe was alone. But he had already quickly tackled one of the hunters, rolling on the ground with him and lunging his knife into his chest. Blood spurted from the wound and onto Rafe's clothing, and quickly he got to his feet, holding his knife out toward the other four. All came at him at once. Rafe kicked out, landing his foot under the chin of one and sending him sprawling, and at nearly the same time he whirled with his knife, slashing across the face of another. That one went down screaming, holding his face as blood poured through his fingers. By then one of the two remaining men had slashed his blade across Rafe's middle, slitting his shirt and the skin under it.

Rafe grabbed the knife hand of the second man, jerking him forward and slashing down, cutting at least half way into his arm so that the man cried out and dropped his knife. The one who had already slashed Rafe came back at him again, ducking and stretching out his arms in challenge.

"Someone do something!" Maggie said, sure she was yelling, but the words came out in a weak cry. Edward left her side, but Maggie kept her eyes on Rafe as he and the remaining man lunged at each other. Finally Rafe dove at the man's legs, flipping him up and over his back before he realized what was happening. Maggie had never seen a man move so swiftly. She knew Rafe's fury came from knowing she had been hurt. He was fighting on her behalf, and she loved him for it, but she did not feel worthy of having him die for what had truly been an accident. The knife had been meant for him, and he knew it, which probably made him even more angry.

The last opponent landed hard on his back, and apparently he'd had the breath knocked out of him, for he lay there just staring up at Rafe and not moving. Rafe kicked his knife from his hand, then leaned down and slashed his throat. Even the men gasped at the sight. Rafe stood there bleeding and panting, then turned to the first man he'd kicked in the groin. The man was on his knees and going for a handgun he wore. Rafe pulled his own gun and fired, leaving a hole in the big man's forehead.

"Heavenly Father," Reverend Krueger muttered.

Rafe turned and stumbled toward Maggie, who stood there grasping her upper left arm, afraid to move it for fear of how much it would hurt. Rafe came closer, and the reality of what had happened began to sink in as Maggie again looked down at the knife sticking out of her shoulder. "Get it out!" she asked, her voice squeaking with terror.

"Get her into the wagon," Rafe ordered, covered with blood himself. "Leave the knife in until I come in to take it out myself. She'll bleed like hell once it's pulled out. Get some needle and thread. I'll stitch it myself."

Needle and thread!

"I'll douse this belly wound with some whiskey," Rafe was saying, as things began to go black for Maggie. "It's just a surface cut. Somebody take care of the dead bodies, and the rest of you men keep an eye on the ones still alive."

Somewhere in the distance Maggie heard Jack shouting, wanting to know what had happened. He'd heard a gunshot. She remembered men lifting her into her wagon, remembered Edward crying.

"Oh, God, Maggie, don't leave me! I need you so!"

Chapter Nineteen

"Damn! I never meant for things to turn into such a mess!" Maggie heard Rafe's voice nearby.

"I should have expected that sonofabitch would try to knife me in the back! That's what whiskey does to a man who's been too long in the wilds. I'm damned sorry, Edward. That was goddamn stupid of me! I was trying to *avoid* something worse happening!"

"You couldn't help it. You were just doing your job. Just don't let her die!"

"I'm not God, but I know she *will* die from loss of blood or infection if I don't do this right. Help me cut off this side of her dress. We can't move her arm to try to get the dress off that way. We'd just make the blade work itself around more and cause her more pain. Once we get the dress cut off, I'll cut the straps of her camisole. We've got to work around the blade. Then the minute I pull it out, you've got to douse it with whiskey and put clean cotton cloth over it and press, and I mean press *hard!* Hold it there while I get things ready to sew up the wound."

Maggie felt a jerking sensation as her clothes were cut away, and dark pain tore through her left shoulder and the entire left side of her back, so severe she felt sick. She screamed at Rafe and Edward to stop, begging Rafe not to take out the knife. "I'll die!"

"No, you by-God won't," she heard Rafe answer, the tone of his voice making the words come out in a determined, almost angry statement. "Don't you *dare* die on me, Maggie McCahan! Gretta!" he shouted louder. "Get Hazel and come in here and hold her arms!"

"Damn you!" Maggie screamed. "Both of you leave me alone!" Why was she saying that? The pain and terror were making her feel like a woman apart from her true self.

"Go ahead and scream and cuss, Maggie-girl. Sometimes it helps. I ought to know."

Maggie gritted her teeth, opening her eyes to see Rafe threading a sewing needle. She didn't care at the moment that his clothes were dirty, his face bloodied, or that the front of his buckskin shirt was cut and stained with blood; or that he'd suffered all those injuries and had got into a scuffle that could have cost him his life, all because one of those men had accidently landed his knife into Maggie McCahan. She had damn well seen what Rafe Morrisey could do when he was mad, but for the moment her only concern was the fact that he intended to use that big needle on her!

"Don't you dare touch me with that needle, Rafe Morrisey, or I'll—" She had no idea how to end the statement. Rafe smiled, making her even angrier.

"You'll what?" he asked. "What could you possibly say to intimidate me, woman? You'll *hit* me?" He frowned mockingly. "Now *there's* a real threat." He looked at Edward. "She ever hit you?" he asked.

Edward smiled through tears, realizing Rafe was only trying to lighten a grave situation. "Beats me up all the time," he answered.

They all chuckled, including Gretta and Hazel, who were now inside the wagon.

"I hate you!" Maggie screamed at Rafe, tears on her cheeks. "I hate *all* of you!"

"Oh, I reckon' you do, Honey," Hazel told her.

"Here, Love," Edward said, holding a bottle of whiskey near her lips. "Drink some of this."

Maggie gulped down the whiskey, too eager to mask the pain to even be affected by the fire that moved down her throat into her belly.

"I'll be damned," Rafe said, taking the bottle and sniffing it. "Good stuff, too. The way she drank that down, I'd have figured it was watered down." He looked at Maggie. "I guess we're all finding out the truth about you, Mrs. McCahan. You're a lush!"

Maggie's mouth flew open, but things were beginning to swim before her eyes. Deep inside she knew what Rafe was trying to do, but it wasn't going to help the pain all that much. Again blackness tried to envelop her, and again her eyes closed.

"Get ready with the cotton," she heard Rafe say. Then she felt him touch the knife still embedded in her shoulder. "Nooo!" she screamed. Rafe jerked out the knife, and she felt fiery whiskey go into the wound. She screamed again and tried to move, but she could not. People were holding her down. Someone was pressing hard on the wound, making the pain worse. She heard what she thought was someone else screaming at them to "Stop it! Stop it!" But whoever it was continued to press tightly.

"Damn it, Maggie, you're tearing my heart out," she heard Edward say.

"Let go and I'll start sewing," came Rafe's voice.

The pressure lightened.

"My God!" Edward exclaimed.

"Just what I was afraid of," Rafe said. "It's not going to be easy sewing it up with that much blood."

What blood? *Her* blood? She felt the ugly piercing of the needle then, and again she tried to make him stop. Pain made her keep her eyes squeezed shut, but she knew it was Rafe who wielded the needle. Pain from both the stitching and the wound seemed to course through her entire body.

The screams abated to deep sobbing. Who was that? Surely it wasn't her. Finally the piercing stopped. Someone moved her to a slightly sitting position. "Let's get it wrapped tight," came Rafe's voice. Her camisole was pulled away from her breasts. Someone began wrapping something around her breasts and on over the wound, across the opposite shoulder, around the wound again, wrapping for what seemed like several minutes before she was lowered onto the mattress again.

"That's about all I can do," Rafe said. "The rest is up to someone with more authority. Might not hurt to pray."

Did Rafe pray? She didn't even know if he believed in God.

"Keep her still. When there is loss of blood like this, they need to drink plenty of water. I don't even know why, except that it must help replace the blood. I only know from years of treating things like this and from suffering my own wounds that plenty of water helps. Actually, she'll crave it for a while."

"Whatever you say," Edward answered. "I'll have Gretta and Hazel stay with her once we get going again. I have to handle the oxen."

"You did well, Edward."

"I never should have brought her out here."

"She's quite a woman."

"Poor Maggie," Gretta said softly.

"She's a fighter," Hazel said. "She'll come through."

Why was everyone talking as though she was not even there?

"I think you're probably right," Rafe said. She felt someone squeeze her hand, and through her deep pain and agony she instantly felt a degree of comfort because she knew the touch was from Rafe.

"I have things to tend to," he said. "I'll make sure the men left alive out of that bunch get the hell out of here. We'll have to watch things for a while. They might decide to get their revenge by stealing some of our stock . . . or one of the women. You women stick together when you have to tend to personals."

"Yes, Sir, Mr. Morrisey." It was Gretta's voice. "What about you? Zat man cut you."

"He just nicked the skin as I moved back. I threw some whiskey on it."

Maggie felt the wagon move, and just that little bouncing, apparently from Rafe climbing out, brought pain that made her groan. How was she going to bear the trip once the wagon started rolling again, bouncing and swaying over rocks and holes? And how was she going to make it through this without the comfort of Rafe's arms? Right now she could think of nothing that would help ease the pain more than Rafe Morrisey lying beside her, holding her, feeling his sure, strong embrace.

"Don't you die on me, Maggie."

Someone was stroking her hair back from her forehead. She opened her eyes to see it was Edward. He was sobbing like a child.

Rafe stood in the darkness watching the wagon where Maggie lay in pain. He drew a deep breath against the tears that wanted to come for realizing *why* she suffered. Maggie McCahan had taken that blade trying to warn him. It had been hell bringing her more pain by having to sew her up, without being able to hold her close, tell her he loved her, that he was sorry, that he wanted to hold her forever and stop all the hurt.

The men he'd killed had been buried, and Reverend Krueger had insisted that the "sinners" be prayed over. Rafe had not attended the "funeral." All he'd wanted was to kill the whole lot of them. At least the rest had left the area. Still, he intended to keep an eye out for them when they left the fort and headed into the desert. Right now his main concern was Maggie. How strange that after all these years of no interest in any women except whores or loose Indian women who could satisfy his baser needs, that he should feel so drawn to Maggie, a woman of obvious wealth and status. He realized he really hardly knew anything about her except that she was rich, that she didn't belong in this rugged environment, and that she was married to a man who could never possibly appreciate her as a real woman. There was a loneliness in her eyes that tore at him, and he knew the reason for it; but there was nothing he could do about it, and it was driving him crazy.

He threw down the thin cigar he'd been smoking and walked to her wagon, knocking lightly on the gate before peering inside. A lamp was lit, and Edward still sat beside Maggie, who seemed to be asleep. Edward looked at Rafe, and Rafe could see his eyes were red and swollen.

"She's my best friend, you know," he told Rafe.

Rafe could not help feeling sorry for the man, who he suspected was genuinely trying to be a proper husband. "I know."

"We've been friends since we were very young. Everyone knew we would marry one day."

Rafe wondered what it must be like for a person to live a lie his whole life. He supposed he'd already started learning, for he would have to do the same thing, pretending not to be in love with this man's wife. "Why don't you take a break, Edward? There is still some coffee over the fire, and there is nothing you can do right now to make her feel any better. I'll sit with her a while, check things over."

Edward sniffed, looking down at Maggie. "I don't know. I hate to leave my Maggie." He touched her hair, then looked back at Rafe, new tears on his face. "She's my best friend," he repeated. "She understands me."

Does she? Rafe wanted to ask. *Does she know that you cheat on her with men? Have you thought about how such a revelation would utterly destroy her?* "I know, Edward. Come on out. I'll sit with her a while, and I'll let you know if she asks for you. When I leave, you should try to get some sleep, away from Maggie. She'll rest better without you or Gretta moving around in the wagon."

"Oh!" Edward wiped at his eyes. "I didn't think of that. Yes, of course." He leaned down and kissed Maggie's forehead, then climbed out. Rafe climbed inside then, moving as carefully as he could. He crawled up to Maggie, wanting desperately to lie beside her the rest of the night.

"Maggie?" He touched her cheek and forehead with the back of his hand, relieved that so far there seemed to be no fever. The next three to five days were crucial. If she didn't show signs of infection by then, she might get through this without one. The last thing he wanted to do was have to burn out infection and bring her that kind of pain, let alone the scar it would leave on her milky white skin. He'd seen just how beautiful it was, had seen her full, firm breasts, breasts he ached to touch . . . to taste lovingly while giving her the pleasure he suspected she'd never known with Edward.

Her eyes fluttered open, and she just stared at him a moment. "Rafe," she whispered.

He leaned down and kissed her cheek. He took hold of her right hand and squeezed lightly. "You saved my life, Maggie." He was surprised to see a hint of a smile on her lips.

"Just . . . paying you back . . . for saving mine in the river. Now . . . we're even."

He grinned. "I guess you could say that. But I didn't suffer pain saving you. And if you hadn't called out, they'd have buried me today. You keep surprising me, Maggie McCahan. When I first met you in St. Louis, I figured you to be a woman who would never last through a trip like this, but you just keep right on. And right now you have to be stronger than ever. Don't you give up now. Hell, we're more than half way to California. Nothing but a desert and more mountains ahead of us."

"Is that . . . all? It should . . . be easy, then."

Rafe grinned more. "Sure." He kept hold of her hand. "I love you, Maggie. I know I have no right saying it, and I know nothing can ever come of it, but I love you. I'm saying it because I *have* to say it. Once we reach California, I'll get out of your life. But I'll never forget you, Maggie."

She closed her eyes, a tear slipping down the side of her face. "Nor I you," she whispered.

Rafe glanced at the back of the wagon. No one was there. He leaned down then, kissing Maggie's forehead, her eyes, her cheeks, then gently kissing her mouth. "Don't you die on me, Maggie-girl."

How strange, Maggie thought. Edward had said those very words, but with desperate neediness and childlike fear. When Rafe spoke them, she felt a strength she couldn't find with Edward. This man could survive just fine without her. Edward could not. Rafe was a man who could take charge, and when he told her not to die it was almost like an order. With Edward it was a childish plea not to leave him alone to face the world. "I'm . . . trying," she answered, "but it hurts . . . so bad."

"I know. I've felt it."

"I've never . . . seen a man fight . . . like you did. Jack . . . was right. You can be . . . mean as hell."

Rafe laughed lightly, relieved that she could manage to joke a little. It was a good sign that she truly was fighting and not giving up. "They just pissed me off," he answered. "They hurt my Maggie."

Maggie opened her eyes and studied his handsome face. How she wished she truly was "his" Maggie. But that could never be, and she felt so disloyal to Edward for even thinking it. "Are you . . . all right? They . . . cut you."

"It stings, but it's not deep. I'm all right."

"Your face . . . has bruises."

"That's nothing new," he answered with a grin. "I'd better get going. People will wonder."

Their gazes held, and Maggie wanted to tell him she didn't care what people thought. "Touch your cheek . . . to mine first," she asked him. "I'd ask you . . . to hold me . . . but it hurts too much . . . to be moved."

His heart ached for her. He glanced out the back of the wagon again, then leaned down, kissing her mouth once more and touching his cheek to her own, keeping it there for several seconds. "You can always come to me, Maggie, for anything. Remember that, even if it's just to talk. When we reach California, I promise to let you know how to find me if you need to. Promise me that if you need help in any way, you'll come to me."

"I promise," she whispered.

"It's our little secret, just between you and me."

"Our . . . secret."

He kissed her mouth once more, squeezing her hand before reluctantly letting go. He carefully moved to the back of the wagon and climbed out, and Maggie drew a deep breath, feeling comforted in a way Edward had not been able to comfort her. She soon fell into a deep sleep, no longer afraid. She wouldn't die. Rafe Morrisey wouldn't let her die.

Chapter Twenty

I doubt that I will ever again suffer the kind of pain I have suffered from this knife wound, Maggie wrote, glad the wound at least was in her left shoulder so that she could still use her right hand. The pain penetrated her whole arm and hand, as well as her back. It even hurt to laugh.

We have been followed by a Sioux hunting party for several days, but they have turned out to be harmless, more curious than anything else. We have done a little trading with them, and they did bring us a deer in trade for more cloth. The meat was badly needed, but I fear I will have nothing left to have more clothes made once we reach California. By the time I order more cloth and dresses, I will be in rags.

She winced with pain as she shifted against the quilts and pillows propped behind her. How she wished she could make an entry about Rafe, but still she only wrote about the fight he had gotten in and how she had been stabbed, trying not to make it too obvious that he'd gone after the man who had thrown the knife not just because of the accident, but because it had been Maggie McCahan who had taken the wound, Maggie McCahan, the woman he loved.

She had been two weeks healing now, and though everyone

had breathed a sigh of relief that there would apparently be no dangerous infection, the pain still plagued her whenever she tried to move her arm. Rafe had demanded she move it for fear of permanently losing the use of it, and he'd had Gretta and Edward help him take her arm and exercise it for her. She was sure her screams could be heard back home in Pennsylvania, but she knew Rafe was probably right in forcing her muscles into action. She dreaded every evening's treatment, but what must be done, must be done.

They had gone on to Fort Hall, where they had been able to take on more supplies before heading into the desert of what Rafe said most called Nevada. The way he had described this next trek of their journey, no one looked forward to it, but there was no other way to get to the Sierras and on to California.

Rafe told us we could have taken the Hastings Cutoff, she wrote, *which would have shortened the journey by heading south around Great Salt Lake and through the salt desert beyond, but he told us that way is even more miserable than the way we are going. Problems the Donners experienced there are the reason they arrived too late going into the Sierras, the reason they ended up stranded in those mountains for the winter.*

No one wanted to take the chance of suffering the same fate as the Donners, so they had taken Rafe's advice and followed him to Fort Hall. The country they passed was spectacular, with splendid, snow covered mountains all around, yet the land they passed through was wide open, barren, hot. And getting hotter. Rafe had told them that getting from Fort Hall to the Sierras would be their greatest test, for it was a long, long, seemingly endless journey, monotonous, lonely, barren, and dangerous for the animals because of the endless heat that Rafe described as "second only to the devil's cairn."

It is nearly August, she continued, *so we will be crossing the Nevada desert in the worst time to be caught there, but there is no choice of timing if we are to get through the Sierras before winter visits their peaks. At best, we will go through those mountains in September.*

They were camped in high, rocky country southwest of Fort

Hall. Edward sat outside around a campfire with some of the other men, and she had no idea where Gretta had gone. Lately she had often left her side in the evenings—to "be alone," she would explain. Maggie's faithful maid and friend had "given up" on Rafe, so she had declared, and she had "things to think about."

Maggie missed her company, for even when she was by her side Gretta seemed preoccupied. She had finally admitted she had been talking often with someone new, that she had become quite taken with him. She had told Maggie she knew everyone would think it was wrong, but that she believed it was very right, that she belonged with this man, that he could show her a whole new world once they reached California, a world of excitement and riches. When Maggie badgered her into telling her who this man was, she had been shocked to learn it was none other than the slick, handsome Buck James!

The whole situation made Maggie very uncomfortable, and she had warned Gretta she should stay away from Buck, who everyone knew by now was not really married to Jenny. The two had had several arguments since Jenny was snakebitten, and Jenny had blurted out again that Buck was not her husband. Reverend Krueger had grumbled about the situation nearly every day, perturbed that they must travel with two people who were "living in sin." Gretta was convinced Buck had only been helping Jenny, who he'd said had been accused of theft in Chicago and faced prison there. He had told Gretta he was taking her to California to help her start a new life.

Maggie had no idea if that was the truth, and she'd warned Gretta to be careful of both Buck and Jenny, who seemed to be a jealous, tempermental young woman with no scruples. Not only that, but the young woman had gradually begun behaving more and more irrationally, getting into screaming arguments—not just with Buck but with others—accusing people of gossiping about her, of hating her, judging her; swearing she hated this country with her whole being, that she could not wait to be rid of the whole lot of them, including Buck, once they reached California. She had become bitter and angry, and most felt the trip itself had simply taken its toll on Jenny's nerves. All of them suffered one way or another from the same ailment, but most had so far been able to control their moments of ''craziness'' brought on by danger, monotony, weariness, hunger, sore feet, missing home, aching for the comforts of civilization, and in general sometimes being a little sick of each other's company. This journey had been a trying experience for all of them, and had spelled tragedy for some.

Still, Gretta had apparently been won over by the smooth-talking Buck, and perhaps that, too, was due to the boredom of the journey, the need for a change brought on by a need for relief from day after day of backbreaking work and struggle. Maggie worried that her frequent absences at night were due to secretly meeting Buck after dark. Gretta seemed rather ignorant when it came to men, and Maggie feared Buck James would cajole his way under her skirts and then break her heart.

I am worried about my Gretta, she wrote. *I have come to think of her almost as my younger sister, even though there is little difference in our ages. I think of her that way because she has become a good friend, but she seems to need guidance in her thinking.* Did she have any right writing about Gretta's choice in men? At least Gretta was single and had the right to pursue any man she wanted. She herself, on the other hand, had fallen in love with a man who was not her husband. A married woman should not be having these thoughts of love and desire for someone else. Other than that kiss, she had not acted on those feelings, yet she felt almost as guilty as if she had slept with Rafe. Who was she to judge another woman's needs and motives?

She put down her pen, closing the journal. Gretta still was not back, but she had to try to sleep, anyway. Because it was cold tonight in the high country and it hurt too much to try to change into her gown, she simply scooted down into her make-shift bed and pulled a quilt over herself. She closed her eyes, but sleep would not come. Men, including Rafe, talked and laughed around the campfire outside. Maggie wondered if Rafe hurt as much inside as she did, and she supposed it was just as bad for him. She would never forget the concern and love in his eyes every time he checked her wound, never forget the comfort she had taken when he'd knelt over her and touched her cheek with his own, kissed her so gently and with such reassurance.

Now she was healing, and there was no legitimate reason for him to come to see her. She listened to him explaining what it would be like in the Nevada desert—she did not look forward to that part of the journey—but everyone's thoughts and discussions were interrupted by shouting somewhere in the darkness, followed by a gunshot, a scream, another gunshot.

"What the hell—" One of the men outside had shouted.

Gritting her teeth against the pain, Maggie sat up and moved to the back of the wagon. "Edward?"

"I'm right here."

"Where is Gretta?"

Edward came to stand at the back of the wagon. "I don't know. Rafe went to see what all the commotion is about."

"I'm worried about Gretta. I told you I think she's been seeing Buck James."

There came more shouts, a woman screaming and cursing. Moments later Rafe dragged Jenny into the light of the fire. She was crying and still cursing him, ordering him to let go of her.

"These people have to decide what to do with you!" Rafe told her, giving her a shake.

"Don't be so rough with her, Rafe," Willard Haggarty told him.

Rafe was obviously angry. He held out a small handgun. "She shot Buck James, and Gretta Wheeler!" he told those who had gathered nearby.

Maggie gasped. "Gretta!" She leaned farther out the back gate to see better. "Is she still alive?"

Rafe glanced at her, remorse in his eyes. "They're both dead. I'm sorry."

Everyone mumbled and gasped. "Dear God!" one woman exclaimed.

"What do we do now?" another asked.

"We shoot or hang the person who murdered them," Rafe announced. "It's the law out here. It's the way it's done. If we don't keep some kind of order, near the end of this journey we'll all be shooting each other. This trip can make a man—or woman—crazy! Without some form of civilized living, people can become animals!''

''But . . . we can't hang a woman!'' one of the men protested.

''She's a murderer!''

''She's simply lost her mind,'' Edward put in. ''I have lost a valuable servant, and my wife has lost a good friend, but killing yet another person won't solve the situation.''

''Go ahead and hang me,' Jenny screamed at them. ''I don't give a damn! I caught Buck with that whore Gretta! She *stole* him from me! Buck was the only person who ever cared about me!''

''Then why did you kill him?'' Susan Haggarty yelled.

''He *deserved* it, for cheating on me! He wouldn't marry me, but I by God wasn't going to let him have any *other* woman! We were supposed to work together once we were in California, get married there, run some gambling tables, have a good life. Then that damn Gretta started blinking her big blue eyes and strutting for him.''

''That is enough of that talk!'' Reverend Krueger told her.

''And you!'' Jenny screamed. ''I'm sick of you, looking at me like I'm some kind of harlot, judging me like you're God. You're *not* God! You're just a plain man like every other, a man who thinks he knows something about the Bible. You're no better than the rest of them! I've seen how you look at me, *Reverend,* and your thoughts have not been so pure, *have* they?''

The reverend gasped, staring at her wide-eyed, amazed by her accusation.

''Matthew!'' his wife exclaimed.

''The woman is crazy!'' he shouted. ''She's trying to make even more trouble!''

''Which is why we have to do something about her,'' Rafe told them. ''Normally in these situations everyone votes on what to do with the culprit. It's not my decision to make. I can only say what *should* be done.'' He dragged Jenny over to a wagon wheel and took down some rope. Jenny kicked at him, and Rafe told others to come and hold her while he tied her wrists behind her back and then to the lower portion of the wheel so that she could sit down. He explained that in her present state of mind she could not be trusted. When he finished tying her, he turned to the rest of them. "I'll let you discuss what you want to do. Then I want all of you to sleep on it and vote in the morning, *after* we bury Gretta Wheeler and Buck James. I'm going to lay them out somewhere and cover them. It's not a pretty sight. She shot them both in the head."

He walked off into the darkness, and everyone stood staring at Jenny, who hung her head and wept. Maggie sat back in the wagon, her chest pained with grief. "Gretta," she murmured. "Poor, dear Gretta." They had become so close on this journey. It had been hard enough to bury Maria. It would be doubly hard to leave Gretta's lonely grave behind, here in the middle of nowhere.

Chapter Twenty-One

The men were up half the night discussing what should be done about Jenny, and through it all Maggie wept. So many had died, and it was bad enough losing them to sickness and accidents. But for poor Gretta to be murdered! If only she had stayed away from Buck James . . . and if only she and Edward had never brought the poor girl along in the first place. She could have stayed and worked for one of Maggie's sisters, or for her mother. But Gretta had *wanted* to come, and like most others she had had big dreams about finding a whole new life in California. What was it about people that made them think that changing their environment would change their lives? Her own would be the same wherever she went with Edward, unfulfilled, struggling to be a good and loyal wife out of duty.

Morning came too soon, and Edward helped her change into a clean dress. He brushed her hair and pinned it at the sides, and to her surprise he actually seemed to enjoy fussing with it.

"What are they going to do with Jenny?" she asked.

"We still are undecided, except for one thing. None of us has the courage or desire to have her shot or hanged. My God, she's a woman."

"She is also a murderer, Edward; but I, too, cannot comprehend killing her in return. God knows it's the stress of this journey that made her do what she did. And how do we know the snake venom didn't do something to her brain? She hasn't been the same ever since she was bitten."

"I never thought of that."

Edward helped her climb out of the wagon, and they walked over to where everyone stood around the graves the men had dug early that morning. The bodies were covered with blankets to help keep the dirt off their faces when the graves were filled, and because Rafe felt none of the women or children should view their faces because of the wounds.

"Oh, Edward," Maggie wept, turning away and crying on his shoulder. "Poor Gretta. I will never look upon her pretty face again, never hear her chatter, never laugh with her again."

Edward embraced her, for the first time in a comforting way. "I am so sorry, Maggie. You have lost so much coming out here."

Rafe watched them quietly as Reverend Krueger spoke over the graves, reading scripture, then breaking into the hymn, "Shall We Gather By The River?" Others joined in singing, followed by a final prayer before two men began filling in the graves, dug as deep as possible to avoid being dug up by wolves.

Gone. So quickly gone. Maggie wondered if her heart would ever stop hurting. It was as though God meant to wipe out every last remnant of home. Having Maria and Gretta along had been a little like having part of her old life still with her. Now there was just Edward. She would never see her precious mother again, her sisters, nieces and nephews, her father, her favorite church and friends. And she could never be with—

No. She had to give up all thoughts of Rafe. He was yet another cause of added heartache. She walked with Edward to the meeting about what to do about Jenny, who earlier had been untied by Rafe and led at gunpoint to a place where she could relieve herself, then tied again until after the funeral. She was glum and sulky, and she had said nothing all morning. Rafe untied her again and allowed her to come to a campfire and eat, but she ate only one biscuit and drank a little coffee. She remained sitting by the fire while everyone gathered around her again for a final decision. Rafe folded his arms and faced them, scanning the group of weary travelers. "Have you decided what to do with Jenny James?"

"My name is Jenny Hansen," Jenny said sharply then. "I already told all of you I was never married to Buck James."

"Why don't you tell us something about yourself?" the reverend asked. "Maybe it would help us decide what to do with you."

Jenny looked at the fire, resting her elbows on her knees. "I was abandoned at ten years old, left to fend for myself in the streets of Chicago. My parents were both alcoholics, and one morning they just disappeared and never returned."

Immediately everyone began to feel sorry for her.

"When you're ten years old you don't know much about people or how to survive, but believe me, you learn quick, and all the wrong ways. I stole to eat, and I worked some of the crummiest jobs imaginable in order to have a place to sleep. By the time I was twelve I was . . . selling my body in order to survive."

Women gasped.

"What's that mean, Mama?" Joey Maddox asked. Beverly hurried her children away.

"The only reason I did that was because . . . because a gang of boys taught me early on what women were supposed to be for," Jenny continued, "except I wasn't a woman. I was a kid. After that I didn't have much respect for myself so I figured, what the hell, I'll just do it for money. I was pretty, so I had plenty of work, you might say."

A couple more women turned away, shaking their heads.

"Later I went to work in taverns," Jenny continued. "That's where I met Buck. He was a cardsharp. He cheated, and he was good at it. I started helping him, sending him signals about other men's hands. He paid me a percentage of his take. One night one of the players caught on, and he tried to have Buck arrested. He managed to escape, and I was fired. Later I got caught stealing because I needed money for food. I went into hiding, and later Buck found me, said he wanted to go west and start over in California, asked if I wanted to go, too. I agreed because I was sick of the streets of Chicago and scared of being arrested. Buck knew we would have to lie and say we were married so decent folks on a wagon train would accept us. Buck took me for granted, thought of me as just another one of his many conquests, never really cared about me personally, just used me in his con games, and for . . . other things. He never knew I loved him. I don't think he even understood about loving anyone.'' She stopped a moment and choked in a sob. ''My God, I loved him. I really did. You have . . . to believe that. I always knew he'd never . . . love me back . . . but we were going through so much hell to get to California . . . I just figured he would at least wait until we got there before he turned his attention to other women. And I thought . . . with what we were going through on this trip . . . maybe he'd learn to love me along the way . . . make a respectable woman out of me. Then I figured out he was sneaking off with Gretta whenever he got the chance. Last night I was sure they were together, so I looked for them. I found them in the grass, and I just . . . I couldn't stand it. I snuck away and got my handgun. I always carry one. You have to when you live in the streets of a city. I took it back and I . . . I just . . . shot them.'' She broke into harder weeping, putting her head in her hands. ''I shot them . . . and I can't change that now. My God, I've lost Buck! I've lost Buck!''

She sat there sobbing, and a storm of emotions moved through Maggie. She was sure it was the same for the others. Jenny had led a terrible life, and the strain of the journey had added to her already delicate emotional state, causing her to do something totally irrational. Still, she had planned it, had gone and gotten her gun and deliberately shot two people who were no threat to her. Maggie thought how horrible it must be to be left alone in a place as big as Chicago at ten years old.

''Let her go,'' she said.

Everyone looked at her.

''Are any of us in our right minds at this moment?'' She glanced at Rafe, then at the rest of them. ''I, for one, have not felt like myself since leaving home. This journey takes its toll on people, not just physically, but emotionally, mentally. And who are any of us to accuse?'' She looked at Reverend Krueger. ''Wasn't it Jesus who said that he who is without sin can cast the first stone?'' She looked at Rafe again. ''I am not perfect. I am not without sin.'' She looked at the others again. ''Neither are any of you. I want nothing to do with accusing this woman, sentencing her. Nor do I want my husband to be a part of it. Yet we are the ones who have lost the most here, a faithful maid, a close friend. We have known Gretta for years. She will be dearly missed. But another death will not make up for her loss.''

She turned away, urging Edward to come with her. They walked to their wagon and waited while the others talked. It was decided that Jenny should either be abandoned where they were, given a horse, food and water, and general directions back to Fort Hall. Or, she could stay with them to Goose Creek, where there was a small trading post where she could wait for the next wagon train to come along and go with them to California. She was asked what she would prefer.

''I would rather have a horse and food and go back,'' she told them. ''We all know there are thousands of people on this trail. I am bound to run into another wagon train if I follow the trail backward. I'll tell them my . . . husband . . . died, and that in my grief I decided to go home; that I realized I could never make it and changed my mind, then ask if I can travel with them. There should be no problem finding someone willing to take me.''

They all knew she meant some lonely, single man who would be more than happy to have a woman along to cook for him, among other things. There was certainly a generous supply of such men on their way to California.

''All right,'' Maggie heard the reverend say. ''She wants to leave now, so someone offer a horse. You women get a few supplies together for her.''

''She can take my roan,'' Rafe spoke up. ''He's gentle and dependable. I can manage without him. I have three other horses.''

Maggie was grateful for the offer, after the rough way Rafe had treated Jenny. She understood why he'd had to do it. If a man didn't stay in control of his travelers at this point, they would all be fighting and shooting each other before reaching California.

"Get your things together," Rafe told Jenny. He looked around at the others. "I'll need the offer of a saddle. I don't have one to spare."

"I have some in my supply wagon," Edward said from where he stood with Maggie. "I will provide one."

"Good. Bring it over to where my horses are tethered."

Everyone obeyed his orders, and soon Jenny was mounting Rafe's horse, food, blankets, and what personal things she could pack into canvas bags tied onto the horse behind her. She looked at all of them once more, holding her chin proudly, and Maggie felt sick inside at how lonely and frightened and full of grief the young woman must be.

"Thank you for letting me live," she told them. She looked at Maggie. "I'm sorry about Gretta." With that she turned and rode off, heading east. They all watched in silence until she was out of sight. Another casualty. A casualty of a different kind, but still a casualty. Maggie prayed Indians would not get hold of her before she came upon another wagon train.

Chapter Twenty-Two

Maggie began walking again, as by the time the wagons reached the Raft River the trail would become one of mostly climbing for a good sixty-five miles, according to Rafe, before dropping to an easier journey along the Humboldt River and the Humboldt Sink—"One of the hottest and most boring stretches you will see on the whole journey," Rafe had told them, "but at least easier than mountains. It will give the animals a bit of a break before we begin the climb over the Sierras."

Maggie had to smile at the name Raft River. After fording river after river, some of them several times, every crossing a danger in one way or another, she had dreaded yet another. But the Raft River had turned out to be hardly more than a stream, easy to ford, certainly too shallow to float any raft.

After several days they passed what Rafe said others called the City of Rocks, and Maggie wished she could properly describe the sight in her journal, for it was something no one back east could imagine without seeing it for themselves.

The opening to this spectacular rocky area are twin rocks that spiral upward like a cathedral, she wrote. *I can think of no other way to describe how they look, and they are as majestic as the gates of heaven. Rafe has told us that some people are actually beginning to call them Cathedral Rocks rather than City of Rocks. Through this area we mostly climb, frightening, dangerous heights through high divides. It is too bad it is so much work, and that we have no time to stop and truly appreciate the beauty of this country. It is impossible to describe it. One must see it for oneself. I will miss home and my loved ones forever, but I must admit I am seeing things I never dreamed I would see in my lifetime. Some days I hate it, but most days I love it for its beauty, for such country reminds me that there is a God, and that He will keep us safe.*

She had to believe that. She had seen so much tragedy and death, and she did not doubt there was more to come before reaching the western side of the Sierras. She could only pray it would not involve her and Edward . . . or Rafe. She had not even written about what had happened to Gretta. She planned to one day copy this material and send the copy home to her family. She did not have the heart to tell them how Gretta had died. Let them believe she was still alive. She never dreamed she could miss hired help so much, but on this journey she had come to see people in a much different light, had come to depend on Gretta in ways she never would have depended on her at home.

Now she was what at home would be called a true pioneer woman, for she was doing everything herself, including cooking. It seemed she was constantly apologizing to Edward and the other men for ruining something in one way or another, but she was learning from her mistakes, and also learning that perhaps she could actually enjoy cooking once she was in a home of her own and had a real cookstove. She decided that at least once a week she would cook a meal all by herself.

Every day we climb and climb, then descend again. The descent is always more dangerous than the climb, because of the weight of the wagons pressing against the poor mules and oxen. Rafe tells us that once in the Sierras, there will be places where the only way to lower the wagons is to tie ropes to them and snub the ropes around trees so that they are lowered slowly. I worry about the animals. The faithful beasts are growing weary, and the worst is yet to come. California is only one desert and one more range of mountains away. So close, and yet so far.

Maggie had to smile at the thought of what her mother and sisters would think of her now. She no longer cared about her hair, and it was impossible to bathe as often as she would like. Because the journey and the work involved were so hard on clothes, she tended to wear the same dresses over and over. By now none of the women cared what their dresses looked like, and there was no sense wearing out everything they owned. Some had to be saved for when they finally reached their new home.

There was no sense in using any kind of facial makeup, but Maggie did at least daily use the creams she had brought for her skin, although she wondered how much good they did under the brutal Western sun. She wore slat bonnets like the other women, doing what she could to keep that sun off her face. Her hands were beginning to show the effects of the sun and hard work. Her once manicured nails were broken off and worn down, and gathering wood for fires and helping care for the animals had left dirt buried in cracked skin and under nails.

Following the Humboldt River, or what some call Mary's River, is just as boring as Rafe told us it would be, yet it is a great relief from the rocky country from which we just came, and a good break for the animals before climbing the Sierras. Rafe tells us we will follow this river, crossing it several times, for nearly four hundred miles! The land around it here in northern Nevada is dry and desert-like, and there are no large animals, only jackrabbits and coyotes, and an abundance of rattlesnakes. We have to constantly watch for the snakes, and already Rafe and Jack have killed several; but at least here there is drinkable water and grass for the animals along the river. Rafe says it would have been much different if we had taken the Hastings Cutoff to try to save time, as that goes through a salt desert where hardly any of the water is drinkable.

Water and grass aside, temperatures soared to the point where it seemed as though they were literally being baked in an oven. This was the longest stretch of flatland of the entire journey, and in August it was a furnace. In spite of no climbing, it began to take its toll on the animals and wear on the nerves of the travelers, for to think they would ever reach the Sierras seemed hopeless. They began traveling mostly at night because of the torturous heat of day, but often they kept going day *and* night, for now timing was crucial. Rafe warned again that the earlier they reached the Sierras, the better.

Tempers often flared, and Rafe tried to keep people calm when they camped by telling stories about California. It was difficult for Maggie to sit and listen . . . and watch. She could not help studying his every movement, the way he used his hands, strong but gentle hands. She watched his mouth, the full lips, the handsome smile. She watched his dark eyes, studied his nose, how it was straight and masculine, perfectly set in his handsome face. She wanted to feel his full lips kissing hers again. How could one kiss that took place nearly two months ago remain so memorable? His kisses after she had been hurt were light and comforting, but the kiss he'd given her that one memorable night. . . .

She looked away as he told yet another story about the mining camps. It was so hard to watch him. This yearning, this unrequited desire, was sometimes too much to bear. She almost looked forward to the day when they reached their new home and would finally have to part. At least then she would not be forced to look at him every day, hear his deep but gentle voice, watch the skilled way he rode a horse, shot a deer or a buffalo, fought an enemy. She would not have the chance to study his very masculine physique, to wonder what it must be like to lie beside him in the night. She would not have to suffer this horrible guilt for having such thoughts, for betraying her husband by having them. Rafe Morrisey would be out of her life for good.

Endless, endless, endless. That was what this area called the Humboldt Sink was like. There was literally no horizon, because there was nothing on that horizon to use as a marker. There was only the river, which wound and meandered across what was otherwise dry, grassless land. It slithered and twisted along like a snake, and because of its many curves it had to be forded several times in order to continue traveling in a straight line. Sometimes they followed the right bank, then the left, then the right again.

Gunshots were a daily event, as more snakes were killed. Children were kept in wagons because of them.

At times we are visited by Indians, Maggie wrote. *At first they were Shoshoni, but as we go farther west, Rafe tells us the ones we see now are Paiute. We call them Diggers, because they apparently subsist mostly on some kind of roots they dig from the soil. They are quite peaceful, not to be feared, but they are notorious thieves, and we have to watch everything closely. They are quite filthy, but at this point none of us can say we are much cleaner. Cleanliness, nice dresses, lovely hairdos, are all something we only dream about now.*

We have been trudging through this endless desert for nearly a month, but at last, a few days ago, we saw the Sierras come into sight. At first we thought we were only seeing clouds on the horizon, but Rafe told us we were looking at mountains. Today we could see he was right. We could make out the peaks, and we could even see through our spyglasses that there was snow on some of them. How strange to be in such a hot, dry place and see snow. It can only mean we will at last be in cooler country when we reach them, but we have to hope that snow is only the remains from last winter, in places where it never gets warm enough to melt. I long for cooler temperatures, but I do not wish to be stranded by a snowstorm in the Sierras the way the Donner party was stranded.

Anticipation of heading into the Sierras was met with both joy and dread. The joy came from knowing that once over those mountains, they would at last arrive in the soft, green valleys of California. The dread came from knowing that getting over those mountains would be even rougher than getting through the Rockies had been.

Tragedy struck again only days from their leaving the desert. It began with a bloodcurdling scream from Beverly Maddox, followed by a gunshot. Wagons had been halted for noon camp.

Rafe ran back to the Maddox wagon to find Beverly sitting in the grass holding six-year-old Joey, and Terrence Maddox standing over another rattler he'd shot with his handgun, the same handgun with which he'd accidentally shot himself in the foot.

Joey had been bitten. Rafe had to literally tear Joey from his mother's arms in order to try to save him the same way he'd saved Jenny from her snake-bite. Beverly was beside herself, wailing like a crazy woman, for she had already lost her youngest son. The poor woman had already left one grave on this hellish trail, months past, a little grave she would never be able to visit again; and she had suffered through watching her husband having his foot chopped off. Now another son's life was threatened, and after weeks of endless monotony. She was close to uncontrollable, and two other men had to hang on to her to keep her still while Rafe worked frantically over Joey. Terrence Maddox watched in obvious agony, and Lucille Krueger took five-year-old Minnie Maddox to her wagon in an effort to calm the crying, frightened little girl.

Rafe did all he could, and because they were so close to the Sierras and the day was still young, they had to continue. Joey was propped up in the Maddox wagon, and Beverly Maddox sat with him as they continued on, her husband riding a horse alongside the wagon, as he had done since losing his foot. The man had not talked much since the accident, and some said he was suffering from severe depression over losing the foot.

By nightfall Maggie had to make another sad entry in her journal.

We lost little Joey tonight. Rafe said it was because he was so young and small. The snake's venom got to his brain much more quickly than Rafe could suck it out, and the venom is powerful, too powerful for such a little boy to overcome. Beverly Maddox has lost a second child, and we are all worried about her. There is no consoling her, and tonight she lies across her son's grave, vowing she will not leave it in the morning. She already left one son behind. She swears she will not leave another, and I fear Rafe and the other men will have to forcefully drag her away.

That night Terrence also went to visit the grave, and all thought he had only gone there to comfort his wife. It was not until they heard the two gunshots that they knew, without going to see, what had happened. Terrence and Beverly Maddox had apparently agreed they could go on no longer. Terrence had shot his wife, and then himself.

Of all the things I have witnessed, this is the worst, Maggie wrote. *My heart is so heavy I can hardly bear it.* She could not explain it was already heavy from loving Rafe and not being able to fulfill that love. That in itself would be hard enough on the heart. This latest tragedy made it feel as though a vise had been clamped around her heart and was being screwed shut. She felt she could hardly breathe as the Maddox's were buried and Reverend Krueger prayed over them. Little Minnie was kept away from all of it, and Lucille Krueger explained as best she could to the little girl that her parents had gone to be with God.

The Kruegers agreed to take Minnie as their own and raise her, and everyone appreciated their kindness, having no doubt that they would make a good and loving home for the child.

Three more graves, Maggie wrote. *I can only pray that there will be no more before reaching California, and that if there are, they will not be for me or for Edward. Mostly I pray there will be no more tiny graves left behind. There is nothing more heartwrenching than putting a child into the ground. I want children of my own, but right now I am glad I do not yet have any. There will be time enough for that once we reach California.*

Soon enough it would be time to restart a normal married life with Edward. They had not made love since before leaving for California, and for the most part the journey had been too wearing for them to care. Now, because of all they had been through, with little time to just lie and talk about their future, Edward seemed more and more like a stranger than a husband, and he seemed to grow more distant. Maggie attributed it to the strain of the journey and the horror of the deaths they had seen; as well as the guilt she knew Edward suffered for bringing her along. Still, sometimes it seemed he wanted to tell her something. He had not said so outright. She only sensed it.

Wearily, full of grief over the tragedy of the Maddox's, they went on, leaving the Maddox wagons behind but taking the animals, which might be needed as they climbed the Sierras and other animals gave out. They divided the Maddox's supplies, and Lucille Krueger gathered family items that might be important to Minnie as momentoes when she was older. They found the address of Beverly Maddox's parents, and Lucille promised to try to get a letter sent back to them. What a terrible letter that would be for the poor woman's parents to read. Maggie prayed such a letter would never have to be sent home to her own mother.

Chapter Twenty-Three

"Our last leg before the mountains will take us through what is called the Forty Mile Desert," Rafe told everyone at the meeting he called. "I know everybody is worn to the bone, and it's worse for the oxen, but when we hit the true desert, there will be no stopping to camp, no rivers or watering holes. There will only be a couple of stops to rest the animals for a while, and then we go on, day and night."

"My God, Man, how can we do that, and *why?*" Graydon Howell spoke the words. "We've just gone through four hundred miles of near desert, and we're about crazy. At least through all that we had water!"

Rafe rubbed at his eyes. "Mr. Howell, you can't waste time in the desert. We will fill every single water barrel and other water containers and we'll spend tomorrow cutting grass, as much as we can load into the wagons. For the next forty miles there will be neither one for the animals. Even if we fill every single container, we'll still run out before we reach the mountains, I guarantee it. I've done this enough to know. The reason we don't stop is because it's important to get through the desert as quickly as we can, and because of the heat and lack of water it's important to get in a lot of miles at night. We'll lose a few more animals, but a few is better than all of them. We'll pass some water farther on, but it's no good. It stinks of sulphur, and it's hot. You will even see a few geysers. If it weren't for the hellish heat, they would be interesting sights. Beyond the geysers and springs is the worst leg of all. Sand so soft the animals will sink to their knees in some places. The men will have to help the animals by pushing on the back ends of the wagons. It won't help much, but it's better than nothing. Some of the animals won't make it through that part. It can't be helped. After that it's a downgrade, so the animals will get a break. Then we'll come to the Truckee River, trees, water, grass. It will seem like heaven by the time you get there, I can promise you that."

Everyone looked at each other, none of them looking forward to this part of the journey. "There's no way around it?" the reverend asked.

Rafe shook his head. "Not unless you want to lose valuable time and get into the mountains too late. Believe me, struggling through the desert is better than getting snowed in in the Sierras."

Maggie pushed a strand of hair back off her face, which was bathed in perspiration. "What must be done must be done. We'd better get started gathering grass." She turned to Edward. "Get a couple of blankets, Edward. We'll load grass onto them and tie it up in the blankets."

Edward nodded and followed her, and Rafe grinned at how lately Maggie seemed to have taken charge of things. She kept up the women's spirits by explaining how she had probably given up more than any of them, describing her life back in Pennsylvania, which had been much more glamorous and wealthy than even Rafe had imagined. He found it astounding that she had so far mastered this journey, survived a cholera epidemic, faced the death of close friends, fought mosquitoes and Indians, survived a life-threatening knife wound, struggled through furnace-like heat without complaining. The damn woman was a true pioneer, a hell of a wife, and would one day be a damn good mother. He just wished he was the one who could be husband and father. Edward would never successfully fill either role, and if their sex life was what he imagined, he might never *be* a father.

What a waste of a good woman, he thought. He had considered staying in California himself this trip, maybe starting ranching there. Still, even if he could have her, that would not be much of a life for Maggie McCahan. She was used to much finer things, and probably planned to live life that way again once they settled in San Francisco. Even if she was free it was probably foolish to think it could ever work between them, no matter how much she loved him. He had to stop dreaming about something that could never be, and he knew she was already doing the same.

Rafe had not exaggerated. If ever Maggie felt like giving up, this was the time. There was no rest, and, many miles before they should be out of the desert, there was no water. Maggie could think of no other part of the journey that had been as hellish as this. The heat was so intense that it carried up in waves off the hard desert floor. It seemed as though it was searing her eyeballs, and her lips began to crack. Animals began to fall, so many that Edward finally had to give up his extra supply wagon altogether so that the oxen could be shared with others who lost so many oxen or mules that their wagons could not be pulled. Maggie's heart went out to Edward, who blinked back tears as he trudged on without his precious supplies. Reaching California with them in tow had meant everything to him.

''Perhaps the ship will be there with the things you had sent by sea,'' she encouraged him.

''Maybe. But some of those things would have been used in building our new home, Maggie.''

''After this journey, anything will be a welcome home, Dear. A simple cabin will seem wonderful. Anything, as long as it doesn't have wheels on it.''

He shook his head. ''I had such great plans, Maggie. I knew it would be hard, but I never thought it could be this bad.

You've lost so much. You look and work like any common pioneer woman."

"I *am* a common pioneer woman right now, and there is nothing wrong with that. I'll be fine, Edward. And we have plenty of money and plenty of good things coming by ship."

He shrugged. "I suppose."

Maggie studied his sunburned face. His lips were also cracked and dry, and there were tiny blisters on his nose and cheeks. He had the kind of skin that would never be dark. A ruddy red was as far as it would go. She realized then that the sun didn't seem to bother Rafe at all. Although in this furnace everyone wore hats if they didn't want to get their brains cooked, much of the time Rafe did not otherwise wear one. His skin only grew darker, and it never looked burned. That was the Indian and Mexican in him, she supposed, and if his father lived in New Orleans he was perhaps French. One of her father's business friends had been French, and he had been quite dark and handsome. She realized she had never asked Rafe about his father's heritage. Edward was Scottish, and her own grandparents on her mother's side had been English. It was her father's parents who had been French, and from whom she had inherited the trunk.

What an odd thing to be thinking about at a time like this, she thought. But then one had to think about *some*thing, or go crazy. She wanted to rip off her clothes, but she suspected the sun on bare skin would be a worse agony than staying dressed. She told herself to concentrate on the fact that Rafe had promised there would be water and shade at the end of this nightmare. So far he had been right in everything he predicted.

After days and nights of grueling travel they reached the deep sands Rafe had told them about, and more animals gave out. Maggie could not help thinking how easy it would be to just sit down and shoot herself and turn to bones, like the bleached animal bones they had passed along the way. Dying had to be better than this. The single men headed for the goldfields had to give up one of their wagons, as did the Kruegers. They had gone from nineteen to twelve, and they were not yet over the Sierras. The animals struggled through the deep sands, up another ridge, finally down, down, down.

Everyone took hope in the sight below. Water! Trees! Grass! Shade! Some of the men began whistling and shouting, and when they neared the bottom of the frighteningly steep grade women and children began running toward the river. Maggie joined them.

Finally! After days of burning hell, blessed relief! She and others simply walked into the river fully clothed and fell face-forward into the wonderous cool liquid. She could think of nothing she had experienced in her entire life that had felt this good. The air was filled with screams and laughter, children splashing each other, wives splashing husbands.

Edward lay back in the water beside her, giving out a yell of satisfaction. ''We've done it, Maggie! All that's left is the mountains!'' He threw water at her, and Maggie screamed and laughed. For a brief moment she loved him totally as he embraced her. ''Maggie, my Maggie. My God, you've surprised me, the way you've gotten through all this. A man could not ask for a better friend.''

He kissed her cheek. Maggie could see other couples embracing, kissing on the lips.

''I'm going to unhitch the oxen so they can come all the way in and cool off,'' Edward told her. He left her, then, and Maggie wanted to scream at him to stay, to hold her. She wanted to hug, to celebrate longer. She wanted to be held, to savor the moment, to feel like a woman again. Her smile faded as she watched him walk away, and she turned back to the water, sitting down in it. She looked around at the continued splashing as children reveled in the cool water, and she saw Rafe. His shirt was off, his brawny muscles rippling as he fell back in the water. Katie Howell came up beside him to splash water in his face.

''Hey!'' he cried in mock anger, splashing her back. Pretty, blond Katie splashed him back again, and Rafe laughed, standing up and swooshing water at the girl in huge handfuls. Katie screamed more, trying to splash back, but Rafe's waves of water kept her ducked away from him. Finally, laughing, she begged him to stop. She smoothed back her hair and waded closer to him then, saying something Maggie could not hear. Rafe said something back, then nodded toward shore, as though telling her to get out of the water. "You get too cold after all this heat and you'll get sick," he told her.

"Would you care, Rafe?"

"Of course I'd care. I care about everybody on this train."

"Do you care . . . extra . . . for some of us?"

Rafe just looked at her a minute. "You'd better keep an eye on your younger brother and your sisters. Your poor mother has already lost two children. I'd hate to see her lose more."

"She'll lose *me* someday soon through marriage," Katie answered. "I'm a woman now, you know."

She stuck out her chest as though to make sure he noticed how large her breasts were, and they *were* quite large for a fifteen-year-old's. Maggie felt a knife-like jealousy tear through her, and she felt silly for feeling it, as though she were a young schoolgirl herself, vying for a man's attention.

Rafe just shook his head and turned away from her to swim farther out into the river. Maggie looked away, wading out a little farther herself. She wanted to cry at the thought of Rafe being attracted to Katie, but then why shouldn't he be? She certainly had nothing to offer him herself. Katie was young and pretty . . . and free.

Something tugged on her dress from under the water then, and Maggie frowned. She let out a little scream when strong hands grasped her about the waist and jerked her under the water. Lips covered her own in a quick kiss under the water, and then she was freed. She bounced back up, gulping for air, and Rafe came up right beside her.

"Sorry about that. I couldn't resist. I'm just happy you made it all right."

Maggie shook water from her ears and face, smoothing back her hair. "It seems we have met this way before."

Rafe grinned, and she thought how utterly dashing he looked with his hair wet and slicked back, his teeth looking extra white against his dark skin. "I believe we have, Mrs. MacCahan."

Their gazes held, both needing and wanting to say so much.

Rafe turned and pointed to a thick stand of pine trees along the edge of the river, then moved closer so he didn't have to talk too loudly. "There is a rock formation in the midst of those pines. A nice private place. Come meet me there tonight. We haven't talked in a while." He didn't even know why he had asked her when things were so hopeless. He only knew this was their last break before heading over the Sierras. Then they would be in California, and he would have to leave her for good. The thought tore at his guts.

Maggie looked around. "I don't know—"

"Please come there, Maggie. We'll not get another chance to talk."

No! It was as wrong as it could possibly be. "I'll try," she answered, as though having no control over her thoughts or actions. "Are you sure you won't be meeting Katie there?"

"Katie?"

"I saw her flaunting herself for you."

He laughed. "You jealous?"

She stiffened. "Of course not! I have no reason—"

He caught her arm. "Katie is a kid. I'm not that crass or that stupid. You know what and who I want, Maggie. Meet me tonight."

He swam away, and Maggie waded toward shore, feeling numb. She tried wringing out her dress as best she could, then walked over to help Edward finish unhitching the oxen.

"This must feel so good to the oxen," she told Edward.

"Damn right." He smacked one on the rump and let it amble into the river. "Damn good to everybody." He took a deep breath, throwing back his head. "I'm going to sleep well tonight, Maggie, better than I have slept in weeks."

"Yes," she answered. "I believe I will, too."

Chapter Twenty-Four

The nights were hardly any cooler than the days, but Edward had been right in saying he would sleep better this night than he had in weeks. Maggie, however, lay wide awake, debating over whether to go and meet with Rafe as he had asked. Apparently he felt the same way she did, that there was still so much to say and so little time left to say it. A rough struggle was ahead of them, getting over the Sierras, and then they would be in California . . . and back to the reality of normal life. She would go her way . . . with Edward . . . and Rafe would go his. She had no idea where that would be.

Crickets and coyotes joined forces in night songs, and far, far away she heard a wolf howl. It was a lonely sound, and it seemed to epitomize her own feelings. She wanted to howl like that wolf, to cry out her loneliness. She wanted to be held, in the way that only a man like Rafe could hold her. Did she dare let him?

She sat up, and Edward did not move. He breathed deeply in exhausted sleep. The entire camp was quiet, everyone relishing the break from the awful desert trek, the relief of water and trees. Maggie moved to the back of the wagon, and because of the heat, she did not put on a robe. She wore only a thin cotton, short-sleeved gown. It was dark, so no one, including Rafe, could see much of her, anyway. Besides that, he had already seen her breasts when he doctored her for the knife wound. She wondered how closely he had looked, if he had deliberately let his gaze rest on them so that he could remember them. The thought made her angry . . . yet it also stirred a forbidden desire somewhere in her deepest places.

She climbed out of the wagon, and she thought how nice it was that no mosquitoes bothered them. There had not been a problem with mosquitoes since coming into this place called Nevada, and she smiled at the thought that it was even too hot for the mosquitoes. Too hot and *dry*. This was strange and beautiful country, this West—Colorful rocky mountains, waterfalls, hot, bubbling pools and steam-fed geysers; rich, rolling prairies laden with game and buffalo; high, flat, endless plains; sand hills and canyons, red rock and granite, forest and desert, sagebrush and rattlers, blue skies and violent storms, eagles and grizzlies; Indians and mountain men. She had seen it all, and it had done something to her. She was a changed woman, and she wondered if she could ever be the same now even if she did get to go home. Somewhere deep inside she was actually falling in love with this West. She *had* to fall in love with it, because there would never be anything else for her now. She could only pray California was as beautiful as everyone claimed.

She looked around and saw no one, although she knew Wolf Hunter was watching things. It was his night to keep watch. He was Rafe's friend. He would think nothing of her going to meet Rafe. She found her way by the full moon to the place where he had said she should come. "Rafe," she whispered. She gasped when strong arms pulled her close, pushed at him when his full lips met her mouth, but in seconds she moved her hands along his bare arms and shoulders to wrap them around his neck.

How could she resist the wonderful comfort of these arms? How could she turn away from such a warm, soft, delicious kiss? It had been forever since she was kissed this way, and that kiss, too, had come from Rafe Morrisey. The kiss lingered, neither of them wanting to stop, both relishing its sweetness.

Rafe kept her crushed against him as he went to his knees, and Maggie realized he already had a blanket spread in the grass when he laid her back on it. She moved her hands down his back when he finally released the kiss, moving his gentle lips to her ear, licking her earlobe, kissing his way down her neck, kissing and licking her throat.

Maggie realized he wore no shirt. Was he wearing anything else? Why was she letting this happen? He hadn't even spoken one word yet. "Rafe, don't," she whispered. She damn well didn't mean it, and he knew it. He only groaned, moving his lips downward, kissing at her breasts through her gown, while at the same time pushing up on the gown from its hemline.

"My God, Rafe, we can't do this," she whispered.

Still he said nothing. Why was she raising her hips and letting him pull off her drawers? She drew in her breath when he moved his hands over her bare thighs then, kissing at the hairs on her lovenest, kissing her belly, pushing the gown ever upward, kissing her bared breasts. Edward had never done these things to her, never seemed to truly relish her womanness. Edward had never taken her nipples into his mouth, licked and sucked at them this way.

How was she to stop this madness? It felt wonderful, magical, exotic. Never had she felt like such a true woman as now. Never had she truly *wanted* a man to make love to her, to be inside of her, as she did now.

He knew it. He covered her mouth again, and his fingers traced their way between her legs, seeking her moistness. He touched her in a place Edward had never touched, and never had she known such ecstasy. He made little circular movements that made her want to open herself to him, made her want more. This was Rafe! He was touching her most private places. This rugged, experienced, handsome but lonely man was ravishing her, and she was letting him do it. She wanted to touch him, feel his magnificent muscles, the very maleness of him. She ran her hands over his back, down to his hips, and that was when she realized he was completely naked.

She should be angry that he had been so sure this would happen but she could not be, because she wanted this just as much as he did. He was not taking advantage this time. He was only taking what she was gladly offering, wrong as it was.

She felt a stunning pulsation deep within her, a marvelous, totally pleasurable throbbing that made her start to cry out. Rafe stifled the urge with another kiss, pressing his fingers tightly against the place he'd just toyed with.

"Try not to cry out," he told her.

Those were his only words as he moved on top of her, and in the next moment she was filled with his glorious manhood, his hot, hard shaft much bigger and more satisfying than anything she had felt when Edward made love to her, if it could even be called making love. He had a way of making her feel as though she was only performing a duty for him.

It was impossible *not* to want to cry out at Rafe's deep, rhythmic thrusts. She gritted her teeth, breathing through them almost as though in pain. And she *was* partly in pain. It had been months since a man was inside of her, and Rafe Morrisey was going deeper, into places Edward had never touched. He took up one corner of the blanket and drew it over so that she could put it in her mouth and groan into it, muffling the sounds.

Rafe raised to his knees then, grasping her hips and burying himself deep and hard, moving in a fast, desperate rhythm that made her reel wildly with desire. She never realized it could be this way, this exotic, this thrilling, this satisfying.

This was wrong . . . as wrong as it could be . . . yet so right. After all, she loved this man in ways she had never loved Edward, and Rafe Morrisey loved her. He *had* to love her, or she could never live with what she was doing. It was just something that had to be done or she would go crazy. And so it was done. Rafe groaned as his life spilled into her, and Maggie could feel the pulsations. She had never felt anything like that with Edward, and now she wondered if sometimes he had only pretended to release his life into her.

Rafe held himself there for a moment, then slowly breathed out and leaned down, kissing her eyes, her cheeks, her throat, her lips. "I'm sorry," he whispered. "I'm so sorry. I didn't mean to come inside of you. I meant to pull out first. My God, I could get you pregnant."

Maggie touched his face, ran a hand through his long, dark hair. ''I think it will be all right,'' she whispered. ''My mother told me once—'' She was glad for the darkness so he could not see how embarrassed she was. ''It's . . . almost my time. My mother told me a woman usually does not conceive when it's that close.''

Rafe sighed, lying down beside her and pulling her into his arms. ''Still, I took a terrible chance.''

''I took the chance with you. I hope God can forgive me for what I've done.''

''All you've done is give yourself to the man you truly love, and who loves you in return; a man who appreciates the woman you are, who would love to possess you fully, heart and soul and body.''

''Please don't talk that way, Rafe. I can't bear it.''

''It's the truth, and you know it.''

''I could never leave Edward. It would destroy him. He depends on me, now especially.''

Deep inside a voice screamed at him to tell her the truth. But *that* could destroy *her*. Edward had been a lifelong friend. He had no right to destroy such a relationship, to plant the seed of hate. She still loved Edward, and he had no doubt Edward loved her.

He closed his eyes and relaxed beside her. ''I have probably only made you more unhappy. Even if I could have you, I could never give you the life you deserve.''

''Maybe I don't want the kind of life you think I want. Right now I don't know *what* I want, except that I hate the thought of having to say goodbye once we get to California.''

He turned on his side and kissed her, and she ran her fingers over his hard-muscled arms, his broad chest.

''I'll pay a visit to San Francisco now and then, see how you're doing,'' he told her. ''Just in case you need me for anything.''

''No. It's best I never hear from you again. We've done what had to be done, and now we have to face reality. We can't ever do this again. I will have a hard enough time living with this, facing Edward.'' She reached up and traced her fingers over his lips. "I love you, Rafe. I love you in a way I could never love Edward, but I do love Edward, too, and he is my legal husband. I cannot leave him, because I know what it would do to him. I won't be responsible for that."

Tell her. No. *He* could not be responsible for *that.* "I love you, Maggie McCahan."

Maggie could not help the tear that trickled over her cheek and into her ear. "Love me tomorrow, Rafe Morrisey. Love me in all your tomorrows, so that there is never a today. There can't be a today."

Maggie sat up and found her drawers. She slipped them on and stood up. "I never should have come out here. I knew what would happen, what *had* to happen. It's done now, and it is all we can ever have. It hurts. It hurts worse than that knife wound, worse than burying Gretta, or leaving my family behind in Pennsylvania. Nothing has ever hurt this much." The tears started to come again. She adjusted her nightgown and shook back her hair, and Rafe rose to stand beside her. He pulled her into his arms.

"I hurt, too, Maggie, almost as bad as when I had to bury my wife. I was younger then, and I loved her. But not the way I love you, as a man of experience who knows what he really wants. Too bad we were both too late in learning that."

She stood there relishing the embrace for as long as she dared. One moment longer and she would be letting him make love to her again. They had taken enough of a chance as it was. "I must go, Rafe."

"We didn't even get a chance to talk."

"Neither of us *planned* on talking. We both know that." Maggie breathed deeply of his scent, a rugged smell of leather, sage, fresh air. Back home, before this hellish trip, she would not have given such a man a second thought. She had to believe that was all that was wrong. She truly was not herself. She would get over this once she was settled in with Edward and living the way she'd been brought up to live. Yes, she could forget him. She could get over him. Tomorrow. She would love him tomorrow. Never today.

Chapter Twenty-Five

The contrast between the desert and the Truckee was astounding. The weary emigrants went from flat land with an endless horizon and burning heat to the roughest terrain they had yet encountered, the journey now a steady climb. The Truckee flowed out of the mountains, sometimes in roaring force, over boulders and through canyons, and the water was swift and icy cold. The river had to be forded several times, a bone-chilling experience that caused Maggie to curse the very water that had earlier been so cherished. The trail began to follow narrow makeshift roadways along mountainsides, sometimes to frightening heights and often dangerously narrow pathways. Here the drivers had to be most experienced in order to keep the oxen and mules from balking, perhaps panicking, which would send wagons and animals tumbling to their deaths hundreds of feet below.

Everyone breathed in relief whenever they moved into forested hills where there were no narrow cliffs, but still the journey was ever upward, climbing, climbing, climbing, sometimes twisting away from the river, then back again, across the river, climbing again, over the river again.

We are headed toward Bear Valley, which some call Emi-

grant Gap, Maggie wrote. *There is still a lot of dangerous climbing ahead, over a pass, our last truly rough and dangerous trek, so Rafe tells us.*

If only she could write the flowing words of love she wanted to write about Rafe. *I have truly fallen in love for the first time,* she wanted to write. *He is more man than any I have ever seen or known, with a body as supple and muscled as a panther, a temper wild as a grizzly when protecting his mate, a face as handsome and proud as an eagle, and he reminds me of all those things, for he is partly a man of the wild, wearing buckskins, keeping watch like a wolf, leading the emigrants with skill and a knowledge of this wild land. I love Edward, but I love Rafe Morrisey in a whole different way. In his arms I am a true woman and I enjoy being that woman, letting him take his pleasure in me, while I in turn take my pleasure—*

"Stop it," she whispered. Instead she wrote a description of the land itself. She could appreciate the beauty of this area better if she were not so weary and hungry. Supplies were again low, and they were conserving in case of a freak snowstorm.

I cannot begin to describe the beauty here, she wrote. *How I wish I were a poet, or a better painter. There is just no describing it to those who have never seen it, the purple and gray rocks with snow in their crevices and on their northern edges; deep canyons through which the river rumbles and roars; colorful wildflowers, deer flitting about, rich green pine trees set against a deep blue sky. This is truly God's country, and I am not sure man was meant to be here. There are not even any Indians about.*

She had to write, to stay busy, tired as she was. To be idle was to have time to think, and to have time to think meant thinking about Rafe, longing for him, dreaming about being in his arms. Would he turn to whores, or maybe some other emigrant woman one day to relieve his loneliness? Would he marry someone else?

She set aside the journal and forced herself to lie down. They were camped in a fairly flat area in a pine forest. Tomorrow, according to Rafe, would be the hardest climb. They would head for the top of the pass. After that it would be a steep descent, so steep wagons would have to be lowered by rope part of the way. Maggie could not decide which was more stressful—the monotony and the heat of the desert, or the constant fear that one would fall to his or her death.

The ascent continued, a constant climb. Maggie wondered where each next step would come from, and she genuinely felt sorry for the animals, having to drag all that weight behind them. All day long she could hear men shouting and cursing, whips snapping.

"Get up there!"

"Keep going"

"Ha!"

"Keep it up! Move it!"

"Come on there, Peggy!"

"Don't you give out on me now, Jeremiah!"

Nearly all the animals were named, and each loss along the way had become another thing to mourn.

The teams were on another narrow trail with a dangerous drop to one side when a mule belonging to one of the Howell wagons balked and fell to its knees, refusing to rise again. All wagons behind it had to stop, including the three McCahan wagons. Maggie walked at the head of the line with other women and children, who, because of the danger of wagons getting loose, were forbidden to walk behind any of them. She heard shouts, and Rafe dismounted and hurried past the women and the three lead wagons, telling them all to keep going. It wasn't much farther.

The others went on, but Maggie was worried about Edward. She leaned against the rocky mountain wall as the lead wagons went past her, then walked closer to the wagon where the mule had collapsed. She realized then that it was Katie's pet mule, Beaner. Rafe was shouting orders to unhitch the animal as fast as possible.

Graydon Howell hurriedly worked to get the harness off the dying mule, and much as they all hated to do it, it had to be gotten out of the way. "I can't shoot it first," Rafe told Howell.

"The gunshot would echo extra loud right here and could startle the rest of the teams. It wouldn't take much for them to panic, and you know what would happen then. We have to throw her over the edge, Howell. It's the only way."

Maggie put a hand to her chest, feeling terrible sorrow. Howell shook his head. "I can't do that to her."

"You have no choice. You have your family to think of. We have to get off this ledge, and she's in the way."

Graydon Howell sniffed and wiped at his eyes. "The poor thing made it this far. She's Katie's special pet. Let me try to get her up."

"Just a couple of minutes."

Graydon knelt down beside Beaner and began trying to cajole the animal to its feet. Maggie felt like crying herself, and she looked at Rafe, who was frowning with concern. He met her gaze. The deep longing to be together only deepened every time she looked into his dark eyes. Where would he go when they parted? What would he do? They still had not truly "talked," and now they would probably never get the chance.

"You should be up there with the rest of the women. It's dangerous here."

"I'm not going up until I know Edward is also on his way."

"Beaner!"

The shouted name came from Katie Howell, who had realized what happened and had come running back down the ledge. Rafe hurried forward and grabbed her. "Stay calm, Katie! You don't dare stir up the rest of the animals!"

"I can help get her up!" Katie tore away from him and went to the mule. "Beaner, get up! Get up!" She had seen other animals shot. She could not bear for that to happen to this one, too, but it was obvious the mule was not going to get up on all fours again. Her father explained what had to be done.

"No!" she exclaimed. "I won't let you!"

"We have no choice, Katie-girl."

"No!" Katie rose and faced Rafe. "You bastard! I won't let you do that to my Beaner!"

"Katie!" Graydon Howell rose and grasped the girl's arms. "What in God's name is wrong with you, talking that way!"

"I'm tired of him telling us what to do! He's just an ignorant, uncivilized half-breed with no feelings. He doesn't know anything about families and pets and love! All he knows is horses and sweat and wandering this godforsaken country like a wild animal, and I won't let him kill my Beaner!"

Maggie was astounded at the words. She could not read the look on Rafe's face, and she wanted to scream at Katie in his defense, but she didn't dare, not just because of how it would look, but because this was not the time or place to get into a shouting match. Some of the other animals were getting restless, sensing a feeling of panic, finding it difficult to stand still with so much weight dragging behind them.

"If we don't get rid of the mule right now and get going, some of the other animals will start to give up," Rafe warned Howell. "We've got to get her to the edge and get her over."

"No! No! How can you be so cruel!" Katie screamed.

"Damn it, Girl, shut up!" Rafe told her. "Control your daughter, Howell!"

Howell grabbed Katie and held tight while Rafe knelt down and urged Beaner to try to rise. All the animal could muster was to wiggle enough so that Rafe was able to let it begin wiggling to the edge.

"I can help," Edward said. He had come up from his wagon to see what he could do. "Hazel Schultz said she can keep my oxen calm for a few minutes."

"Get hold of the other side of her bridle," Rafe told him. "We have to drag her to the edge."

Edward nodded, and because of Katie's screaming and struggling with her father and the smell of death in the air, the rest of the mules began braying and scuffling, making the Howell wagon rock slightly. The rest of the way down the line men began having trouble hanging on to their animals, all of them sensing something was terribly wrong. Rafe and Edward dragged the ailing mule to the edge as best they could, and just as Beaner started to go over, Katie broke loose and ran to the mule, grabbing at it and tripping on the hem of her dress at the same time. Maggie watched in horror as the girl went over the edge with the struggling mule. Edward grabbed for Katie, and he, too, went over.

"Edward!" she screamed, running to the edge, only to be caught by Rafe.

"Stay back! The edge is beginning to crumble!"

"Edward!" she screamed again.

"Stay right there, damn it, Maggie!" Rafe told her. "I'll see if there is anything I can do!"

She looked up at him in tears. "My God, Rafe! What have I done!"

No one but Rafe knew what she meant. Had Edward been killed because of her "sin?" Rafe turned away and crawled to the edge to look down. "Edward!" he called. He could see Edward clinging to the stump of a pine tree that jutted out from the drop-off that was otherwise nearly straight down, with few barriers to keep an object from falling several hundred feet into the canyon below. He could see farther down, where Beaner and the young girl who loved her both lay on a wide, flat rock.

"Help me!" Edward screamed.

"Get some rope!" Rafe yelled, scooting back from the edge. "And a spyglass, if anybody has one! I think I see the girl and the mule. I don't think they're alive, but Edward is hanging on to a stump." He glanced at Maggie, who covered her mouth with her hands.

"Edward," she muttered. "Please help him, Rafe."

He knew what she was thinking. He could easily let Edward fall and call it an accident, and the thought had already crossed his mind. But Maggie would always wonder, and she could never possibly love him and stay with him after something like that. He probably couldn't even live with himself, much as he loved Maggie and wanted her to be free.

Someone came running with a rope, and Rafe shouted for the others to get the wagons moving and try to get to the top of the pass before the animals got too restless.

"Katie!" the girl's mother screamed. She had been watching from farther up with the other women and had come running when she realized what had happened. "What about my Katie! What's happened to her!"

Graydon Howell hurried to Rafe's side to peer over the edge.

"Keep back!" Rafe yelled. "Just get your wife and your wagon up the pass! There is nothing you can do for your daughter."

"What if she's still alive!" Howell shouted in panic. He handed Rafe a spyglass, and Rafe crawled back to the edge, more rocks and debris breaking away.

"Hurry!" Maggie could hear Edward screaming. "I can't hang on much longer!" She watched in terror, wondering if Rafe, too, would go over, and she would lose both of them. She could just imagine how terrified poor Edward was at this moment. And her heart went out to Katie's mother when Rafe turned back and handed up the spyglass.

"Your daughter is dead, Mr. Howell."

"No! No!" Katie's mother screamed.

"Mildred, you'll frighten the animals," Graydon told her, grasping her arms.

"How do you know she's dead for sure?" Mildred demanded of Rafe.

"Ma'am, I know. I'll explain later!" Rafe quickly tied a loop in the end of the rope. "Right now you've got to get up that pass! Do as you're told, or more people will die! I've got one man alive down there, and I'm bringing him up." He handed one end of the rope to Graydon Howell. "Tie that to your wagon axle. We've got to get Edward up as quick as we can before the rest of these animals panic and cost more lives!"

Mildred Howell screamed that she would not budge. Someone had to go after Katie. "We can't just leave her there! We can't! The wolves will eat her! She has to be buried!"

"That's impossible!" Rafe yelled, trying to reason with the woman while at the same time keeping an eye on Edward. "I saw her through the spyglass, Mrs. Howell! Her skull is broken! There is no doubt that she's dead, and there is no way humanly possible to go down there and get her. I'm sorry, but that's how it is!"

Howell finally had to slap Mildred to make her calm down. She shoved away from him and stormed back up the narrow path, screaming that she hated her husband, hated Rafe, hated everyone on the the train, hated this god-awful country. Maggie wished she knew what to tell the woman, but there was no consoling her.

Rafe lay at the edge of the roadway yelling down to Edward, while Graydon Howell tied one end of the rope to his wagon axle as Rafe had asked.

"Try to grasp the loop! Slip it under your arms!" Rafe hollered.

"If I let go I'll fall!"

Maggie ran to the edge to look down, gasping at the sheer drop and the sight of Edward clinging to a stump that could pull loose at any time. "Edward, try! You've got to try!"

"Damn it, Maggie, get back! Get back!"

Maggie gripped her stomach, feeling sick at the incredible drop and the thought of poor Edward dying that way, dying with his dream. Rafe was still screaming at him to grab the rope, and finally the rope went taut.

"He's got it!" Rafe stood up and stepped back to start pulling, and Graydon joined him, both men pulling hard while Maggie watched with gripping pain in her chest. At last she saw Edward's head, his hand. Rafe crawled back to the edge, grabbing his hand, and just then more of the edge broke away. Maggie screamed in terror as Rafe clung to Edward. Frayed from rubbing on a sharp-edged rock during Edward's climb, the rope broke.

"Oh, God! Oh, God!" Maggie moaned as Rafe hung on with all his strength, and Graydon hung on to Rafe's ankles, ordering Maggie to tie what was left of the dangling rope around Rafe's ankles. Maggie quickly obeyed, hardly able to see for her tears. Rafe began scooting back, clinging to Edward's wrists with powerful hands and arms. Slowly Edward came higher again, struggling to find a place to put his feet in order to help himself up.

Maggie watched, feeling the irony of the situation. Her lover saving her husband's life. And she loved them both.

"Keep the rope tight!" Rafe yelled to Howell. Gritting his teeth, he kept pulling, and finally Edward was fully on more solid ground, panting, sweating, dirty, and disheveled. Both men lay there breathing hard, and Rafe rolled onto his back. After getting his breath, Edward got to his knees and touched Rafe's shoulder.

"Thank you, Rafe. What would any of us do without you?"

Maggie felt sick at the irony of the statement. "Edward," she called out.

Edward stood up and walked over to embrace her. "I'm all right, Love, just scratched and banged up. Poor Katie! Poor, poor Katie! It's a horribly long fall. She can't possibly be alive. I don't know how I managed to grab onto that stump."

Maggie hugged him, consumed with guilt. "Thank God you're all right."

Edward pulled away and wiped at sweat on his brow. His shirt was ripped and dirty, his face dirty and scratched, and blood showed at the rips in his shirt, where his skin had been scraped. "You had better go on up with the other women," he told Maggie. "We've got to get these teams the rest of the way up."

Maggie nodded, glancing at Rafe, who had got to his feet and was dusting himself off. She realized what must be going through his mind. Saving Edward had only ensured that he could never be with Maggie. Edward turned and put out his hand to Rafe.

"Thank you again. There are no words to tell you."

Rafe glanced at Maggie, then nodded, taking Edward's hand. "Sure." He let go of Edward's hand and walked back to help the others. Edward kissed Maggie's cheek and left her to handle his own team, and Maggie wearily headed up the pathway toward the pass that would soon lead them downward again . . . to Bear Valley, and California.

Chapter Twenty-Six

Poor Mildred Howell just sits and stares, Maggie wrote. *After having to leave her daughter, Katie, behind us, lying dead in a canyon, she collapsed, for she had already lost another daughter and a son. The Howells started this journey with six children, and now they have three. We put Mrs. Howell into a wagon, where she just sits and does not speak. No one knows what to do for her. How sad that this had to happen when we have only that one last mountain pass to conquer before finally coming into the valleys of California.*

The words were the ending to Maggie's diary entry about the accident and how Rafe Morrisey had saved Edward from certain death, risking his own life to do it. He could so easily have let go and simply claimed he could not hang on, and Maggie loved him all the more for the honorable man that he was.

She set her journal aside and rose, looking back at the higher mountains now to the east. It had taken several days to come down those mountains, since much of the descent was handled by tying ropes to wagons and snubbing them around trees to help keep them from breaking tongues and tumbling down the mountain over the heads of the animals pulling them. It was a long, slow process, but at last they reached bottom . . . and home.

So, this was California. She had yet to write about this place called The Sacramento Valley, and it would be difficult to describe its beauty. Perhaps it only seemed greener and warmer and more beautiful than it really was simply because it was so wonderful to at last be here and be finished with their journey. This land was wide and flat and endless, its grass a rich green from recent rains. Willard Haggarty was ecstatic over the soil, claiming he could farm here and become every bit as rich as those who went looking for gold. Last night he had carried around a sample of the dirt he'd dug up.

"Look at this!" he kept repeating, showing it to everyone. "*This* is the *real* gold! Sutter has the right idea farming and ranching here, building a sawmill! He's already upset that so many people are flooding through here that they're ruining his crops, and I don't blame him."

Maggie didn't blame him either. This must have been quite a lovely, peaceful place before gold was discovered. Now thousands of people tramped through here, panning for gold in the creek, others heading into the nearby mountains to dig. They had passed prospectors on their way down, and gold fever literally shone in their eyes. Already Edward was making the rounds talking to prospectors to find out what items were most needed, and Maggie sat alone on a wagon tailgate, enjoying the warm California sun, watching some of the children from the wagon train play. Little Minnie Maddox seemed to have adjusted just fine to life with the Kruegers. Already the men who had come along to look for gold had left the train and gone off on their own. And over the next two or three days all others would go their separate ways, for all their separate reasons. For now they were content to camp and rest, and to celebrate getting through the Sierras without a major snowstorm burying them alive.

It is mid-October, Maggie added. *Edward and I have been traveling for six months.* Six months, and so far away! Mother, Father, Sarah, Elizabeth, Catherine, all her friends, her old life . . . so far, far away . . . and now so unreal. Where was the old

Maggie? She had been left behind somewhere. In her place was a young woman with dry hair and skin, and no color on her cheeks except what the sun had given her; a young woman with hands that were cracked and calloused, her fingernails broken and dirty; a young woman wearing a plain, gray cotton dress and living out of a wagon, the only true remnant of her old life being her grandmother's trunk and the special items inside. She had given her expensive wedding dress and diamond earrings to an Indian! She had an ugly scar on her left shoulder from a knife wound put there by a mountain man. She did her own cooking, such as it was, did everything for herself now, certainly things she never would have done or been expected to do back home. She had nursed her husband through cholera, her lover through an arrow wound.

That was the strangest part of all, the one thing most different about this Maggie. She'd taken a lover on the way west, betrayed her faithful husband. It could be called nothing else but adultery, and yet nothing in her life had seemed more right at the time. Her marriage to Edward seemed all wrong. But she could do nothing about it. She would not accept the status of a divorced woman, nor would she hurt Edward by leaving him at this crucial time in his life, just when he was readying to realize his biggest dream.

She put down pen and journal when she saw Rafe approaching. She sat sideways on the wagon gate, leaning against a sideboard. Rafe climbed up and sat down facing her, and they both just looked at each other quietly for several seconds. Maggie thought her heart would burst at the realization that after these last few precious hours she might never see Rafe Morrisey again. "What do we do now?" she asked softly.

"I was going to ask you the same thing."

She blinked back tears. "Go our separate ways. We have no choice."

"Don't we?"

She looked down and shook her head. "No."

"You know you'll never be happy with Edward."

She quickly wiped at a tear. "I know. But I won't be abused

or unloved. Edward loves me very much. He has always been good to me, and he always will be.''

He uses you, Maggie, as a cover. Rafe sighed and rubbed at his eyes. ''I can never offer you the life to which you are accustomed,'' he told her. ''Is that it?''

She choked in a sob. ''You know it isn't!''

There followed several more long seconds of silence.

''All right,'' he said. ''I believe you. But that's easy for you to say right now. It won't be long before you're living that way again. And once you are back to that life, you'll know where you belong . . . and where I belong. Out of your life.''

Maggie could not help breaking into tears. She covered her face and wept. Rafe wanted to cry, too, just looking at her. He ached to hold her, but someone might see, and what good would it do? It would only prolong the pain, renew the desire.

''Maggie, I want you to know I love you. Don't ever think I used you. This isn't something that happens to me every time I lead a train west. It just . . . happened. I am as confused about it as you are. And I'm just as sorry about it, as far as making you feel guilty goes. You shouldn't feel that way. We both had a need, and as long as love was involved, there was nothing wrong with it. I will always love you. I will never forget you for the rest of my life.''

She only cried harder.

''Please tell me you aren't pregnant.''

She shook her head, turning to take a handkerchief from a box of her daily clothes. ''No.'' She blew her nose and wiped at her eyes.

More silence.

''Where will you settle?'' Rafe asked.

She blew her nose more. ''Probably in San Francisco. Edward feels the area will grow dramatically because of its location on the ocean where supply ships can come in. He wants to leave for there tomorrow and see if the ship bringing our own supplies might be there. It's been six months.'' She wiped at her eyes more. ''It has had plenty of time, unless it sank going around the Cape. That happens often. If the ship isn't there, things won't be quite as easy as we planned.''

Rafe sighed again, and Maggie suspected he was fighting his own urge to weep.

"I can't bear the thought of you riding off alone, Rafe."

He folded his legs and leaned forward, resting his elbows on his knees. "I've been alone most of my life. I'm used to it."

She met his eyes, so dark, so handsome, and misty with tears. "Are you? I doubt anyone gets used to being alone."

He forced a grim smile. "I've got Jack, and Wolf Hunter."

"You know what I mean."

He looked down and said nothing. Why couldn't he bring himself to tell her? It just didn't feel right to him. Maybe from now on Edward really would try to be a proper husband. He had to give him that chance, much as it burned his gut to picture Edward making love to Maggie. But he was her legal husband. If only there were something about the man he could hate, it would be easier. But he was a likeable, kind, caring man, unusually generous and accepting of others of lower class, for a man of such wealth. What right did he have to destroy the man's marriage and life by telling his wife what he'd witnessed? Maybe it had ended with David's death. Maybe there was just something about it he didn't understand, but in his book what he'd seen was repulsive and wrong, a hideous betrayal of a good woman's love. But then his affair with the man's wife was also a betrayal.

"I wish you well, Maggie. You know that."

She nodded. "Where will you go? What will you do?"

He shrugged. "I'll go back. Do it all over again."

Her eyes widened in surprise. "I can't imagine making that trip all over again!"

"This was my third one."

Maggie gasped, finding it incredible that any human being would want to ride that trail more than once. "Oh, Rafe, the heat, the snakes, the mountains, the desert, all the death!"

He met her eyes, forcing another meager smile. "All part of the job. Besides, I can't stay around here. With you here I can't stay anywhere in the whole state of California. I wouldn't trust myself. I'll start back tomorrow, before winter starts getting too rough in the Sierras."

"Rafe, you just got here! How can you bear the thought of going back all that way! And winter will be setting in *everywhere* soon, including the plains and prairies! You could die out there!"

He forced a light laugh. "I've done it before. A man on horseback can make it in half the time it takes to bring a wagon train out. I'll run into other wagon trains on the way, so it isn't like I won't find help at different times. Besides, Jack and Wolf Hunter will go with me. We usually try to get at least as far as Fort Bridger or Fort Hall. If we hole up there for the winter, we can still get back to Independence in time to pick up a new wagon train. And it's decent money. I don't even have to spend most of it. The emigrants usually cook for us."

"What good is the money if you never settle down and enjoy it?"

"I don't know. I just figure the day will come when I'll know what I really want to do, how I want to spend it . . ." He hesitated before finishing. "Who I want to spend it with . . . or on. After meeting you it's going to be a long time before I can ever give my heart to any other woman, if ever."

Maggie wanted to beg him not to lie with whores, but what right did she have to ask him? She couldn't bear the thought of it, or the thought of him loving someone else, but there was nothing she could do about that. "Will you come and visit us when you come back next year?"

He nodded. "I'll try to find you."

"Edward would like that, too, I'm sure."

Their gazes held for another long, silent moment. "God, I love you, Maggie. I told you once that I would stay around in case you needed me, but it would just be too hard."

Her tears came again. "And you know that I love you, Rafe."

He reached out and took her hand, squeezing it. "I won't be around in the morning when you leave with Edward."

She nodded, covering her mouth as more tears came. "I understand."

"You stay strong, for me, Maggie. Understand? You're one

hell of a woman, much stronger than you know. You'll do okay out here. Edward is the luckiest man alive. I just wish he realized that and appreciated you fully. I wish he could—''

''Don't, Rafe. Please don't say it. Just go.''

He sat there a moment longer, squeezed her hand again. ''Good-bye, Maggie McCahan.''

She raised her eyes, hardly able to see him for the tears. ''Good-bye, Rafe Morrisey. God be with you.''

''And with you. If anything goes wrong, even if something happens to Edward, you stay right where you are, understand? Wait till I come back and find you. If I'm not back by next November, you'll know something happened to me and I'm not coming.''

She nodded. ''I'll wait. I'd wait for you forever.''

''We'll do like you said, Maggie. We'll love each other tomorrow.''

She shook in a sob, nodding again. ''Tomorrow.''

They looked at each other a moment longer, and Rafe climbed down then, squeezing her hand once more before forcing himself to turn and walk away. Maggie watched him mount his horse and ride off, then stretched out on a feather mattress and wept until she began to wonder how there could be any tears left.

Chapter Twenty-Seven

We barely made it to San Francisco before our drivers ran off to the goldfields, Maggie wrote. *Never have I seen such frenzy and rush as there is here. I am told it was worse last year when the first thousands came to this place because of gold. In the harbor sit hundreds of ships left there by their crews, who ran off with passengers to look for gold, leaving the ships' captains with no one to help. Even some of the captains deserted. The term "gold fever" is not at all an exaggeration. It has caused this city, which they say only two years ago was just a tiny log cabin settlement, into a burgeoning, bustling city that has already been incorporated and boasts several thousand citizens. There are bankers here, lawyers, doctors, teachers, ministers, grocers, sailors, suppliers of all sorts, farmers, blacksmiths. The list goes on and on, thousands of people from all walks of life. Edward could not have picked a better place to come and start over, and already he has grubstaked several prospectors, in hopes of becoming part owner of several gold mines if they should be successful in their hunt for their glittery treasure.*

Maggie went on to explain the meaning of grubstake, and the thought of how many thousands of money hungry ruffians were in this city made her nervous. Edward had begun lending money to prospectors for purchasing proper mining equipment, with agreements that he would get a share of any gold they discovered. He also had made money supplying other miners with various necessities, and he had struck a deal with a ship's captain to purchase a good deal of the clothing and mining equipment he had carried by ship to California. The ship Edward had reserved still had not arrived with their personal furnishings and building materials for their new home, as well as the supplies Edward had planned to bring here and sell.

What worried Maggie was the fact that so many men knew Edward had money. He had hired an old man, Wade Grisham, to keep guard over his three wagons while Edward visited the docks in order to buy supplies that could be taken to the gold camps and sold for "tremendous profit," according to Grisham. The old man had been in one of those mining camps, where he claimed men would "pay five whole dollars for a loaf of bread." And where "a man could get rich just off the gold dust left in his pockets and on the floors of the saloons."

Maggie had no desire to see one of those gold camps. San Francisco was wild enough, an uncivilized young city full of a grand mixture of wealthy men and cutthroats; wives trying to establish churches and schools, and wild, painted women who hung over balconies and stood in the doorways of saloons. There was not a paved street to be found, but already the wealthy were building fine homes in the higher hills. Some of those wealthy were those who had come here with their pockets already full of money, like Edward; and some were those who in one short year had gone from a common life to the life of wealth.

She had written about all of it in her journal. *The problem is,* she added, *most of those who discover gold sell their claims to people like us who have the money to properly get the gold out of the bowels of the earth, purify it, and get it to the banks for profit. Already I am hearing stories about men selling their claims for what they think is a lot of money, but for what is a paltry sum, to the already wealthy. The rich get richer, and the poor common man who sells his claim spends his money quickly and ends up with nothing.*

Maggie spent her days sorting supplies and writing in her journal, or reading—anything to keep from thinking about Rafe. She had tried going into the city, but she was afraid of its rugged, raw nature, and the looks of some of the men who wandered its streets . . . and even some of the women. She felt as though everyone was sizing her up for her vulnerability, trying to decide if they should hit her over the head for her purse.

The days were filled with the sounds of clattering wagons, barking dogs, the belching steam whistles of ships at the docks, and constant pounding as hundreds of buildings and homes were being constructed all at the same time. Maggie did not doubt that contractors and carpenters who had come here would make far more money than most of the prospectors.

The nights were worse—and sleepless for Maggie. That was when thieves and drunks roamed the streets at random, and Maggie did not trust old Wade to stay awake and properly guard her. Edward seemed not the least worried, and he slept soundly at night. Maggie could not help thinking how much safer she would be in a place like this if she were lying next to Rafe instead of Edward. Every night the air was filled with laughter and screams, piano music, and occasional gunshots. Wade had said it was worse in the mining camps, and she did not doubt it. How could so many thousands of people, mostly men, congregate in one place, with no law, and be expected to behave? Most of the men here seemed to be a rather heartless, savage, ill-mannered, and unpolished lot as a whole, and poor Edward did not fit in at all. He was too kind, too eager to make friends. She worried about him constantly. She suspected someone like Rafe could handle himself just fine in this environment, but this was unlike anything Edward had ever known.

Wade's excuse for not staying in the mining camp where he'd tried his hand at prospecting was that he was just too old to put up with all the noise and the danger, although he said most camps were instituting some bit of law. A man could be hung for claim jumping. That apparently was the worst crime that could be committed, higher than fighting, stealing, rape, or even murder! Wade claimed he was too old to enjoy his wealth for long even if he did discover gold, and that finding it was also much harder than those who came here thought it would be. Some of the men in the camps had been looking for nearly two years, and still had not found their "pot of gold."

"Oh, it's up there, all right," he had stated more than once. "Some really have found it, but there's thousands more who never will."

Every day Edward went to the docks to meet the ships, and already he had purchased more wagons, heavy supply wagons, which were fast filling with stores to be taken to the mining camps. Every night Edward carried on about the kind of profit he would make from this first load, after which he would come back and open a supply store and stock it with the merchandise he'd ordered shipped out of New York City. Once he'd established the store, probably more than one, he would hire men to take more supplies into the camps, grubstake even more prospectors, establish loans, probably open his own bank.

No man had ever been more excited than Edward about his future, his accomplishments, the pride he felt in the decision he had made, which he was confident now had been totally right.

"There isn't one place east of the Sierras that offers more opportunity than San Francisco," he had stated more than once. "I wish my father could see this. By the time I am through, his own wealth will seem paltry next to mine!"

So, Maggie thought, as she sat with the wagons on a little knoll above most of the town's madness, *I have put up with all of this so that Edward can be richer than his father.* That had not quite been the way she had looked at it when she had agreed to come here with her husband to help him realize his dream. She had truly felt sorry for the way he'd been treated, truly understood why he would want to come here and strike out on his own. But it seemed that "gold fever" had hit even Edward, in a strange sort of way. Just to succeed in building his own little empire out here and to share his dream with her no longer seemed to be what was most important to him. Now it seemed money itself was the most important goal—not just to realize a comfortable living all on his own, but to outdo his father in every way, especially in wealth. Already he had begun writing letters home, sending them off on any ship heading back to the States. Maggie had also written a letter, telling her mother and sisters of their safe arrival, trying to explain what San Francisco was like, and promising to send copies of her journal as soon as she had time to copy it all down.

She wondered if the letters would ever really arrive, if her mother would ever know she had made it to California. The memory of the trip west would remain vivid in her mind the rest of her life, more vivid because of Rafe Morrisey. Where was he now? Was he thinking about her? Would he really come and see her next year? That seemed like such a long, long time away, and pain gripped her heart every time she thought of it.

"Maggie!"

She looked up to see Edward coming, and she smiled for him. He rode a horse, and behind him two supply wagons followed, driven by men with sense enough to work regular jobs rather than chase a dream.

Edward urged his horse into a faster gait and came closer, dismounting and lifting her down from the wagon gate. "I think I have everything I need for a trip into the camps," he told her, grinning. "By the time I return, Maggie-girl, I'll have just as much money in my pockets as if I had discovered gold myself!"

Maggie glanced at the drivers, who were being greeted by Wade. One of them looked back at her and looked her over as though she were a cold beer he was getting ready to drink down. There was something about him she immediately did not like. She looked back at Edward. "I don't like the thought of you going into those camps, Edward. You heard what Wade has told us about what it's like. You're walking into a den of lawless men who would rather have their supplies free, and you know what that means, let alone the fact that you will be taking a lot of money along."

"Don't you worry about me. I've hired good men for protection, and I am paying them well. I'll be all right, Maggie. And listen! I have been talking to a banker by the name of Ben Skeller. He and his wife have a lovely home in a place some are calling Nob Hill, up where we've seen some big houses being built. He has agreed that while I am gone you can stay with them. You will be much safer there. I have hired a contractor to begin building my first supply store, right in the center of town, so when I return, my love, I will finish the store and stay here for a while, and I will build you a beautiful home! That is a promise. It will be the fanciest home on Nob Hill, and you can hire as many servants as you think you need! In the mining camps I will establish sub-stores, find good, honest men to run them, men to take even more supplies into the camps. It's amazing, Maggie, the money that can be made here! I've never seen anything like it!"

He talked so fast that Maggie had trouble absorbing everything he was telling her. She would be staying with perfect strangers while he was gone! He had made so many plans already, without even speaking to her about them.

"Edward, I don't even know these people—what is their name?"

"I told you. Ben Skeller. His wife's name is Mary. We're going up to visit them this evening."

"Edward!" Maggie put a hand to her hair. "Have you taken a good look at me lately? I'd be going up there looking like some common, poor settler woman! I have no way of properly fixing my hair, my face—and all my dresses are wrinkled ruins! I refuse to go to the hideous public bathhouses they have here, and—"

"Don't worry about it. I have explained the whole situation to the Skellers. Believe me, Love, they understand. They came here by ship, but it was just as hellish a trip. Ben Skeller told me his wife would be more than happy to provide you with a nice room all your own, a private hot bath, and you can borrow her personal maid until you find one of your own. Out here they use mostly Orientals for such services. I know they're a strange lot, but they're quite good at what they do, quite fastidious, I am told."

"Edward, please slow down! I am having trouble absorbing all of this."

He only laughed. "It's wonderful, Maggie. I have never been this happy in my entire life, and so much of it is due to your patience and friendship!" He kissed her cheek.

Friendship? Since arriving here they still had not made love. Although Maggie was basically too weary to care, a little part of her was disappointed that Edward seemed not at all interested in the one thing most men would be wanting after six months of abstinence.

"Edward." She took him aside where no one could hear, and she put her arms around his neck. "Edward, I need a day or so to get used to all these plans you have made. You forget that you haven't talked to me about any of this. I knew you would go into the mining camps, but I didn't know you would go so soon and leave me with strangers."

He put his arms around her waist. "Maggie, Love, I'm sorry. I am just so excited. This is all so much better than I had imagined! I promise you, as God is my witness, I will build you the grandest home on Nob Hill when I return, and by then you will have made friends with the wealthier, more refined women of San Francisco and will have settled in just fine. In no time at all you will be living the life you were meant to live."

"Edward, stop worrying about how I will live. I have been living a much different life for six months, and I am just fine. It's *us* I care about. That whole trip was so grueling, and we hardly ever had a chance to relax together, to just *be* together. And since finally arriving in California, I've hardly seen you at all! Can't you stay for a week or so before going into the camps? I feel like we are strangers."

He frowned, kissing her cheek. "I'm sorry, Maggie. It's just that it is important for me to get on this right away. I've waited and dreamed for six months, and now I am finally here. Mr. Skeller will watch for the ship that is bringing my supplies from New York, and he'll see that my things are warehoused until I get back. It's all set, Maggie." He gave her a brief hug. "We'll be back to normal in no time."

Maggie rested her head on his shoulder. "Edward, can't we at least get a hotel room, just for tonight? I'm sure that the excuses for hotels here are all full, but you could pay someone to let us have their room—"

"Maggie," he interrupted, pulling her away. "Love, if we get a room alone . . . well, you know."

"I *do* know! It's what I *want,* Edward. It's been so long since we made love. I want to be with my husband the way every wife should want to be with her husband. Edward, don't *you* want it?"

Edward reddened. "Maggie! You brazen woman, you!"

She smiled, but also blushed. "You know what I mean, Edward. I love you. We've been apart that way for much too long. We had a good reason. Heaven forbid that I should ever have gotten pregnant on that trip. But we are here now, and you'll only be gone a few weeks. Even if I got pregnant—"

"No, Maggie. I still think that risk is a bad idea. What if . . . what if there were complications? That happens sometimes with a first baby, I'm told. I would never forgive myself if something happened while I was gone."

"But you won't be gone that long, and I am perfectly healthy, probably healthier and stronger now than when we left. And the timing is right. I mean, my mother taught me—"

"No, Maggie. We . . . we can't. Not yet." He grasped her arms, then leaned forward and kissed her cheek. "You understand, don't you? I just don't want to leave you with that on my mind. It's just better that way. There will be time for all of that when I return."

For all of that? He made it sound as though it was some kind of chore for him. The pain of disappointment ran deep. Never had she needed her husband more than now, yet he was more distant than ever. It would be so much easier to accept his denial if he at least acted as though it was difficult for him, but she saw not one spark of desire in his eyes, and it had never been more clear than now that he truly saw her as just a good friend. What was worse was that he did not even seem to need her in the way he had needed her before. Perhaps it was because he was truly away from his father's hold now, truly independent. His father was not standing over him and constantly belittling him.

She wanted to cry over the sudden, intense loneliness and homesickness she felt . . . combined with a terrible need to see Rafe, talk to him, feel his strong, reassuring arms around her. She could not help the tears that came to her eyes.

"Maggie! My goodness, Love, I didn't mean to hurt your feelings. You know I love you, Maggie." He pulled her close. "You're the best friend a man ever had. You're my Maggie."

She choked in a sob. "I miss you, Edward. I need you."

"And you shall have me, all of me, as soon as I return. I promise."

He gave her a solid squeeze, and Maggie felt as though she was being hugged by a brother rather than a husband. She pulled away. "Please be careful, Edward. This is a dangerous place full of dangerous men."

"I am perfectly aware of that, Dear. I told you, I've hired good, dependable men. The supply wagons are packed and ready to go. We will meet the Skellers tonight and you will live in total comfort while I am gone, with a woman of your own class to talk to."

Edward gave her a peck on the cheek and a smile, then left her to give instructions to the men he had hired. Maggie wanted, needed, to sob openly, but she stifled the need, not wanting to make a fool of herself in front of these strangers. The effort made her feel sick, made her head ache. What hurt the most was realizing that she would never know the comfort, the satisfaction, the fulfillment as a woman in Edward's arms that she had felt with Rafe Morrisey. Things would be like this for the rest of her life, a marriage of friendship, not one of desire.

She straightened, taking a deep breath to calm herself. The only way to bear this was to believe that things *would* be better when Edward returned.

Chapter Twenty-Eight

"Do come in, Dear!"

Mary Skeller stepped aside to allow Maggie and Edward entrance.

"Forgive my appearance, Mrs. Skeller," Maggie said. "This was the best I could do." She had pulled her hair back into a bun and applied cream to her sunburned face. She wore a soft blue day dress brought from home, one she had left packed during the trip. "There was no way to press my dress, and—"

"Oh, nonsense," Mary Skeller interrupted. "Do you think I don't remember what it was like getting to this place? You will take a room here and my personal maid will help you out. You will be back to your old self in no time."

The woman put an arm around Maggie and led her toward the parlor while Ben Skeller, a tall, robust man, came out from his library to greet them. He stopped and introduced himself to Maggie, taking her hand and squeezing it. She felt a little uncomfortable with the way he looked her over, but the man seemed friendly and gentlemanly, and he quickly turned away to greet Edward with a vigorous handshake.

"Glad to help! Glad to help!" he told Edward when Edward thanked him for offering his home to Maggie.

"When they smell gold, there is no stopping them, is there?" Mary told Maggie. She led her into the parlor.

"No, there isn't." Maggie walked up to the brick fireplace. A cool mist had moved into town in late afternoon, leaving a chill in the air. It felt good to stand in front of the fire. "You have a lovely home, Mrs. Skeller."

"Oh, please call me Mary, and this home is comfortable, but not nearly as nice as what we had back in New York. This place is just temporary. We plan to build a much bigger home over the next year or two. There is so much building going on, and it is difficult to find the kind of builders we need, let alone how long it will take to have marble shipped from Italy and special wood from South America." Mary sat down near the fire. "From what Edward told my husband, the two of you apparently come from quite wealthy families yourselves."

"Yes," Maggie answered, thinking how unimportant that seemed to her now. She faced Mary and sat down in a rocker across from her. "I feel as if that life was just a dream. At the moment it seems so unreal."

"I know what you mean. There are many of us in your situation, Maggie. May I call you Maggie?"

"Of course." Maggie studied the woman as she spoke. She was older, probably old enough to be her mother. Mary was stout but not fat, her brown eyes set narrowly in her otherwise round face. The woman seemed friendly enough, kind and willing to help, but as Maggie watched her thin lips move as she babbled on about San Francisco and what it was like just one year ago when they arrived, Maggie hardly heard the words. She could only wonder what she was doing here, wonder what had happened to the Maggie she'd been when she left Pittsburgh. Even Edward was different. They had arrived here almost as strangers, and now they *lived* among strangers. Tomorrow she would be completely alone in this wild, untamed city, and sometimes she wanted to scream.

". . . are other women of our class here, so we try to socialize as much as we can. Perhaps you would like to come with me tomorrow to Jean Reynolds's home.'' Mary waited for an answer. ''Maggie?''

Maggie looked at her, somewhat startled. ''What? Oh! I'm so sorry, Mary. I just have so much on my mind.''

''I know, Dear. I'm sorry I am carrying on this way. You know, when one is away from their own kind for so long, it is so refreshing to be able to talk with another woman who understands.''

Maggie nodded, not really agreeing wholeheartedly. She didn't really feel she was any different from any other woman who arrived here. And after having an affair on the way, maybe she wasn't even any better than the whores. But then, she had not allowed Rafe to make love to her just so they could both satisfy a need. She had allowed it because she truly loved him with all her heart and soul, and she had to believe it was the same for Rafe, or she could never forgive herself. She only wished she could feel the same way about Edward, or that he at least felt the same way about her. If only he loved her in the way Rafe had, she could bear this marriage. She could return his love.

''Yes, it is nice to share the company of a woman who understands,'' she told Mary, feeling obligated to agree. The woman was only trying to be friendly, and, after all, she would be living under the same roof with her for several weeks. ''It is so kind of you to open your home to me this way, especially when you hardly know us.''

''Oh, Ben says your husband presented fine credentials, a bank certificate worth several thousand dollars, which he deposited in my husband's bank, along with some valuable jewelry he wants Ben to keep for him. And he had papers signed by several prominent businessmen in Pennsylvania, some with whom Ben was familiar.''

Maggie frowned. ''I didn't even know he had brought such letters.''

''Oh, well, I suppose he didn't want to bother you with such things. It's one of those men things, you know. I suppose he thought he should be prepared for a situation like this, knowing he would not be able to build you a home immediately, and not knowing, of course, what you would find when you arrived. Heaven knows there is not a hotel in this city yet that a truly decent person would want to stay in. Here you will be away from the maddening crowd, so to speak, and from the thugs and rapists."

"Rapists!" Maggie's eyes widened in disgust.

"Oh, Dear, don't worry. This house is well guarded. You must realize the things that go on when you have so many thousands of men in one place with no law. But the city council is working on bringing some order to all of this. Ben is part of that council. Don't you worry. In no time at all San Francisco will be just as refined and orderly as any city back east. We will see to it. Come now. I have asked my cook to prepare a grand meal for you. It has probably been many months since you sat at a table and ate off of china. We do have much to talk about, sharing memories of home and all. Our home was upstate New York. In fact, it still is. Our sons are managing everything there for us, Ben's businesses, our home and all. We do intend to go back one day, after Ben has established himself here. Wherever there is opportunity, that is where you will find my Ben. It seems your Edward is the same, and he is still young. He is lucky that way. What a future he has ahead of him!"

Mary's taffeta skirts rustled as she rose and took Maggie's hand, and Maggie struggled to keep up with the woman's rapid ramblings about San Francisco and her family. She followed Mary into a rather small but grandly decorated dining room, where a large table was beautifully set with fine china.

"Do get Ben and Edward, will you, Serena?"

"Sí, Señorita." The pretty young Spanish woman to whom Mary had spoken hurried out, wiping her hands on her apron as she went.

"Most of our help is Spanish. Two years ago they still thought they owned California, you know, but it belongs to us Americans now. We have to be careful. We can't trust all of them yet. There are also a lot of Chinese here. Strange people, indeed, but actually they are quite good workers. A Chinese man does my laundry and mending, and he is quite dependable.'' Mary offered Maggie a chair. ''Oh, it will be so nice to have company. My husband is gone so much, and you will find it will be the same for your Edward. We women have to stick together or go insane. Look at this china, dear.'' She held up a beautiful dinner plate, a white background with a design of many colors that Maggie thought quite beautiful, a very unusual pattern she had never seen before.

''It's lovely.''

''Oh, I just so love it! It was made in China.'' Mary laughed lightly, and Maggie detected a nervousness in the laugh. ''China made in China! Isn't that funny?'' She laughed harder, and Maggie forced a smile, still befuddled by too many things happening too fast. When she met Mary's eyes, she thought she detected tears, but the woman acted so happy and gay she could hardly believe that was what she saw. Just then Edward and Ben entered the room, both men all smiles.

''What do you think, Maggie?'' Edward asked. ''Isn't this a pleasant home? And it's only temporary, for the Skellers *and* for you. They plan to build a much finer home higher up on the hill, and that is where I, too, plan to build. Ben said he would pick out a good spot and claim it for us. He will keep the bulk of what is left of our money in his bank until I return, and I guarantee I will return with much, much more. I promise to stay then, Darling, and not leave you alone again for a while.'' He leaned down and kissed her cheek before sitting down beside her. ''I have to go this time because I need to see for myself, Maggie, what items sell the best, what is needed, what the best deals are, things like that. I am so happy you understand.''

Everyone seemed to be talking but Maggie herself, and she didn't know quite what to say. She only sat and listened as the conversation continued while dinner was served by Serena.

''Isn't she lovely?'' Ben asked, indicating their waitress. ''I bought up Serena's father's plantation, promised he could keep running it and keep half the profits.'' He looked at Serena as she set a bowl of vegetables on the table beside him. ''Didn't I, Serena?''

Maggie was astounded to see the man pat Serena's bottom

as he made the statement. She did not miss the hint of disgust in the woman's eyes as she answered calmly. "*Si, Señor.*" It seemed to Maggie that the woman was practically gritting her teeth. She glanced at Mary, who simply looked at her plate and said nothing, her cheeks showing a hint of crimson.

"These Mexicans didn't much like us coming out here at first, but they've learned who has the power," Ben told them. "Our coming here will improve their lot to much better than the way they lived before."

Serena cast him a look of contempt and walked back into the kitchen. Maggie had not forgotten the way Ben had looked at her when she first arrived, and, friendly or not, she did not trust him. They moved through the mechanics of eating, and Ben carried on about a transcontinental railroad, an idea Maggie thought impossible.

"Oh, the government is already thinking along those lines, Mrs. McCahan, er . . . Maggie. Is Maggie all right?"

"Yes."

"Well, there is talk of it in Congress. Heaven knows we need a better way to get back and forth than by drowning off the Cape or dying in the sweltering heat of the desert or the Plains. The best answer would be a railroad that connects California to the East. I promised Mary she could go back one day, and by God I'll keep that promise."

"I promised Maggie the same thing," Edward told him. "But I must admit, I cannot imagine how they would bring a railroad over those mountains."

"Tunnels, my boy, tunnels! You wait and see. They will do it. All we have to do is get a president interested. Oh, I'm not saying it will happen overnight. It will take years, but it will happen."

Maggie was sure the man was talking through his hat. He seemed to carry on as nervously and rapidly as his wife, both of them apparently eager to please and to make an impression. The conversation turned to the trip west, what it was like by land, and Mary kept shaking her head in wonder that they had survived.

"We had an excellent guide," Edward told them. "Rafe

Morrisey was his name. I don't know where he went after we got here, but he was a good man. He even saved both our lives—kept Maggie from drowning in a river crossing, and saved me from falling into a canyon."

"My goodness!" Mary daintily wiped at her mouth with a cloth napkin. "Well, we have certainly seen a lot of men like that, mountain men, trappers, scouts, all of them a strange lot, loners; most of them never do settle."

Ben chuckled. "Unless it's in a brothel for a night."

"Ben!" Mary chastised him for such talk, and Maggie assured them it was all right.

The evening moved too swiftly. Edward brought Maggie's belongings upstairs to an extra bedroom, setting them on the floor. "Well, Dear, what do you think? They are nice people, aren't they?"

Maggie closed the door. "I am not fond of Ben Skeller, but I do like his wife, except that she babbles on like a squawking chicken."

Edward laughed. "Ben is a little overbearing, but he's a good man. He has been a big help already. It's good there are already people like him here who can help us. And look, a real bed!" He patted a four-poster that sat under a window and was covered with a blue satin quilt. "This should feel wonderful tonight, especially after sleeping on a feather mattress in the floor of a wagon for six months. I am just glad—"

"Edward! Can't you please stay a few more days?"

He came closer, grasping her arms. "You know that I can't, Love. I promise to return just as quickly as possible. In the meantime, take advantage of this. You can relax, bathe, have a personal maid, eat well, learn about the city, meet some of the other wealthier women socially, live almost as grandly as you lived back home. And I promise you will live more grandly than that, eventually. Right now I have men and wagons waiting, and it is important I learn all the ins and outs of this business quickly so that I can be competitive. It really won't be so long, Dear."

"Edward, we really hardly know these people. How can you leave your wife with near strangers?"

He sighed deeply, moving his arms around her again. "Maggie, all the way here you have been so brave and strong and helpful. Please don't start behaving this way. You've seen how nice Mary Skeller is, what a lovely home they have. And I have seen Mr. Skeller's bank and businesses. The bank is a two story building with a vault that is well guarded. He owns two warehouses and a shipping line. He has expanded the shipping line to include trade between California and China. These people are *our* kind of people, Maggie, wealthy, mannered people who understand where we come from. I thought you would be happy with all of this. You've been so supportive this whole trip. You should be overjoyed that we made it here relatively unscathed and that things are going so well. At last the danger is over, and I can begin doing what I came here to do, while you are able to return to a life of comfort and luxury." He kissed her cheek. "You'll feel much better when our ship arrives with more of our personal possessions and all the things I ordered to start building, as well as supplies to open up some stores. Everything will be better when I am here full-time and we have our own home."

They were alone in the room, yet still Edward showed no sign of needing her sexually, or even wanting her that way. She felt like a fool asking him why. It would make her feel like a harlot to ask him again if they could make love. She wanted him to stay here with her tonight, sleep with her; but if he did not offer, she would not bring more embarrassment upon herself by asking. How silly, she thought, that she should be embarrassed to ask her own husband to stay with her tonight. "Do you still love me, Edward?"

He frowned, touching her hair. "Maggie! Such a foolish question! You're my Maggie, my friend. I *married* you." He closed his eyes. "I'm so sorry, Maggie. You know how much I need you, how much I love you. I just . . . I don't want to take any risks, not now that we have come this far. I promise with all my heart that we will get back to a normal life when I return. You're just . . . you're having trouble adjusting to all of this. I can understand that. I'm sure Mary can help you there.

She's been through it. So have a lot of her friends. Once you meet them all, you'll feel much better.''

A tear slipped down her cheek, and Maggie nodded. ''Maybe I will. Please be careful, Edward. You're all I have now.''

He smiled. ''And you're all *I* have.'' He grasped her close. ''I have to go, Love, before I *do* decide to stay. I am staying with the men tonight so we can leave first light. I've hired a good crew, some who have already been to the gold camps. We'll be fine, and I'll come back just as soon as I can.''

Maggie pulled away. ''Be careful of the one big one, the one with the red beard and a funny scar over his left eye. I only saw him for a minute, but there was something in his eyes . . .''

''Brady? That's all they call him. No last name, or maybe that *is* his last name. Heavens, Maggie, you should be glad he'll be along. Two of the men I hired are his friends, and they tell me nobody is meaner or more dependable when it comes to fighting of any kind, gun, knife, whatever. I'm paying him well to guard my supplies, my money, and me. No one is going to mess with me as long as Brady is around, so rest easy, Love.''

She wiped at tears. ''Well, I don't like his looks, and I don't trust someone who goes by one name. Surely you realize that half the men who come out here are probably running from the law someplace else. I think you are wrong to trust men you have only known two or three days, including Ben Skeller.'' She turned away. ''I love you, Edward, in ways you will never know. And I have given up more than you know to be here with you. I just wish you wouldn't leave right away like this.''

Edward touched her shoulder. ''I know it's been hard for you, Maggie.'' He sighed. ''Maggie, my Maggie. I do love you so. Give me a kiss, Love.''

Maggie turned, and he kissed her mouth, his lips cool and pressed tight.

''We've been through so much over the years, haven't we?''

She studied his eyes. She knew very well that he loved her. Yet something was missing. Perhaps she would never understand what it was. ''Yes, we have, Edward.''

He wiped at her tears. ''Good-bye, Maggie.''

''Good-bye, Edward. God be with you. I hope . . . I hope all your dreams come true.''

He grinned confidently. ''They will. And so will yours.'' He squeezed her arms, then turned and left. Maggie walked to a window to look out at the sprawling tent and wooden city of San Francisco, wondering if she could ever truly call this place home.

Chapter Twenty-Nine

Five weeks have passed, Maggie wrote, *with no word from Edward. Ben Skeller tells me that is not such a long time at all. There are hundreds of camps in the mountains and along the streams. Still, it seems to me that it would not take long for Edward to sell what he took there. I am worried, but everyone tells me I should not be, that it is just the newness of this place that has me edgy.*

Perhaps they were right. But Maggie could not shake the ominous cloud that hung over her head, nor could she get the picture of the big man with the red beard out of her mind. She stayed occupied by joining Mary and other women of "their kind," as Mary put it, in working to raise money for more churches and better schools. Along with the prospectors that continued to pour into San Francisco came teachers and ministers, some who also were there to look for gold, others truly dedicated to serving those who came.

It was either keep busy or go crazy. There was no "in between." Maggie's stay with the Skellers was reasonably pleasant, although sometimes Mary's jabbering made her nervous. She was not terribly fond of Ben Skeller, pleasant and jovial as he was. Something about him made her uncomfortable, although he said and did nothing to give her reason for her feelings. It was just the way he looked at her sometimes that bothered her. Still, this was a pleasant home, and already Ben had a bigger home under construction. It did feel good to be in a room built on solid ground, rather than one that rocked and swayed on wheels.

Memories of the loss and heartache of our journey west still plague me, she added, *but as I become more settled here they are becoming more bearable. Now I can bring myself to write down the fact that we also lost our Gretta along the way. It has taken me until now to be able to write about it, I miss her so.* She blinked back tears as she finished by saying Gretta had died from a fall. How could she write the truth? To write the truth would be a dishonor to Gretta's memory. And, after all, hadn't she had her own affair on that journey? Something about her life felt so "unfinished" now. It would have helped so much if Edward had stayed.

She put down her pen and studied the flowered wallpaper in her bedroom. This was a small but lovely home, each room decorated in a different color, with plants in expensive vases that sat on expensive, imported tables. She was just beginning to more vividly remember what life had been like back in Pennsylvania, although here there still were no brick streets or large, brick buildings, still few of the conveniences of home.

She rose from the handsome cherrywood desk at which she had been writing, and walked around the mahogany four-poster bed to a window, parting the lace curtains to look across the hills where more homes were under construction. There seemed to be activity everywhere, from the docks far in the distance to the nearby pounding and sawing. One thing she did like about California was the near-constant sunshine, the lovely warmth during a time when back home the weather would be gray and cold and wet. She could enjoy these beautiful new surroundings, if only she were happy and fulfilled within.

Somewhere out there were two men that she loved, and for the moment she had no idea where either one was, or if they were safe. She felt she was hanging between two worlds, one woman split apart, part of her belonging in this world of wealth with a "proper" husband, whether she loved him or not; part of her actually missing the more common life she had led on the trail west, and the rugged, wild man who had led her to this place. She realized now how good it had felt to contribute to the aid of others, to help care for oxen and mules, do her own cooking, help gather buffalo chips and wood for fires, to know people like Hazel Schultz and Lucille Krueger. She wondered how little Minnie Maddox was doing, wondered if others would find and help preserve all the graves they had left behind . . . children, mothers, fathers, friends, lovers. She thought about that poor mule, Beaner, and her faithful young mistress, Katie, both lying together somewhere in a canyon in the Sierras.

The tears came then. She missed them all. And she actually missed that life. She looked down at her precious trunk, which now sat under the window. She sat down in front of it, touching the faded flowers painted on the lid. This trunk had made it all the way across this land with her, over prairie and plain, mountain and desert, across many rivers, through a tornado, cholera, snakebites, mosquitoes and Indians. Before that this poor old trunk had come all the way across an ocean, from France. If only it could speak.

She sniffled and wiped at tears as she opened it, breathing deeply of the lilac smell inside that came from dried lilacs from home, which had been wrapped in linen handkerchiefs and placed inside for freshness. The smell reminded her of home and her precious mother and sisters, whom she would never see again. She studied some of the contents—expensive jewelry, a bible her mother had given her, an imported mink coat, two of her most expensive ball gowns, a pearl necklace, satin shoes, her dolls, a music box. . . . Her wedding dress was gone, and heaven only knew where it was by now, probably cut into a thousand pieces.

She closed the trunk, and as she did so it seemed to represent her two lives. The things inside of the trunk represented the Maggie who once existed in Pennsylvania. The trunk itself represented the strong, durable Maggie who had come west, the Maggie she never dreamed she could be before she left home. The old Maggie loved Edward McCahan. The new Maggie loved Rafe Morrisey.

She quickly wiped her eyes when she heard voices just outside below the window, a group of women all jabbering at once. She rose and looked out to see that some of the women Mary had called together for coffee and rolls this morning had arrived. There they were, dressed in their finest day dresses and hats, the wives of wealthy men who had come here to take advantage of the prospectors' hard work and become even wealthier. Her own husband was part of the plan, and she supposed that made her a part of it, too.

The women were at the door now, and Mary was greeting them. Two more were arriving in a buggy. Maggie hurried to a mirror to fix her face, and she studied her own very proper day dress. It was time to go downstairs and help Mary "entertain." She liked most of these women well enough, and all had been friendly and helpful; but she felt so different now, as though she just simply did not belong with such women any longer. She wondered if she would spend the rest of her life with this constant wrestling in her soul making her so undecided. The women were here to discuss another church and to meet the wife of a Presbyterian minister.

She would rather be alone this morning, but Mary seemed to enjoy being surrounded by company, and Maggie had no choice but to oblige her. She took a deep breath, enjoying a last few minutes alone in her room. She walked back to the window, wanting to put off the inevitable just a few more seconds. Two more women were arriving. On a distant hill she could see yet another wagon train heading into town. She could just imagine how relieved they must feel. Surely they had had a terrible time in the mountains, where just a few days ago those here in the bay area could see snow had begun to fall, as it was visible even at this distance.

Ahead of the train rode a man—in buckskins—she could tell even from her window. The sight brought pain to her heart. Oh, how she missed Rafe! Would she ever really get to see him again? Their affair seemed like just a distant dream now, and sometimes she wondered if any of it had been real.

"Maggie?"

Mary was knocking at her door.

"Most of the women are here, Dear. Please do come and join us."

Maggie turned away from the window. Today she would be the proper, wealthy Maggie . . . Edward's Maggie.

"What do you think, Jack? Did I do the right thing?"

Rafe and Jack lay in the Nevada desert, studying a sky brilliant with stars. Wolf Hunter had gone off to be alone, something he often did at night. *Not the sociable sort,* Jack had commented more than once.

The night was dead quiet, with only the occasional *yip* of a coyote. Most emigrants headed for the goldfields had already gone through here, and instead of more wagon trains Rafe and Jack now came across only graves and discarded furnishings, broken down wagons, and animal carcasses.

Jack took a moment to answer Rafe's question. "Well now, my friend," he finally said, "I don't generally stick my nose into other men's affairs, but when it comes to havin' a spark for a married woman, my advice would be to leave it alone. I think you did the right thing by leavin'."

Rafe sighed, surprised he had told Jack about Maggie. The only thing he had not told the man was what he had seen between young David and Edward McCahan, before David drowned. Now he was plagued by doubt, wondering if he'd been wrong in not telling Maggie, wrong in leaving her behind. Still, it was what *she* had insisted must be done. Perhaps if she knew the truth—

"I hope I did," he answered Jack. "I did promise her I would come back next fall and see how she was doing."

"Well, there you go. That's good enough, I'd say, considerin' her situation. You might find her settled and happy, and then you'll feel better about the whole thing."

"She'll never be truly happy with Edward."

Jack stretched his legs and scratched at his beard. "Now, how do you know that? You figure after havin' a big, handsome, wild man like you that nobody else can satisfy her?" Jack chuckled, and Rafe rolled his eyes.

"Damn it, Jack, this is serious."

Jack turned on his side and rested his head on his hand. "Hell, I know that. You're hurtin'. I ain't never seen you hurt this way except when I first met you, after your wife was killed and you was in the war. Hell, Rafe, the woman is *married!* And it was her choice that you go away and let her *be* married. You said yourself she grew up with the man, and they was best friends. Why do you think they could never be happy together?"

"Because she never would have turned to me if she was really happy. And because . . . because . . . I saw something when we were traveling with the wagon train."

Jack frowned. "*Saw* something? What the hell does that mean? Did you see the man abusin' her or somethin'?"

"No." Rafe rubbed at his eyes. 'I saw him with . . . David, that young kid they brought along as a servant, the one who drowned."

"What the hell do you mean, you saw him with David?"

"Shit!" Rafe muttered. He sat up and faced Jack. "You know. I . . . *saw* them . . . *together* . . . out in the darkness beyond the campfire." He sighed deeply. "Damn it, Jack, don't make me describe what I saw. It turns my stomach."

Jack slowly sat up. "You mean—"

"Now do you understand why I know she'll never be truly happy and fulfilled with the man?"

Jack shook his head. "Holy Moses," he muttered. "What a waste of a beautiful, strong woman."

"Yeah." Rafe leaned forward. "I can't get the picture out of my head. I thought about telling her several times, but I just couldn't bring myself to do it. I felt it was something she had to find out for herself. When I thought about how devastated she would be, I didn't want to be the one to do that to her. And maybe . . . maybe what I saw was just . . . I don't know. Hell, people do all kinds of strange things on a trip like this, their lives are so changed." He stood up, walking out of the light of the fire. He ached for Maggie, could not stop thinking about her. "I can't go a whole year wondering if she's all right. I should have stayed around. She wouldn't have had to know it."

"Rafe, by now she's gettin' settled in. Her husband has probably opened his supply stores and all them supplies he ordered from back east has arrived, and the Missus is gettin' back into her old life, dressin' fancy, entertainin' San Francisco's wealthy, overseein' the buildin' of some fancy new mansion for herself. Give her another year and she'll forget all about you. Women are fickle that way. If her husband don't satisfy her, she'll turn to some other fancy man, somebody who can give her the best of everything, like she's used to."

Rafe thought about her, the look on her face the day they had said good-bye. "Not Maggie," he told Jack. "She's not like that. She's all quality and honor and loyalty. She's a damn good woman. Edward doesn't appreciate what he has."

"Well, that's for them to work out. Besides, there ain't no way you can get back over them mountains again. Winter's settin' in good up there, so unless you plan to die for the woman you love, you'd better just keep goin' east with me and go back next fall, like you told her you'd do. Showin' up now might be too soon for her."

"Maybe. But something is bothering me. Something still isn't quite right, and it's more than what I told you about Edward. I just feel like I have to go back."

"You can't get through them mountains, Rafe."

Rafe came back and sat down again, reaching into a canvas bag nearby and taking out a flask of whiskey. He uncorked it and drank some down. "A man alone with just his horse and a pack horse could still do it."

"You know better."

Rafe took another swallow of whiskey. "I only know that I love Maggie McCahan, and if she needs me, I intend to be there for her."

Chapter Thirty

Maggie finished fixing her hair, preparing to go to Jean Reynolds' home and help care for her overnight. Jean, one of the older women in Mary's circle of friends, had become very ill, and no one quite knew what the problem was, except that she was losing weight very fast and had grown so weak and was in so much pain that she had taken to her bed. All the women in what they now called The Ladies' Guild were taking turns helping to care for her, since she had no children to look after her. Today had been Mary's turn, and this evening Ben was there with her, the men all trying to soothe Jean's husband, who was an engineer for a company that supplied steam engines that were used in gold mining operations. Gus Reynolds was beside himself with worry.

Maggie pushed a comb into the side of her hair. Ben was to come for her later. She had already eaten and had only to put on her shoes. She decided she would wait and do that when Ben arrived. Satisfied with her green striped day dress and the way the combs were fixed in her hair, she walked over to her desk to make another journal entry, which would include the fact that much of the time she did her own hair now and was getting quite good at it. She did not like to have to use Mary's personal maid all the time, as the poor woman had enough to do, and she still had not hired a maid of her own. She had grown so accustomed to doing for herself on the way west that she discovered she rather enjoyed it and was having trouble growing used to someone doing everything for her again.

She sat down at her desk and had begun writing when she heard the door close downstairs. She frowned at the sound of Ben Skeller's voice. He had come back earlier than she thought he would. She could not make out what he was saying, but she supposed he was talking to Serena, advising her of Jean's condition. In the evening Serena would be the only servant left. She lived in a little room at the back of the house. The cook had gone home after serving Maggie earlier. She did not feel well, and Maggie was sure Ben would eat at the Reynolds home with Gus, so she had let her go.

She got up from her desk and walked to her dressing table, sitting down in the padded, wrought iron chair to pull on her high-button shoes. While she pulled the tab around each tiny button, she could not stop her thoughts turning back to worrying over Edward. He had been gone three months. Ben continued to reassure her that such a length of time was not unusual for men who went into the gold camps, but she no longer believed him. Edward would not leave her for so long without at least sending someone back with word about how he was doing and when he would be home. She was sure he had not planned to be gone this long. She had insisted to Ben that something had to be wrong, had begged him to send men out looking for Edward, but he had insisted it would be a waste of time and money, that Edward would show up any day now.

Maggie wished she could be as confident. This simply was not like Edward, and he had gone into those camps with a lot of supplies and a lot of money. She still could not get rid of the image of the man called Brady. Old Wade Grisham had gone along with Edward, but he was so decrepit that he would be of no use if the younger men decided to take what Edward had for themselves. She had at least finally convinced Ben just this morning to hire someone to search the camps for Edward, and was anxious to know if he had done so.

She still had one shoe to go when she heard Ben's heavy footsteps on the stairs. She pulled on the second shoe, hurriedly beginning to button it, but could not finish before she heard the expected knock at her door.

"Maggie? It's me, Ben."

"Yes. Just a minute. I only need to finish buttoning one shoe. How is Jean?"

"That's what I need to talk to you about," he called through the door. "You don't need to finish with your shoe. Mary decided to stay the night and let you go over in the morning. Then you can stay tomorrow and tomorrow night instead of going back and forth so much."

Maggie frowned in irritation, since she had taken time to change and redo her hair. She sighed and rose, going to the door and opening it. "Are you sure that's all right? I'm all ready to go."

He reached out one hand and braced himself against the door post. "It's what Mary wanted to do. I hope you don't mind."

Maggie began to feel uncomfortable with him standing at her bedroom door. "No, not at all. How is Jean?"

He took just one step forward so that his big frame filled the doorway. He folded his arms casually and leaned against the doorjamb. "I'm afraid she's a little worse. Of course we don't have a wide choice of doctors out here yet, but the one we do have says it's some kind of cancer eating away at her. There is nothing that can be done about it, he says. It's a terrible way to die, and she's begun to have trouble recognizing people. He says that means it's in its last stages, so she doesn't have long. The only good thing is that it isn't something contagious."

"Oh, dear." Maggie turned away. "Poor Jean. How is Gus holding up?"

"I'm afraid he's keeping himself drunk most of the time. Stewart Hanes is with him right now."

Maggie turned back around, arms folded. A note of warning rushed through her when she realized Ben had stepped a little farther inside, but she told herself it was a foolish alarm. "Well, I am just sorry Edward isn't here. Did you find someone to go and look for him?"

Ben nodded. "I sent two men into the mountains today."

Maggie breathed a little easier. "Well, thank you." There was that look again, the one that made her uncomfortable. His blue eyes raked over her as though sizing her up as a purchase, and there was a flush to his face, made more pink by its contrast to his white hair.

"You, uh, must be getting pretty lonely by now."

"Of course I am. But it's been very nice having the company of Mary and the rest of the ladies."

"Well, that doesn't always cancel all the loneliness, does it?"

"What?"

"Oh, you know what I mean."

Now Maggie's wariness heightened. "No. I don't believe I do."

Ben chuckled. "Maggie, Maggie. You are so young, and so beautiful, and so alone. Personally, I would never go away and leave a young thing like you alone for so long."

Maggie frowned, every nerve end coming alive. "I think you should leave my room, Ben. Perhaps you have been drinking tonight with Gus Reynolds."

He grinned. "Perhaps I have. But not so much that I think I'm being foolish. I've watched you, Maggie. There is a strange longing in those big, blue eyes, and I know what it is you need."

Before she could make a move, Ben kicked the door shut. Maggie's eyes widened in surprise, and she backed away. "You are gravely mistaken, Ben Skeller! And I will remind you that Serena is in the house! If I scream—"

"Serena went to see her mother. I gave her the night off." He stepped closer. "Besides, Serena and I are good friends, you might say. We have an understanding. She lets me visit her little room at night after Mary is asleep, and I let her father stay on and run the ranch I bought out from under him after California became part of the United States. I let him keep enough of the profits so that his family doesn't starve."

Maggie felt sick at the realization of just how evil Ben Skeller was under all his fancy suits and gentlemanly manner. "You *blackmail* the poor woman into thinking her family will be ruined if she doesn't . . ."

"It's the truth, Maggie. And she knows she doesn't dare tell my wife about it, or about you and me, or her family will be ruined."

Maggie's anger and revulsion knew no bounds. "You are a sick man, Ben Skeller! And maybe Serena is afraid to go against you, but *I* am *not!* You can't ruin *me!* I have my own money, and if I have to move out of here tonight, which I intend to do, I will *survive!*"

"And I will remind you that I am in control of that money. Edward left it all to me to handle for him until he returns. Remember?"

Maggie decided it would be wise not to mention she had money of her own in her trunk. "Money in a bank that is in Edward's name. I can take our money *out* of that bank any time I wish!"

Ben frowned. "Oh, I don't think so. Edward told me to hold it until he returns, and he hasn't returned yet."

"He *will!*" It struck her then what the man might be telling her. "Unless you know something about why he *hasn't* returned! Did you really send someone looking for him, or is he already *dead!*"

Ben put up his hands. "Now, wait a minute. Edward went off all on his own. I had nothing to do with it. Yes. I promise you, I sent men looking for him. I just thought that as long as he's been gone so long . . . well, dear Maggie, maybe you would like some male company tonight. No one needs to know. We're all alone."

"*I* would know! How dare you come into my room and suggest such a thing! How dare you threaten me with Edward's money! And how dare you rape poor Serena on the pretense you will destroy her family if she doesn't let you!"

"Rape! Oh, such a strong word, Maggie. She lies quite still and allows me my pleasure, and I don't doubt she takes some pleasure in return. I don't call that rape."

"*I* do! And if you try to do the same with me, I will scream bloody murder, and all the neighbors will hear! They will all know exactly what you are, an extortionist and a rapist! Something told me the first time I met you that you could not be trusted, but I wanted to believe in Edward's judgment! And I wanted to believe you were a decent human being because you allowed me to live here and become friends with your wife. If only the poor woman knew what a bastard she is married to! Now you get out of this room!"

He clucked and shook his head. "Maggie, such language!"

"I learned to use worse on the trip out here, and I, by God, made it here in one piece! I don't intend to suffer something worse now that I'm here than I suffered on the trail west!"

"Worse? Dear Maggie, I am talking about making love to you, making you feel good, offering you strong arms to comfort you in the night, things you haven't had for a long time. I am quite infatuated with you, Maggie. I don't intend to hurt you."

"You would *have* to hurt me! I won't just lie still for you like Serena! Now get out!"

He stepped forward, and Maggie stepped back. She felt the knobs from a chest of drawers poke her in the back, and she remembered that on top of that chest of drawers was a rather heavy ceramic figurine. "Please leave," she warned again, "or you will have scratches and cuts you will have to explain to your wife!"

He only grinned. "Not if you can't move your arms, My Dear. I may be getting old, but I'm still damn strong, woman, and once you feel me inside of you, you'll find out I'm still plenty young in some ways. You will remember what it is you've been missing all this time. You will want to stay here longer, and you will gladly let me into your room at night. But if you would choose to try to tell my wife, I would only tell her that you tried to seduce me. Your reputation would be ruined, and all the ladies of the Guild would shun you. You would start your life here in a very bad light and have a devil of a time making new friends. You would never fit into San Francisco's high society in the way you otherwise would have. Your own husband would probably divorce you. Do you understand why you must let this happen, Dear? I promise to be gentle—"

He reached out to her as he spoke, and Maggie remembered one piece of advice Rafe had once given her. Never hesitate. It took only a second to turn and grab the figurine. She landed it butt end into Ben's forehead, splitting the skin. Immediately he stumbled backward, blood instantly flowing out and down over his eye. He put a hand to his head and stared at her incredulously.

"Now *you* understand why you must *not* let this happen!" she shouted. "Explain that cut on your *head* to high society! I don't give a damn *what* they think of *me,* but I'll make damn sure they know about *you!"* She made a dash around him before he could recover his senses, and she flew down the stairs and out the front door. She ran, away from Nob Hill, away from town, into the falling darkness, and the thick pines in the higher hills. She ran until she simply could not find her next breath, and she collapsed onto the pine needle floor of the woods, rolling to her knees. She bent over, sobbing, feeling more desperate and alone than she ever had since leaving Pennsylvania.

Such betrayal! She had not trusted Ben Skeller, but she never dreamed he was quite the sadistic thief and rapist that he was! Poor Mary! And how could she ever go back now! How would she explain moving out? Where would she go? Ben would probably arrange it so she couldn't even get her money out of the bank! Thank God she had money in her trunk! She could only pray Ben would not rummage through her things and find it.

If only Edward would come back! Where was he? Did Ben really know something about him? Was he already dead somewhere? "Oh, Edward, Edward!" she sobbed. "Where are you? Please, please come back!"

Deep in her heart there was someone else she knew could help her more right now. Rafe would know what to do. And nothing would feel more wonderful right now than to feel his arms around her. She always felt so safe and protected in those arms.

She cried until her head ached and she felt sick. By then it was dark. She refused to go back to that house knowing Ben was there alone. She would wait until morning, and that meant sleeping out here alone tonight.

She curled up on the pine needles, pulling the outer skirt of her dress up over her arms and shoulders. The nights had been very warm and lovely. After all the nights spent sleeping in a wagon or out of doors on the way here, she decided she could damn well survive one night alone in these hills. It was better than facing Ben Skeller.

She undid her hair and used it to rest her face against so that the needles would not poke her face, then settled in, totally exhausted from terror and terrible disappointment in Ben Skeller's betrayal of her trust; and from worry over Edward. She had no idea what she would do come morning.

Chapter Thirty-One

Maggie ached everywhere when she awoke, the night dampness seeming to settle into her bones, and the bed of pine needles not so comfortable after lying on it for hours. She sat up, taking a moment to gather her thoughts, shivering at the memory of Ben Skeller's attempted rape. It could be called nothing else. She grunted with pain as she got to her feet and brushed needles from her hair and dress, realizing what a mess she must be. Pine sap was stuck to one sleeve of her dress, and her hair was in a tumble. Her eyes must surely be swollen from so much crying the night before. But realizing she had survived out here all night made her feel stronger, more determined.

There would be no more crying! She would get through this, with or without Ben Skeller's help! She had survived that awful trip west, and she would survive this! One thing was certain. She would not spend another night in the Skeller house. The only problem would be how to explain it to Mary, although it was quite tempting to tell the woman the truth. She deserved to know. But Mary was such a jabbering innocent, the truth would probably destroy her sweet spirit.

Her first problem was to get back into the house without

being seen. Serena would be back this morning, and perhaps Ben had already gone to work. The bastard! She would damn well find a way to fix him for this! She shook her hair behind her shoulders, picked up the hem of her skirt, and marched back down the hill toward the Skeller home. Luckily it was early. If she walked around the back way, staying in the trees, she could get close enough to the Skeller house to make a mad dash to the back door without being seen. She was surprised at how far away she was, realizing now that she must have run for a very long time to get this far.

Well, she had walked clear across this country, and at times in worse condition than she was right now. She could certainly walk back down this hill and the distance involved getting back to the Skellers'. She did just that, her anger feeding her will and giving her strength. She made it to the back porch, and was relieved to discover the door was unlocked. That meant Serena was back and had let herself in. Maggie walked inside to see the young Spanish woman cleaning up from breakfast.

Serena looked at her in surprise. "*Señora* McCahan! You . . . you look terrible! What happened? How did you get here? I thought you were in your room!"

Maggie closed the door, thinking how beautiful Serena was, a dark, exotic beauty. She had been here long enough to know that the Spaniards held their unmarried daughters in high esteem, and that young Spanish women cherished their virginity until marriage. This lovely young woman must be suffering greatly, literally sacrificing her body for her family. "Is Mr. Skeller gone?"

Serena nodded, frowning. "He had a bad bruise and cut on his forehead. He told me he fell."

"*Did* he now?" Maggie stepped closer, taking a plate from Serena's hand. "I think you know how that cut got there."

Serena's eyes immediately teared, and she stepped back. "You are angry with *me?*"

Maggie closed her eyes and sighed. "No, although you surely knew why Mr. McCahan sent you away."

"I . . . he has much control—"

"He has *no* control! I will see to that, Serena! You will

never again have to lie under that vile, evil man! Do you understand?''

Serena looked at her in wide-eyed disbelief. ''No, I do not! I mean, how can you promise such a thing? And how did you know—''

''Drunk men say stupid things,'' Maggie interrupted. ''And they *do* stupid things. *I* put that cut on Mr. Skeller's forehead, and I escaped his intentions. I slept outside all night. I was not about to come back here and be alone with him in the house.''

''Oh, *Señora,* you poor thing!''

''I found out a lot last night,'' Maggie continued in a firm voice. ''I know what he has been doing to you. It will remain our little secret from Mrs. Skeller. Is that understood?''

Serena nodded. *''Sí, Señora.''*

''On the way here I did a lot of thinking, and I believe I have a plan that will free you from Mr. Skeller, you *and* your family. First I will go and clean up and change. Mrs. Skeller will be home soon, and I will have to go spend the day and night with Jean Reynolds. When I come back tomorrow, I will see to it that Mr. Skeller never bothers you again.''

''But how—''

''Just trust me, Serena.''

The young woman slowly nodded. ''If you can do this, I will be eternally grateful, but . . . my father must never know—''

''Of course not. Whether you tell him or not is your business. Mine is to see to it that Ben Skeller in some way pays for what he tried to do to me last night. Tomorrow I will look for a new place to live. I will move out by tomorrow night, even if I have to stay in the filthiest hotel in this city! And don't you say one word to Mr. Skeller or Mary about my moving, or that you saw me come back this way.''

Serena nodded again. *''Sí, Señora.*

Maggie raised her chin and grinned a little. ''I intend to make Mr. Skeller squirm a little, wondering what I will do next. Do you understand what I mean by squirm?''

Serena finally smiled. *''Sí, Señora.* It is like making him afraid.''

''Yes, a little like that.'' Maggie walked past Serena and up the stairs, going into her room and slamming shut the door. She hurried over to her trunk, opening it and throwing out clothes until she could feel the seam at one corner. She felt for the tiny opening there, then ripped upward, reaching under the lining of the trunk.

"It's still there!" She breathed a sigh of relief to realize her money was intact. "Thank you, God."

She carefully put the clothes back inside and walked over to a mirror, nearly gasping. Serena was right. She looked terrible! It would take a lot of work to appear fine and unruffled when she went to Jean's house today, and how she was going to stay awake was another problem. After last night she felt as though she could crawl into bed and sleep for a week, but there was no time for any of that. There was only time to clean up and change. Serena could help with her hair.

Her mind was made up. No matter what it took, even if it meant losing her status among San Francisco's Ladies' Guild, she was leaving this house, and she would find a way to make Ben Skeller pay, and to force him to leave Serena alone! She would also make sure she got whatever money she might need from Edward's money fund in Skeller's bank. Then she would hire her own men to try to find Edward!

Maggie took a deep breath before entering the Skeller home. It was Sunday afternoon, and Ben would be home now. He was always home on Sunday afternoons, pretending to want to spend time with his wife. Maggie had deliberately stayed longer than necessary at Jean's bedside, wanting Ben to wonder if she would ever show up, and what she would do when she did. She had not set eyes on him since the night of his attack, and he must be very worried by now.

She knew it would do no good trying to accuse Ben in front of Mary. Mary would never believe it. Nor would she believe her husband was capable of rape. Maggie did not intend to accuse him of either. She had other plans.

She mounted the steps and walked inside. It was a lovely day, a good day for revenge. Mary came out from the parlor to greet her, genuine concern in her eyes for Jean. Maggie reported that she was about the same. "She just lies there groaning. I'm not sure she even knows who any of us are," she told Mary sadly.

"Oh, the poor woman! And to die way out here, so far from her real home in Boston. It's a shame, just a shame."

"Yes." Maggie glanced past the woman at Ben, who sat in his favorite stuffed chair. "There are a lot of things in life that are a shame, aren't there, Ben?"

He had been deliberately avoiding her eyes. Now he looked up at her with a scowl and said nothing.

"My poor Ben fell and hit his head," Mary told Maggie. "You must have been here when it happened. You should have told me yesterday morning when you came by Jean's to take my place."

"Oh, I meant to, but he dismissed it as nothing, and I was just too concerned about Jean." Maggie saw relief pass through Ben's eyes, but he appeared to be perspiring. She dearly loved the sight.

"Would you like something to drink, Dear?" Mary asked.

"That would be nice. Some lemonade, perhaps?"

"Oh, yes." Mary waved to Serena, who stood down the hall at the entrance to the kitchen. "Take Maggie's overnighter to her room, will you? And then get us all some lemonade."

Serena nodded, glancing questioningly at Maggie. "Oh, Serena, when you bring the lemonade, fix a glass for yourself and come join us, will you?" Maggie asked. Out of the corner of her eye she noticed Ben sit up a little straighter, and Mary blinked in wide-eyed surprise.

"Maggie, you know we never socialize with the help."

"Yes, I do know. But there is something I need to talk about with you and Ben." She walked into the parlor, removing the pins from her straw hat and using the hat to fan herself as she sat down in a satin chair directly across from Ben.

Mary came in and sat in a loveseat next to her husband. "What is it you need to talk about, Maggie?" she asked, her face flushed with excitement.

"Well, since I have no idea when Edward will be back, I

really just can't live here for who knows how much longer, let alone even longer after he returns, until we build a home."

"Oh, but we don't mind at all, do we, Ben?" Mary's cheeks looked rounder when she smiled, and she turned to her husband with that smile, which clearly irritated him. He kept his eyes on Maggie, his face looking flushed.

"No," he answered.

"Well, *I* do," Maggie told them. "I just don't feel right infringing on you this way. At any rate, you know that Mr. Reynolds is quite distraught and plans to return home after Jean's death, which is quite imminent. I am terribly sorry for both of them, but it is true that this presents an opportunity for me to have a proper home of my own right away, someplace where I can live while waiting for Edward and where we both can live after he returns. We might even wait a while to build a bigger home, since Edward will be absorbed in building his supply stores."

Serena brought in a tray with glasses of lemonade. She set them on a coffee table in front of Maggie, glancing at her curiously.

"Oh, do stay, Serena," Maggie told her. "Sit down."

Serena glanced at Mary, then at Ben.

"I assure you, she is needed," Maggie told them.

Scowling, Ben told Serena to take a chair away from the rest of them. Serena obeyed, wringing her hands nervously after she sat down, not sure what to expect. Mary handed a glass of lemonade to Ben, then took one for herself, as did Maggie, who sipped some of the drink, kept cold with ice Ben paid Chinese men to bring down from the mountains. He kept it packed in straw in a shed behind the house designed especially to store ice.

"You want to buy the Reynolds home?" Mary asked.

"Yes. Actually I have enough money of my own to buy it without touching Edward's money. It will be a nice surprise for Edward when he returns, and Mr. Reynolds has already agreed to it. He is giving me a wonderful offer of only eight thousand dollars, if I will come and stay with Jean through her death and then help him with all the funeral arrangements and such, help him pack, and do a little secretarial work for him in his preparations to leave. Another man from Scott and O'Neal was to come here sometime soon and replace him anyway, so Mr. Reynolds plans to go back east. The poor man is so distraught that I thought I would move over there today and keep my promise to stay with Jean. He so needs the help, and I am the only one who truly has the time to do it. It would relieve the rest of the ladies who have husbands and families and their own homes to take care of. Gus said he would have the paperwork drawn up right away."

Mary put a hand to her cheek. "Oh, I would miss you so, Maggie."

Ben still said nothing.

"Well, I would still be close. Because of Jean's condition, it is imperative that I do this right away. I'm sure you understand."

"Of course." Mary looked at Ben. "Isn't it wonderful of her to offer to do this, Ben? And what a wonderful opportunity for Maggie to have a ready-made home of her own!"

Ben puffed quietly on the pipe he'd been smoking. "Wonderful," he said drily.

Maggie smiled victoriously at him. "Well, it isn't the grand home I plan to build with Edward," she told them, "but it is certainly respectable. And if you don't mind, Mary, I would dearly love to steal Serena from you. You already know that Jean's personal maid ran off with a prospector. She was useless, anyway, always sniveling and carrying on about having to care for Jean, thinking she was going to get some terrible sickness herself. I do love Serena so. She wants to get out of the kitchen and become a personal maid, and she is so good at doing my hair. I could trade Jean's cook and housemaid for her. You need the cook, as you have been using poor Serena for both jobs and have been complaining that you need a good cook. Jean's cook does a marvelous job, and you could train the housemaid as a personal servant. Would you agree to that? I, of course, would have to find another cook, but you would be getting two women for one, and I would feel so much better about that.'' Maggie looked at Serena. ''How do you feel about it, Serena?''

Serena looked at Maggie, who smiled supportively. ''I . . . I would like very much to do this, if *Señor* Skeller agrees.''

Maggie looked at Mary. ''Oh, Mary, do make him agree. It's such a perfect idea!'' She looked at Ben. ''You don't mind, do you, Ben? After all, the house servants really should be Mary's choosing, since you are gone so much. And Jean's cook truly is marvelous. You two would by far be getting the better end of the deal, and we would all be happy.''

''Yes, Ben, I agree. I would dearly love to have Jean's cook.''

Maggie wanted to laugh out loud at the look on Ben's face. By her bringing this up in front of Mary, he was trapped, and he knew it. He had no logical reason to object to her idea, and no control over the money she would use to buy the Reynolds house. Maggie had no doubt he was surprised to discover she had money of her own. He turned and set his pipe in an ashtray on the ledge of the fireplace, then rose. Maggie noticed that his fists clenched a couple of times before he walked past her to the parlor door, casting a dark look at Serena. He looked back at Mary and Maggie then.

''You women do whatever suits you. I am going to lie down. I have a headache.''

''Oh, that's too bad,'' Maggie told him. ''Is it from the fall?'' She did not miss the contempt in his eyes.

''Yes, I suppose it is.''

''Oh, have you heard anything from the men you sent looking for Edward?'' Maggie thought he looked as though his whole body might explode at any moment.

''No.''

He turned and went up the stairs, and Maggie turned to Mary. ''Thank you so much, Mary. I am sorry to take Serena, but I really think this will all work out for the best.''

Mary took her hands and squeezed them. ''I am happy for you, Maggie. Sorry for Jean, but happy for you, and for Serena. She has never seemed very happy here. I can't imagine why. I treat her as kindly as anyone ever treated a servant.''

''Oh, I am happy, *Señora,*'' Serena spoke up. ''You have

been very good to me. But I know that I am not so good of a cook. You will be much happier with *Señora* Reynold's cook.''

''Well, I suppose I will.'' Mary drew in a deep breath and rose. ''Well, we shall have to tell The Ladies' Guild about this. We will let them know you are looking for a cook.''

''Yes. Thank you.'' Maggie also rose. ''Well, I am very tired from my night with Jean, but I do have to go and pack. Mr. Reynolds will send a buggy over for me later this evening.'' She turned to Serena. ''Serena, you should also pack your things. You will go with me tonight.''

''Oh, my, this is all so fast,'' Mary commented.

''And I am not one to put things off, Mary. It's just my nature. Thank you for being so good about this.'' Maggie gave the woman a firm hug and kissed her cheek, then turned to Serena, reaching out and putting her hand to her waist as she accompanied her to the hallway. ''Go ahead and start packing, Serena.''

Serena looked at her with tear-filled eyes. ''I do not know what to say,'' she said quietly.

''You don't need to say anything, Serena. *You* are doing *me* a favor. Did you see the look on Ben's face?''

A look of pride and determination came into Serena's eyes. ''*Sí*. I enjoyed it.'' She embraced Maggie and hurried off to pack her things. Maggie smiled inwardly, holding her chin high as she marched up the stairs to pack. She had one more thing to do to finish her vendetta against Ben Skeller!

Chapter Thirty-Two

Ben Skeller rose to greet Gus Reynolds, his smile fading when he saw the man was accompanied by Maggie McCahan. *Now* what was she up to? "Well, Gus," he said. "You're going to have tongues wagging if you're seen in public too often with Maggie here."

Gus scowled. "Please, Ben. My Jean has only been in her grave for a few days, and Maggie is a married woman who has purchased my home. Everyone knows I have taken a hotel room until my business here is finished. And Maggie is accompanied today by her personal maid. Serena has gone to do some shopping for her."

Ben glanced at Maggie with obvious contempt, then looked back at Gus. "You needn't get so defensive, Gus. I was just joking, trying to lift your spirits a little."

Maggie took a chair near Ben's desk, and Gus sat down beside her. He was a short, slender man of German descent, a man of utmost respect and honesty, who was very direct in his manner. Maggie felt more confident having him with her today. She knew Ben Skeller would not try to talk his way around Gus Reynolds. Gus took a gold watch from his vest pocket and looked at it.

"I have a lot to do, Ben, but I promised Maggie that I would come with her and speak for her. She has purchased the property I own northeast of here, that ranch that was abandoned when we took over California. You remember it. I am shedding myself of all interests here before I go back, and Maggie wishes to purchase the land."

Ben frowned, skepticism in his eyes. "What on earth do you want with that land, Maggie?"

"I just feel that since Edward intends to settle here permanently, we might as well start investing in California. Gus has taken me out to see the property, and it is quite lovely. I have a feeling the land itself will one day be worth much more than the gold in the mountains, and perhaps Edward will be interested in paying someone to farm or ranch the place for him. He might even just want to resell it. For now, I hate to see anyone else get it, so I am buying it. It will help Gus settle his affairs more quickly. I know he is anxious to go back east."

Ben looked surprised as he leaned back in his chair. "Isn't this a decision Edward should make?"

"Well, he isn't here to *make* it, is he? Your men have apparently had no success in learning what has happened to my husband, so that will be my next project, sending someone to find him. And if something *has* happened to him, I need to start thinking about what I should do if I end up alone here. For now, I need to draw out some of Edward's and my money. I *can* lay claim to it, you know. I am Edward's wife, and besides that, some of that money is mine, given to us by my parents when we married. We both have quite a bit more money in a bank back east that will be forwarded in two years, and we stand to inherit much more. And since Edward should make a considerable profit on the supplies he took to the gold camps, there should be no problem using some of the money he left in your bank."

Ben sighed, sitting there silently for a moment. Maggie knew he was irritated at how she brought these things up only when she had witnesses to her statements and requests, so that he had no choice but to give her what she asked for. He shrugged. "How much?"

"Twelve thousand," Maggie answered.

"Twelve thousand!" Ben looked at Gus. "That property is only worth about eight."

"I am perfectly aware of what my own property is worth, and that is what I am asking. Eight. Maggie wants the rest for personal reasons. I have no idea what for, and it is not my business. Just give her what she needs, Ben."

Ben shook his head. "It's dangerous for a woman to be walking around with that kind of money."

"I have plans for it," Maggie told him. "Just get it for me, will you, Ben? You've been *so* good to me, putting me up the way you did. I know this is probably a strain on your bank, but Edward *did* leave thirty thousand with you. I know, because I have his books."

Ben's hands went into fists again. "Those books don't include the fact that I have had to dish out ten thousand to the contractor constructing two supply stores at Edward's request before he left. Perhaps he failed to tell you about that. Another twelve thousand will only leave you eight thousand. He looked at Gus. "I make my money by *lending* money. I don't actually *keep* every dollar people bring in here. Twelve thousand will leave me dangerously short."

"And I am truly sorry about that, Ben, but I want to sell the property, and Maggie wants to buy it. I am going back east, so I will have to take the money with me. I don't know why she wants the extra four thousand, but it matters little to me." Gus took some papers from inside his suit jacket and handed them out. "Here are the signed papers deeding the land to Maggie. I would like to pick up the money today, and Mrs. McCahan also needs the extra four thousand. I am very sorry to put this strain on your bank, but with so many more men still coming in every day, you will build up more in no time."

Ben scowled as he rose. "I'll have my clerk get it. And I do know one thing. We have to get more law and order in this town. I pay plenty of men more than I can afford to keep this place guarded." He glanced at Maggie again. Gus seemed rather stiff and demanding, and he wondered if she had told him about what had happened. His forehead still showed a greenish bruise and a scab where she had hit him two weeks ago.

He left to get the money, and Maggie turned to Gus. "Thank you for coming with me. If you hadn't been along, I am sure he would have come up with some excuse not to give me the money."

"Well, if you had asked for all of it he would have put up more of an argument, and a legitimate one, I suppose. I hope that you find your husband alive, Mrs. McCahan. And I am glad to help you see some satisfaction after what he did to you and to poor young Serena. Ben and his wife have been good to us, but I suspected Ben had an eye for other women, and I knew he was not easy to deal with as a businessman. It was not hard for me to believe what you told me, but I will tell no one else, as you asked, but only for poor Mary's sake. She is a good woman."

"Yes, she is."

Gus reached out and took back the papers. "Too bad he did not look at them, huh?" The man's face still showed circles under his eyes and looked rather gaunt, because of the hell he had been through watching his wife die. But now he grinned. "You are some woman, Maggie McCahan."

Maggie smiled in return, remembering hearing those words from another man. "I guess that is a compliment, so thank you, Gus."

Ben returned several minutes later with a small canvas bag. He threw it down on his desk. "It's all there if you want to count it, mostly gold and silver pieces, some currency."

Gus rose and picked up the bag. "As long as the there are enough greenbacks to cover the actual value in gold. We both know paper money is never worth its face value."

"I made up for it in gold and silver, but you know I have to keep a certain amount of gold and silver in my safe to cover a run on the bank."

"Oh, I don't think that will happen for some time to come. Not with the gold they are bringing out of those mountains." He picked up the heavy bags. "San Francisco is here to stay, Ben, and will grow and grow. You will never lose by having a bank here. If Jean had lived, I would have stayed myself, but without her, it means nothing."

The man blinked back tears and turned away, and Maggie followed him to the door. Then Gus turned back to face Ben. "Oh, by the way, my friend, you will have to hire someone else to run the farm you bought out from under Ricardo Martinez. He will be running his own place now."

Maggie enjoyed watching Ben begin to pale. "What?"

"Yes. Maggie is giving Ricardo the land she bought from me, so that he can own his own farm again. Serena will be moving back with her family and helping run the farm."

Ben struggled not to show his temper in front of Gus. From the look on Gus's face, he was sure she had told the man everything. *Damn* her! He needed Ricardo! It wasn't easy to just go out and find someone to run a farm and ranch as big as his, and most men were more interested in looking for gold, not farming. *Bitch!* She had deliberately used him to take Serena away and give some land back to Serena's father. Ricardo would no longer be under his control.

"Well, how kind of you," he said to Maggie, keeping his voice steady.

"I just think some of the Spaniards here have been treated wrongly. And we do need to do things to keep the peace, don't we? They are here to stay, so we might as well find ways to get along with them. I will need a new personal maid, though. Please tell Mary for me, will you?"

Maggie smiled and walked out, terribly pleased with the look on Ben Skeller's face.

Rafe sat on a wooden bench in front of a tavern, not sure what to do next. He had scoured the docks, the streets, most of the now sprawling city of San Francisco. He had climbed hill after hill, back down again, spending his nights in hotels and rooming houses where a man was wise to take his weapons to bed with him.

He had not been here since the fall of '49, and the city's growth in that nearly year-and-a-half absence was astounding.

The once sleepy settlement was now a bustling, burgeoning city, and so far there was not much order to the place. He hated the thought of Maggie being here, the danger she could be in if she was alone.

So far his search for her, or at least for some kind of business Edward might have opened, had turned up nothing. His next step was to go up to what some were beginning to call Nob Hill. "That's where the fancy folks live," one man had told him. "If they've got money, that's where they're livin'." Still, it seemed Edward would have opened a business by now. No one seemed to have even heard of him, yet he and Maggie would have been here a good four months by now.

Maybe he was not *supposed* to find them. After all, he probably had no business coming back so soon. He had told Maggie he would be back in the fall, and he shouldn't even have promised that much. Maybe she and Edward were settled and happy now. Maybe coming back into her life would only create more problems for her. He had hoped to find Edward first, find out how things were going, maybe not go to see Maggie at all if things seemed all right. After all, setting eyes on Maggie McCahan again might make it impossible to leave her yet a second time. Coming back here might bring him more trouble and heartache than he had bargained for. Yet he'd been drawn here like a thirsty horse to water.

He stretched out his legs and watched the busy street, muddy from a recent rain. He supposed he had better check the homes on Nob Hill, but he felt foolish going up there, a man in buckskins with nothing to his name but three horses and the gear packed on their backs. He did not doubt that some of the women there would slam their doors in his face, thinking he had come to rob them. He couldn't blame them, considering some of the rabble he'd seen in the streets. Brawls were apparently commonplace, and he had inadvertently gotten himself involved in one just last night. He had a bump on his head and sore knuckles to prove it.

He was beginning to wonder if Edward and Maggie had settled here at all, but then in a city that was occupied probably a good ninety percent by people from other parts of the country, it was no wonder most people he talked to didn't know anyone but their immediate friends and family. No one had been settled here long enough to establish a larger branch of friends, and most of those he had talked to didn't have reason to be acquainted with the truly wealthy. He would have to give in and head for Nob Hill. That was, after all, where Maggie belonged.

He started to rise when he noticed a man and woman exiting a bank farther up the street. He noticed the woman because of her yellow dress, which stood out against the muddy street, and the dark suit of the man who accompanied her. All of Rafe's senses came alert. She was too far away for him to be sure, but something about her, the way she moved—yes, he could tell the hair under her hat was dark red!

He stood up, walked a little closer. If it was Maggie, he didn't want her to see him yet. He had to decide if she should see him at all. She climbed into a fancy carriage, and the suited man, who looked much older than Edward, climbed in beside her. He ordered the driver to take them home, and the carriage headed in his direction.

Rafe ducked into an alley and waited for it to pass, then hurried over to where his horse was tied, the pack horses behind it. He mounted up and followed, lagging far enough behind so that Maggie would not notice him. Indeed, the carriage headed into the wealthier district of San Francisco. Rafe dropped even farther behind, keeping his eyes on the carriage. It rounded a corner and he rode past that street, noticing it turned right again. He followed along on a street a block over from them until finally the carriage stopped coming. He headed down a side street, past large brick and frame homes, noticing that even bigger homes were under construction farther up the hill. Seeing the wealth represented here, he felt totally out of place, and even more doubtful about bothering to see Maggie again.

He held the reins to his lead horse and cautiously made his way along the side street until he caught sight of the fancy buggy. It was pulling away from a modest but elegant frame home. The woman in the yellow dress walked up the steps and went inside.

"Maggie," Rafe muttered. This would take some hard thinking. The man who had accompanied Maggie was not Edward. Where *was* Edward? Had something happened to him? If it had, was there a new man in Maggie's life already? He could not blame her if there was. This was no place for a woman alone. And she had no idea if he would ever return to her. Even if he did, he could not hold a candle to the fancy-suited man who had just left.

Maybe she was settling into a whole new life now. Maybe what they had along the trail was just a fleeting thing for Maggie, from loneliness and need. She had obviously fallen right back into her former way of living . . . the way she was *meant* to live.

He turned away, aching to go to the door. But he wanted nothing more than for Maggie to be happy, and maybe she was. He'd heard her laugh about something with the man who had just left. He had not laughed himself since leaving her at Sutter's Fort last fall. Had she so quickly forgotten him?

He decided he would lay low for a while, keeping an eye on things. Maybe reentering her life now would be the worst mistake of his life.

Chapter Thirty-Three

Maggie called Serena into the kitchen and had her sit down. She had never felt better about something she'd done than what she was doing now. She laid the deed out in front of Serena, and the young woman looked down at it, then back at Maggie. "What is this?"

"It's a deed to some very good land northeast of here, across the bay in the Sacramento Valley, one thousand acres of good grazing or good farming land. I got it for eight dollars an acre."

"Eight dollars? How much is that total?"

"Eight thousand dollars."

Serena shook her head. "That is much money. Will you hire someone to farm it? Are *we* going there?"

Maggie sat down. "Not we. *You,* and your family. It now belongs to your father."

Serena frowned in disbelief. "I do not understand."

"I bought it for him. Now he can get out from under the claws of Ben Skeller and have his own ranch. I am giving him another two thousand dollars to buy a good mare and stud horse for breeding, and there should be enough left for seed, whatever he will need most."

Serena sat back in her chair, astounded. She looked wide-eyed at Maggie. "*Why?* Why do you do this?"

"Because you all deserve it, and because it is well worth it to me just to be able to steal good help out from under Ben Skeller, and to make sure he has no more hold over you. I told you he would never touch you again, and he won't. More than that, he had no right taking from your father something that has been in your family for generations."

Serena's eyes teared, and she shook her head. "I . . . we cannot accept this. It is too much."

"Of course you can accept it. You have no choice, Serena. The deed is already in your father's name. That is why I asked you his name a few days ago. I can afford it. And it feels good to use some of the money for someone else. Where I come from, most people only think of themselves. Actually, I need you to *let* me do this."

Serena shook her head, a tear trickling down her cheek. "I do not know what to say."

"The look on your face says it all. Ben Skeller is out of your life, and out of your father's life. It's that simple, and it's what I wanted most of all. You can go back and live with your family. I will find another personal maid. Actually, I don't mind so much doing for myself. I find it challenging and rewarding, and heaven knows I have little enough to do as it is. Tomorrow I will go to the docks and find out what happened to the ship that was to bring the things Edward ordered shipped here from back east. Apparently it still has not arrived."

"The docks are a very dangerous place, *Señora* McCahan, especially for a pretty woman like you."

Maggie smiled. "Thank you for the compliment, but I have a handgun. And after all I have been through, there isn't much that frightens me anymore. My whole life—" she said, hesitating, wanting to cry herself, "has been changed forever. Edward might be dead, and I have no idea how or if I should go back to Pennsylvania . . . or if I even *want* to go back. I hardly know who I am any more." *Or who I love.* She sighed deeply, forcing a smile. "You told me this morning that your brother was coming to take you for a visit tomorrow. Take the deed and the money with you."

Serena picked up the deed with a shaking hand and stared at it. "I am so grateful. This is . . . so amazing. My father lost everything when the Americans came. He only stays and works there because he has been on that land all his life and could not afford to start over. *Señor* Skeller has threatened many times to force him to leave, which would leave our whole family in poverty. Because of this my father and brothers hate the Americans. This will show them that there are some who are good and kind . . . and fair."

Maggie felt a little embarrassed, unaccustomed to doing such things for someone else. "Well, let's just call it a sort of peace offering."

"*Sí, Señora.* My father will want to come and thank you himself."

"You tell him it is not necessary. I fully understand what it will mean to him. And I realized some bit of vengeance from doing this, so my motives were not just generosity and a desire to help. I don't deserve any more thanks than what I see in your eyes right now."

Maggie rose, going to the back door and looking out at some struggling rose bushes Jean Reynolds had planted before she took sick. "I will give you the name of a land agent your father can come and talk to about the location. He will be glad to take your father out and show him the property boundaries. Gus won't be here to show him. He is staying at the Whitlow Rooming House just below Nob Hill, but he will be leaving in just a couple of days."

"*Sí, Señora.* I will give my father the name of the land agent. Are you sure it is all right for me to go back to my family? I should stay and work for you."

Maggie shook her head. "It won't be necessary. I have to concentrate now on finding my husband, and finding out about the items that were supposed to have been shipped here to build our home and to finish the supply stores. When my husband placed the order back east, he was told the freighter would arrive by December, and here it is nearly the end of February.

Gus has had one of his men check every day to see if it is in yet, but so far nothing. I will wait three or four more days, then go and check myself. At the same time I will try to find someone trustworthy to go with me into the gold towns and try to find out what has happened to Edward."

Serena rose. "Into the *gold* towns! *Señora* McCahan, that would be very, very dangerous for a woman like you!"

Maggie shrugged. "Nothing much frightens me any more." She truly wanted to believe that as she turned and faced Serena. "I'll be all right. And as I said, I will find someone to go with me."

Serena shook her head. "I will worry about you. You must come and tell me when you return, and let me know what has happened to *Señor* McCahan. I hope that he is well, *Señora.*"

Maggie nodded. "So do I, Serena." She looked back out at the roses. Some bushes had died, others seemed to be fighting to grow stronger. She felt like those rose bushes, trying to hang on, to be strong. She realized now that on that trail west her strength had not come just from within herself. She had found strength and courage through the presence of Rafe Morrisey. Every time she thought of him pain pierced her heart, and she knew it would be that way for the rest of her life.

Maggie used one of the buggies Gus Reynolds had left with the house to drive herself to the docks. He had sold all his horses except one mare, left for Maggie to use. She was gray with a black tail and mane, an old horse, but still strong enough to pull a light buggy.

Maggie's heart beat harder with trepidation as she drove through the bustling city toward the docks. Every road seemed an obstacle course in hills, and she hoped poor old Betsy would make it back up the steep inclines to get back home. More than that, she hoped she survived visiting the docks. She told herself she could do this, and held her chin high, proud that she had mastered yet another chore she never thought she would do on her own—driving her own buggy. Gus Reynolds had given her a quick course in handling Betsy, and thank goodness,

Betsy was a very mild-mannered, rather lazy mare that was easy to handle.

She ignored a few hoots and remarks from some of the men as she drove deeper into the more seedy area of town, deciding that if she simply ignored their remarks no one would give her any real trouble. She had dressed demurely, wearing a gray linen dress that buttoned all the way up to the neck and had long sleeves. It was very plain, with only a little lace at the neck and the ends of the sleeves. Her hat was black with twisted netting around the crown, the only flare being some pink silk roses at one side. She wore no jewelry, nor even any color on her cheeks or lips, hoping to attract as little attention as possible; but she soon determined that the animals who prowled the docks thought anything in a skirt was worth drooling over and worth a go at trying to find out if she might be there looking for a man to make her feel good.

Many only stared, some whistled, a few made lewd remarks. Maggie stared straight ahead, driving to a building that said merely OFFICES. Perhaps here she could get some answers. She drove Betsy to a hitching post, and before she could even climb down men were there to tie her horse for her. They grouped around the buggy, each offering a hand in helping her climb down. ''I need help from none of you,'' she said curtly, gathering her skirt and climbing down on her own. She kept the buggy whip in her hand, giving all of them a warning look of disdain before marching among them to the OFFICES door. Inwardly she cringed at how close all of them stayed to her, a mob of men who could turn into something worse than a pack of dogs with one flutter of the eyelid. She forced herself to appear nonchalant and unintimidated, but she felt great relief when she got through the door and closed it behind her.

An older man sat at a desk writing something in a ledger. He looked up at her, glancing over the top of a pair of small glasses that sat on the end of his nose. His aging eyes lit up at the sight of her, and he quickly put down his ink pen and rose. ''Yes, Ma'am! What can I do for you?''

Maggie smirked at the thought of how silly men could behave. ''I have been waiting for a ship that should have arrived weeks ago,'' she told the man. ''It was to come here from New York City. The White Whale, it's called, Ship Number two hundred six of the Atlantic Freighting Company. Do you have any idea if it might have arrived in the last two or three days?''

The man's smile faded. ''The White Whale?''

''Yes. Is something wrong?''

The man frowned. ''Why would you be asking, Ma'am?''

''I am asking because it was carrying everything important to me and my husband—enough building supplies to build our new home, thousands of dollars worth of cargo that belonged to us, all kinds of mining equipment, things my husband needed to start a chain of supply stores, expensive antique furnishings that were family heirlooms from France, given to us by my family when we married. Does that answer your question? What do you know of the ship, Sir?''

The man frowned and turned away. ''It's strange you should ask, since I just found out yesterday from the crew of another ship.'' He faced her again with deep sorrow in his eyes. ''The White Whale sank, Ma'am, in a storm off the Cape. She's gone, with all her cargo and crew, except for two who survived and were rescued by another ship that just came into port yesterday with the news.''

Maggie felt as though someone had kicked her in the stomach. ''I hope you are lying.''

''I wish I was, Ma'am, for your sake. But it's the God's truth.''

''But . . . everything on that ship was paid for! Thousands and thousands of dollars!''

''I'm sorry, Ma'am, but she's gone. I don't know if her contents were insured, but it wouldn't matter. Rumor is, Atlantic Freighting is bankrupt. I don't imagine you'd get anything out of trying to sue them, and besides that, their headquarters is way back in New York City. You'd have to go all the way back there to try to get your money.''

Maggie turned away, not wanting the man to see her tears. Edward! This news would kill him. She was sorry for him, but also angry with him, for not investigating Atlantic Freighting better before hiring the company to bring his things to California. If they were bankrupt, then the thousands they had spent on their supplies was simply gone. All they had left was what was in Ben Skeller's bank, a paltry sum compared to the kind of wealth to which they were accustomed. "Are you . . . absolutely certain?"

"Yes, Ma'am. I can find men to testify to the fact, if you want. But I don't know you from Adam. I got no reason to lie about it. It's the God's truth. I'm awful sorry."

She swallowed back a lump in her throat. "Thank you." She walked to the door.

"You be careful out there, Ma'am. A pretty lady like you shouldn't be in these parts."

"It doesn't matter." There was nothing left now but try to find Edward. Maybe they should just go home. The money they had left here was not enough to start the kind of business Edward had intended to start, and even if it were it would take months to get another order through. If they tried to start by buying supplies being shipped in now, it would cost them three times what it would cost to order the same things back east. Once a ship hit the coast of California, its contents immediately jumped in value at least three hundred per cent, because of the great need for anything and everything. Their only saving grace might be the money Edward should have made on the items he took into the mining camps, because of the outrageous prices he could get for them. But had he even reached the camps? She had to know.

She drew a deep breath and opened the door. Out of the motley crew of men who stood outside waiting to get a look at her again, maybe she could find someone who would help her look for Edward. When she went out she lost her hope. How could she possibly trust any of these ruffians? They gathered close around her again, too close. She tried to ignore them, but one of them grabbed her from behind.

"What's a pretty thing like you doin' down here at the docks?" he asked.

Maggie lashed backward with her small whip, striking the man in the face. He cried out and let go of her, and the others laughed. Maggie stepped away and tried to hurry to her buggy, but the angered sailor grabbed her skirt, tearing it away slightly at the waist. Men hooted and whistled at the sight of a white lace slip that peeked out from the tear.

"Leave the lady alone, Blake," one of the men shouted.

"You stay out of this!" The man called Blake cast an angry look at Maggie, a small cut on his forehead bleeding. "Any woman who comes down to the docks alone ain't no lady!"

Maggie was furious at the remark, but she was also secretly terrified, for the man who was baiting her was big and muscular, obviously one who had been in a lot of fights. His face showed several small scars, and his powerful arms, exposed from wearing a shirt that had the sleeves cut off, were covered with tattoos. He wore knee-length pants that were soiled, and at his waist was a wide sash from which hung a sheath that held a threateningly huge knife.

Maggie decided that to act like the fainting, frightened little woman would only entice this man more. Instead she faced him squarely. "You are nothing but an ignorant lout," she told him. The others laughed, and the one called Blake was obviously getting angrier, his face turning a dark red. "You have no idea *why* I had to come here alone, you loathesome animal! And if I *was* here for the reason you think, you would be the *last* man here I would take a fancy to!" She turned to get into her buggy, but immediately a strong hand grabbed her arm.

"Who do you think you—"

"Get your hands off the lady!" came a deep command. The voice sounded familiar. Maggie turned, and immediately her terror vanished.

"Rafe!"

"Who the hell are you?" Blake sneered. He kept his hand on Maggie's arm. Maggie just stared in surprise and joy. There he stood, in those familiar buckskins, his face as handsome—no, more handsome than ever—his long hair blowing with a breeze coming off the ocean.

"I am a friend of the lady you're touching," Rafe answered. "I said let go of her."

The others began to back away, forming a circle around the two men, and the shouting began.

"Take him, Blake!"

"Show him what you can do with that knife!"

"Fight for your woman!" some teased, eagerly egging Blake on.

More similar remarks were shouted, until finally the shouting of the circle of men became a din. Maggie's joy at seeing Rafe was dashed by the realization that a fight was inevitable, a *knife* fight! Rafe! Where had he come from? How had he happened to be here just when she needed him? Blake released the painful grip on her arm and shoved her out of the way.

"Get up in the buggy and get out of here!" Rafe told her.

"But, Rafe—"

"*Do* it!"

Blinking back tears, Maggie climbed into the buggy.

"C'mon, Blake! You can take him!"

"Draw some blood!"

"Cut his balls off!"

"He's a goddamn Indian! Better watch it, Blake! You know Indians and knives!"

The shouting grew so loud that Maggie covered her ears. Her buggy actually got jostled around as men charged around it and some even climbed over it trying to get a closer look as Blake bent over and yanked out his knife, dancing in a circle, baiting Rafe to fight him. Finally Rafe pulled his own knife, and Maggie watched with her heart in her throat as the two men went at it amid the circle of now screaming men. Poor Betsy became frightened and whinnied and pranced around slightly, shaking her head and mane. Maggie picked up the reins and tried to control her, but the horse reared and took off, yanking the reins right out of Maggie's hands. Betsy headed uphill toward home, leaving the shouting mob, and Rafe, behind. The horse ran at a mad pace, while Maggie screamed for someone to stop her. Horse and buggy nearly hit several pedestrians before one man finally ran out to intercept the animal, managing to grab hold of the bridle and hang on, shouting "Whoa!" until finally Betsy slowed down. She finally came to a stop, snorting and panting and shaking her head.

"You all right, Ma'am?" the man asked.

"I think so."

The man handed her the reins, and Maggie looked back toward the shipyard. Even this far away she could hear the shouting. She knew that going back into that den of animals was too dangerous now, and it might only make things worse for Rafe.

She could hardly believe he was actually here. How horrible it would be to finally see him again, only to have him killed trying to defend her!

Chapter Thirty-Four

Maggie took hold of the reins and kept the winded Betsy steady. The buggy sat on the flat area of a street that looked out over the dock area, and she trembled at the thought of what could be happening to Rafe in the midst of all the commotion. Moments later, to her relief, she saw Rafe on his favorite black gelding, riding toward her at a gallop. Some of the men at the dock ran behind him, shouting, fists raised, but none had the transportation to follow.

"Oh, my God!" Maggie exclaimed when Rafe came closer. Blood streamed down his face.

"Get the buggy in motion and keep going!" he shouted. "I killed him! Get the hell out of here!" He galloped past her, and Maggie whipped Betsy into another run. The horse could not come close to keeping up with Rafe's, and Rafe whirled his black gelding and rode back down to her, grabbing Betsy's bridle. He goaded the horse into a faster gait, turning down a side street to get out of the sight of the men at the dock so they could not see where they were going. After two more blocks and another hill, they entered a quieter section of town.

"Rafe, please! Betsy's an old horse. You've got to slow her down. Walk her the rest of the way."

Rafe slowed down, then rode ahead of her for a moment, then back again. "What the hell is wrong with you, going down to the docks alone!"

Maggie was surprised at his anger, considering she had no idea he was even in town. "Because I happen to *be* alone! Someone had to check and see if the White Whale was in yet!"

"The *what?*" Rafe wiped blood from his eyes, but it continued dripping all over the front of his buckskins. A few people began to stare.

"The White Whale! It's a freighter, the one that was supposed to bring all our things from back east. I found out it—." It suddenly struck Maggie all that she had lost. "It . . . sank." She started to cry, then gritted her teeth to keep away the tears. "Damn!" she muttered. She halted Betsy and pounded her fists on her lap. "We've lost everything! Everything! God knows . . . how we'll get the money we still have back east . . . or *if* we'll ever get it. We never thought we would need it. I have some left in the bank here, but—" Now the tears came again. "For God's sake, Rafe, you'll bleed to death! Follow me to my house and let me do something about that cut. And how on earth did you find me at the docks in the first place!"

"I *followed* you there! I was hoping I wouldn't have to interfere, because I didn't want you to know I was even around."

Their gazes held as a mountain of emotions rushed through both of them—joy, anger, confusion, indecision . . . love. Rafe calmed down a little.

"Come on. I already know where you live. Let's get up there and get that nag of yours unhitched so she can rest."

"Here!" Maggie reached down and lifted her dress, ripping away a piece of one of her cotton slips. "Put this on that cut and hold it there!"

Rafe came closer, reaching and taking the cloth, feeling the same rush of happiness at seeing her again as she did seeing him when their fingers touched. He pressed the cloth to the cut on his head and turned his horse and rode off. Maggie snapped the reins and got poor Betsy into something resembling a trot. She followed Rafe, astounded to know he'd already been in town a while and even knew where she lived. Rafe said nothing the whole way. He ordered her into the house when they arrived, then took Betsy around back.

Rafe unhitched her as quickly as he could, smacking her on the rump and turning her loose in the penned backyard where she was kept. He sent his own horse inside the pen, removing just the bridle, glad his other two horses were boarded at the rooming house he'd taken. He felt himself growing dizzy, and he knew it was from loss of blood. He grabbed some gear off his horse and went into Maggie's house through the back door, and she waited in the kitchen with a pan of water and some bandages.

"Sit down," she said anxiously. "I'll wash that cut as best I can and put a little whiskey on it. Mr. Reynolds left some in the house."

"Who?"

"The man who owned this house before me. His wife died, and I had already become friends with them. Gus is going back east and needed to unload the house, with contents, so I bought it."

"Is he the man I saw you with five or six days ago, coming out of a bank?"

Maggie had just wrung out a damp cloth, and she hesitated before putting it to the cut. "You've been here that long?"

He sighed. "Yeah."

"Why on earth didn't you come and see me, let me know you were here?"

"You know damn well why. And where is Edward? You said *you* bought the house, as though he had nothing to do with it."

Maggie pressed the wet cloth to a deep cut that had been struck across his forehead from farther back in the hairline across the left side of his forehead, partly into the brow. "My God, this could have been your eye."

"Tell me about it."

"Why did you kill him?"

"I didn't exactly have a choice. It was him or me. After that I knew I'd better get out quick before his friends turned on me, which was happening fast. And you didn't answer my question about Edward."

"Edward went into the gold camps just a few days after we got here. I haven't seen him since."

"What?"

"That was my next project. Hiring someone to go and find out what happened to him."

"Jesus," Rafe muttered.

"Don't use the Lord's name in vain."

"You're in a fix."

"I know." Maggie ordered him to hold the cloth against the cut and walked to a cupboard to get down a bottle of whiskey. "I've been in a fix one way or another for over ten months now, ever since we left Pennsylvania. I hardly know which way to turn any more. I only know I can't make any more decisions until I find out what happened to Edward." She uncorked the whiskey. "Take the cloth away and tip your head back. It looks like the bleeding is finally slowing." She held a dry rag under the cut to catch the excess as she carefully dribbled whiskey into the wound. Rafe winced and grunted. *Another scar,* Maggie thought. "I might have been able to handle myself," she said, dribbling on a little more whiskey. "I had my whip, and a handgun in my purse."

"Yeah, and there were probably twenty of them and one of you, and you weigh half as much as most of them. Men just off a ship see anything in skirts as something to go after, even if she's ugly as sin. Being beautiful only makes it worse."

Maggie did not reply. The words cut to her soul. It had been a long time since she had heard Rafe Morrisey call her beautiful, even longer since Edward had. She put a clean cloth against the cut. "That will be pretty hard to wrap, but I'll try. By morning you can probably unwrap it and let the air get to it. It will probably heal faster that way. Keep your head back so that stays there until I wrap it a couple of times."

"Yes, Ma'am."

Maggie began wrapping a strip of cloth around his head to hold the bandage in place, and only then did she become acutely aware of how close she was to him, and only then did it hit her that he was really there. "My God, Rafe, what are you doing here? You said you'd come back in the fall."

"I couldn't stay away. I was worried about you. Looks like my instincts were right."

She cut off the excess stripping and tucked what was left of it into the wrappings. "There." She sighed and picked up the bottle, but as she started to put it away he grabbed her wrist and took it out of her hand, uncorking it again.

"Sit down."

Maggie obeyed as Rafe took a swallow of the whiskey, then set the bottle on the table.

"Where were you staying before you bought this house?"

Maggie decided not to tell the whole story about Ben Skeller. Rafe had been in enough trouble today. She had no doubt that if he knew the truth, especially in his present agitated state, he would go storming over to Skeller's house and call him out. With his head wound, he didn't need to be getting into another scuffle, and she didn't want to hurt Mary that way.

"I stayed with a wealthy couple Edward met after we arrived here. They very kindly offered me a room in their home. After a while I began to feel a little guilty living there. I felt as though I was infringing on their privacy, so when I found out Gus Reynolds was anxious to sell, I bought this house. I don't have any servants. I am trying to conserve until Edward returns. Now that I know everything we depended on to open a business here and build a home here has been lost, it is even more important to protect what we have left in the bank. And if Edward has lost everything he took into the gold camps, then we are in an even worse mess."

Rafe studied her closely, remembering all the reasons he loved her, not just because of her lustrous auburn hair and gentle brown eyes. Not just because she was the most beautiful creature he'd ever met. Certainly not because of her money. He didn't much care about that. It was Maggie herself, her courage, her determination to survive, the way she'd faced every obstacle presented to her since she left Pennsylvania a spoiled little rich girl. "I missed you, Maggie."

Her eyes immediately began to tear. "And I missed you. I thought about you every day."

"Same for me."

A tear slipped down her cheek, and she looked down at her lap. "You shouldn't have come. It will start all over again."

"I promise to get out of your life if you find Edward and still want to keep living the lie that you're living."

"Don't say that."

"It's the truth."

She sighed again, twisting her hands together. "Edward needs me."

"Then why isn't he here?"

She shook her head. "Because he's off fulfilling a dream. I came out here because of that dream, because back home we were best friends."

"But never lovers."

"Don't say that."

"In a marriage you have to be both."

She wiped at tears. "Please, Rafe."

He rolled his eyes and sighed. "I'm sorry." He looked down at himself. "I've got to get out of these bloody clothes."

She nodded. "Lord knows there are plenty of rooms in this house where you can change. You can even take a bath if you want."

"I'll just wash." He leaned forward, resting his arms on the table. "You said you were going to hire someone to find Edward. I can't think of anyone better or more trustworthy for that than me."

She met his eyes. "I'd be taking advantage of your feelings for me. It isn't fair—"

"I'm going, and that's that. Hell, I don't have anything else to do now that I've messed up my chance to lead another wagon train out here. It's way too late to think about going back over those mountains again. Besides that, the snow would be over my head in the passes."

"I'll pay you. It's only fair."

"If it makes you happy."

She broke into tears. "I can't believe you're really here."

He reached out and put a hand over hers. "I'm really here. And I damn well am not going to leave you until you know for certain what has happened to Edward and then make up your mind what you're going to do about it. You're not alone any more, Maggie."

She nodded, crying harder as she put her head down against the back of his hand. "I'm so glad you're here. It's hard to do this alone."

"I know." He put his other hand on her hair, lightly stroking it.

"I can't . . . we can't . . . talk about us . . . until I know what has happened to Edward."

"I know that, too. I promise not to sneak up on you in the night like I did on the trail."

She laughed lightly through her tears. "I didn't exactly fight you."

Rafe grinned. "I'll go back to where I'm staying tonight, a boarding house just a few blocks away. Tomorrow morning I'll buy an extra horse and some of the things we'll need for the trip, get everything packed and ready."

"I never said I was going along."

"I know. But you were going to."

She wiped at tears. "How did you know that?"

"Because I know you, and how faithful you are to Edward. You think he might need you."

She smiled and sniffled. "Yes."

"You will have to dress like a very common woman, if that's possible for you. You will have to pose as my wife. It's the only protection you'll have. There are a lot of woman hungry animals up there, but most of them respect a proper lady, especially when she's someone's wife. Agreed?"

She nodded. "Agreed."

"Go to town tomorrow and buy some of the cheapest, plainest dresses you can find. No fancy hairdos. No color on your face. No jewelry."

She nodded again. "Are you sure you'll be all right to leave so soon?"

He grinned wryly. "I've lived through a lot worse. You of all people know that. You take tomorrow to shop and pack and then get some rest. I'll be back the next morning at sunrise. Lock up the house and tell the neighbors to watch it for you."

"I will."

Rafe pulled his hand away and rose, and Maggie thought how much bigger and even more handsome he was than she remembered. Inside a room he seemed bigger than out of doors.

"I'll be back day after tomorrow. Be careful going into town to shop. Maybe you can take a couple of lady friends with you. What about Mrs. Skeller?"

"Yes, Mary would go. She would understand why I need to do this."

"Good. Take her."

Their gazes held a moment longer, and Maggie stood up, facing him. "Thank you, Rafe, for coming back."

"I had no control over it."

She smiled. "I need . . . could you . . . hold me . . . just for a couple of minutes? It's been so long since I had anyone strong to lean against."

He smiled lovingly. "You'll get blood on your dress."

"I don't care."

He put out his arms, and Maggie moved her own arms around his waist and rested her head against his broad chest, closing her eyes and relishing the ecstasy of a simple embrace as his strong arms moved around her. He held her tightly, burying his face in her hair. "I still love you, Maggie."

"And I never stopped loving you."

He kissed her hair and pulled away. "I'd better get going before I break down and break my promise to you."

Maggie looked up at him, and she allowed him to bend close and meet her lips. It was a gentle, loving kiss of promise. He pulled away then and stepped back. "I'll change and bathe at the boarding house." He went to the door, looked back once. "Day after tomorrow."

Maggie nodded. Rafe picked up the change of clothes he'd brought inside, and left. Maggie went to the door and watched him put the bridle back on his horse. He threw his gear over its rump and mounted up. Maggie waved to him as he rode away, and she broke into tears again, tears of relief at the safe, secure and loved feeling she had whenever Rafe Morrisey was in her life.

Chapter Thirty-Five

Maggie realized this was the first time she'd had to truly appreciate the beauty of California and the Sierras, although riding a horse was a totally new experience for her. The first three days were spent literally teaching her to ride as they made their way into the foothills of the Sierras. Back home she had used only buggies and carriages, and on the trail she had only occasionally ridden, and then only sitting sideways.

This was different, and riding astride was creating sore spots in unmentionable places, as well as stretching leg muscles that were not accustomed to being used this way. Whenever she dismounted, it was difficult at first to walk with her legs straight, and her rear end and lower back ached fiercely. But her dilemma was food for laughter for Rafe, and she dearly loved to hear him laugh, loved his handsome smile, the hard lines of his face, the dark skin and eyes, the strong hands and arms, the tall, muscled physique, his graceful stride.

That was the hell of it. She loved everything about him, and having him back in her life again, being out here in the open air and sleeping on the ground, cooking over campfires, brought back all the memories of the trail west and how and why she had fallen in love with Rafe Morrisey. Here he was in his natural element, as much a part of this land as the Indian and the bear. It was not easy to lie looking at the stars at night knowing he was nearby, remembering the ecstasy she had known that one beautiful night she had given herself to him, the glorious satisfaction of all that was woman in her being realized in Rafe's arms.

Yet she loved him more now for staying on his side of the campfire. She knew it must be hard for him, but he made no advances or demands. He had already invaded her most private places once, made love to her in the exotic, virile way only Rafe could make love to a woman, yet now he behaved as though he had never touched her, respecting her wishes not to act on their love or make any decisions until she learned what had happened to Edward.

After taking the ferry across the bay, they rode through rich grassland, past beautiful ranches and farms, and from directions Gus had written out for her Rafe was able to find the land Maggie had purchased for the Martinez family. Serena welcomed them, and her father and brothers were overjoyed to see her, thanking her in Spanish for what she had done. Serena had to interpret everything they said, but it was obvious from the joy on their faces and the mist in their eyes that they were deeply grateful, and Ricardo Martinez insisted he should pay her back. Maggie had Serena explain to him that she was not even sure she would be staying in San Francisco, and that she had only bought the land for him as a peace offering. The memory of the looks on their faces was all the payment she needed, even though now that she realized the kind of losses she was experiencing, the money could definitely be used. They did not need to know that. Let them be happy.

"We'll camp here," Rafe said, interrupting her thoughts. "By tomorrow we'll be passing creeks where there will be small settlements where men will be panning for gold. Farther up we'll hit the bigger camps, where they go at it with pickaxes and dynamite."

Maggie heard a rumble that she now knew was an explosion higher in the Sierras, where men blasted away at mountainsides looking for the precious gold that was not as easy to find as most had thought when first coming here. *They think it's going to be lying on the open ground to be picked up,* Rafe had told her, shaking his head. *What fools.*

Maggie was glad Rafe had not got caught up in gold fever, which seemed to have a way of changing a man's entire personality. It had even changed Edward into someone she hardly knew, and he wasn't even looking for gold. Apparently even those associated with the gold seekers became different men.

She dismounted, glad that at last her muscles and rump seemed to be adjusting to the saddle. She was not quite so sore, and she took pride in knowing how to put on and remove a bridle and how to cinch a saddle. Rafe had taught her how to inspect a horse's hooves and to know when a horse needed new shoes. She had never brushed down a horse in her life, but she had learned that, too, and every night she brushed down the spotted Appaloosa mare Rafe had brought for her. She removed the holster and handgun that were kept strapped around her horse's neck so she would have a gun handy when necessary. Rafe had purchased the gun for her, insisting she should have a more powerful handgun than the little pistol she carried in her handbag, and tonight she would again practice shooting it.

Both tended to the nightly ritual of unsaddling horses, brushing them down, setting up camp, building a fire, spreading out bedrolls. Rafe always took care of the packhorse, unloading it for the night, and Maggie usually cooked, although sometimes they took turns making coffee and heating potatoes or beans, cooking whatever small game Rafe could shoot along the way. Tonight it would be squirrel, a fairly large one Rafe had shot earlier this morning, and which Maggie had helped clean.

She laughed to herself as she ran a stick through the squirel's skinned and cleaned torso and set it over the fire to roast.

"What's so funny?" Rafe asked.

"I'm just thinking how shocked my mother would be to see me cleaning a squirrel and cooking it over an open fire."

Rafe grinned, adding dead pine wood to the fire. "I expect you've done a lot of things that would shock her."

Maggie blushed. Her having an affair with a mountain man

would definitely shock her mother. Now she traveled alone with the same man. Mary Skeller had been rather shocked when she told her she had hired a scout to take her into the mountains, insisting she shouldn't go along, but Maggie had in turn insisted she should be along, in case Edward needed her.

"Just cooking itself would shock my mother, even if it were inside on a stove. Even at her age I doubt she even knows how to boil water." She rose and walked to a nearby creek to wash some potatoes, putting them into a towel to carry back. When she turned from the creek, Rafe was standing behind her.

"Why don't you tell me the truth about buying that land for Martinez?"

Maggie forced a look of innocence. "Whatever are you talking about?" She walked past him to the fire, kneeling down and setting a black fry pan at the edge of it. She began slicing potatoes into the pan.

"You know what I'm talking about, or don't you realize I understand Spanish? I am part Mexican, but that isn't the reason. You don't live in Texas for very long without learning the language, and it's the same here in California. Serena's father said something about being grateful you freed him from being at the mercy of Ben Skeller. You told me you lived with the Skellers a while. Aren't they your friends?"

Maggie kept slicing the potatoes. "Mary is my friend."

"But not Ben? What kind of hold did he have on Martinez?"

Maggie sighed. "Serena used to work for Ben and Mary. She was there when I was. I learned through her that Ben had literally stolen her father's ranch out from under him after the U.S. took over California. There is a lot of bad blood left between some of the Spaniards, *Californios* they call themselves, and the Americans. I just thought that giving some land back to Ricardo Martinez would help keep the peace, and then Serena would be able to rejoin her family instead of having to work for Ben and Mary in order to survive. Ben had allowed her family to stay on the ranch, but they never knew when he might kick them off."

"Why didn't Serena stay at the ranch, instead of coming to work for a man they detested?" Rafe sat down across from her and lit a thin cigar. Maggie finished slicing a couple of potatoes and spread them around in the pan before answering. She glanced at Rafe. He damn well suspected the truth.

"She needed money."

Rafe puffed on the cigar for a moment. "You bought that land for more reasons than just the fact that the Serena and her family had to work for Ben Skeller. It isn't that I don't think you have a generous heart, but I've seen Serena. She's beautiful, and the joy and gratefulness in her eyes tells me there is something more to your story. Is Ben Skeller the reason you bought a different house? Seems to me that a woman alone would appreciate having someplace to stay, another woman's companionship. Why would you want to be all alone, buy a house without knowing what had happened to Edward?"

Maggie closed her eyes and sighed, moving back to sit on a stump. She faced Rafe. "Ben Skeller was forcing Serena to . . ." She looked away. "To let him come to her bed. He told her if she didn't come to work for him and allow him his . . . pleasure . . . he would force her family off the ranch and make sure they never owned a piece of property again. I don't know if he really could have done that much damage, but Serena believed it because he was a rich American, and rich Americans were invading California like flies, stealing ranches and farms for themselves. She was protecting her family."

Rafe shook his head, puffing quietly on the small cigar. "Anything else you're not telling me? Buying that land seems more like a personal vendetta to me than just helping out a Spanish woman you hardly know."

Maggie met his eyes, irritated by his perception. "I like Mary Skeller. She's a sweet woman who is totally oblivious to what a scoundrel her husband is."

Like someone else I know, Rafe thought. "Which means?" he said aloud.

"Which means I don't want you giving the man trouble, or deciding to slit his throat. Mary needs him."

Rafe sat on a log, resting his elbows on his knees. He kept the end of the cigar between his teeth as he spoke. "And why would I want to slit his throat?"

"Because he was literally raping Serena."

Rafe shook his head. "I've only met the woman once. I agree the man is a bastard for what he was doing, but there is something more, Maggie. What did he do to you?"

Maggie could see anger beginning to smoulder in his eyes. "He tried the same thing with me. Mary was gone for the night, helping nurse Jean Reynolds before she died. Ben came into my room and made advances. That was when I learned what he'd been doing to Serena. I hit him over the head with a small statue and ran out of the house." She walked back to the fire to stir the potatoes. "I slept outside all night in a grove of pines. I decided then and there to get out right away. Gus wanted to sell his house because his wife was dying, so I bought it, and I stayed there with the excuse that someone needed to help care for his wife until she was gone. I've been there ever since."

Maggie watched Rafe stand up with a sigh. He paced, obviously thinking, and obviously angry. "I should have stayed nearby."

"You couldn't have done anything. How would it look if I had gone running to you with every little problem? I am a married woman."

"And your worthless husband left you there to face things like that all alone! Hell, he couldn't have known shit about Ben Skeller! How long did he know him? One day? Two days?"

"Please, Rafe. Don't talk about Edward that way. He means well."

"Edward looks out for *himself!* You're nothing more than a friend to him. He doesn't love and respect you the way any normal man loves and respects his wife!"

"What do you mean, any *normal* man?"

Rafe held her gaze a moment, then turned away. "I only mean it isn't normal to be so neglectful of a beautiful and generous woman like yourself."

"Edward is a very good man in many ways. You saw that on the trail west. He was courteous and helpful, and he had nothing but praise for you. He admired you greatly. And he did not behave as though he was any better than the most common person along. I grew up with men like Edward, and believe me, arrogance is their number one quality, if you can call it a quality. Edward has never been arrogant. And he has always been good to me. This was just something he had to do, and he was afraid it would be too dangerous for me."

"It *is* dangerous. The only difference is that I can protect you. Edward would be useless in that department."

"Please don't insult him."

Rafe rolled his eyes. "Begging your pardon."

Maggie turned the squirrel, wanting to change the subject. "Where do you think we should look first for Edward?"

"No telling. All we can do is start asking questions, hit every camp we can, and talk to men at creeks along the way."

"He had a big man with a red beard along as a guard, another man he hardly knew. I didn't like the looks of him. The hair on his head was red, too, and it was long and shaggy, with an unwashed, uncombed look. Rafe hired him because he was big and strong and was supposed to be good with a gun. I have no idea where he found him. He was called Brady. He's someone men would remember, as well as the big supply wagons my husband brought along. I just hope Edward doesn't go home while I'm gone and panic. If he came out looking for me, we could spend weeks traipsing around these mountains looking for each other."

"It would serve him right."

Maggie scowled at him. "Why don't you watch this food while I go practice shooting again?"

Rafe rose. "Think you can handle it this time without my help?"

Maggie also rose, putting her hands on her hips. "I know how to load and aim, and I can set up my own target. I don't need your help in every little thing I do, Rafe Morrisey."

He grinned. "Yes, Ma'am. Just offering."

Maggie softened. "I really appreciate all of this, Rafe. This isn't any easier for me than it is for you."

He knew exactly what she meant, and it created an ache in

places he would rather not feel. "I'm not so sure about that. You aren't a man."

Maggie reddened and turned away, feeling suddenly flustered. She left him to get her gunbelt and handgun, walking farther away and picking out a target. Maybe shooting a few rounds would help keep her mind from things she should not be thinking about.

Rafe knelt down by the fire, watching her in the distance. She looked almost comical, such a slender, pretty thing holding out that handgun with both arms and shooting. She shouted with joy once, when she actually hit the wide tree trunk she was shooting at. A piece of bark flew off.

Rafe grinned. Damn, he loved her! And traveling this way together was like living as man and wife, especially considering how easy she was to talk to. It would not be difficult posing as a married couple when they made it to the gold camps. The only hard part about this job was keeping his hands off Maggie McCahan.

Chapter Thirty-Six

Each gold camp seemed the same as the last—wild, noisy, muddy, crowded, peppered with tents and shanties, sewer-ridden creeks, beautiful mountains turned ugly from explosions and gold tailings dumped into piles. They were rampant with saloons and bawdy women who wore bright colors, their painted faces peering out from under plumed hats. At night the air was filled with the sounds of piano music, singing, laughing, dealers at roulette wheels calling out numbers, screams, gunshots now and then, and the constant explosions, as well as the noise in some of the smelting plants that had already been erected. The camps were basically ugly places full of people who held a constant hope for the dream of a lifetime, a dream only a few of them would ever realize.

It was quite obvious to Maggie that she could never have come here alone, or even with someone she had hired, since she could not have trusted a stranger. Rafe was the only person she could trust implicitly, and she was more grateful than ever that he had come along. He posed an intimidating stance wherever they went and whoever they faced, and so far no one had given him any trouble, although there had been more than a few whistles and remarks when she walked by. Still, no one had dared lay a hand on her. Just as Rafe had told her, as long as these men believed she was his wife, for the most part they respected that and they gave her no trouble.

Still, there were always the drunks, and drinking could make a man do crazy things. And apparently most of these men figured that as long as they were away from their wives and sweethearts, they did not need to bathe or shave. The stench was overwhelming at times, especially when they were in a crowd.

At night she and Rafe camped a good distance away from the saloons and bawdy houses, keeping to themselves, but by day they hit the saloons and supply stores, as well as the mining camps themselves. Some of the locations were dangerous for Maggie, but Rafe refused to leave her behind, alone. Everywhere they went they asked the same questions, describing Edward, the wagons, the man named Brady, some of the other drivers. It took nearly a month of traveling and exploring, climbing steep passes, fording cold, rushing streams, and talking to miners, prospectors, businessmen, even prostitutes, everyone they could, before a slender, fancy-dressed gambler caught Maggie's eye. He was sitting at a card game in one of the hundreds of saloons they visited, and when he took out a gold pocket watch to check the time, Maggie recognized the tune it played, a lovely waltz that had been Edward's favorite. She had given him just such a watch when they married.

She could not help staring at the watch, and she moved closer, while Rafe spoke with the bartender. The gambler looked up at Maggie and caught her staring. He grinned, looking her over appreciatively, running a hand through his already slicked-back hair.

"Something I can do for you, Ma'am?"

"Yes. I'd like to know where you got that pocket watch."

The man shrugged. "I bought it."

"When? From whom?"

The gambler beamed. "Well, now, let me buy you a drink and we can talk about it." He started to close the watch.

"Wait! Is there a picture inside?"

The man grinned. "Yes. A very pretty—" He frowned,

studying her closely. Then he popped open the watch again and looked at the picture inside. He looked back at Maggie. "By God, it's you!"

By then Rafe had noticed Maggie had singled someone out, and he walked over to stand beside her.

Maggie closed her eyes at the sound of the waltz. Edward! She had been so happy on her wedding day . . . until her disappointing initiation into womanhood. "That is my brother's watch," she told the gambler. "Please, I *must* know where you got it."

The man shrugged. "Bought it off a big guy with red hair and beard. He had all kinds of stuff in a wagon, a regular traveling supply store."

Maggie looked up at Rafe. "Brady!' she said, her eyes tearing. She looked back at the gambler. "What color were the wagons painted?"

The man looked her over, then looked up at Rafe. "She your wife?"

"Yes."

"Not bad! You could make a bundle letting her work in here."

"Just answer her question. What color was the wagon?"

The gambler closed the watch again. "Blue. The wagon beds were blue, and on the sides were painted the words McCahan Supplies. I don't know why that stuck in my mind. I guess because the man who had it called himself McCahan when he shook my hand."

Maggie felt rage. "His name is *not* McCahan! *My* maiden name is McCahan, and my *brother's* name was Edward McCahan. *He* owned those wagons. He's been missing for four months! Did the man you saw mention anything about anyone else? Was there anyone else with him? My brother is about your size, with light hair and blue eyes."

The man shook his head. "Didn't see anybody like that."

Maggie's heart fell. That could only mean one thing. She turned away, clutching at pain in her chest.

"Any idea where the man headed?" Rafe asked.

"Nope. He just went on, selling things to others. It was a

long time ago, nearly three months, I think. He's probably sold everything by now and maybe gone back for more, or maybe sold the wagon, too.''

''There was more than one wagon.''

''I only saw one.''

''Where was this?''

''Sorry. I don't remember. These mountains are peppered with gold camps, and I've been to most of them. I don't remember which one I was visiting when I bought the watch.''

Rafe nodded. ''Thanks for the information.'' He turned and put an arm around Maggie, leading her outside.

''Oh, my God, Rafe. He killed him. I know Brady killed him!''

Rafe took her into an alley and pulled her into his arms. ''We don't know that for sure, yet.'' *He could have decided to stay up here . . . with a man.* How could he tell her a thing like that?

''Edward would never leave his wagons or split them up like that. And I know in my heart the man called Brady was not to be trusted.'' She rested her head against his chest and cried. ''Deep inside . . . I suspected . . . but to know for certain . . . oh, God, poor Edward! What if he suffered? And what if his body was left to the wolves? He had such big dreams, and after all we suffered to get here . . .'' She wept harder, and Rafe held her, hating her suffering.

''Let's do more asking around. We'll explore every damn camp, maybe find some of the other drivers, maybe even find the bastard you said was called Brady. I'll beat the sonofabitch until he tells us the truth about what happened to Edward.''

She looked up at him. ''The watch! I have to have that watch! It meant so much to him, Rafe, and it would be some little thing I would have left of him. I've known Edward since I was old enough to have a memory. Please try to get him to sell that watch. I can pay much more than he probably paid for it.''

Rafe sighed, leaning down to kiss her cheek. ''All right. Let's go.'' He led her back into the saloon, and the gambler looked up at them with a scowl at being interrupted again.

"Now what?"

Maggie wondered if she would begin choking. There was so much smoke in the small room. A prostitute sat next to the gambler now, her breasts nearly popping out of the bodice of her dress. She wondered how often Rafe had lain with such women, and it made her cling tighter to him.

"My wife wants to buy the watch off you," Rafe told the man. "It's all she has left of her brother."

The gambler turned away, looking at his cards and folding. "Forget it. I like the watch. It's solid gold."

"I don't give a damn if it's attached to your balls," Rafe answered. "You either sell it, or I'll take it."

Even Maggie gasped at the remark, and Rafe gently pushed her away as some of the men at the table scooted back their chairs. Rafe did indeed have an intimidating appearance. The prostitute sat there grinning, and the gambler looked back up at him.

"Who do you think you are?"

"I *think* I'm Rafe Morrisey, and I *think* I could pull my knife and slit your throat in just under one second. Now, how much do you want for the watch, or do I have to rip it off your bloodied vest?"

The gambler just stared at him several silent seconds, the rest of those in the saloon having quieted to watch the confrontation. The prostitute looked Rafe over as though he was a delicious treat. "Oh, hell, give him the damn watch, Stan," she finally said. "He doesn't look to me like the kind you should consider messing with."

"Wise advice," Rafe told him.

The one called Stan sighed deeply, finally unhooking the chain from his satin vest and pulling the watch itself back out of the vest pocket. "Three hundred dollars."

"What did you pay for it? Fifty, maybe? Seventy-five?"

"You want it. You can pay what I ask."

"And you can go to hell." Rafe rested his hand on his knife.

Stan rolled his eyes. "All right. Two hundred."

"I'll pay him," Maggie told Rafe.

"It's too much."

"Not to me. I just want to pay him, and get out of here."

Rafe glanced sidelong at her, irritation in his eyes. "If that's what you want."

Maggie reached into her handbag and took out several gold and silver coins, counting out two hundred dollars. "Give me the watch."

Scowling, the gambler handed it over to her.

"Now you have more to gamble with," Maggie told him. She wiped at tears and tugged at Rafe's arm. Reluctantly, Rafe followed her out.

"I wanted to bash his head in!" he grumbled.

"I know. And if you had, there would probably have been an all out brawl. I can't afford to lose you, Rafe Morrisey. Do you want me left alone up here? And how can we keep searching for the man called Brady if you're wounded or dead?" She put the watch into her purse.

"You shouldn't have let so many men see you take gold coins out of your handbag. Now they're all wondering how much more you might have on you. We'd better get the hell out of this camp and head to another one."

"Fine."

"It's almost dark, but we can get at least part way out of town before it's too dark to see. We'll go back to camp and pack up."

Rafe walked so fast Maggie had to practically run to keep up with his long legs. "Thank you for getting the watch back," she told him.

"Don't mention it."

It took several minutes to reach their camp.

"Rafe!" someone called out.

Rafe stopped and turned.

"Tarnation! Where the hell you been, you half-breed buzzard?" The man who had spoken the words stepped closer.

"Joe?"

"That's me."

"Tobacco Joe!" Rafe left Maggie to greet a man who Maggie could smell from several feet away. He spit a wad of tobacco juice before grabbing Rafe's hand, laughing as he greeted him

"I seen you back there at the tavern. Didn't say nothin' 'cuz I didn't want to interrupt what was goin' on and spoil your attention. That there gambler don't know how lucky he is, does he?"

"Joe, you smelly old man, what the hell have you been doing with yourself?"

"Oh, I been doin' some pannin' for gold, did a little diggin', too, but that's too much work for me. I'd rather be on a horse on the open plains, huntin' and scoutin'. Say, did you really take yourself a wife? And how in hell did an ugly thing like you get a woman good-lookin' as this one?"

Joe came closer, and Maggie struggled to not wrinkle her nose. He was obviously nice enough, and a good friend of Rafe's.

"Well, it's a long story," Rafe told him, "and better not told here where someone might hear us. We're heading away from this camp yet tonight in case of trouble."

"Good idea." Joe tipped his hat and bowed. "Howdy, Ma'am. Name's Tobacco Joe. It's been so long since anybody used my last name, I done forgot what it is!" He laughed, and Maggie was obliged to reach out and shake his hand. She glanced up at Rafe, who grinned, realizing what she must think of Joe.

"Joe here saved my life once, fighting Indians. I've scouted with him a few times. He's a good man, Maggie, trustworthy." He looked at Joe. "Joe, this is Maggie, and she is a very proper, well-bred woman. So try to watch your manners around her, and don't spit in front of her."

"Sure enough."

"Listen, we've got some more searching to do, and I could use somebody to stay with our gear when we go into these camps. You know how these places are rampant with thieves. Think you could do that? Maggie will pay you."

"Hell, I'd do it for free just to jaw with you again. It's been a long time. You're lookin' good as ever. Where'd you get that scar on your forehead?"

"It's all part of the story. Go get your horse and gear and meet us back here."

"Well, I think I'll just do that. Be talkin' to ya'."

Maggie watched the man walk away, then turned to Rafe. "Rafe, he stinks!"

"You think I don't know that? I'm part Indian, remember. Indians have keener noses than you whites," he teased. "It hurts my nose worse than yours. But he's a good man, totally trustworthy, and we need him. I hate leaving our gear unguarded. We'll take Joe with us, and he can guard it for us. Besides that, he's an extra man in case of trouble. He can fight like a mad grizzly, and he's good. You'll just have to try to put up with the smell, but I'll see if I can't get him to take a bath."

"That would be a great relief." Maggie helped him pack, and they loaded everything onto their horses and the pack horse. They mounted up, and already Joe was returning with a horse, followed by a mule packed with more gear.

"We got a lot of catchin' up to do, Friend," he said. "And I've got somethin' to tell you that will interest you right good."

"What's that?"

"Well, I heard what you said the first time you was in that saloon. I was gonna' follow you out then, but a pretty gal with tits big as watermelons offered to buy me a drink, and I couldn't—" He hesitated. "Oh, I'm damn sorry, Maggie. I shouldn't have said that in front of you."

Maggie felt as though her face was on fire, and she pulled a jacket closer around her bosom. "I suppose it's all right. I understand you have to get used to being in the company of a lady."

"I guess so. Anyways, I heard what was said between you and that gambler. After you come back in, and I seen how upset your wife here was, cryin' and all, and willin' to pay so much for that there watch, I knew how important all of this was to you. Well, I'll tell you, Rafe, I think I might know where the man with the red beard is."

Maggie instantly forgot how repulsive the man was. "What!"

"Hell, if it's the same man you was talkin' about in that there saloon, I dug for gold right beside him for a while, up at a place called Bonnie's Gulch, only about five miles from here. He thinks he's onto somethin', so he's probably still there. He had all kinds of the best equipment—stole from your brother, I don't doubt. He even had a nice wagon with him, painted blue. He sold most everything, he said, except what he needed to do his own prospectin' with. Anyways, we could go a ways and camp for the night and be there sometime tomorrow."

"Oh, Joe, you're a godsend!" Maggie told him.

"Well, I don't know about that. I just know what I know. It might not even be the same guy, but from your description and the gambler's, I think it is. And I heard you say the name Brady. That's what this man calls himself. What did he do?"

"I think he killed my—brother," Maggie answered. She decided it was Rafe's decision to tell him whatever he wanted to tell him about their relationship.

"Well, then, let's go find out. Ole' Rafe here, he's got ways of makin' a man talk."

"You don't know what this means to us, Joe," Rafe told him. "We've been searching for a month." He reached across his horse and shook Joe's hand again.

"Glad to help an old friend."

Joe headed out, and Rafe looked at Maggie, who smiled through tears. "At last maybe I'll have an answer," she told him.

Rafe nodded, wondering what it would be, and wondering what would happen to their own relationship once they knew.

Chapter Thirty-Seven

''No! It's got to be all the way,'' Maggie insisted.

Tobacco Joe stood beside a cold, rushing river in his long-johns. ''But, Ma'am, I ain't scrubbed that way in years! I *always* take my baths in my underwear.''

''The fact that you have not had a real bath in years is obvious.''

''But this way I wash my underwear, too.''

''It doesn't work that way, Joe. Not with me. You will take off the underwear and take the bar of soap I have given you, go into that water and wash the *right* way! Then you will scrub your underwear and lay it out to dry. Surely you have at least one change of clothes and underwear.''

''Yes, Ma'am, but I save that for emergencies, and I ain't never had one come up that was worth cleanin' up for.''

''Well, you do now! Strip off the rest of those clothes and clean yourself up, including your hair and beard.''

Joe looked at Rafe, obviously begging him to do something about this. Rafe only laughed. ''The woman has spoken, Joe. She appreciates your help, but she just can't tolerate the smell. Hurry up with that bath so we can get to that gold camp by nightfall.''

Joe stomped his foot. "Tarnation!" He turned in a circle, then faced Maggie, who stood at a distance because she couldn't bear to get too close. "You got to turn away and not look."

Maggie rolled her eyes. "Believe me, I don't *want* to look!" She glanced at Rafe with a grin. "You make sure he does what he's supposed to do."

He nodded with a grin. "You and I could take a skinny-dip ourselves," he suggested.

The thought brought an immediate rush of desire that irritated her. There was nothing she would enjoy more, other than sharing her bed with Rafe Morrisey. But she folded her arms and gave him a warning look, saying nothing. Rafe just laughed and went to make sure Joe did what he was supposed to do.

Maggie walked back to the campfire and added some wood to keep the coffee hot and the bacon cooking. A moment later Rafe came over to the fire, telling her not to look.

"I've got Joe's underwear," he told her. He reached around her and picked up a piece of wood that was burning only on one end. "You can look now," he told her a moment later.

Maggie turned to see him holding the longjohns while fire licked its way up the legs. When it reached his hand he dropped the underwear and let it keep burning. "They weren't worth washing," he told Maggie.

Maggie just shook her head and glanced over at the river. "You sure he's using that soap?"

"Yes, Ma'am. I made sure before I stole his underwear."

It was then they both heard the click of a gun being cocked. Their smiles faded when four men stepped into the open from where they had been hiding behind rocks and brush. Rafe and Maggie both immediately recognized one of them as a man who had been sitting at the gambling table last night when Maggie paid the professional gambler for Edward's watch.

"Hello, pretty lady," he said to Maggie.

Rafe stiffened, moving his hand to his knife.

"Don't be thinking of using that thing," one of the others warned him. "All we want is the rest of the money the two of you are carrying. You be good, and we'll leave it at that.

Otherwise, we'll have to kill you and do a little skinny-dipping ourselves with the wife here."

Maggie looked up at Rafe, who was obviously sizing them up, and she was afraid for him. All four men were armed, one with a rifle, the other three with handguns. None were as big as Rafe, but when a man held a gun on someone, his size didn't much matter. "All we have is what I carry in my handbag," Maggie lied to them. "That's why I keep it with me at all times."

"Well, Lady, I don't believe you, but it's a start. *Get* it!" The man who spoke was the one they recognized from the night before. He ordered one of the others to tell the "old man" to get out of the river and come up here where they could keep an eye on him.

Maggie knelt down to pick up her handbag.

"I'm buck naked!" she heard Joe protesting.

"Who cares?" his abductor answered. "Get out of there and come up here where we can watch you."

"Tarnation!" Joe said again. "At least let me wrap a towel around myself."

"Go ahead."

Maggie rose, glancing at Rafe again. He looked down at her out of the corner of his eye, looking first at her handbag, then at her. She knew what he would want her to do if they were going to get out of this. These men wouldn't want just the money. They would want her, too, and they were not going to have her.

"Hand it over!" the apparent leader demanded, indicating her handbag.

"No," she answered, deciding to feign a silly, flustered woman. "This is my favorite handbag. You can have the money inside it, but not the purse."

One of the others laughed. "Ain't that just like a woman? They don't give a damn about money. It's the *purse* it's in that counts," he said mockingly.

They all laughed as Maggie reached inside her handbag. "Just hold out something I can put the gold and silver into," she said, stepping closer.

Rafe felt sick at the pit of his stomach. He knew what she was thinking of doing, and she was being brave as hell. He had to be ready. If she got hurt or killed over this. . . .

"Put them in my pockets, Honey," the skinny one told her, "way down deep."

They all laughed again, and Maggie stepped very close. "If that's the way you want it." She reached into the handbag and took out some of the coins, shoving them into his pocket as deeply as she could, deliberately getting close to his privates to distract him. "Is that deep enough?"

The man drew a deep breath, and now the others were also distracted. Rafe looked at Joe, and Joe grinned, also realizing what she was trying to do. Maggie reached into her handbag again, and they were all so concentrated on her and the way she was lookng the skinny one right in the eye as though to tempt him that none of them noticed that this time she pulled out her tiny pistol. In one swift second she jammed its barrel against the center of the skinny man's chest and fired, and before he even had a chance to fall she dropped to the ground and rolled away.

As soon as Rafe heard the small crack of her pistol, his knife was out and landed into the chest of a second man. He was not wearing his handgun at the moment, so he literally dove into a third man before any of them realized what was going on. Joe dropped his towel and fired at the fourth man with a handgun, which, unknown to his abductor, he'd picked up along with his towel.

Rafe wrestled with the man he had tackled, trying to get his gun away. The man was on his back with Rafe's knee in his belly, and Rafe held the man's wrist with both hands, squeezing hard. The man writhed beneath him, using his free hand to pull a small knife from his pocket.

"Rafe! He has a knife!" Maggie screamed

Rafe let go with one hand and grabbed the man's other wrist just as he started to plunge the small knife into Rafe's side. With one swift surge of determination and strength Rafe shoved the knife hand downward while still bracing the gun hand away from him. Because of the way the man had been holding the knife, it landed in the man's belly when Rafe pushed down. The man cried out and dropped his handgun, and Rafe reached out and grabbed it. He cocked and fired, shooting the man square in the chest.

Maggie gasped and stared as Rafe got up and stepped back.

"You okay, Rafe?" Joe asked.

"I'm all right. I'm just damn mad that we weren't keeping better watch." Rafe looked over at Maggie. "Are you okay?"

Bewilderment on her face, Maggie walked over to where the man she'd shot lay flat out, a small bloody hole in the middle of his chest. "Dear God, I've killed a man!" she said, stepping back. She looked at Rafe. "I've killed a man!"

"He deserved it," Rafe told her. "You were protecting yourself. Don't think for one minute they would have just taken the money and left. They would have taken you with them, and you'd have been wishing *you* were dead." He turned to Joe. "Let's get these bodies over behind those rocks so we can eat and get out of here. And get back the money Maggie put in that bastard's pocket."

Maggie watched them drag off the bodies. "Eat?" she muttered. She put a hand to her stomach. Rafe yanked his knife out of the chest of the man he'd stabbed, and he wiped the blood off on the man's shirt, then shoved the knife back into its sheath. It was then the reality of their differences struck Maggie like cold water being thrown into her face. Here was Rafe the mountain man, the scout, the man who could kill without remorse. And yet he had such a kind, caring side. He'd risked his life more than once on the trail west protecting the people under his supervision. He'd saved Jenny from snakebite, saved her from drowning. He had been purely the gentleman on this trip, having complete respect for her wishes; yet there was this wild side, that little part of him that liked a challenge, that quick, skilled, vicious side that made him unlike any man she'd known before coming out here.

She sat on a log staring at the bacon, which was beginning to burn. A moment later Rafe was pulling the pan off the fire, and then he sat down beside her.

"This is just the reality of life in a place where there is no law, Maggie. You are used to law and order, but it doesn't exist out here, at least not yet. Men can turn into animals without the law to keep them in line. You did nothing wrong in shooting that man."

He moved an arm around her, and she faced him, studying the hard lines of his face, the scar on his forehead from a fight in which he'd killed yet another man. "How many men have you killed, Rafe?"

He frowned, pulling his arm away. "If you count the Mexican War, I would have no idea." He stared at the fire, aware of what she was thinking. "I'm not an Edward, Maggie. I'm nothing like any of the men you're used to. You know that." He faced her again. "But I don't kill for pleasure, and if you think it doesn't bother me, it *does*. No decent man kills another man without some remorse, or without wondering if he's going to burn in hell for it. But God gave us common sense and the will to survive. Sometimes that means killing someone. And I don't think God would have wanted me to let those men just take our money and you, and have me do nothing about it. It isn't in me, Maggie. I am what I am."

Maggie nodded, studying his eyes. "I know. And I love what you are. It's just . . . sometimes I have to get used to it all over again. And right now I'm just upset to realize *I* have killed a man."

He sighed, taking her hand. "It's okay."

Maggie looked away, and Joe was coming out from the rocks where he'd laid out the last body. "Oh, my God!" Maggie exclaimed.

Joe stood there naked as Adam. "You folks okay?" he asked.

"Don't you think it's time to put some clothes on?" Rafe called out.

Joe looked down at himself, only then realizing he'd lost his towel in the whole affair. "Tarnation!" he screamed. He covered himself with his hands and backed up, going behind the rocks. "Get me my clothes!" he yelled.

Rafe looked at Maggie, and in spite of the trauma of what had just happened, she could not help a grin, then light laughter. She rested her head on Rafe's shoulder and he moved an arm around her, kissing her hair. "Let's eat something and get the hell out of here," he told her. "Maybe by tomorrow you'll finally have your answer about Edward."

Maggie turned to kiss his cheek. "Thank you, Rafe." Close. So close. Rafe's lips met hers in a light, sweet kiss that turned a little deeper before Joe called out to them again.

"Hey, you two! I'm standin' here buck naked! Damn it, Rafe, get me some clothes! I ain't never gonna' live it down that your wife done saw parts no woman except the whores has ever seed! I'm sorry, Maggie. I was just so caught up in things, I didn't even realize!"

Maggie held Rafe's gaze for a moment, then laughed lightly. "You had better get his clothes. And tell him it's all right. Tell him I was so worked up myself that I didn't even notice." She couldn't help wondering what Rafe must look like, standing in naked glory by the light of day. She had never actually seen all his nakedness that one dark night they had made love. She turned away, and he left her to get Joe's clothes. Maggie put her head in her hands, chastising herself for the thought, again wondering at her own emotions and actions. What was Maggie Dumont McCahan doing in the foothills of the Sierras, shooting at robbers and forcing a smelly old mountain man to take a bath and then not even ruffled at seeing him buck naked? Who was this Maggie who cooked over campfires and fell in love with wagon train scouts and stood defiantly against would-be rapists, this Maggie who slept outdoors with nothing but her hair for a pillow? Who was this Maggie who had walked all the way to California, who dared to go alone to the docks of San Francisco? And what should she do if they found Brady and knew for certain that Edward was dead?

Chapter Thirty-Eight

They reached Bonnie's Gulch by late afternoon, and the main camp was as wild and wooly as all the others they had visited. Bawdy women strolled the streets, mingled with satin-vested gamblers and bearded, soiled prospectors. A few mules roamed freely, and the street was a churned mess of mud and animal dung. Piano music filtered out of taverns and whorehouses, even though it was far from nightfall, and more explosions could be heard higher in the mountains.

"That man called Brady, he staked out a claim up in that there region," Joe told them, pointing to a jutting of flat rock high up in the mountains. "It's a pretty good climb, but we can make it most of the way by nightfall, if you're willin' and able to keep goin'."

"I am anxious to get this over with," Maggie replied. "I need to know what happened to my husband."

Joe frowned. *"Husband?"*

Maggie closed her eyes at the error.

"I'll tell you on our way up," Rafe told Joe. "Maggie's just posing as my wife to help keep the men away."

Joe looked her over. "Well, I sure as hell can understand that. If'n I had ideas about her, I sure wouldn't want to go up against a big buck like you. A woman up in these parts who ain't hitched is askin' fer trouble, unless it's trouble she's lookin' for.'' The man laughed and headed his horse and mule through the main camp. A few men hooted and whistled at Maggie, in spite of the fact that she had begun wearing a pair of pants under her dress so her legs wouldn't show and she always wore a light jacket to help hide her breasts. She had purchased the pants at a different camp, having to purchase the smallest size she could find. She wore miner's boots and a floppy hat, with her hair pulled straight back into a tail at her neck. She looked down at her chapped hands and broken nails, and she wondered if Edward would even recognize her if they did happen to find him, let alone having to tell him she had killed a man.

One obviously drunk man staggered up to Maggie's horse and grabbed her thigh. ''Hey, Honey, you're new!''

Maggie raised her foot and kicked him hard in the face, sending him sprawling against a watering trough. A group of men who had been standing around him broke into hoots and guffaws, and another one headed toward Maggie. Immediately Rafe whirled his horse and rode into the man, knocking him down. He pulled his handgun and cocked it.

''Anybody else want to mess with my wife?''

''*Wife!*'' several of them said the word almost in unison.

''That's right. Next one who touches her gets turned into a woman himself with my knife.''

They all backed off, and Rafe stepped his horse over the man he'd knocked down and trotted the black gelding faster to catch up with Maggie and Joe. ''You're getting pretty damn good at defending yourself,'' he told Maggie.

She grinned. ''Thanks for taking care of the rest of them.''

They rode side by side as they continued toward the steep trail that would take them to the camp where they hoped the big man called Brady was still prospecting. ''Are you prepared for the worst regarding Edward?'' Rafe asked.

''I am. I have already considered him dead more than once. I just need to know for certain.''

Rafe lit a cigar. ''Then what?''

Maggie faced him. "I don't know. I suppose a lot of that depends on you."

"Does it?"

"Doesn't it?"

Rafe looked ahead. "Maybe. I just think there are some things you need to know . . . not about Edward, but about yourself."

"What do you mean?"

"I mean the life you have lived out here has all been out of necessity and survival. But just how natural is it to you? I think that if Edward is dead, you need to go back, Maggie."

"*Back!* To Pennsylvania?"

Rafe nodded.

"No, thank you! I will not go all the way back there, back over the mountains and the desert and—"

"That's the life you grew up with. You need to go back and find out if you really can leave all that behind. You have to go back and see your mother again, your sisters. You have to remember what it was like, and what you'd be giving up by staying here. You have to know if staying here is just a fantasy that will wear off after a while, if you would start missing the way life used to be, the way it won't be here for years."

"Are you saying you don't want me to stay?"

He smoked quietly before answering. "You know I do."

"Yet you'd let me go?"

"For your own sake. We're worlds apart, Maggie McCahan. Maybe too far apart to last. You've learned a lot coming out here, grown, changed, become stronger. But most people return to what they're born to. Besides, I know you. Out of respect for Edward, you wouldn't want to remarry right away."

More silence ensued.

"Is that a proposal?" Maggie finally asked.

"In a roundabout way. Kind of a pre-proposal, I guess. Right now it's pointless to even talk about, and probably not right."

"No, it isn't. But I understand what you're trying to say. We both have a lot to think—" Maggie gasped. "Oh, Dear God! It's one of Edward's wagons!" She kicked her horse into a faster run.

"Maggie, wait!"

Maggie did not even hear Rafe's shout. There it sat, next to a tent, the wagon bed painted blue, the name "McCahan" painted in white on its side, although some of the letters were partially worn away. Immediately other memories came flooding in, memories of the joy on Edward's face when he first told her of his plan to come to California and be his own man; memories of the trip west and how good he had been to her; memories of a man starting toward his dream with four freight wagons filled with supplies for the mining camps. Edward had truly thought he was doing the right thing leaving her with Ben Skeller. She could not blame him for what had happened.

She reached the wagon before Joe and Rafe, and she dismounted, running up and touching it.

"Hey! Who's out there?" It was a woman's voice.

Maggie ran around to the end of the wagon, where she was confronted by a large woman with red lips and rosy cheeks, green eyelids, and a pile of blond hair that was obviously bleached and had once been done up in a fancy style, now hanging in a frazzled mess. She wore only a slip and a lacy camisole that revealed a voluptuous bosom, and she was not a bit embarrassed for Joe and Rafe to see her that way.

"Where did you get this wagon?" Maggie demanded.

The woman looked her over, and when Rafe and Joe got closer she rested her arms on the top of the wagon gate and leaned out so that her breasts nearly spilled out of her camisole. "What the hell do you care, Honey?"

"It belonged to my husband! He's been missing for nearly four months!

The woman looked up at Rafe and grinned. "You fellas got a need? I've got this wagon fixed up pretty nice in here, nice feather mattress."

Maggie felt like vomiting. "Answer my question!"

The woman scowled. "Hey, Lady, I've got a living to make. And that big, dark, handsome man riding behind you is the best looking hunk of male I've seen up here." She looked back at Rafe. "I would just about be willing to give you a go-round for no charge. I have a feeling *I'd* benefit as much as you."

"If that's what you want, then answer the lady's question," Rafe told her, riding closer.

Maggie looked up at him, a wave of anger and jealousy shooting through her when he leaned closer, kissing the fat woman's cheek. Surely he was deliberately teasing her.

"Where did you get this wagon?" he asked.

The woman grinned. "Bought it off a big man with a red beard a few weeks back. It's a lot more comfortable than a damn tent. At least it's off the ground." She looked him over, and Maggie half expected her to begin drooling. "And you know what?"

"What?"

"It kind of rocks when a man is going at it, you know?"

Rafe nodded. "I know."

The fat woman laughed.

Rafe puffed on the cigar a moment, and Joe rode up beside him, eagerly eyeing the woman's huge breasts.

"Did the man who sold you this wagon say anything about where he got it?" Rafe asked her.

The woman shook her head. "I figured it was his. He called himself McCahan, you know, like the name on the side."

"Nobody else with him? No other wagons?"

"No. Just him and some mining supplies. Someone must have grubstaked him, because he had all the best equipment."

"That equipment belonged to my husband!" Maggie snapped. "The man with the red beard is *not* named McCahan! His name is Brady, and he *stole* this wagon and all the equipment from Edward McCahan!"

The woman shrugged. "I wouldn't know about that. All I know is I gave him a free night for it, and then he headed up the mountain."

"Have you seen him since?" Rafe asked.

"No."

"That most likely means he's still up there," Joe put in. "I don't think there's another way out."

Rafe nodded. "Thanks for the information," he told the fat prostitute. He pulled back his horse.

"Hey! I thought you wanted a free ride."

"I'll take one!" Joe told her.

"Joe! We have other things to tend to first," Rafe said.

Maggie turned away and mounted her horse. Rafe rode closer to the fat woman again. "Maybe another time, Honey."

"Oh, I'm so disappointed. Can't I change your mind?"

To Maggie's dismay, the woman pulled her camisole down to reveal large, pink nipples.

"Whoooie!" Joe yelled.

Rafe just grinned. "Got more important things to do first. I might be back."

The woman glanced at Maggie defiantly, then looked back at Rafe. "I'll be waiting."

Rafe gave Joe's horse a light kick on the rump. "Get your eyes back in your head and lead us up to that camp. We don't have time for this right now."

Joe shook his head. "You drive a hard bargain, friend. I'm givin' up an awful lot for you, and I mean an *awful* lot!"

Maggie rolled her eyes as she rode up beside Rafe, and they followed Joe out of the camp. After several minutes Maggie spoke up. "Are you really going back there?"

Rafe laughed lightly. "Hell, no. I don't care to die from whatever diseases women like that can give a man."

Maggie felt a secret relief.

"You didn't think I *meant* it, did you?"

"I don't know. You're a man, and I am beginning to wonder if such things are all men think about. In places like this it certainly seems so."

Rafe took a last puff on his cigar and threw it down. "I only think about it in relation to you."

Maggie suddenly felt as though her own breasts were naked, and she pulled her jacket closer around them. Her nipples actually ached with a desire to be touched and tasted by Rafe Morrisey. Guilt for thinking such a thing at this time made her feel ashamed. They had just found one more clue that most likely meant Edward was dead. "You have probably been with a lot of women like that."

Rafe shook his hair behind his shoulders. "A time or two. It's been several years since my wife died."

"Have you been with that kind of woman since . . . since . . ."

"No. You must know that. If you don't, then why am I helping you?"

Her eyes teared. "I'm sorry. Seeing that wagon . . . I don't know. I'm so confused. It will help so much just to know the truth about Edward."

I hope you never know the whole truth, Rafe thought.

"All right, you two," Joe called out from up ahead, "how about tellin' me what the hell it is between you? What's this about you not bein' married and us lookin' for Maggie's husband? You still ain't explained it."

"I'll explain when we make camp," Rafe answered. He left her to ride up beside Joe, and Maggie watched him, memories flooding in as Rafe told Joe part of the story about the trail west and how they had come to be such good "friends." It soon became too dark to go any farther up the trail, which was getting steeper and narrower. Rafe decided they had better camp for the night, and they found a small area that flattened out a little, enough to bed down and tether the horses, although there was little grass for the horses to eat.

"We can make the top by mornin'," Joe told them. "It's pretty flat for a ways, with a high wall of rock all along, with holes blowed into it. Some of them ought to be in there pretty deep by now . . . dangerous work."

"Does Brady have friends up there with him?" Rafe asked.

"None close. Just other prospectors that are workin' their own claims up there. They all sort of look out for each other, but ain't none of them close enough to get in on another's fight, if that's what you're askin'."

"That's what I'm asking. And you let me take care of Brady. Maggie needs the truth, and I'll get it out of him."

"Oh, I don't doubt you'll do that."

They dismounted to make camp, and Maggie looked out at the scenery below, only then realizing how high they had already come. It seemed they could see for miles. The ground shook from an explosion somewhere, and Maggie wondered how much would be left of these mountains by the time man was finished digging out their bowels to find their precious gold. Poor Edward hadn't even wanted the gold. He had simply wanted the chance to build his own little empire. But he wasn't made for this land. It was men like Rafe who were made for it.

Chapter Thirty-Nine

The pathway along which Joe led them became precariously narrow, and the morning was spent watching every foot ahead, with no chance to think about what they would do about Brady or anything else. The climb took total concentration, and that the prospectors had managed to get up here with all their equipment was a wonder. Yet when they reached the top Maggie could see the scattered tents of a secondary camp, a little gathering place of all who mined up in these parts.

Now she could hear picks clanging, hear the swish of rockers that were sloshing gravel through their screens, leaving only larger minerals, including nuggets of gold, or what the prospectors *hoped* would be gold. Everywhere she looked men were working in one way or another, with shovels or picks, rockers or pans, and the entire side of the mountain, which at this point became more of a gradual, grassy slope before turning back into precarious rock formations, was dotted with tents and shacks.

"Up there," Joe pointed. "That's where he was, last I knew."

"Come on," Rafe told Maggie. "You can tell us if he's the same man who left with Edward."

"I already know he is." Maggie felt her heartbeat quicken at finally being so close to knowing the truth.

"Got to be careful. Up in these parts men hang claim jumpers. You don't want to be mistaken for one," Joe warned Rafe. "Brady has probably made friends by now."

Rafe and Maggie followed Joe along a narrow pathway past other claims, and men turned to look, this time not so much to stare at Maggie as to give a watchful eye for possible claim jumpers. They reached a shack beside a hole that had been blasted into a sheer rock wall behind it.

"That's Brady's shack," Joe told them.

There did not seem to be anyone around.

"You two stay here and keep watch," Rafe said. "Have your guns ready—even you, Maggie. Use that bigger six-gun I gave you, not that little pop-gun you carry."

"It worked just fine yesterday morning," she reminded him.

Rafe studied the way her auburn hair blew in little wisps around her face, and the picture of her sitting there in that big hat and wearing miner's boots would have made him smile, if not for this grave situation. God, he loved her. "You held it right against his chest. From a distance the thing is useless. Just do as I say." He unbuckled his own gunbelt and slung it over his horse. "But only use your guns to hold off others who might try to come to this guy's aid. I don't want Brady killed . . . yet. He's the only one who can tell us the truth about Edward."

Maggie nodded. "Be careful, Rafe. He's a giant of a man."

Joe pulled a rifle from its boot on his horse and rested it across his lap. "Come on up here closer to me," he told Maggie. "Now that I smell better, that shouldn't be so hard."

Maggie smiled and rode up closer, and they both waited, watching the other miners scattered about below the site.

"You love him, don't you?" Joe asked Maggie.

She swallowed, nervous about what might happen. "Yes," she said quietly. She looked toward the cave entrance. "That is part of the reason we have to know what has happened to my husband."

Rafe came out of the small cave. "There are tools in there, but no Brady."

"Somebody looking for me?" A big man with a red beard came walking down a pathway from somewhere above his own camp, and Maggie felt instant hatred at the sight of him, as well as fear for Rafe. Big as he was, Brady was even bigger and broader.

"Brady!" Joe called out. He dismounted and walked up to greet him, and Maggie looked at Rafe. Both realized Joe was trying to take the wary looking Brady off his defensive stance. The man was carrying a pickaxe. "Hey, old friend, you remember me?"

Brady grinned. "Sure, Joe." He shifted the pickaxe to his left hand and shook Joe's hand. "You smell a mite better than what I remember."

"Well, I done took a real bath!"

Both men laughed, and Joe lured Brady closer.

"Stay on your horse," Rafe said quietly to Maggie.

"Say, I got some folks here who want to meet you," Joe was saying. "They've got somethin' to ask you." He brought Brady within an arm's length of Rafe. "This here is Rafe Morrisey, a scoutin' friend of mine." Rafe shook his hand, sizing him up. "And the pretty woman there—well, maybe you remember her?"

Brady studied Maggie a moment, looking puzzled. "Well, Ma'am, you look familiar. Am I supposed to know you?"

"You only met me once," Maggie answered, "when my husband, Edward McCahan, hired you to help guard his supplies . . . supplies he brought into these mountains four months ago to sell at the mining camps. He has never been heard from since. We are wondering if you know why."

Brady's smile faded. He looked from Maggie to Joe, who was still grinning, then to Rafe, who was not.

"How about some answers?" Rafe said with a commanding air.

Brady backed up. "What's going on here?"

"Where is my husband?" Maggie asked. "We already know you were going around with one of his supply wagons and claiming to *be* Edward McCahan! I am in possession of a gold watch you sold to a gambler in another camp. The watch belonged to my husband. It even has his initials engraved on the back of it, and my picture inside!"

Brady looked up at her. "Your husband . . . he sold everything . . . but it took a while, traveling to all the different camps and all. Then we . . . we were attacked by thieves. They killed your husband and took the wagons. They thought I was dead, too, but I lived. I buried your husband and I . . . I kept that watch—figured he owed me something for my time helping him."

"You're a lying sonofabitch!" Rafe told him. "We know you were in possession of at least one of those wagons because people *saw* you with them, and you were posing as Edward McCahan and selling the supplies yourself! One of those wagons is down at the main camp right now, housing for a fat whore who bought it off you for sex. How about going over your story one more time!"

Brady's face began to flush. "I don't have to tell you *anything*! You ain't the law. There's *no* law in these parts! It's every man for himself!"

"Is that why you figured you had the right to *kill* Edward McCahan? Where's all the money, Brady? He had a lot of money on him, and made even more selling those supplies!"

In an instant Brady raised his pickaxe, and Maggie screamed when he swung it at Rafe; but Rafe was ready for him. He jumped out of the way in time, then quickly rammed into Brady before the man could again raise the axe. He managed to barrel the man to the ground, and Joe grabbed the bridle of Maggie's horse, pulling it back farther as the two powerful men wrestled on the ground.

"Help keep watch!" Joe told Maggie. "Have that six-gun ready. Some of these men might think we're claim jumpers."

Maggie was torn between terror for Rafe, wanting to watch and make sure he wasn't hurt; and the necessity of turning her horse and watching for others. Joe ran his horse over to a pine tree to tie it, then came back, rifle ready. All the while Rafe and Brady fought viciously. Brady had lost his grip on the pickaxe, but after managing to kick Rafe off him, he scrambled over to pick it up again. Before he could raise it, Rafe landed into him again, grasping that arm with both his hands while pressing a knee against Brady's throat.

With his free hand, Brady pulled a knife from its sheath at his side and rammed it into Rafe's left thigh. Rafe cried out and fell away, and Maggie turned, screaming at the sight of blood on Rafe's thigh, at the same time seeing Brady getting to his knees and raising the pickaxe again. Joe made ready with his rifle, but Rafe quickly rolled away, the pickaxe slamming into the ground just inches away. Rafe immediately slammed into the man again, landing vicious blows to the man's big belly, then catching him flat in the nose when he bent over, sending Brady sprawling onto his back with blood splattered all over his face.

Joe quickly grabbed the pickaxe and tossed it out of reach, then ran over and picked up the knife Brady had dropped when he had picked up the axe again. Rafe grabbed Brady by the shirt front and jerked him to a sitting position.

"All we want is some *answers,* Brady!" he growled. "The *truth!* We need to know the *truth!*"

The only reply was a big fist slammed into Rafe's face.

"Oh, my God," Maggie choked.

"Hey! What's going on!"

Maggie turned around again to see several men approaching. Nervously, she took her handgun from its holster around her horse's neck and raised it, so upset that she was afraid she would pull the trigger without even wanting to. "Stay back!"

Joe walked to the edge of Brady's camp, rifle raised. "We're just tryin' to get the truth out of this man called Brady," he shouted. "We think he killed this here woman's husband and stole his money and supplies."

"Claim jumpers are hanged!" one of the men yelled.

"We don't want his goddamn claim!" Joe shouted back. "All's we want is the truth out of him as to what happened to Maggie McCahan's husband!"

The men came closer, angry looks on their faces.

"It's true!" Maggie shouted at them. "My husband has been

missing for four months, and he had left San Francisco with four wagons of supplies. He had hired Brady as a guard." She could hear punches and grunts behind her, and she felt sick for Rafe.

"You men stay put," Joe warned. "Otherwise you can decide among yourselves which one of you wants to be first to get a bullet in his belly. Ain't nobody gonna' finish this fight except the two men that's already in it."

Maggie glanced back, and she groaned at the sight. Rafe's left pantleg was soaked with blood and his face was also a bloody mess, as was Brady's. Both men were beginning to stagger. Rafe landed another blow to the side of Brady's head, and the big man stumbled against his shanty. He grabbed a hatchet that was propped against the small building, and he came at Rafe with it.

Maggie wondered if Rafe could even see the weapon, for all the blood in his eyes, but he must have, for he drew his hunting knife. He had not wanted to use a weapon himself if it could be avoided, but now he had no choice. He tossed the knife, and it landed in Brady's right shoulder. The man screamed out and dropped the hatchet, and Rafe plowed into him once more, landing Brady flat on his back and yanking the knife from his shoulder. Instantly the knife was pressed against Brady's cheekbone, the tip of it just under his eye.

"Now!" Rafe seethed. "The *truth,* Brady, and if you move even *slightly,* your eyeball will be cut out of its socket!"

Brady lay there panting, and he rolled his eyes downward, trying to see the blade. "He's . . . dead," the man panted.

"*How! When!*" Rafe pricked the skin under the man's eye.

"Couple months ago!" Brady answered instantly. "He'd sold . . . most of his stuff. Even sold the empty wagons so's we wouldn't have to . . . take them back. Men bought them . . . for the canvas . . . and used the wood to build shanties. The other men that . . . came with us to help . . . they dropped off along the way as things got sold and they wasn't needed. It . . . got down to just me and Edward."

"So you decided that as long as there weren't any witnesses, you would just get rid of Edward and take his money and supplies, right?''

''Something . . . like that.''

Rafe leaned closer. ''Now, you're going to say this quiet, so McCahan's wife can't hear, understand?''

Brady just swallowed, then groaned when Rafe sank a knee into his groin. ''How did you kill him? Where is the body? Did you bother to bury it?''

Brady gritted his teeth when Rafe cut a little deeper under his eye. ''A place . . . called Jackknife Pass,'' Brady half whispered. ''Above Jackknife Landing. It's . . . another gold camp. I got him with an axe in the back . . . then threw him over the ledge. His body is . . . down there somewhere . . . what's left of it.''

''You backstabbing sonofabitch!'' Rafe growled. ''I should cut your eyeball out just for my own satisfaction!''

''Wait!'' Brady panted. ''He ain't worth it!''

''What do you mean by that!''

''That woman . . . she's best rid of him. He wasn't no . . . real man. He was . . . hell, I used him before I killed him. We'd been . . . you know . . . hell, man, up in these parts . . . where there ain't hardly any women . . . a man does what he has to do. He was willin', so I . . . took advantage.''

''You slime!'' Rafe hissed. He cut a gash under the man's eye, and Brady cried out. ''Don't you say one word about that to another soul! Understand?'' Rafe got off the man and told him to get up. Brady rolled to his knees, blood running from the wound in his shoulder and from the cut under his eye. He held his left hand to his eye, and his right arm hung limp as he managed to get to his feet. Rafe shoved at him so that he stumbled closer to the crowd of men that had gathered. ''Tell them!'' Rafe demanded. ''Tell them who murdered Edward McCahan! I'll leave it up to the rest of these men as to what to do with you. The only law up here is *camp* law, so it's their call!''

Brady looked at the group of men with his uncovered eye, and Rafe pressed his big blade against the man's back. 'Remember what I told you,'' he warned.

Brady took a couple of deep breaths. ''I . . . killed a supplier named Edward McCahan . . . up at Jackknife Pass,'' he admitted. ''He was . . . this woman's husband. I . . . worked for him.''

Mumbles moved through the crowd of men, some asking each other what they should do. Maggie looked away, a heavy pain rushing through her at finally knowing the truth.

''Where is the money you took from McCahan?'' Rafe asked.

''Robbed. That's the God's truth. All I had left . . . was that last wagon . . . and some good mining tools. Bandits got the money . . . between Jackknife Pass . . . and here. You can look through my shack if you want.''

Rafe shoved the man toward the crowd of men. ''You decide what to do with him!''

''Hang him!'' some of them shouted.

''We have to hold court first!'' another advised.

''Break out the whiskey and let's have a trial!'' another man yelled.

Several men grabbed hold of Brady and hauled him away, followed by men shouting, fists raised.

''They latch on to anything for excitement,'' Joe said as he watched them leave.

''Will they really hang him?'' Maggie asked.

''You can bet on it,'' Joe answered.

Maggie's eyes stung with tears. ''Good.'' She put away her handgun and dismounted, going to where Rafe had sat down on the ground, holding his ribs. ''Joe, help me,'' Maggie ordered. ''We've got to do something about his leg.'' The buckskin pants Rafe wore were designed to lace up the sides, so Maggie began unlacing them far enough down so that she could pull them aside and expose the wound in his hard-muscled thigh. She looked into Rafe's eyes as she waited for Joe to get some bandages. ''What can I say? He could have killed you.''

''You had to know the truth. That's why I didn't dare use my knife or a gun the way I would have liked to. I couldn't kill him.''

''I know.'' Maggie leaned forward and touched her cheek to his own bloody one. ''Thank you, Rafe. At last I know the truth.''

He nodded, still panting from his ordeal. He wiped blood from his lip. "We'll have Joe take us to Jackknife Pass. I'll try to get down there and find the body and bury it. He told me he . . . shot Edward." How could he tell her the man had slammed Edward in the back with an axe? "Then pushed him over the edge."

Maggie closed her eyes and bowed her head. "My God," she whispered. "Poor Edward. Poor, sweet Edward."

Rafe decided this much was all she needed to know. He would never tell her the rest. She had suffered enough.

Chapter Forty

Maggie, Rafe, and Joe had to ride through the secondary camp to get back down the mountain, and as they did so it was impossible to miss the sight of Brady's body hanging from the sturdy branch of a huge Ponderosa pine. His "trial" had taken place quickly, with much celebration, apparently, for there was still a considerable amount of drinking, gambling, and laughing going on. Maggie looked away from the grotesque sight—Brady's head snapped into a sideways position, his face still covered with blood from where Rafe had cut him, blood also covering the right side of his shirt.

Dead. Edward really was dead. Joe was going to lead them to where Brady claimed he'd left the body. She didn't want to see it. She only wanted Rafe to try to identify it, at least by the clothes, if possible, and to bury what was left. All she could think about now was the night they had lain in bed and Edward had told her of his dream.

I'm thinking of leaving, Maggie. . . . West. California. All for this. To end up with his flesh being eaten by vultures, a good deal of his money gone, his supplies lying at the bottom of the ocean somewhere off the southern tip of South America. Gretta and Maria were gone, and so were all of Edward's dreams. And in spite of her disappointment in the marriage, she still had lost the truest friend she'd had growing up. It had always been Edward and Maggie, even when they were little.

Why couldn't she cry? Perhaps it was because she had already been prepared to learn he was dead, or maybe it was because she had already cried out all that was left in her. Maybe she had emptied herself that night she slept alone in the woods hiding from Ben Skeller, or the day Rafe had ridden out of her life the first time. Right now she just felt empty, lost, displaced. Edward was gone, and she had dragged Rafe into her life without even knowing quite what to do with him . . . except love him when that love was forbidden.

They headed down the mountain and even made it through the main camp before finally finding a spot to hole up for the night. It was obvious Rafe needed the rest. Maggie spread out his bedroll for him, and he limped over to it, wincing with pain as he eased himself down. Joe took care of the horses, and Maggie soaked a rag with cool water and gently applied it to the bruises and cuts on Rafe's face.

"I couldn't have done this without you. I'm so sorry you ended up hurt like this, Rafe."

He managed a weak grin. "I didn't figure I'd get a man to confess to murder with a smile."

"Still, you didn't have to do this."

"Yes, I did. You know damn well I did."

Maggie sat back on her heels. "Are you sure you want to go to Jackknife Pass?"

He closed his eyes. "We have to. Neither one of us will truly rest easy until we find the body and bury what is left of it. Do you want me to take off his wedding ring and give it to you?"

Maggie felt sick. "If you can. Don't force yourself to do something that is too repulsive for you."

He patted her hand. "I've seen and done just about everything there is for a man to see and do. I'll get the ring."

"How is your leg?"

"Aches."

Another scar, she thought. He was tough, tough and resilient brave and skilled. She could just imagine the looks on her family's faces if she brought such a man home with her. "Rafe, I can't go back."

He opened his eyes. "You have to. It's impossible to get through the higher passes yet. Too much snow. But the sooner the better. If you go by ship, you can get around the Cape before the really bad weather sets in, which is usually around July, sailors tell me. You'd be a couple months ahead of that kind of weather. By the time you reached the Atlantic, the weather there should be the best—late summer weather as you head north, pretty calm seas."

Maggie put the rag back into a pan she'd been using. She drew up her knees and wrapped her arms around them. "Oh, Rafe, it's such a long voyage. I would be too lonely. Can't you come with me?"

"It wouldn't be the same. You need to go back alone, to be with your family again, back into the life you always knew before this. You need to be without me so that you can truly decide if you can get along without me in your life."

"I already know that I can't. And to go all the way back . . ." Tears filled her eyes. "That world is like a distant dream now."

"I know. And you will never settle in your mind where you belong until you go back to Pennsylvania."

"But I might never find you again. I let you go once, and it was so painful. I can't walk out of your life again."

"You'll find me, if you decide that's what you want. As soon as the snow is melted enough, I'll head back east by land. By next spring I'll be back in Independence. I'll find another job leading a wagon train west. If you want to go back, just go there. Be sure to hire a good escort to get you there. If you show up by May fifteenth, I'll know it's to go back west with me. If not, I'll know you have decided to stay in Pennsylvania."

Maggie cried quietly. There was so much to mourn. "I don't know. I just don't know."

"Do it, Maggie, for us, for yourself. Before I left I found two families who have changed their minds and want to go back home. They are going by a ship that leaves April tenth. They figured that would be the best timing, and I hoped we'd be back in time for you to take the same ship. It looks like we'll make it. They would be good folks to travel with, Maggie, and I remember you telling others you had been to Europe when you were sixteen, so you're familiar with traveling by sea."

She met his eyes. "You apparently already have it all planned."

"I thought about it almost constantly from the day I left you at Sutter's Fort, what we should do if we saw each other again. Then when I found out Edward was missing, and before we left to come up here, I asked around at boarding houses and homes to see if I could find someone going back. Once home, if you decided not to continue your life with me, you would at least be safe, with the people who love you and can help you live the way you deserve to live."

She looked at her hands. "I don't think I could ever live that way again. Please come with me, Rafe."

Their gazes held in the anguish of knowing the truth, and of knowing they must part once more. "I don't belong there. You know that. If you decide to come with me, I'd like to settle in Oregon, away from all this madness. I have money saved. Lord knows I've never had anything to spend it on, except a good horse once in a while. I'd like to do some ranching in Oregon. It wouldn't be an easy life, Maggie. Remember that. Think really hard about it before you leave the luxury of Pennsylvania again."

More tears came. She had not been able to cry over Edward, but she could cry over Rafe. She lay down beside him, resting her head on his shoulder. "I can't think about it now. I just can't. Oh, God, Rafe, poor Edward. What a terrible way to die. I don't think he ever knew truly happy days in his life besides the day he headed west and the day he headed into these mountains with his supplies. He had such big dreams."

Rafe pulled a blanket over both of them, glad he had never told her the truth about her husband. Now she would never have to know.

* * *

An eagle flew overhead, its cry as lonely as this place. Far below a river tumbled in a roar that echoed up through the Canyon, and even though this pass was nowhere near the top of these mountains it was still cold and windy, and Maggie shivered. Farther ahead snow still blocked the pass, but there was another mining camp above that. Apparently Edward had been trying to get there, and it made Maggie sick to realize that Brady probably deliberately talked him into it, telling him they could make it through. That way he could get Edward alone, someplace where there would be absolutely no witnesses but the wolf and the eagle. What a lonely, lonely way to die. She could only pray that Edward had died instantly when he was shot.

What made the mourning worse was to realize how much she loved Rafe, and yet she knew he was right that she should go home, if Pennsylvania could even be called home any more. And now her faithful Rafe, even though he was in pain, had descended the cold, windy canyon wall, dangling by a rope that Joe maneuvered by winching it around a lonely pine tree. He had been determined to get to the floor of the canyon so he could search for the remains of a body.

Maggie had insisted he did not need to go. Because of wolves and hungry birds, there was probably nothing left. Or perhaps the river had risen from melting snows, to the point that it had washed everything away. But Rafe refused to go back to San Francisco without this final proof, and he knew what it would mean to her to have something more of Edward to keep forever.

She ducked back inside the tent Rafe and Joe had erected for protection from the wind, and she lay down, feeling weary . . . so weary. Rafe and Joe had come prepared with wolfskin jackets and hats when first coming into the mountains, but she had had nothing warm enough for this, so before coming up Rafe had purchased a buffalo robe from a supplier at the base of the pass, and now Maggie wrapped herself in it.

Another amazing first, she thought. Maggie Dumont McCahan, belle of the posh ball her mother had held for her when she turned sixteen, was now lying in a makeshift tent in a snowy pass in the Sierra-Nevada Mountains, wearing a man's pants and miner's boots, a plain gray dress, and wrapped in a buffalo robe like an Indian woman. The constant howl of the wind and rumbling of the river below made her want to cover her ears, and finally she fell asleep, wondering how many more days it would take poor Rafe to find something, praying he was all right. He had been down there for three days, and Joe said he had better come up soon, since one never knew when a spring snowstorm might come, and it would bury them right where they were. Maggie didn't care if she died up here, as long as Rafe made it back and she could die in his arms.

She had no idea how long she had slept when Joe tapped the bottom of her feet. "He's comin' back up."

Maggie sat up, rubbing her eyes, wondering how terrible she must look by now and glad she had no mirror along. She crawled out of the tent and walked over to where Joe was using a horse to pull on the rope. After Rafe's descent, he had tied the rope around the saddle horn of his horse every morning, ready for when Rafe returned and needed help being hoisted up. They had already made their plans. Maggie would watch over the edge, and each time Rafe reached a point where he could stand and wait, Joe would untie his end of the rope and bring the horse back to the edge and tie it again. Then he would walk the horse away from the edge once more, as far as it could go without running into yet another canyon wall opposite the ledge where they were camped. The ascent would take a good hour of going back and forth, gathering up whatever length of rope had already been used each time. They could all only pray that the places where the rope was tied together with more rope would hold.

Maggie watched. Rafe wore the backpack and shovel he'd gone down with. Had he found anything? She signaled Joe each time Rafe gave the hand signal that he could stop for a while. She knew this had to be painful for Rafe because of his leg wound, but finally, after a couple of heart-stopping moments when rocks fell or Rafe lost his footing, he made it to the top, crawling past the ledge and flopping down wearily in the snow, panting.

"I found him," he told Maggie. He grunted as he lay back in the snow, physically spent.

"Oh, Rafe, I'm so sorry it took so long." She took hold of one hand, removing his glove and rubbing the hand vigorously to warm it, but he pulled it away and reached inside his wolfskin coat. He fumbled around a moment, then pulled his hand back out. He held up a gold wedding band.

"I told you I would get this for you if I could."

Maggie could not help the tears of mourning then. Here was her final proof . . . all that was left of Edward McCahan. She took the ring and closed it into her fist. She lay across Rafe's chest and wept.

Chapter Forty-One

Maggie packed her best dresses in the trunk in which she had brought them to California. She had worn them only a few times, during her stay with Mary Skeller, when they had meetings with The Ladies' Guild. She had not been here long enough or become a big enough part of San Francisco society to bother ordering more ball gowns and fancy evening dresses, or to have any made for her. Now these dresses from home would *go* back home, along with the trunk that had come here all the way from France. Now it would make another journey by ocean.

The thought of leaving tore at her soul when she thought about all she had been through getting here just last summer. They had come with so much, and now it was all gone. Even Edward was gone, along with a good deal of their money. She would return home with only a few thousand dollars, her grandmother's trunk, and two extra bags . . . and her journal. She could not bring herself to read any of it right now, to remember things that hurt too much to remember.

She had talked Mary Skeller into encouraging Ben to buy the house from her, again using Mary to wring more money out of Ben. She had also taken what was left of her and Edward's own money out of Ben's bank, and again most of her money . . . along with Edward's wedding ring . . . was hidden in the lining at the bottom of the trunk. She would not need the few items of furnishings and dishes in the house that were hers. She would leave them.

She looked at herself in a full-length mirror. Rafe was coming tonight, for a last talk, a last good-bye. Tobacco Joe had stayed behind at one of the mining camps, and despite the short time she had known him Maggie knew she would never forget him the rest of her life. So many people had come in and out of her life in the last year, people she would remember forever. She had learned how painful good-byes could be.

Now another good-bye, the hardest of all. After returning from the mountains a week ago, Rafe had left her alone, respecting her wishes to *be* alone, giving her time to make ready for her return to Pennsylvania. But both knew they must see each other once more, and she had left a message at his boarding house to come here this evening. She looked closer in the mirror, hoping she had not put on too much color. She hardly needed any on her face now, for the western sun had put some there, as well as a couple of new wrinkles, she was sure. She even had a few freckles on her nose. She had filed her nails, but all the scrubbing in the world couldn't get the dirt out of some of the little cracks around her fingers and the edges of her nails. She decided the dirt would have to work its way out on its own. And generous amounts of hand cream still did not quite soften her hands to where they had been before she left Pennsylvania. They looked stronger now, but much drier, and she'd developed callouses where she had handled reins daily.

She turned in the mirror. At least she had her figure. That had not changed. She wore a soft, pink cotton dress, not terribly fancy but well-fitted, and pink went well with her auburn hair and her complexion. The dress had short sleeves, with white eyelet ruffle trim around the sleeve caps and the modest neckline. For once Rafe would see her looking closer to the real Maggie McCahan, *sans* the miner's boots and floppy hat and buffalo robe! She had given the boots and pants away at the last mining camp they traveled through, but she kept the buffalo robe. It was rolled up and tied. She would take it home and show it to her family.

There came a knock at the back door, and she knew who it would be. Her heart pounded faster as she descended the mahogany staircase and walked over the polished wood floor of the hallway that led to the kitchen. She opened the door, and she drew in her breath at the sight of him . . . Rafe. He wore a neat white shirt and black pants, a string tie, and black jacket. Never had she seen him dressed this way and looking quite this handsome. He removed a new black hat, and his long hair was clean and shiny, pulled straight back into a tail.

"My goodness! I did not expect this!"

Rafe looked a little embarrassed. "Other than taking you to the docks tomorrow, this is the last you'll see of me. I thought I'd put on my best for you, maybe help entice you to be waiting for me next year in Independence." He brought a hand from behind his back and handed out a bouquet of flowers.

"Oh, Rafe." She stepped back, allowing him in. "You know you don't need to do anything to make me want to come back any more than I already do." She took the flowers and smelled them. "They're very pretty. I wish I had more time to enjoy them." She walked to a cupboard and took down a vase, setting the flowers in it and setting it on the kitchen table. "I still am not positive I am doing the right thing by leaving."

Rafe closed the door, and Maggie met his eyes. *Dear God, if a man can be beautiful, you are beautiful,* she thought. He had the most wonderful smile, his teeth even and white, his lips just the right fullness. . . . Desire swept through her like a storm, and both of them knew what must happen tonight. "Thank you for the flowers."

His dark eyes moved over her in a way that nearly made her tremble. "I just thought . . . hell, all we've been through, the way we feel about each other . . . yet I've never done something as simple as give you flowers." He sighed, hanging his hat over the post of a chair. "You look beautiful, Maggie, but then that doesn't take much."

She actually felt herself blushing. "Thank you. Would you like a drink? Or tea? Gus left some wine in the icebox, and since ice is delivered up here frequently, I bought some to keep what's left in there cool. The wine should be cold."

He removed his jacket. "I think we could both use a little wine."

She smiled, going to the icebox to take out the bottle. She uncorked it and went to the china cabinet to take out two wineglasses. Gus had left everything behind, even Jean's china and glasses. She set the glasses on the table and filled each one half way with white wine. "I'm not much of a drinker. I've never tasted this, so I can't guarantee how good it is." She set down the bottle and took a chair. "The women of The Ladies' Guild say their husbands think California has a wonderful climate for growing grapes. The Spanish have already been doing it for who knows how long, and they think this state could one day give France a run for its money in quality wine."

"They do, do they?" Rafe sat down and picked up his glass. "I see you learned enough back in Pennsylvania to have a mind for business."

She picked up her own glass. "I grew up around people whose only conversations revolved around business, money, investments, industry, and such."

Rafe held out his glass. "Here's to a safe voyage home."

She held out her glass and touched his. "And to your own safety while we are apart."

They touched glasses and sipped some of the wine. Maggie was pleased that it was sweet and cold.

"Speaking of how you grew up," Rafe said, "I remember the stories you told along the trail, of balls and theaters, governors and company presidents, finishing school . . . the grand wedding you had in your parents' mansion."

Her smile faded. Edward. She looked at her wine. "Yes, it was a wedding fit for a princess, and I felt like one that day. It seems like such a long, long time ago now."

Rafe could not help wondering what her wedding night was like. Surely she had been a virgin. It made him sick to think how clumsy Edward must have been at making a woman out of her. He was probably a virgin himself, at least when it came to women. "Maggie, I didn't mean to bring up memories of

Edward. I only wanted to point out the kind of life you led back there, the kind of life you will go back to. You are still young, and you are incredibly beautiful. Any number of very wealthy, probably handsome, and single men are going to be after your hand. I won't blame you one bit if you accept one of them and stay in Pennsylvania. I mean that.'' He drank more wine.

Maggie studied his strong hands, thought about his vicious fight with Brady, remembered when he slit the throat of the man who had landed his knife in her. Such a contrast he was to the kind of men he had just mentioned. ''None of them could compare to you,'' she told him.

''But I can never offer you what they can.''

Maggie set her glass down. ''Rafe, I have learned so much out here, about myself, what is and is not important to me. I don't think going back home will make any difference now, but you're right that I need to go and find out for myself. The only think I can guarantee right now is that I love you, with all my heart and soul. I think I fell in love with you the first time I set eyes on you in Saint Louis. Maybe I don't need the things you think I need. I have discovered that I can survive just fine on the simplest terms. I have learned to do my own wash, do my own hair, my own cooking.'' She smiled, picking up the wineglass again. ''I have learned not to care that my nails are broken and dirty. I have killed a man, trudged through wild mining camps wearing a man's pants and boots, slept in a buffalo robe. I have even cleaned a squirrel! My mother and sisters will die when they hear what all I've done.'' She drank down more wine, and Rafe finished his. ''I just want you to know,'' Maggie continued, ''that all that wealth and fancy living back home . . . I don't think I could be happy with all that if I couldn't be with the man I truly love. I would rather give it all up and be with you. The most important lesson I have learned is how much more important real love is than things.''

''Well, you'll never know until you go back.''

She studied his eyes, his face, not wanting to forget one

thing about him. "I need to know what your plans are, for when I meet you in Independence."

"My plans? It's like I told you. I'd settle in Oregon, build a ranch there."

"I will have money, Rafe. I can help you have anything you want."

"I don't want you for your money."

She smiled. "I know. But as long as I have it—"

"Maggie, all the money in the world still won't make life in a place like Oregon the same as it is in Pennsylvania. It will be a long time before streets get paved and theaters are built and—"

"I know."

"And where I intend to live, we won't exactly be living near a city of any size. You're used to cities."

"Not any more. Stop trying to talk me out of coming back, Rafe."

"I just want you to be sure."

"And there has never been anyone else for you since Nina?"

His eyes took on a longing look. "No." He reached out and took her hand. "And I was pretty young then."

"I don't even know how old you are now."

He grinned softly. "I am thirty-two. I've never asked you age, either. It has never really mattered."

"You have nine years on me. I'm twenty-three."

"It's strange, isn't it? How two people can know practicall nothing about each other, yet still be attracted to each other?'

Maggie thought about Edward. She had known him all he life, yet had never been attracted to him in the way she wa attracted to Rafe Morrisey. "Yes, I guess it is. I think som things are just meant to be."

He squeezed her hand. "Maggie . . ." He sighed, actuall seeming nervous. He rubbed the back of her hand with hi thumb. "I can't just let you go tomorrow. Not without . . showing you how much I love you . . . not without giving yo one last reason to come back."

Maggie stood up and came closer. She grasped his head an pressed it against her bosom. "Why do you think I wanted yo to come here tonight?'' She placed her cheek against the top of his head. ''I . . . the timing is good, Rafe. It should be safe, and I also need to show you how much I love you.'' She stroked her hand down his hair, removing the leather tie that held it. ''Make love to me, Rafe. I *need* you to make love to me.''

She drew a deep breath when he turned his face to kiss at her breasts.

There was nothing more to say. His lips moved up her neck, to just behind her ears, where he licked her softly. They trailed over her cheek to her lips, and he rose, crushing her against him as he met her mouth in a savage kiss. Maggie could hardly get her breath for the want of him.

Chapter Forty-Two

The first time their need was so urgent there was not even time to undress. They had needed this for much too long, and Rafe wondered if she realized the absolute pain he had suffered by keeping his hands off her all the time they had traveled together. The ache inside him was furious. He carried her up the stairs to one of the bedrooms. He didn't even know if it was hers. He only needed the bed. She met his kisses just as wildly as he gave them, and it took only seconds to rip off her drawers and unbutton his pants and longjohns. He literally cried out when he rammed himself inside of her. He reached inside the bodice of her dress and camisole and grasped a full breast, pushing at it until he worked it out of her camisole. He savored the nipple as though he could take nourishment from it, and he pushed as deep as he could.

Maggie in turn could not get enough of him. She cried out his name, grasping his hair and bending slightly upward to push her breast into his mouth, wanting to please him, give him anything and everything a man needed from a woman. He raised up then, ramming his hard, hot shaft deep into places Edward had never reached. Quickly Maggie felt his life spill into her as she grasped his powerful arms and arched up to greet him.

Rafe leaned close then, kissing her deeply, almost reverently. "Don't move," he told her. He climbed off the bed and undressed, and Maggie watched. She *wanted* to watch. Edward had never even let her see him completely naked. Everything was done under the covers and in the dark. But a wild, untamed man like Rafe Morrisey had no qualms about showing his magnificent physique, and it was still light enough outside that she could see him well.

His body was glorious. Every part he exposed as he undressed only made his virile qualities even more evident. The scars on his face and torso bespoke a man who knew how to handle himself, who had faced war and other dangers and had survived. The scar on his left thigh was proof of how much he loved her. His stomach was flat, his buttocks and thighs firm, and for the first time she saw that part of man that she had never really set eyes on. Already he was swollen again, ready to mate again, and there was nothing she wanted more.

He crawled onto the bed and began unbuttoning her dress. She closed her eyes and let him undress her . . . dress, slips, stockings, shoes. He unlaced her camisole and opened it, grasping and massaging her breasts, rubbing his thumbs over her taut nipples.

"You're the most beautiful woman I've ever seen," he told her. He pulled down the covers and helped her scoot up longways on the bed so that her head lay on a pillow.

"I've never wanted a man to see me this way before," she admitted. She sat up slightly, running her hands over his arms and shoulders, leaning up to kiss his chest. "And I have never wanted to see a man this way." She closed her eyes and met his mouth again. He ran his tongue deep, laying her back on the pillow and moving a big hand from her breasts down over her belly, running a finger into the crevice of that most secret and sacred place Edward had hardly ever touched. He moved in a circular motion, bringing out something sweet and wonderful and exotic, something that made her want to open her legs. She groaned when he ran his fingers deep inside of her and back out again to keep toying with that magical spot she'd hardly known existed before Rafe Morrisey came along. In moments she was almost screaming his name as a wonderful pulsation ripped through her, and she arched against his hand.

The first time they had done this she had to be still so no one would hear them, and because of the darkness they could not enjoy the sight of each other's nakedness. But this time Maggie could truly experience every wonderful touch, and cry out her pleasure. Rafe moved between her legs and pulsed into her again, and Maggie wondered if anything on earth could bring a human being more pleasure than this. Instinctively she wrapped her legs around his torso. He raised up again, his own arms wrapped under her hips so that the rest of her body was arched back, exposing her in naked glory. Never had she wanted to be so brazen and unfettered. She gloried in every quick thrust as he moved in sweet rhythm. Could there possibly be any better expression of love than this? The only thing that could show it more was a willingness to die for each other, and she knew Rafe Morrisey would die for her in a moment if he had to. And the day she stepped into the path of the knife meant for him, she knew she would also give her life for him if she had to.

They had been through so much, suffered so much, learned so much about each other. All she had been through had been worth it, if it meant coming to this moment.

His life spilled into her once again, and he groaned with the release. He lay down beside her, pulling her into his arms, enjoying the way her long, thick, auburn hair tumbled out of its combs and pins.

"I love you, Maggie McCahan."

"And I love you, Rafe Morrisey."

They laughed, they kissed, they rolled together, they got up and washed and went right back to the bed, where they explored each other with fingers and lips and tongues. Rafe taught her positions she never knew a man and woman could use to make love. She most enjoyed his magnificent body hovering over hers. He could break her in half, yet he was so gentle. She allowed him to touch and taste every part of her, amazed at her own abandon. But how could she resist the exotic splendor of his tongue softly exploring that part of her that belonged only to Rafe Morrisey, for no other man, not even Edward, had claimed her this way? For tonight she was his to do with as he pleased, and not once did she feel it was a "duty." It was pure ecstasy.

He stayed all night, and it was the most glorious experience of Maggie's life. God, how she loved him!

Somewhere in the early morning they actually fell asleep, but bright sunshine coming through the window woke them. They turned to each other, both exhausted but terribly fulfilled . . . and terribly hurting at the realization that today they must once again part.

"It won't be forever," were Maggie's first words. "I'll meet you at Independence next spring."

Rafe moved on top of her, and Maggie thought her heart would break at the sight of tears in his eyes. "Promise me."

"I just did."

"I love you, Maggie."

"And you know how much I love you. I have never belonged to any man the way I belong to you. Promise me you won't go to the whores while we're apart."

He looked her over lovingly. "There isn't another woman alive who could please me the way you do. I'll have no desire for any of them, whores or proper women."

"I can't bear the thought of you being with anyone else."

He grinned through tears. "Then don't think about it. It won't happen. It's the same for me, you know. I can't bear to think about some fancy, rich man sweeping you off your feet."

"He wouldn't be you," she whispered. Her own tears came then, and Rafe met her mouth in another fiery, sweet kiss. This time their lovemaking was gentle, slow, sweet, almost painful, a special good-bye. Deep, so deep. She arched up to him with aching desire, wanting to always remember what this was like. Too soon the sun rose higher. The freighter on which Maggie and the two families returning east would leave in two more hours.

"I can't go," Maggie wept.

Rafe forced himself to sit up. "You have to, Maggie. It's just something that has to be done. We probably never should have done this, but this, too, simply had to be."

Maggie felt numb. She got up and washed, dressed, pulled the bedclothes off the bed and left them in a pile. She didn't much care what whoever bought this house would think of a bed left unmade. She was never coming back here. Oh, the pain of it! The pain of all of it! The memories, the suffering. They hardly spoke as she finished fixing her hair. She pinned on a hat, pulled on a cape that matched the soft green dress she wore today. She packed everything, carried her two lighter bags downstairs, where Rafe waited in the kitchen. He was dressed in buckskins again, and he sat at the table staring at the two empty wineglasses. Whoever came in after she left would wonder about the two glasses, but she didn't care about that, either.

Rafe looked up at her, and her heart ached at the look on his face. He really believed she would not return once she was back home. "I love you, Rafe. Always remember that."

He nodded. "I'll get the trunk."

"It's so heavy. I'll help." Maggie followed him back up the stairs, and together they lifted the trunk . . . the trunk, with its faded yellow flowers . . . the trunk that had traveled clear across the ocean to America, and on across America itself. Her end became too heavy, and Rafe tilted it so that it half slid down the stairs, with him controlling the bottom end. When he got it to the bottom he lifted it himself and carried it to the kitchen, then scooted it out the back door.

"I rented a carriage yesterday," he told her. "That's what I came here in. I'll go hitch it back up to the horse."

Maggie couldn't speak for the lump in her throat. She watched out the back as he hitched the carriage and gave Betsy some fresh hay and water. Betsy would stay with the house. Ben had promised to care for the horse. Rafe's horses were boarded. Rafe dragged the trunk to the carriage and managed to lift it into the back. He came back to the house and picked up her other two bags.

''Got everything?''

Maggie nodded.

Rafe glanced at the flowers on the table. Soon they would wither and die. Would her love for him also wither and die once she was back home?

Maggie followed his gaze and went to the table, taking the flowers out of the vase. She had forgotten to water them, but now she was glad. They were dry enough to pack. ''I want to put these in the trunk. They will dry out, but I don't care. I will keep them forever.'' She reached into her pocket and placed a door key on the kitchen table. ''I told Mary I would leave the back door unlocked. I said my good-byes to them already. I told them I had someone to take me to the docks.'' Her voice broke on the last words, and she hurried out the door. Rafe followed, setting down her bags and closing the door, then carrying the bags to the buggy. Maggie was unbuckling and unlocking the trunk. She slipped the flowers inside and re-locked it, then climbed up onto the carriage seat. Rafe climbed up beside her and snapped the reins, heading the horse down the many hills that led to the docks.

The drive took nearly a half hour, and Maggie sat rigid the whole time, saying nothing. They reached the ship, and they went through the mechanics of greeting the two families who would also take the freighter home. Rafe was right. They were very nice people, two married couples, both with children. Maggie hardly heard their names or their explanations of why they had come and why they were going back. She could think of nothing but the fact that today she would leave Rafe Morrisey standing on the docks of San Francisco . . . alone. Because of the dangers of this land west of the Mississippi, it was very possible she would never see him again. She was unaware of the hustle and bustle at the docks, the deep calling of the ship's steam whistles, or the fact that one of the sailors took her bags for her, and two more took her trunk. The families with whom she would travel walked the wooden plank that led to the ship, and Maggie turned to Rafe.

"I can't say . . . good-bye. I told you once . . . to love me tomorrow. Please do love me tomorrow, because one of these tomorrows we will be together again." She could not stop the tears that flowed from her eyes.

Rafe grasped her face between his hands. "I love you *today,* Maggie, and I will still love you tomorrow. I'll be waiting for you."

"But . . . you have to go all the way back," she wept. "Something . . . could happen . . . wolves, bears . . . Indians . . . robbers . . . the weather . . . the desert—"

"Maggie." He forced a smile for her. "Come on, Maggie. Hell, I've been facing those things for years. You know nothing can stop me from being in Independence next spring."

She wrapped her arms around him and cried against his chest. "I'm so afraid I'll never see you again!"

"It's the same for me, Maggie. I have to pray you have a safe voyage." He kissed her hair. "You have to get on board now, or the ship will leave without you."

"I can't, Rafe, I can't."

"Please, Maggie. Don't make this harder than it already is."

She looked up at him, and there were tears on his cheeks, also.

"Go, Maggie. Go see your mother and your sisters. Go find the life you once knew, and be sure you can give that up."

Her whole body jerked in a sob. Rafe leaned down and kissed her lightly, then led her onto the ship.

"God be with you, Rafe," she sobbed.

He gave her one last embrace. "And with you, my Maggie." He turned and hurried down the gangway, and immediately two sailors pulled it in. There was no going back and getting her.

Maggie stood on the deck and watched him, wanting one last, long look at the tall man in buckskins who wore his hair long like an Indian . . . and part of him *was* Indian. Was last night real? The delicious ache deep in her belly from nearly constant lovemaking told her it had been. She watched and waved for as long as she could keep him in sight. "Good-bye, Rafe," she whispered. When the ship got so far away she could no longer see him, she sat down on her trunk, which was still on deck.

On shore, Rafe watched the ship become smaller and smaller, and he realized his heart ached worse now than it had when he'd buried Nina. He wiped at the tears on his face, hoping that making her go back had been the right decision.

Chapter Forty-Three

Maggie told herself she should have known this could happen. She should be devastated, ashamed, but she was not. All the way home, months at sea, when she should have felt so alone that she wanted to die, this was all that had saved her. God meant for it to be. This was her link to Rafe. He was still with her. His life was growing in her belly, and she didn't care who knew, or that she would arrive home six months pregnant.

She'd had to let out her dresses as much as their seams llowed, and one of the women with whom she traveled lent er a couple of her own dresses. She was a couple of sizes igger than Maggie, and her dresses were not as fitted, since hey were simple, homemade garments, so at least they gave er room for her growing belly, and Maggie was grateful for omething more comfortable. Although she was not huge yet, he had grown enough to warrant giving up on binding undergarments and dresses that had simply become too small.

She was not going to do anything to risk losing this baby. afe would be so happy if he knew! When she met him in ndependence, she would be bringing him a son or a daughter, nd she couldn't wait to see the look on his face. They would ave more, many more. She had been so certain it was impossible to conceive that night they spent together, for she had just finished her period. But who could predict nature, and maybe God meant for this to be. If for some reason she never saw Rafe again, she would always have this child to remind her of their love.

By the grace of God, the freighter had made it to New York with no mishaps, and to see the city was almost a shock to the system after spending a year in the wide open spaces of the uncivilized West. She took ferries and trains and coaches, finally another train to Pittsburgh. And all the way she saw cities, tall buildings, factories and smokestacks, farms with huge frame homes rather than sod and log houses, cattle instead of buffalo, rows of corn instead of high, wide, treeless prairieland filled with wildflowers.

This was all so different, and hardly seemed familiar any more. Now she found the smoky air and the litter in Pittsburgh's brick streets distasteful. Bricks and cement, steel and smoke. She ached for the pristine mountains, the Nebraska sand hills, the sparkling water of a tumbling waterfall. Instead, the water from a recent rain stood in gray puddles along the curbs. Tall brick buildings were her mountains, and the hills were covered with homes.

She hired a cab to take her home, and it was only then she felt nostalgia, as the horse and cab pulled up to the front of her family's stone castle. As she waited for her things to be unloaded, she studied this place where Maggie Dumont had grown up, its pinnacles and towers, lanterns and tracery windows. What would Rafe think of such a place, with its carriage porch and balconies, Tudor arches? What would he think of the grand ballroom on the second floor, where her sixteenth birthday party had been held, and where she had married Edward?

The thought of Edward brought her back to reality. She was really here, at the place where they had walked and talked over the years, even played when they were little. For all her disappointment in him as a husband, Edward had been a good man. Never in his life had he spoken a mean word to her, or been physically cruel. He'd been a good husband in the only way he knew how to be one, and she had always been able to trust in his friendship. He had spent his whole life unhappy, under the thumb of a father who'd never loved him.

The cab driver set down her trunk and her bags. She reached into her handbag and paid him, then pulled her wool coat closer around herself. It was October, the same time one year ago that she had arrived at Sutter's Fort in the beautiful Sacramento Valley. Now here she was, back at the starting point. The colors were beautiful—orange and yellow, red, and still some green. She had always liked the autumn season here, but now she wondered how many thousands more were just now arriving in California. How many had died along the way this year? How many more graves?

Everything was so different. So different. She thought she heard someone shout, and suddenly her mother appeared at the huge wooden front door, then stepped farther out into the sunlight. "Maggie?"

Tears filled her eyes. "Mother!" Maggie ran to her.

"Oh, Dear God!" her mother exclaimed. "Maggie! Maggie! What has happened! What are you doing here!"

They embraced, and it was only then that Maggie realized Rafe was right. She had needed to come back here, if for no other reason than to see her family once more, to explain, and yes, to truly know in her heart that this place could no longer be home for her.

"Mama," she wept.

The entire family sat in the parlor listening to Maggie read her journal—her parents, her sisters and their husbands, all her nieces and nephews, even a few of the more prominent of Pittsburgh's society, Edward's father and brothers, and their families. Maggie knew of no better way to describe her trip west and what it had been like for her and Edward than to read the daily entries in her diary. It tore at her own heart to go over all of it again, especially remembering the part Rafe played in that incredible journey. How she wished she could add the details of their affair, but so far her mother and everyone thought the baby she carried was Edward's. She had been home only two days, and the news of Edward's death seemed to be enough for them to bear right now. Let them think what they wanted. When things quieted she would tell her mother the truth, that this baby belonged to the leader of their wagon train, the man mentioned only casually in her journal. All the while her heart ached at needing to see and touch him again, and she wondered how she was going to survive until spring.

Yesterday we lost the young man, David Whittaker, whom we had hired as a servant . . . He drowned . . . Wilena Marks has married Stuart Purdy . . . She wondered how they were doing, where they had settled. *Everyone has recovered from cholera and bee bites, and Susan Haggarty's broken arm is healing . . . At last Edward and I can be together again, but poor Gretta must sleep alone, now that Maria has left us . . .*

Everyone listened in total rapture, some of the women crying when they learned of Maria and Gretta's deaths. Maggie was glad she had not written the truth about how Gretta had died. No one need ever know. She cried herself when she reached that part, and when she read her descriptions of the land.

The terrain has changed dramatically since leaving Fort Laramie. We have left the wide-open, treeless country and the sand hills of Nebraska Territory and have entered an even more beautiful area, hilly, rocky, strange formations . . . Our captain—She hesitated. Rafe! How she ached for him!—*promises it will be cooler when we reach the mountains.*

She went on to read about their encounter with the Indians and giving their leader her wedding dress and a pair of diamond earrings. Nearly everyone gasped, and Maggie explained why she had no choice. She read about Rafe's injury and how she helped nurse him herself.

"You nursed a half-breed scout?" Sarah asked.

Maggie met her eyes. How could she understand? "He saved my life, don't forget."

"I know, but . . . heavens, Maggie, I can't believe the things my little sister suffered, and the things you've done."

Maggie smiled sadly and went on reading. *We are now into the most beautiful country I have ever seen, surrounded by rocks and pine trees, forging through majestic mountains. It is a terribly dangerous area, and if not for Mr. Morrisey's and Jack Latham's skill in getting us through these mountains, we would surely all perish . . .*

Even she could hardly believe some of the things she read. Elizabeth nearly fainted when she read about Terrence Maddox's foot being cut off.

"Dear Lord, Maggie, do you think the children should be hearing all of this?"

Maggie looked at her mother, who had made the remark. Her father listened silently. He'd had little to say. "Mother, of course they should hear it. All those people are helping settle a whole new piece of America. Some day this will be important history, and they can hear it firsthand. I want to copy all of this, and I want you to keep it forever."

"Of course, Dear, but . . . you talk as though you won't be iere. Why copy it when you will be here yourself to hand it lown?"

Maggie looked down at the journal. No, not yet. "I just want here to be a second copy, in case something should happen to his one." She read on, reaching the section about the desert. *Ve are told it is beastly hot, and there will be no shade and ardly any kind of life for several hundred miles. Most of the vater is no good, for it is salt water. I am sure we will all be lad to reach the Sierras, no matter how dangerous they are. Ieaven help us.* She read about Rafe's fight and her knife vound, and everyone gasped.

"Can we see the scar?" one of her nephews asked.

"Johnny, of course not!" his mother chided. "That is a very rivate thing!"

"Oh, Maggie, such things you have suffered!" Catherine ld her.

"And you look so different," Sarah spoke up. "You've rown in a different way. You aren't our little Maggie any ore. You're so much stronger."

Maggie wished she could tell them about her experiences in e mining camps, traveling with Rafe and Tobacco Joe, wearg pants and boots. But to do that she would have to tell the truth of how Edward had died, and she did not want them to know it had been such a cruel death. She had told them he'd gone to inspect a mine he was interested in buying, and he'd died in an accidental dynamite explosion. She'd told them that he had died instantly.

"Did you actually cook for yourself?" Elizabeth asked. "Over open campfires, like Indian women?"

"Yes, I did. I even know how to skin and clean a squirrel, and I can shoot pretty straight and ride a horse astride."

More gasps.

At the opening to this spectacular rocky area are twin rocks that spiral upward like a cathedral, she read on. *. . . they are as majestic as the gates of heaven . . . One must see this for himself. . . . some days I hate it, but most days I love it for its beauty, for such country reminds me that there is a God, and that He will keep us safe.*

She read to her captured audience for another half hour. *We lost little Joey tonight. Rafe*—His name caught in her throat, and she had to take a moment to regain her composure. She hoped they all thought her near tears were over Joey, not because it hurt to even say Rafe's name. *Rafe said it was because he was so young and small. The snake's venom got t his brain much more quickly than Rafe could suck it out. . . Beverly Maddox has lost a second child, and we are all worrie about her. There is no consoling her*

"Oh, dear heavens!" Sarah wept when Maggie reached th part about Katie and her mule, and the children listened wide eyed when she told about Edward going over the edge wit Katie and the mule, and how Rafe Morrisey helped save him

"Poor Edward," his brother, Mark, remarked. "Goin through all that to get to California, only to die in a min explosion."

Maggie dabbed at tears. *Poor Mildred Howell just sits an stares,* she read on. *After having to leave her daughter, Kati behind us, lying dead in a canyon . . .* She thought abo Edward. He had died a similar death. *. . . she collapsed, f she had already lost another daughter and a son . . . How s that this had to happen when we had only that one last mounta* *pass to conquer before finally coming into the valleys of California.*

She closed the journal and told them what California was like, the wonderful weather, the wild, untamed city of San Francisco and all the building that was taking place. They would never know about Ben Skeller's attack, or that she had bought land for Serena's family. What they had heard was shocking enough.

"Thank God you are back with us, Darling," her mother declared. "Such horrors. I can't imagine how you survived it all. Once the baby is born, you can get back into society again. We will take care of you for as long as necessary, until you find a husband. Tomorrow I will have my manicurist come and do something about your hands, and—"

"Mother, I don't want any of that. Not yet, anyway. I just want to sit and think. I don't want a lot of company after tonight, and I don't want any parties or social gatherings. I don't want people staring at me as though I am some kind of unusual statue. And I don't want any special pampering, except for a good doctor. I want to be sure nothing happens to this baby."

"Of course, Dear. You have been through so much. I'm sure you just need a lot of rest and time to get over poor Edward's eath."

Charlotte had her servants serve tea and cookies, and Maggie quietly watched the children devour the pastries. Her father ad said little throughout the evening. Actually, he had said ttle since she'd arrived home, other than to welcome her with strong embrace and tears in his eyes.

"Maggie," he called to her now. "Come into my study for moment."

Maggie set her journal aside and rose, following the man down the oak paneled hallway to his study, where everything nelled of books and leather and tobacco. Henry closed the door and told her to sit down. Maggie obeyed, a little confused. Henry sat down behind his desk. "How about the truth?"

Maggie felt a slight jolt in her chest. "What?"

"The truth, about Edward, and about that baby. How did Edward *really* die?"

Maggie looked down at her lap. "Why do you think it was any other way than what I told you?"

"Because, my youngest daughter, I have always known when you were not being totally honest. I can see it in your eyes. And I heard something in your voice, every time you mentioned that Rafe fellow. What is it you aren't telling me?"

Maggie drew a deep breath and faced him. "Something I intended to tell you and mother after all the commotion was over. The baby I carry is Rafe Morrisey's baby," she declared.

Henry closed his eyes as though feeling pain. "Dear God, Maggie."

"I am not ashamed of it. Rafe is a gentle, loving, skilled, brave man who saved my life more than once. He helped me through some terrible experiences. After my baby is born I am going back to him. He is meeting me in Independence in the spring, and we are going to Oregon."

Henry sighed and leaned back in his chair. "You woul really go through that trip all over again?"

"I would. For Rafe. And because I am not the same Maggi who left here, Father. I don't belong here any more. And onc mother's society women find out the truth, I won't be welcome I am sorry if this will bring a black spot on the family, bu people do not choose to fall in love. It just happens."

How could he tell her the truth about why he understood He'd once been in love with another woman for years, but h had remained bound to Maggie's mother. It had been a arranged marriage, and Charlotte was a good woman. "I kno love cannot always be controlled," he answered. "Did Edwa know about this?"

Maggie was surprised at how well he was taking the new "No. He never knew. And I would have stayed married to hi and true to him if not for his death. He died in a mounta pass. He had taken supplies to the mining camps to sell, a one of the men he'd hired to go with him ended up killing hi He shot him and threw him over the edge of a canyon. I do want anyone else to know how he died. Rafe risked his o life to help me find out the truth and to find the murderer, who almost killed Rafe, too. Then Rafe went to the place where Edward had been killed and he climbed down that canyon wall to recover Edward's ring for me and to bury what was left of him. Edward had actually died a couple of months before that." She looked down at her belly. "This baby is the result of . . . something Rafe and I shared after Edward died. It was Rafe who told me to come home and make sure I could really leave my old life for good. He has no idea I am carrying." She looked at her father again. "I am sorry if this is going to bring shame to the family. But now that I am carrying, I have more reason than ever to go back to Rafe. I just worry about how Mother will take this, and my sisters."

Henry folded his arms. "You truly love this man?"

She blinked back tears. "More than I ever loved Edward. Edward was a good friend, but in many ways—" She felt a flush coming to her face. "In many ways he was not such a good husband. But he was kind to me, always attentive and considerate. He just . . . was not the man Rafe Morrisey is. But if he had lived, I never would have left him. And this . . ." She touched her belly again. "This never would have happened."

"Tell me all about this Rafe Morrisey. I want to know I won't have to worry about you. And if you must do this, I will explain to your mother and sisters for you."

Maggie smiled, grateful for the offer, and seeing her father in a new light. In all her years growing up here, he had always been a rather silent presence, the wealthy breadwinner who went off to his world of business and manufacturing, somehow magically providing them with everything they could ever want. He was still a handsome man, always immaculate, his graying hair only making him look more distinguished. She told him about Rafe, surprised she could talk so easily about him to her father. Maybe as a man himself, he could understand a man like Rafe.

"You are an astounding young woman, Maggie, much stronger than I ever dreamed any of my offspring could be, considering the way you were raised. Your story is incredible, and to consider making that trip all over again only shows me how much you love this man. He was right telling you to come back here first, and I respect him for that. I will give you a good share of what would be coming to you if you stayed here until I died. It will help you get a good start in Oregon."

"You don't have to do that—"

"I want to. I want my Maggie to be happy. I wish I could meet this man."

"You could accompany me to Independence."

He nodded. "Perhaps I will."

Charlotte knocked on the door. "Henry, dear, when are you going to come back out with Maggie? The children have questions for her." She opened the door, and Henry turned his attention to his wife. "Send them all home for now, Charlotte."

"Whatever for?"

"Because I told you to. I have something to tell you, and I think at first we should be alone when I do it."

Charlotte looked at her daughter in obvious confusion. "Are you all right, dear?"

"I am fine, Mother."

"All right. If you say so." The woman left them to explain to the others that they must leave for the present. Maggie met her father's gaze.

"Thank you, Father."

"True happiness only comes when you follow your heart, Maggie-girl."

Maggie caught a distinct loneliness in his blue eyes, and she realized she hardly knew her father at all.

Chapter Forty-Four

Doctor Barringer was called out in the middle of a blizzard. It was January 15, 1852, three o'clock A.M., and Maggie Dumont McCahan's water had broken. She was delivering her baby. Henry battered his way on horseback through blinding snow to reach the doctor's office several blocks away, while Charlotte ordered one of her maids who had had children of her own to sit with Maggie.

Charlotte Dumont had insisted that society must believe this baby was Edward McCahan's child. When Maggie left in the spring, it would be explained that she had gone to Chicago to live with an uncle, Henry's brother James, and his wife. People would be told that Maggie felt there were too many sad memories for her in Pittsburgh, because of growing up here with Edward. She wished to go someplace new and start over.

Maggie's sisters and their husbands were sworn to secrecy, threatened with losing their inheritances if they ever told the truth. Henry had objected to the lies, and he knew it hurt Maggie. She felt no shame. But to ease her mother's mortification at her daughter being impregnated by a half-breed scout only weeks after her husband's death, and since Maggie was not even legally married to the man, Maggie had agreed to go along with her mother's story. This was an out of wedlock child, conceived under conditions that Charlotte could only see as adultery. Charlotte was kind and understanding toward Maggie, but she had begged that Maggie and Henry stick with the story of why Maggie would leave.

It is for your sake and the sake of the child, she had told Maggie. *What if this Rafe fellow is not there waiting for you come spring? What if you have to raise the child alone, find a new husband who would be a father to it? No man will marry you if he knows the truth of how this child was conceived.*

Maggie did not *want* any other man, especially one who would blame her for what happened, and who would consider her son or daughter a bastard child. This baby was conceived in love, and he or she would be loved and adored forever. Still, at the moment Maggie cared only about the awful pain of childbirth going away. She wanted to be brave about this, but not even the pain of her knife wound could compare to the pains that ripped through her insides now. How she wished Rafe was here, and she prayed everything would go right, that their baby would be healthy and strong.

Henry finally returned with the doctor, who began giving orders. Maids went running, and Charlotte paced. Henry sat in his study smoking a pipe and cringing every time he heard Maggie scream, and the gardener, who had little to do this time of year, was sent into the freezing storm to let Maggie's sisters know she was in labor. Maggie had no idea how many hours went by, except that it had been dark when she went into labor and now she was aware that it was daylight, although she heard talk all around her that it was still blowing and snowing outside

"I am the only sister who could come, Maggie." It wa Sarah's voice. When had she arrived? "Hal brought me. Th nanny will stay with the children. Elizabeth and Catherin decided to stay home with their little ones because of th weather."

It really did not matter who was or was not here. None c them could take away the pain. Only the sight of Rafe's fac could make her feel better, but he was not here. What if h died somewhere in the mountains or out on the plains in son terrible blizzard? What if a grizzly attacked him? What if Indians had killed and scalped him? A snakebite could kill him, or a fall, or a river. Cholera or smallpox could wipe out entire wagon trains.

She heard the doctor telling her to bear down. Why did he have to tell her? Her muscles were contracting and bearing down all on their own. She could not stop it. She knew she was screaming, but she could not stop that, either. Finally she heard the magical words.

"It's coming! Push, Maggie! Push!"

It was Sarah giving the command. The pain turned to something deeper, something that could not quite be called pain, and yet it seemed to be taking the life out of her. "It's a boy!" someone shouted. Then all conversation became mumbled.

"Get him cleaned up."

She heard a smack, a baby's cry. Someone said something about afterbirth.

"She is bleeding too much." A man spoke the words.

"Oh, Dear God! Judith, get some ice!"

Judith was one of the maids. Why did they need ice?

"Towels! Get more towels before she bleeds into the mattress!"

Before *who* bleeds into the mattress? Maggie saw Rafe coming now. He'd come to see the baby. Rafe! Oh, so handsome! So loving! Oh, to touch him again, feel him holding her again! Someone handed him a baby, but her own arms were empty, and she felt a sudden panic. Rafe! He had lost his first wife and baby. Would it happen again? The vision of Rafe and the baby began to fade, and then all was blackness.

"Maggie? Maggie, can you hear me?"

Maggie opened her eyes to see Sarah standing at the foot of her bed. "Yes," she answered weakly. "Where is . . . Rafe?"

Sarah came closer. "Maggie, you're in Pittsburgh, remember? Rafe is not here. You had your baby, Maggie—a boy! He is strong and healthy, and he needs his mother's milk . . . and a name. We have been waiting for four days for you to get stronger and tell us what you want to name him. And we have been feeding him goat's milk while waiting for you to come around. Maggie? Do you hear me?" Sarah took hold of her hands. "You scared us to death! We thought we were going to lose you, but Dr. Barringer finally got the bleeding to stop, but you have been unconscious these four days. It's so wonderful to see you open your eyes and speak."

"I . . . want to . . . see my baby."

"All right, but for one more day you will have to lie very still. You lost a tremendous amount of blood, and Dr. Barringer said that when you finally came around you were to lie very still."

Maggie gripped her sister's hand as tightly as she could in her condition. "Never . . . give my baby away . . . if I should die. Someone would have . . . to tell Rafe. And someone would have to . . . keep him . . . love him . . . make him feel wanted. Don't . . . put my baby in . . . an orphanage!"

"No one is going to do that, Maggie."

"I have . . . to see him."

Sarah rose and kissed her cheek. "I will get him, but for now you can only look at him. You can't hold him." Sarah left, and Maggie heard her ordering a servant to go and tell Charlotte that her daughter had finally come around. "And send for the doctor," she ordered. She left the room and returned moments later with a bundle in her arms. She came close to Maggie and bent over, opening a blanket and exposing ten tiny toes, and ten little fingers, a rosy-cheeked baby with dark hair and reddish skin.

Maggie studied the wiggling, kicking infant. "Son," she said, smiling weakly. "Rafe . . . has a son."

"Yes. He is strong, Maggie, and he eats as though there is no tomorrow."

Tomorrow. Love me tomorrow. Was it spring yet? "Henry . . . Raphael. Put that . . . on the birth certificate . . . Henry Raphael."

Sarah hugged him close. "Father will be happy to hear that."

"He . . . understands. Father understands."

"Understands what, Maggie?"

"He just . . . understands." Maggie studied the baby through blurred vision, noticing only one thing, and it made her smile. His hair was straight, and black. He was going to look like his father . . . his *real* father. She decided she would not die. She had survived too many other things to give up now. She was Rafe Morriscy's woman, and he would be waiting for her in Independence.

It was six weeks before Maggie recovered from near death, and because she was bedridden and the baby was so tiny and vulnerable to colds or sicknesses others might present, Charlotte had a good excuse for putting off allowing friends to see the child.

"Oh, he has such black hair," the woman would tell her friends. "But you know, Edward's mother had black hair. His real father, I am told, was the one who had light hair like Edward's was. You just never know what colorings are going to come out in a child. Just look at my own daughters, all different!"

Already she was telling people that Maggie had decided to move to Chicago with her Uncle Jim and Aunt Laverne. Maggie simply accepted her mother's choice in how to handle the situation. That was mother. In private Charlotte had fallen in love with her sweet grandson, but she was too fragile and too wrapped up in etiquette and proper behavior to be able to emotionally handle gossip and scorn. Her circle of wealthy lady friends was very important to her. And Maggie did not want to spoil that for her in her aging years.

As for herself, Maggie would have no qualms about announcing to the world whose baby this was. She wanted to *shout* it to the world, and every time she held her beautiful son to her breast she saw Rafe in his big, dark eyes, his hair, his strong little legs, and the strength of his grip.

By mid-April Maggie was prepared to leave for Independence when little Henry's grip suddenly became weaker. The baby would not eat, and he ran a low fever. He developed a cough and began losing weight. Something was wrong!

"Consumption," the doctor announced, after two weeks of constant terror for Maggie that her baby would die.

No! Consumption meant *certain* death! The lungs simply wasted away. Adults died of consumption. How could such a little baby survive such a thing? She held her son almost constantly, refusing to leave him for one moment. She gently urged him to suckle at her breast, talked to him constantly, told him about his father, and prayed. Never had she prayed like this, offering her own life for her son's. Surely this child of Rafe Morrisey was strong enough to overcome anything. She would not believe it was consumption. It was something else, something he would conquer.

Days and nights became the same. Maggie hardly knew the date or time, and she could not bear to be away from her son one minute, in case he should stop breathing without his mother holding him close to her heart. The baby's agonizing sickness lingered for a month, and the time to leave for Independence passed. Maggie's faithful old trunk was packed, but it still sat near the bedroom door. She did not dare take her son out that door, let alone out into the chilly, damp spring air, and expose him to other people and the elements.

Rafe! He would think she had changed her mind. If he left and took another wagon train west, how would she ever find him? He would never know she had never stopped loving him, never know he had a son, and that it was because of that son that she could not meet him as promised. It was the end of April before Henry Raphael Morrisey magically woke up without a fever. The poor, frail boy grinned at his mother when she picked him up, and to her amazement he seemed hungry. She put him to her breast, and he eagerly suckled there. His breathing sounded more clear, and she realized only then that for the first time in over a month he had not coughed even once all night.

Of *course* he would live! This was Rafe's son, and *her* son! Hadn't Rafe told her more than once how strong she was? Even her father had said so. How could a child of hers, fathered by a man like Rafe, not be just as strong? She closed her eyes and held him close, and she thought what a joyful entry she would be able to make in her journal. Her baby was getting better.

Her mother came into the bedroom to find her crying. ‘‘Maggie! Oh, dear God, he isn’t—’’

‘‘No, Mother. He’s better! He’s hungry, and his fever is gone! He didn’t cough all night!’’

Charlotte smiled, coming to sit down on the bed. ‘‘Oh, Maggie, I am so glad.’’ She pulled the blanket away and watched her grandson take his nourishment. ‘‘His color is better, too.’’

‘‘He’s Rafe’s son. He’s strong, Mother. Some day he will be as big and strong and handsome as his father.’’ She covered the baby again and wiped at tears. ‘‘What is the date today?’’

Charlotte rose. ‘‘I believe it’s April twenty-eighth.’’

Maggie closed her eyes. ‘‘Dear God,’’ she whispered. ‘‘Most wagon trains have left or are leaving by now. Rafe will think I’ve changed my mind, and if he goes back west, how will I ever find him again? If he thinks I’m not coming, who is to say what he will do, where he will go?’’

‘‘Well, Dear, there might still be time—’’

‘‘No. I don’t dare take the baby anywhere for at least another month. He needs time to get stronger, gain some weight.’’ Pain pierced her heart. Rafe! It hurt so much to realize how he must be feeling right now, thinking she was not coming, after all. ‘‘Rafe said he would wait until mid-May. You can’t wait any longer than that and still get over the Sierras ahead of the snows. What am I going to do? Even if Father sends someone to find him, they will get there too late.’’

Charlotte sighed. ‘‘Well, dear, I will never quite understand any of this.’’ She rose and looked down at mother and baby. ‘‘Maybe it is for the best. Maybe you really *should* go to Chicago and start over. Maybe you aren’t meant to be with the baby’s father after all. You can still pass him off as Edward’s—’’

‘‘No, Mother. I won’t do that. I have to find his father.’’ Maggie closed her eyes, new tears coming. ‘‘I have to find Rafe.’’

Charlotte folded her arms. ‘‘Well, then, if this man truly loved you the way you think, then perhaps he will come looking for you. It certainly would not be difficult to find Maggie

Dumont McCahan in Pittsburgh. Everyone in the city knows who we are.''

Maggie met her mother's eyes, smiling through her tears. The woman loved being rich and well-known. ''He won't come, Mother. He'll think I've chosen to stay here, and he has great respect for whatever decision I would make.'' Her smile faded. ''He won't come.'' She leaned down and kissed the baby's head. ''I may never find Rafe, but I will always have this little boy, this little symbol of the man I loved with all my heart, this little reminder of the most beautiful night of my life.''

Charlotte just shook her head. Such talk! What had happened to her little girl? All the handsome, available, wealthy young men who would dearly love to have her hand, and she sat there pining away for a buckskin-clad, half-Indian scout who probably never really loved her in the first place. Poor, dear, heartbroken, abandoned Maggie.

Chapter Forty-Five

It is May 14, 1852, Maggie wrote, *and four-month-old Henry Raphael Morrisey is healthy again, his legs fat and strong and constantly kicking, his grip tight, his eyes bright, and his smile captivating. He is every bit his father, but now I fear the boy will never know Rafe. Unbeknownst to me, Father sent a messenger to Independence to try to find Rafe when the baby was too sick for me to go. My joy at learning this was dashed when just yesterday the messenger returned alone. My heart is ready to break. If not for my precious son, I would want to die.*

How was she ever going to find Rafe if he had gone on without her? The messenger had said there were so many thousands of people in St. Louis and Independence that it was impossible to find just one particular man. Maggie wondered how hard he had really tried. There were surely scouts wandering about, and many of them would know Rafe. The messenger had said he had asked such men, but none had seen Rafe.

What if he was dead? What if something had happened to him over the winter? Or what if. . . . No! He wouldn't have lied to her. He wouldn't have changed *his* mind, would he? Maybe he felt she was better off if she never saw him again, and if a man like Rafe did not want to be found, then he *would* not be found. He knew the whole west. He might go to Texas, even to Mexico. Or he might go to Canada, or stay somewhere in the mountains. If he thought she had changed her mind and was not coming, he might do the same thing, out of a broken heart.

What was she to do? If only he knew he had a son. Her nights were spent remembering . . . remembering the trail west, a man in buckskins, the prairie sun, the majestic mountains . . . a night by a river, in Rafe's arms . . . and the last night they spent together . . . the sight of him standing on the docks as her ship sailed away. Every bone and fiber of her ached for him, and longed to let him know he had a son.

She knew of nothing else to do but go to Independence herself. If Rafe could not be found, she would return to St. Louis and stay at one of the finer hotels or at a reputable boarding house until spring, and then she would try again.

The very next day she voiced her idea to her mother and father, calling them into her father's study after putting Henry down for a nap. Her father sat behind his desk, listening calmly, but Charlotte was immediately appalled at the idea.

"Oh, Maggie, please go to Chicago. James and Laverne will gladly take you in."

"I don't need to be 'taken in', Mother. I am perfectly capable of taking care of myself. Besides, I will never feel comfortable here *or* in Chicago, now. I've become too independent . With the money I will have I can start my own life someplace new, perhaps open a clothing shop or—"

"Maggie! Why would you want to *work!* All you need to do is find some nice rich young man and—"

"I *had* a nice rich young man, Mother, and I was not happy. Sometimes finding the right young man has nothing to do with his breeding or schooling, and certainly not his wealth. Don't you understand? If it can't be Rafe, then I don't want *any* man at least not for a long, long time."

"But . . . little Henry will need a father."

"He needs his *real* father, and I plan to stay in St. Louis and go to Indendence every spring until I find out what happened to him.''

Charlotte sighed in exasperation. ''Nothing has turned out the way I planned for you,'' she said despondently. ''I thought you would marry Edward and stay right here and have children and be a part of the family and the community like your sisters.''

''Charlotte, Maggie was *never* quite like her sisters. You know that.''

''But . . . she's our *Maggie,* our baby girl.''

''Why don't you leave us alone for a little while? Maybe I can talk her into going to Chicago.''

Charlotte rose, her taffeta dress rustling as she walked to Maggie's chair and leaned over to kiss her cheek and give the baby a peck. ''I will go have Rose start dinner.'' The woman gave her husband a warning look, hinting with her eyes that he had better be successful, then left, closing the door behind her. Henry leaned back in his chair, studying Maggie quietly for a moment.

''It won't do any good to try to talk me out of this, Father.''

''I know. You are too much like your mother . . . stubborn and independent . . . and very proud.''

''Independent? I wouldn't call mother independent.''

''I know. Charlotte is not and never has been independent.'' He closed his eyes and took a deep breath. ''But your mother was.''

Maggie frowned, trying to understand what on earth he was telling her. ''You aren't making any sense.''

He leaned forward, resting his elbows on his desk. ''Maggie, dear, you are a much stronger woman than the one who left here over a year ago. And I think you are strong enough to understand and accept what I am telling you. Charlotte is not your mother.''

Maggie just stared at him a moment, then felt the shock move through her in one sudden charge. ''I'm . . . adopted?''

''In a sense. But there is one thing about the adoption your mother knows nothing about. You really are my daughter. Charlotte is innocent and trusting enough to think it is just a coincidence that you resemble me, but it is because you are my flesh and blood, and, my darling daughter, no one understands better than I how easy it is to marry someone because everyone expects it, but to lose your heart to someone else.''

Maggie took a moment to find her breath. ''I . . . my mother?''

Henry put his head in his hands. ''She was beautiful, but she's gone now. She died in childbirth. It was about the same time your mother was told she would never have any more children. But she wanted more, so I told her I had gone to an orphanage and found a charming little baby girl she might like to adopt. And so we did.'' He looked at her with tears in his tired eyes. ''Now you understand why *I* understand your love for this Rafe Morrisey, and why you could love him in spite of Edward . . . and why I understand that you have to try to find him.''

Maggie was at a loss for words. It was such a strange feeling to suddenly discover her mother was not her mother at all!

''Charlotte loves you like her own. She has no idea you are the product of her husband's love for another woman.''

Maggie rose and walked to a window, struggling to grasp the reality of what she was being told. ''Who was she?''

''It doesn't matter now, Maggie. She's dead. She bled to death at birth, and for a while I was deathly afraid the same thing would happen with you. Thank God you survived. You're so damn strong, Maggie. I am more proud of you than any of my other daughters. And I want you to have what your real mother never got to have—the man she loved. You go to St Louis. Just be sure to write us and let us know what is happening, especially if you find Rafe.''

Maggie could not help the lump that came to her throat. She wanted to hate him for cheating on the woman she thought of as mother. And yet she knew exactly how it must have been for him, if he truly loved her real mother, and it was obviou[s] he did. He would not otherwise have kept the child she bor[e] by him.

''I'm sorry, Maggie. I never thought I would have to te[ll] you, but your present situation makes it seem important. Pleas[e] don't tell Charlotte that you know she is not your real mothe[r]

She loves you very much, and she is so easily hurt. She went on a prolonged vacation in Europe about four months before you were born, and because of the timing, I met her at the docks when she returned and told her about the newborn I had found for her. She agreed we would tell your sisters the baby was ours, that she had had the child in Europe. Your sisters have no idea you were adopted.''

Maggie took several quiet minutes to let the revelation sink in. She saw her father in an entirely different light now, and herself. There were so many different kinds of love. ''Thank you for telling me,'' she said, fighting tears. She met his eyes. ''I am sorry myself that I am just now getting to know my father. I guess we don't expect our parents to have . . . human frailties. I am just glad you have always been good to mother. And I need to know . . . please tell me there was never anyone else.''

He sniffed and cleared his throat, obviously trying not to show his deepest emotions. ''There was never anyone else,'' he answered. ''I loved her very much, Maggie.''

Maggie nodded. ''That helps.'' Maggie could see how unhappy and heartbroken her father must have been all these years. ''I'm sorry she died, sorry for how hard that must have been for you.''

He rose. ''Oh, I've mustered through a good many disappointments and challenges in my life. You will do the same, Maggie. And if this Rafe Morrisey is worth his salt, and he is still alive, he won't give up on you.''

''He won't, Father. I have to believe that. That's why I have to go to Saint Louis.'' Maggie stepped closer, reaching out to embrace him. Henry took her into his arms, and she thought how sad it was that she should just now truly get to know and feel closer to her father, when she would have to go away again.

''Stay a little extra, will you, Maggie? For your mother *and* for me. If it's too late to meet Rafe, and since my man couldn't find him, there is no hurry. You said yourself that if you are going to find him there, it will be next spring. And if something went wrong, if there is some explanation of why he could not be there, then *he* will find *you,* Maggie.''

She wanted to believe that. Poor Rafe. What was he thinking? Was he even alive? Would it really do any good to go to St. Louis now?

''If the man loves you anything like I loved your mother, he will go to the ends of the earth to find you, Maggie, even if it means finding out you no longer want to be with him.''

Maggie rested her head on her father's shoulder. It was a nice thought. ''I'll stay a while longer,'' she told him. ''And now I am more glad than ever that I came back, glad to know the truth. It helps me understand everything so much better. I just pray that coming back doesn't mean I will never see Rafe again.''

Henry patted her shoulder. ''Then you must keep praying, Maggie. That is all there is left to do.''

Rafe made his way along the bricked street, marveling at the big homes, wondering just how crazy he was for being here. If he hadn't arrived late to Independence, he would not be doing this, but he had to know . . . he had to know. He had checked at just about every hotel and rooming house in Independence and St. Louis, and no Maggie McCahan had stayed at any of them. What must she be thinking by now? Here it was June tenth!

He realized it was very possible he was in for the greates disappointment of his life, and maybe this was unfair to Maggie He had, after all, told her not to come if that was her choice and he would respect that choice; but what if she *had* bee there and he had missed her? Would she have come back home What if she had chosen to go on west with a wagon train? H had checked every passing wagon train between Fort Larami and Independence. She had not been on any of them.

His heart pounded a little harder when he came to the mansio that had been described to him by the man at the newspap office. ''Dumont? Hell, everybody in the state of Pennsylvani and probably plenty in Washington, knows about Hen

Dumont! Why in the world is a man like you looking for the Dumonts?''

Why in the world, indeed? In a neighborhood like this he stuck out like a sore thumb. He'd worn his buckskins because he damn well wanted to, and if Maggie didn't like him this way or was embarrassed to have him show up at the door like this, well then he'd know she had returned to the old Maggie. He drew a deep breath and rode his black gelding to a hitching post, then dismounted and tied it. Today he wore his hair tied at the side with a beaded hairpiece, determined to show all the Indian that was in him. These people had better know he wasn't going to cut his hair and fancy himself up just for them. He was not here to make an impression. He was only hear to find out what had happened to the woman he loved.

He walked up a brick walkway lined with beautifully manicured flowers and shrubs. In spite of all he'd learned about Maggie, what he saw now was far more extravagant than he had pictured. There was wealth, and then there was WEALTH! ''Jesus,'' he muttered. This was crazy. He considered turning around and just leaving, but what the hell? He was here now. He might as well get it over with. He would not be surprised to discover Maggie looking elegant as a queen, with some rich bastard on her arm. He would be dearly tempted to land a fist into the man's face, but then it wouldn't be his fault. What normal young man would NOT want Maggie Dumont McCahan in his bed?

He stepped up to the huge, oak double front doors and gathered up the courage to use the knocker. A sour-faced, balding man in a suit answered. ''Yes?''

''Are you Henry Dumont?''

The man smiled wryly. ''Hardly. I am the butler.''

''Is Dumont in?''

''*Mr.* Dumont is in.''

''Get him,'' Rafe said, already growing impatient. The man left, and Rafe stood there with fists clenched. *The butler,* he thought. *I should have known.* It seemed to take forever before a tall, very distinguished-looking, graying man came to the door. Rafe was startled to realize how much Maggie resembled him in the eyes, and around the mouth. This had to be her father.

''Mr. Dumont?'' He was ready for a scathing look, but the man's eyes lit up almost like a child's.

''My God!'' he exclaimed. ''You're *Rafe,* aren't you?''

Rafe was taken aback by the man's reaction. ''Yes, sir. Rafe Morrisey. Is Maggie here?''

The man's smile broadened, and he burst out laughing. ''Is she here?'' He laughed more. Rafe began to feel angry, until Dumont put out his hand. ''Of course she's here! My God, man, where else would she be, knowing *you* wouldn't know where else to *look* for her!''

Confused, Rafe grasped the man's hand, stunned by the firm, genuine handshake he got from Henry. ''I don't quite understand.''

''Oh, my good fellow, there is a *lot* you don't understand!'' Henry clasped his other hand over the top of Rafe's. ''My God, you're as handsome and strong and rugged looking as she described you! Is it really true you've fought Indians and grizzlies, and hunted buffalo and such?''

Rafe felt a little embarrassed, and his heart began to race at the realization that Maggie was here and was apparently hoping he would show up. ''Yes, Sir, but . . . Maggie. Is she all right? Is she . . . I mean, if she decided not to meet me, I'll understand I'll just leave—''

''My God, no, Rafe! My daughter is going to be—'' H laughed again, still shaking Rafe's hand. ''Oh, dear man, sh is going to be awash in tears. Come in! Come in!''

This was far more than Rafe had expected. He followed th man inside, looking up at a chandelier that hung three storie above. The huge marble and oak entranceway opened into on big, grand room with a balcony above, a staircase windin down on both sides.

''Follow me!'' Henry told him.

Still a bit confused, Rafe obeyed, walking across the marb floor of the great room and following the man into one several rooms on the main floor that surrounded the great roo

Henry's footsteps echoed against the walls, but Rafe wore moccasins and made not a sound.

"This is my study," Henry told him, ushering him into a large room with tall windows and floor-to-ceiling bookcases. He closed the door. "I will get Maggie in just a minute. Luckily her mother is gone right now. You and Maggie can have some privacy. I will bring her here and leave you alone." He picked up a gold box from his desk and held it out. "Cigar?"

Rafe looked around, his nostrils filled with the scents of tobacco, leather, and old books. He looked down at the box. "No, thank you, sir. I just want to see Maggie."

"Of course you do." Henry stepped back and looked him over. "All I want to know is if you still love my daughter."

"Of course I still love her. That's why I'm here. I was late getting to Independence, sir. I didn't abandon her. I got involved in a pretty vicious fight with Sioux Indians. One of them landed a warclub in my skull that left me unconscious for several weeks, and struggling with my memory for another three weeks after I came to. I was taken to Fort Laramie, and the Army doctor there said I had a concussion, something about a cracked skull. I had to stay down for quite a while. In fact, I left before I should have, but when I remembered I had been on my way to meet Maggie in Independence, I couldn't let another day go by."

Henry looked him over again. "Well, you certainly *look* fit! Just wait until Charlotte and my other three daughters see you!" He laughed again, shaking Rafe's hand once more. "Maggie has been worried about the same thing as you, Rafe. She also was unable to make it to Independence on time. She was afraid you would think she had decided not to come, and then you would give up on her and leave. I told her that if you really loved her and were worth your salt that you'd come for her, and you did!" He released his grip. "Maggie couldn't make it, Rafe, because the baby—" He hesitated. "My God, you don't know!"

"Know what?"

Henry walked around behind his desk. "Sit down, Rafe."

"I'd rather stand, Sir. I just want to see Maggie."

"I'd better explain first that you have a son, Rafe Morrisey."

Rafe felt an indescribable force move through him. Was he dreaming all of this? "A son?"

"Maggie arrived here pregnant. We all thought, of course, that it was Edward's, but she later explained it was yours. She named him Henry Raphael, and he's a handsome, bright, strong little boy now—five months old. But Maggie almost died having him. She came close to bleeding to death, but she pulled through. She's a damn strong woman, Rafe."

"You don't have to tell me that, Sir."

Henry rose again, unable to either sit still or stand still, for his joy. "The baby got sick, Rafe. We all thought he was going to die, but Maggie wouldn't give up on him because he was all she had left of you. His sickness was the reason she couldn't come and meet you. It took him weeks to recover, some kind of lung infection. But he's fine now. Maggie was going to—"

"My God, please get her!" Rafe interrupted.

Henry chuckled. "I'll do that. I'll let her tell you the rest. You two certainly have plenty to talk about." He shook Rafe's hand once more, grasping his arm at the same time. "All I need to know is that you love Maggie and will take care of her as best you can and protect her with your life."

Rafe's eyes teared. Maggie had had a baby! "Yes, Sir. Don't ever question that."

"Fine." Henry squeezed his hand and left, and Rafe turned and leaned against the desk. "My God!" he groaned. Poor Maggie, realizing on that long voyage home that she was pregnant! He was amazed at how her family had handled the situation. He hated the thought of her having the baby alone, without him. He should have been here. He breathed deeply against tears. A son! Maggie had given him a son!

Maggie straightened from covering little Henry when her father knocked on the door to her room. "Maggie?"

She walked to the door, putting a finger to her lips when she opened it. "I just got Henry to sleep."

"There is someone downstairs to see you. He's in my study."

Maggie frowned. "Who is it?"

"I'm not sure. He says it's very important."

Maggie pushed a piece of hair behind her ear. She had not had it styled yet this morning, and she wore a plain day dress, having spent the morning trying to get a restless Henry to take his morning nap. "I haven't done a thing with myself this morning. I haven't even taken my bath yet."

"Well, you certainly can't keep company waiting for something like that now, can you? Don't worry about how you look. You know you are beautiful no matter how you're dressed or how your hair is done. Don't be rude. Go and see what he wants."

Maggie thought her father looked a little strange, the way he'd looked sometimes when he'd hidden a special present for her when she was little. "All right." She moved past him and down the grand staircase, curious. She walked to a front window first, hoping she could tell by the horse and carriage who was here. When she saw the horse that was hitched outside, she thought she might stop breathing.

"Rafe!" she whispered. It couldn't be, could it? She would recognize that black anywhere! She looked across the great room toward her father's study, and there stood a tall, dark, handsome man in buckskins. "Oh, Dear Heavenly Father," she squeaked. "Rafe!"

She ran across the marble floor, and Rafe came part way out to greet her. In seconds she was swept up in his strong, familiar arms, breathing in the scent of fresh air and sage and buckskins, crying out his name over and over, unable to embrace him tightly enough. He swung her around, carrying her back into the study with her feet dangling off the floor.

"Maggie! My Maggie!" he groaned. "I couldn't make it—"

"Neither could I! Rafe, I had a baby, *your* baby!"

"Your father told me." He kissed her hair, her cheek, her neck. "I'm so sorry, Maggie, sorry I wasn't here, sorry you went through that all alone."

"It didn't matter. I had something of you. Oh, Rafe, he's beautiful!" She spoke through sobs. "But I almost lost him."

"I know. Your father explained everything. I couldn't make it in time, Maggie. I was wounded in an Indian fight. There was nothing I could do—"

"But you came looking for me!" Maggie leaned her head back, drinking in the sight of him. "Rafe. My beautiful Rafe."

He kissed her tears, then moved to her own quivering lips, meeting them in a long-awaited kiss that reminded him even more dramatically of why he had come here. Maggie! She was real. She was here in his arms. These were her lips. Between hungry kisses he managed to speak. "I never stopped loving you, Maggie . . . never stopped thinking about you . . . not for one minute."

"It was the same for me." More kisses. Oh, the glory of being in his arms again! He was here! He was really here! "Oh, Rafe, it was all worth it, everything we've been through, if it meant having this moment. I know now, Rafe. I know I can't stay here. I want to be with you, go wherever you choose to go. It doesn't matter, as long as we can be together, have more babies."

The suggestion brought a surge of desire for both of them. Another kiss followed, deeper, hotter. Rafe finally forced himself to push her away slightly. "I think we'd better find a preacher right away, get a hotel room for the night."

A trembling Maggie wiped at tears. "Yes. Yes, we'll get married right away! This afternoon! I'll send messengers to get my sisters and their families. I can't wait for them to meet you! They'll have so many questions, and my nieces and nephews will be terribly fascinated. I read all of them my journal." More tears came. "All the memories came flooding back. And I knew, Rafe! I knew I could do it all over again as long as I was with you." She kept hold of his hands. "Come and see the baby, Rafe! Come and see your son!"

Maggie kept hold of his hand, eagerly pulling him out of the study and up the grand, carpeted staircase to a bedroom upstairs, and to a large, canopied bassinet. "He's asleep, but for once I don't mind waking him up again." Maggie reached into the bassinet and opened the blanket, picking up a chunky, dark-haired baby whose eyes were closed. His face squiggled in irritation at being disturbed, and his little fists flailed in the air. Maggie handed him out to Rafe. ''Henry Raphael Morrisey,'' she said. ''We almost lost him, Rafe. But I never let go of him once while he was sick. I kept him close to my heart, and he came through. He came through because he has Rafe Morrisey's blood in him.''

Rafe could barely see the child for the tears in his eyes. ''Not just mine, Maggie. His mother is just as strong in her own way.'' He took the baby and held him close against his chest. ''My God,'' he groaned. ''We have a son.''

Maggie came closer and embraced both of them. ''How strange, the pathways life takes us down,'' she said softly. About two years ago this time she was marrying Edward, believing she would stay right here the rest of her life. What a boring life, indeed, that would have been.

Rafe kissed her hair. ''Montana, Maggie. I decided I'd like to go to Montana. Oregon is already getting too settled, and we both know we don't want to go back to California. There is a hell of a lot of unsettled country in Montana. A man can lay claim to enough land fit for a king.''

Maggie looked up at him, studying the face she had pictured only in her dreams for so long. ''Then we will go to Montana.''

The entire Dumont family stood on the docks. Henry had explained to Charlotte that she would simply have to accept the fact that people would find out about Maggie and Rafe and would have to accept it. They were man and wife now, and he had no doubt that going off to the wilds of Montana was more inviting to Maggie than all the theaters and balls in the country. She was with the man she loved.

More good-byes. How Maggie hated them, but this time she could bear it. This time was for something good. Something wonderful. She was going west again, with another new husband. But this was all so different than that first time she'd done this. Her heart soared with happiness. She held her baby son in her arms. She had Rafe by her side. They would take the same journey along the Ohio that she and Edward had taken, but they would go up the Mississippi and the Wabash Rivers to Chicago, where they would buy a wagon and all the necessary supplies. They would head west then, taking a northern route to Montana.

She was not afraid. She did not dread the inconveniences. If anyone could get her there safely, Rafe Morrisey could. And once they were there, she would not be afraid to face the hardships, or the hard work it would take to help Rafe build a ranch. She was by God sure now that she could do just about anything she set her mind to.

She said her good-byes, and this time the hardest good-bye was to her father. He understood better than anyone why she had to do this.

Rafe's horses were already aboard, along with his saddle and gear. Maggie's trunk was carried on deck . . . the old trunk with the faded yellow flowers on the lid. It was going on another journey, and this time they were truly going home. Inside the trunk was her faithful journal, and last night she had made more entries.

I am Mrs. Rafe Morrisey, and I can admit to the world that I love Rafe, that my child is his, she had written about marrying Rafe. She had wished she could write about their wedding night, what it had been like. But that was not something for her grandchildren to read! *I feel like the most fulfilled woman who ever walked,* she wrote instead. That was enough.

The wedding had been a week ago, and the next several days had been spent meeting people and preparing to leave. Last night she had made her newest journal entry. *Tomorrow, June seventeen, eighteen and fifty-two, we leave for Montana, and I am not afraid. Now my tomorrows are bright and full of hope. And today . . . today I can love Rafe freely and with all my devotion. I no longer have to wait until tomorrow to love him.*

I hope you have enjoyed *Love Me Tomorrow*. For information about the many other books I have written and books to come, send a self-addressed, stamped envelope to me at P.O. Box 1044, Coloma, Michigan 49038. I will send an updated newsletter and bookmarks. Please send letter-size envelopes, not little ones.

Or you can contact my home page at:

http://www.parrett.net/~bittner.